Modern praise for a classic from ✍ **W9-AEG-694**

Quatrefoil is among the finest works of all gay fiction produced within living memory. Originally published in 1950, it was regarded as the best novel about love between men up to that time. It may still be the best despite the old-style, overpopulated "closet" in which it is set. . . It is a pleasure to read English of this calibre. It could only have come from a rich and fruitful mind.
—Ed Harold, Connecticut *Dignity*

_____

The love affair is as powerful and satisfying today as it was in 1950, or in 1965 when I first read it.
—Richard Pollack, in the New York *Native*

_____

The charm of this book lies in showing us the values of the day. The attraction is the suspense, the plot twists, the risks and the successes. . . As a historical representation of the times, *Quatrefoil* is significant. As an enjoyable intrigue-love story, *Quatrefoil* is successful.
—David Fields, in *This Week in Texas*

_____

As valid now as it was thirty years ago, and highly recommended.   —Jesse Monteagudo, in *The Weekly News*

_____

This is a must read for anyone in the gay community. *Quatrefoil* is, by far, the most important work dealing with the intricacies of gay life that I have ever read.
—*This Month in Mississippi*

_____

One of the most intelligently written of gay novels.
—Roger Austen, in *Playing the Game*

QUATREFOIL

cover art by Tony Patrioli,
from his book *Mediterraneo*

QUATREFOIL

a novel by
James Barr

Boston · Alyson Publications, Inc.

Introduction and author information copyright © 1982 by Alyson Publications, Inc.
Epilogue copyright © 1991 by James Barr.
Cover photo copyright © 1984 by Tony Patrioli. All rights reserved.

This is a trade paperback from Alyson Publications, Inc.,
40 Plympton St., Boston, MA 02118.

First Alyson edition: May 1982

New Alyson edition, with epilogue: August 1991

ISBN 1-55583-016-1

To

R. A. S.

INTRODUCTION

Those of us who had grown up in the years from 1920 to 1950 had found them to be — as Dickens said — both the best of times and the worst of times. It was a span of years when everyone stayed deep in the closet, save those who had been caught *in flagrante delicto* and been publicly disgraced or fired or disciplined in some way. Still, those of us who could maintain our secret lived under an extraordinary protective umbrella: the ignorance and naiveté of the American public which — save for the pockets of sophistication in the metropolitan centers — spread far and wide over the rest of the land. And under the umbrella we lived and moved and made love and enjoyed our beddings, told our jokes and in general found life happy.

Because of our parasol's protection, the view of homosexuality — if indeed it were ever thought of — was very quaint in America. It was based on the assumption that all people raised in civilized Christian countries knew better than to fall in love with persons of the same sex. Knowing better, then, the narrow fundamentalist mind made two astonishing leaps of illogic: (a) people did not do such things, and (b) such things must be nonexistent. Oh, yes, perhaps in Paris or those wicked foreign cities, but never in God-fearing macho America the beautiful! We existed under the shadow and cover of such naiveté — and only when the audience grew more sophisticated did our long ordeal begin once more.

Quatrefoil, published in 1950, dealt soberly and intelligently with homosexual love; it soon proved to be the best novel up to that time concerned with love between men.

It was not the first of the books on a homosexual theme. Eagerly we had bought, read, and treasured certain novels of the 1920s, '30s, and '40s. The gay and delicious little giggling gewgaws of Carl Van Vechten delighted us, filled as they were with their *double-entendres* and secret jokes for homosexuals. There were a few short stories by Willa Cather and Sherwood Anderson, as well as two great classic novellas — Thomas Mann's *Death in Venice* and André Gide's *The Immoralist*. Following these in the 1930s came a number of wooden productions, portraying the homosexual scene as giddy or semi-tragic or downright awful — with the protagonist always getting killed or committing suicide, thus showing the guards of public morals that Sin, especially homosexual Sin, always came to a bad end. In this group were *Goldie, Butterfly Man, Twilight Men, Strange Brother,* and a creepy campy little horror called *A Scarlet Pansy*, all of which ended in death, disorder, or disaster.

The 1940s were a little better. During this decade authors found themselves able to write a trifle more sympathetically about their homosexual protagonists. Charles Jackson's *The Fall of Valor* enjoyed great popularity, and there were rumors that it would be turned into a movie, but it never was. Gore Vidal's *The City and the Pillar* was certainly the most explicit novel of the decade; in it two young men, for the very first time in American fiction, not only undressed together but actually kissed! Truman Capote, Carson McCullers, John Horne Burns, Ward Thomas, Harlan MacIntosh, Nial Kent and others produced novels with homosexual themes showing varying degrees of talent and forthrightness.

We read all of these novels, and even marked especially attractive passages. Sometimes with moist eyes and tremulous lips we assured our friends that here was a "must read." But we were still closeted, and currently with greater stress than ever, for our beloved umbrella had become a thing of shreds and patches as the nation's knowledge and sophistication increased. It now hardly protected us at all. The publication of Kinsey's *Sexual Behavior in the Human Male* in 1948, although it did much good for our cause, also stripped away the last tatters of silk, to leave only the metal ribs above us. It remained then for Senator McCarthy with his rumors and accusations to shatter everything and to send us scurrying deeper into our closets than ever, to escape utter destruction.

The protagonists of *Quatrefoil* realized this, and with subterfuge and skill waged an eternal battle to remain closeted, for they were both in the Navy, the young Ensign Froelich and the older Commander Danelaw. They successfully concealed their love for each other, living by a deceit which was forced upon them, dangerously skirting discovery and escaping it only by clever fabrications and skillfully invented fictions, compelled to stand guard over every gesture from pinkie and limp wrist, to sibilance in their voices and lilt in their inflections In some ways *Quatrefoil* was a wonderful treatise on how to live happily in the closet in 1950.

The world of Froelich and Danelaw is thus somewhat puzzling to the modern reader who comes across it thirty years later. He finds it difficult to understand. Yet here laid out in *Quatrefoil* is a graphic and accurate picture of the secrecy and concealment that was necessary in those days. For these reasons *Quatrefoil* is valuable, and for the fact that it is among the best-written homosexual novels of the time, a genuine classic, an appealing romantic love story.

There are some flaws in the book, to be sure, but they are made tolerable by the good writing and the positive approach. There are many superficial and condemnatory words about homosexuality in the novel — such as "ugly," "indecent," "diseased," "vile," and "corrupt" — but the standards of the times made it necessary for them to be used.

Ensign Phillip Froelich is a handsome and romantic young man, and Commander Danelaw an attractive, wise, and knowledgeable mentor for him. Both of them are people one would like to know. All the characterizations in the book are firm, some more developed than others; and the novel is strained through the consciousness of Froelich. Thus we see clearly enough into the minds and personalities of the other characters. We can admire, although not necessarily agree with, his firm determination — common to so many homosexuals in the past — to be an individual, standing alone, finding all the answers within himself and never identifying with any group. The two protagonists of *Quatrefoil* are sane and well-balanced, evidence of Kinsey's statement that homosexuality is simply another channel taken by man's sexual instinct, as "normal" for him as for any other mammal.

Standards shift whenever people progress. The changes that have occurred since 1950 are almost unbelievable. The world of Timothy and Phillip was one without adult bookstores, x-rated movie houses, orgy backrooms, amyl nitrate, LSD or Quaaludes. There were no photographs of unclothed males, save those in posing-straps or loin-cloths, nor were there any homosexual organizations. On radio and television there was a rigid code of behavior to be followed when a man and a woman were alone, and you could not say words like "pregnant" or "whorehouse" over the air or in movies. The homosexual, when he was portrayed, was a stereotypical one — limp-wristed, plucked, marcelled, and effeminate. But Timothy and Phillip were not. Although their lives were troubled, they triumphed, and their story is a tribute to the human spirit.

—Samuel M. Steward

xii

QUATREFOIL

PART

1

❖▸◈▸◈▸◈▸◈▸◈▸❖

Seattle

Summer—1946

1

◆·◇·◆·◇·◆·◇·◆

There was fog at midnight, as gray as storm-shadowed ocean, as cold as salt spray exploding across a derelict's bow. But in storm and spray there is the challenge of combat. The fog offered no challenge. Relentlessly it moved over the Oregon coastline like the unhinged jaw of some gigantic, feeding reptile. The listing ship moored against the dock was being scrapped instead of having her battle wounds repaired, for the war was over. This was June, 1946. Once more the world was safe. Not for democracy or anything else this time, just pleasantly safe.

A naval officer, wearing a long coat and a garrison hat whose visor shadowed his eyes and carrying two heavy bags, emerged from the ship's superstructure and walked unsteadily toward the sailor on duty at the gangway. He set the bags down and returned the watch's salute. He was tight.

"Good morning, sir," the watch said. The greeting was ignored.

"You may log me off your ship as of now," the officer returned.

3

His voice was young and he enunciated so distinctly that he seemed to speak with an accent. He had that ludicrous dignity of the meticulous drunk. "I was detached yesterday evening at sixteen hundred," he continued. "I am carrying out my basic orders to report to Seattle. I'm taking an early bus. Get your log information from your captain. Is that clear?"

"Aye, aye, sir."

The officer saluted the quarterdeck, picked up his bags, and turned to leave the ship when the sailor with a teasing note of insult in his voice said, "The crew will be disappointed, sir, finding you gone in the morning. Almost a French leave you're taking, isn't it, sir?"

The officer turned and waited. He said nothing but his eyes glittered dimly. Immediately the sailor sobered. "I'm sorry, sir."

Silently the officer stepped down to the dock. In five steps the impudent sailor and the ship faded into the unreality of fog. Still, the officer realized that the brief episode was significant. It was a forecast of the scorn he must now expect from Navy men. He was pariah.

The thought had a peculiar effect on him. Deep within him, within the secret places of him, he felt a terrifyingly familiar phenomenon take place. It was as if a monster had stirred and sent upward a lazy, powerful tentacle to break the surface of his mind. The monster was called melancholia by those who knew about such things. Sweat broke from his armpits and he shivered as he sucked the cold fog deep into his lungs. There was no horror to compare to the horror this thing could inspire in him. He had endured it for months and he must go on enduring it until . . .

But the black tentacle sank languorously down into his mind. The monster was not ready to strike. That would come later when he was sober, defenseless. Now he relaxed a little despite the fact that his bags were heavy and his steps unsteady. He could see a scant ten feet before him, yet he had at least another

4

two hundred yards to go before he reached the place where the bus would stop.

Where the wooden dock met the oiled road that led to the highway, a tall figure stood, a part of the bulky shadows. The officer was upon it before it moved toward him. Although he was startled, he gave no sign. For an instant the figure towered above him and by the rush of blood in his throat, he knew that it was the one man aboard the ship he was leaving that he could not face without fear. The big sailor fell in step, relieving him of his bags.

"Thanks, Manus," the officer said stiffly.

"Good morning Ensign Froelich," the sailor replied.

The officer felt the sailor's eyes on him. He knew their expression, queerly penetrating and insistent, as blue as smoke from brush fires that clouded the sun on warm autumn noons back home. They could say much, supplementing ordinary words, giving time the timelessness of a dream. But the young officer had not known what they said until one night out of Pearl Harbor when the two men had found themselves pitted against each other, fighting to keep their footing on a storm washed deck. Because of that moment their friendship, forbidden by naval regulation between officers and the men they commanded, no longer existed. For that eerie scene, the officer knew that the man beside him was now contrite. The officer mourned the loss of a friend. What the man beside him felt, he would not guess.

"I thought you'd leave early," Manus said half-accusingly.

"It was better not to risk a scene at the last."

With that they were silent until they reached the roadside cafe outlined in pink neon where the bus would stop. Then the bags were put down and they went inside, the sailor holding the door for the officer. From the cashier, the officer bought a ticket to Seattle while down the counter a few steps the sailor got two cups of coffee and carried them to a table where he waited for the officer to join him. Turning from the cashier, the officer

5

hesitated as he saw the sailor waiting beside the solitary table, then moved toward him. Politely the sailor waited for his companion to be seated first.

Nearby, where the slick counter made a bend, a man was drinking coffee. He seemed to watch the newcomers with more than idle interest. The sailor, evidently intent on the officer, had not noticed the civilian, but Ensign Froelich, his senses sharpened by liquor, had been aware of the man's intent gaze from the first seconds he had entered the brightly lighted room. He did not return the stare at first, nor did he do so as he approached the table, but in that instant when he pulled his chair under him, he gave the man one swift, shrewd glance.

Of the man's features, Froelich noticed little. Instead he saw the handsome suede jacket with a dark fur collar. It was the kind of coat civilian fliers sometimes wear. Almost simultaneously he noticed the man's hand, or perhaps it was his ring. For a moment, as the stranger lifted his cup, it stood out in fine relief. There was a polished surface of emerald the size of a thumbnail set in carved, yellow gold. As the light overhead caught it, an unexpected flash of bright green leaped obliquely from the heart of the stone, sending out a tremor of sensory pleasure to the officer. The hand was wide and thick with long, blunt fingers—the hand of a surgeon or an architect. But feeling the stranger returning his look, Froelich looked down at his coffee.

"You don't have to stay, Manus. I can get my bags," he said shortly.

"I wanted coffee anyway," Manus returned. His tone was unnatural, hurt. The officer understood the reason. He had addressed the sailor by his surname instead of the nickname he had once used. He took no joy from wounding his old friend. He acted from necessity.

For a while they were silent; then the sailor blurted, "I had to talk to you before you left, sir. I had to explain."

"No one can explain such a thing. We won't talk about it."

6

"But will you write and let me know what happens to you?" Manus persisted.

Froelich's eyes narrowed as he looked up quickly. "For Christ's sake, Manus," he lashed out savagely, "what do you think—" The expression on the sailor's face froze his caustic words. The fist which he had formed to emphasize his words relaxed in confusion. "Sorry, Manus," he muttered. "I didn't mean to foul up."

Without warning, the voice of the cashier bawled, "Seattle bus arriving!" As if reacting from shock, they stood up.

"No," Froelich said. "Don't come out." The officer tried to make his voice harsh, but it broke under the effort and as a result he grasped the sailor's rough hand, saying with averted eyes, "Goodbye, Stuff, and good luck." He called the sailor by the old, familiar nickname and grinned the old, familiar grin.

The sailor smiled uncertainly, his grip tightening momentarily before they separated. "Goodbye, sir. If you need . . ."

But the officer had turned away, walking out of the cafe without a backward glance.

Outside, an ancient bus, its hood wet with fog, had drawn up a few yards from the cafe entrance. Froelich picked up his bags and carried them to the bus and waited for the driver to get down. At last the door opened and the driver, his hat pushed back, got out to light a cigarette and look over his prospective customer. The driver's attitude of insolence cleared Froelich's mind like a hard, cold wind.

"There ain't no seats," the driver announced, his voice the rattle of a sack of rubbish. He flipped his match away importantly.

"I can stand," Froelich answered, offering his ticket.

"Against company rules," the driver grated back.

"The hell it is!"

"You callin' me a liar, chum?" the driver asked slowly.

"Not a liar," Froelich said coolly, "a goddamned liar, chum." For a moment they stared at each other. The driver gave

7

ground first. "You ain't gettin' on this bus without . . ." He hesitated over his limited choice of words.

Froelich let him flounder for a moment before he supplied, "Without a slight consideration for yourself. I have to get to Seattle, you have the only way, and this is civilization."

The driver nodded. Froelich reached for his wallet. "Tell me," said the officer, "what do they call you?"

"What d'ya mean?" Now the driver was alert, ready to bolt back inside and drive away if he heard the wrong answer.

Froelich smiled. "I like to know the jackals from the hyenas."

As he selected a bill from his wallet, he felt a restraining hand on his arm. Quickly he glanced up into the face of the civilian he had noticed in the cafe. He had not heard anyone leave the cafe.

"Excuse me," the stranger said, "but I'm on my way to Seattle. I'd be glad for the company." The man's voice was somehow relaxing, reminding the officer of the dry rustle of willow leaves over a summer lake.

Froelich studied the man briefly before he nodded. "Thank you. I appreciate your offer."

But as he noticed the driver looking at them sourly, his smile faded. He faced the man squarely as he creased the bus ticket down the center. Balancing it on his thumb he flipped it against the driver's chest and saw it spiral down into the mud at their feet. "There's your ante, you son-of-a-bitch," he said softly. "Cash that in!"

Then, with no haste, he picked up his bags and followed the civilian to a parked Lincoln cabriolet. He stowed his bags in the back and got in. The car backed and turned, throwing its lights on the bus driver who was stooping to pick up the ticket.

"Every man has his price," Froelich said. "That's a bargain."

"Is that why you insulted him?" the civilian asked.

Froelich laughed curtly. "Not really, I suppose. It goes deeper. Carlyle might have said I haven't transcended that man's level." He paused, glancing at the emerald flashing dimly in the light of the dash. "Or if you prefer something more flamboyant,

8

Wilde might have said there was a certain violence in the air, some red star too near the earth."

The words hung between them like bait as the powerful car swung out of a curve, its twin blades of light cutting into the sodden body of the fog. The man at the wheel turned to give the young officer a searching look and found a strange, soft deadliness in the youthful face. He looked back to the road.

"And have you anything against Oscar Wilde?" he said.

"I?" Froelich's voice was surprised. "Not at all. I might even say I admire some of him."

"And what would that be?"

"Oh," he replied thoughtfully, "some of his drawing room pieces. The Importance of Being Earnest—that sort of thing."

"And his other works, Salome, De Profundis?"

"I don't know," the younger man said slowly, tilting his head a little. "Once I thought only a genius would have attempted what he did."

"Which was?"

"To translate such monstrous emotions into as tangible a medium as words. It's rather like strolling a python on a length of ribbon."

In these words Froelich knew that he was revealing a good deal of himself, yet he felt the need to establish an attitude before this man. This would account for the turn of their conversation and for his own deliberate reference to a man whose name was connected with homosexuality. There was something about the expensive jacket, the ring, and the man's obvious interest in him that stimulated certain unwholesome connotations in the young man's mind. Not that he could accuse the man of any abnormality, but should his intuition become apparent later, he would have established his first defense, a bulwark from which he could fight. The civilian was laughing at his last observation. The sound was low, solid, pleasant, even nicer than his drowsy voice.

"I can see the trip to Seattle will not be dull," he said with amusement. But sobering abruptly he asked, "And Wilde, the man?"

"I don't admire him," Froelich said flatly.

"As a homosexual, of course."

"That doesn't really matter," he shrugged. "But since he was, why didn't he choose suicide, for his family if no other reason?"

"Then protection of family is ample excuse for suicide?" the man asked, turning his eyes on him again.

Froelich stirred uneasily, realizing that again he had revealed something of himself that should be kept hidden. He laughed. "Forgive the emptying of a fool's wounds. I shouldn't talk when I'm drunk."

"That's an unusual expression," the man said, falling in with his desire to change the subject.

"Is it? I must have read it somewhere. I've read a lot lately."

"The Navy must be a very restful organization."

"I've been relieved of all duty for the past ten months while awaiting a general court martial for insubordination. The death penalty can't be passed on a naval officer on foreign soil." They were both silent, their eyes on the gray, swirling road.

"It can't be that serious if you're free now," the stranger said.

"Oh, I'm now AWOL. I'm on my way to Amphibious Headquarters at Seattle for trial." With some horror, Froelich heard his voice go hollow, and he saw that the civilian shot him a sympathetic glance.

"There's a drink in the dash compartment if you want it."

"Thanks, I do." He opened the compartment and took out a flat silver and leather flask from which he inhaled delicately. "Courvoisier," he said with appreciation. He tipped the container and held the first swallow in his mouth a long while, closing his eyes. Though he did not know it, his face clearly expressed a sensuality that was not foreign to it. At last he swallowed with reluctance and breathed deeply through his mouth. "I'd forgotten that liquor can be kind going down," he said softly, inhaling from the flask again.

10

"So you don't like the Navy?" the man at the wheel pursued.

"I didn't say that. I'm indifferent to it."

"And facing a general court martial?" he answered unbelievingly.

"I stepped out of line," Froelich answered swiftly. "Now I'll take my punishment. I could have prevented the incident. I didn't."

"Why?"

"I was bored, I think. I expected the Navy to be high adventure, a chance to swing on God's coattails. The adventure was there, but men without imagination can make anything monotonous. If a breed of supermen ever inhabit the earth, they'll be Amazons, not mere men."

"You're quite a philosopher."

"I'm quite tight."

For several miles they were silent. They seemed to be driving out of the fog and the big car picked up speed. The landscape was hurried but restful and Froelich allowed his mind to dull against the sharp edge of catastrophe he must face in the morning. He put his head back against the seat. Later as the car swerved, he felt his cheek touch the leather upholstery. In the soft light the hands on the wheel looked capable, strong. Apropos of nothing, he murmured, "You know, I like you."

"I'm flattered," the voice held amusement.

"You shouldn't be. When I'm not drunk, I'm a swine."

Froelich yawned at the man's low chuckle and thought of the warmth of brandy and emeralds. He slept.

"We're here," a heavy, half-familiar voice awoke him.

Phillip Froelich felt a strange hand on his shoulder and he opened his eyes abruptly. He was bewildered, stiff, and sickeningly sober. The gray light of day stung his eyes, but he kept them open. He wondered where he was. His cheek was pressed trustingly against a jacket that rose and fell with breathing that was not his own. His hands rested on it tenderly as they might

11

rest on a pillow, and he realized that he had been sleeping in the curve of someone's arm. As recognition rushed over him, he sat up, extremely embarrassed by the intimacy of his position, his drunkenness, and his words of the night before.

"You needed sleep," the low voice said.

Slowly the young officer raised his eyes and felt them jerk wide with surprise. His companion, whom he had thought to be a civilian the night before, was wearing a blue Navy overseas cap with the gold device of a lieutenant commander. He had a handsome, aloof face, one that would not be forgotten easily. Nor was he attempting to conceal the amusement on it now.

"You're a naval officer, too," Froelich stammered.

"Forgive me," the man laughed. "I should have introduced myself last night, but I wanted to hear you talk. I knew you wouldn't if you knew I was a brother officer." His tone made fun of the term. He held out his hand, but Phillip ignored it.

"If you don't mind, sir." He felt that he had made a colossal fool of himself.

"As you prefer," the commander said. "Shall I help with the bags?"

"I can manage," Phillip said, getting out of the car.

As he dragged his bags out and set them on the curb, the commander leaned forward so he could see him and said, "Across the street there is the Ferry Building. You can get a launch to Amphib Island on the hour. That's where you want to go. At the main gate, ask for Lieutenant Bruner. You'll have to see him first." The man smiled and waved his hand. "Goodbye and good luck, young fellow. You're going to need it, I imagine."

"Thank you, sir," Phillip said stiffly. With a too smart salute, he stepped back on the curb beside his bags and the car rolled past him. But the real significance of the man's information did not strike him until the car was half a block away. Then he muttered to himself, "Name of God! He must be stationed at the base, too, to know so much about it. A fine start I'm off to!"

2

◇◇*◇*◇*◇*

*I*t was ten hundred, or ten hours past midnight as the Navy calculates time, when Phillip Froelich left his bags at the main gate of Amphib Island and started for Officer Classification. Despite his increasing nervousness, he walked with a natural air of arrogance, his eyes narrowed against the bright morning sun. The night's fog had exhausted itself in rain at dawn, leaving the air cool and clean. After the thick, drugging heat of the tropics he had left, he found this blue-green world of sea and mountain delightful.

The island that the base occupied floated serenely just off the flat curve of city which rose straight up from her gray docks to end in gleaming rivulets of white houses among abrupt green hills. To the left were the dim Olympics, to the right the bold Rainier, her shadowed snow face the rough caricature of a constipated Queen of Spades. Between the city and the island, ships rode at anchor. Phillip would like to have lingered, but he walked briskly on apparently unaware of the activity of a great naval base about him.

Phillip was twenty-three. He looked eighteen. He was deceptively slender and rather tall, but his gray uniform concealed flat, severely co-ordinated muscles that made him far more powerful than the average man of his height and weight. Only in his disciplined carriage and lithe step did he reveal any hint of strength. His face, a light umber from the tropics, was smooth, carefully purged of any emotion. Yet beneath its mask lay a frightening ambition, the desire for perfection. Later it would harden into simple greed, but now its extreme youth saved it from being either ludicrous or terrifying.

He had no difficulty finding the office he wanted. In the reception room he announced himself to the first of three round-shouldered yeomen. "Ensign Froelich to see Lieutenant Bruner." His voice was clear and hard. He pronounced his name "Froylick."

"Just a moment, sir. I'll see if he is busy. Won't you sit down?"

Phillip shook his head impatiently. The sailor disappeared inside the door at the back of the room. The other sailors paused and stared at him until he gave them a sharp glance; then they went on with their typing. Very likely they were familiar with his case. He could thank his last captain for that. For ten months the man had written letters to every command in the Pacific to have him transferred from the ship. Overseas those letters had been a source of laughter, but now Phillip began to see the possible effect of such ridiculousness on his future. This was civilization. Worse, it was the Navy.

He lighted a cigarette and looked disapprovingly around the room. It was typical of American bases of operation all over the world, hastily erected, giving the dual impression of great expense and haphazard crudity. There were leather chairs, fluorescent lights, glass topped desks, and gleaming chromium in odd touches—all in contrast to sheet rock walls, bare nailheads, and overhead beams of unpainted pine. The deck of unfinished cement caught and held every grain of dirt. The only other

14

thing that impressed him was a collection of pin-up pictures scattered over the bulkheads with the brilliance of a color wheel. Pictures of women—impossible women—caught in the artificial poses of charades, as provocative and believable as houris. The collection was one of the largest and lewdest he had yet seen.

The yeoman returned. "Lieutenant Bruner will see you, sir." Phillip nodded and walked to the door with confidence he did not feel.

Lee Bruner was about thirty-five and gat-toothed with a plump face topped by a froth of blond hair as kinky as a length of unraveled Manila line. He was mawkishly well tailored, his snug uniform touched off with gold instead of black buttons. The sheen of his shoes matched his silk tie. Froelich hated him instinctively; so he gave him his friendliest smile.

Bruner stood to shake hands and did not sit until Phillip was seated. Then he settled back in his chair and put his feet on the wastebasket—to create an air of informality, Phillip supposed. He offered a cigarette. Phillip refused. These amenities allayed none of the boy's wariness.

"You're settled in officer's country, I suppose?" Bruner began.

"No, sir. I came here immediately upon arriving."

"That wasn't necessary. You could have waited until afternoon."

Phillip let that pass, thinking how annoying the man's accent was.

"How was Iwo Jima?" Bruner pursued.

"It was—trying, sir," Phillip replied carefully, but he thought, *Now what kind of fool question is that?*

"I was in on the Salerno push," the lieutenant volunteered, "but that was before your time in the Navy, I suppose."

It wasn't, but Phillip said nothing. An idea had struck him. This politeness, the feet on the wastebasket, had a purpose. Bruner wanted him to talk, to reveal some key that would class him as to the type of culprit he must be. Phillip's smile tightened. Too often he had seen junior officers socially castrate

15

themselves with stupid prattle upon reporting aboard a new ship. Often it took weeks to erase these first impressions. So Phillip returned the officer's gaze innocently until the man leaned forward and pulled a sheaf of papers to him.

"I guess we'd better have some facts about you now," he said. "Your full name is Phillip Eugene Devereaux Froelich. Some mouthful."

"I was named for my grandfather," Phillip replied rather haughtily.

"I see. You're here awaiting a court martial for insubordination to your commanding officer. You are guilty of striking him. Right?"

"No, sir."

"Suppose you tell me your side of the story. Begin with when you entered the Navy."

Phillip nodded and thought a moment before he said, "When war was declared, I was a freshman in college in Oklahoma, my native state."

"Then you aren't from the East?" Bruner asked. "Your accent."

"I'm from Oklahoma. I entered the Navy's reserve officer training program and continued to go to school, studying banking and finance."

"With an eye to what?"

"Entering my family's bank when I was graduated."

"Your family are bankers?" Bruner was impressed.

"Not in the size of the East," Phillip said. "We aren't affiliated with a chain. We are independent in a town of fifty thousand."

"What is the name of it?"

"The town or the bank?"

"Both."

"My home town is Devereaux, named for my grandfather. The bank is the Devereaux National."

"I see. Go on."

16

"Later I was sent to Missouri as a V-12 trainee, and then to Midshipman School where I was graduated in 1944. I was number one man in my class. I have served on two ships, an AKA and the landing ship which I just left. My fitness reports have been excellent until the episode with my last captain."

"I know. We've checked on you closely already."

Phillip noticed that the lieutenant's tone had become businesslike, as if he wanted to match him for clarity and efficiency. To Phillip this was a small but significant triumph. It meant that the man could be led. Phillip wanted to—needed to—use this man. He had to handle him, not only because his commission depended on it but also because it was a matter of private policy to size people up and then outplay them with their own weapons. But it was going to be hard. He hated this man, and lately what he hated he had insulted. He suspected that Bruner was incompetent in his job. If he were right, he could never respect him as a man.

Bruner was saying, "And now about this charge of insubordination. I'll be in charge of preparing your case for the investigating authorities and the court martial that will follow so you may speak frankly."

Phillip searched for the exact words he wanted. He wanted to create a subtle impression of slightly outraged decency, yet complete fairmindedness. "It was on one of the last operations against the island before Japan surrendered. About six hours after the first landings, the auxiliary ships had an inter-ship communication from our flag to transfer officers and men to those landing craft suffering casualties. Our ship was to send two officers. I volunteered to go."

"Why? Trouble aboard the AKA?"

"No. I wanted to be nearer the action than I had been."

Bruner raised an eyebrow and Phillip pretended to ignore it. He could not explain to this charlatan that he wanted a chance to equal his father's exploits in the first World War.

"I reported aboard the landing ship with my gear," Phillip

continued. "I disliked the captain from the moment I met him. He is a full lieutenant. His name is Pratt. The ship was dirty and the crew sloven and sullen. At first I put this down to the nine casualties they had suffered that morning. Actually that had nothing to do with the state of things. It was a result of them. Captain Pratt had confused his orders and had gone ashore too soon, landing the heavy construction equipment he was carrying in the midst of fighting units on a black beach." Bruner shook his head solemnly. "The captain immediately made me supply and communications officer and navigator, and gave me the responsibility of cleaning up the ship. He made the other officer who reported aboard with me a watch officer. That was all. I stood watches, too."

"Why do you mention this?"

"I think it shows the captain's unusual way of allotting authority."

"Go on."

"I began my duties by cleaning up the ship. Because there was much to do, I worked alongside the crew as another hand, loading ammunition, repairing bulkheads, cutting free the debris on deck, and so on. The captain called me into his cabin and told me that to work with enlisted men was unofficerlike. He told me that I was to give the orders and that was all. I think he was jealous that I had got the crew to work, but I did as he said. As a result, work slowed down noticeably. Enlisted men are rather like mules at times—not that I blame them. The captain then complained that I was getting nothing done. I started to work with the crew again, realizing that I was caught in the middle of a long-standing feud between the captain and his men."

"And the officers?"

"Spineless. Content to cower before the captain and complain to his back." Phillip saw Bruner's eyes grow cold. "The captain said nothing more of the situation for a few weeks. During that time the crew took a sullen pleasure in playing me as a favorite against the other four officers and the captain. Perhaps you know their methods: 'Will you censor this special letter, Mr. Froelich?' 'May I go ashore on the next blue beach and trade for souvenirs?' They were not subtle. The captain seemed to resent it."

Bruner interrupted. "Don't you believe in ordering men to do their jobs, Mr. Froelich? Or didn't you believe in taking your captain's orders?" His voice was cool.

"I can take orders, sir," Phillip returned, "but we were working under emergency conditions and it seemed silly to carry on a tradition when half the effort involved would have accomplished the purpose with no friction. At the time, the problem seemed to be one of leading men, not driving them."

Bruner nodded reluctantly. "It is a matter of individual concern among captains if the officers work with their crews," he admitted.

"I'm used to manual labor," Phillip hurried on. "I work on my father's farms. I am neither afraid nor ashamed of getting dirty."

"The fact remains that you ignored your captain's orders and now you are about to go on trial for insubordination while under enemy fire. The charge is comparable to treason," Bruner said pompously. "Go on."

"We were then assigned to unload equipment from the auxiliary ships and to land it on the proper beaches. If we ever needed co-ordination between officers and men, it was then. The captain was, I believe, incompetent. He had difficulty in translating the simplest message. He could not handle his ship. One day, while he was at the con, he broached the ship on its side on the beach during high tide. The forward port compartments were flooded for three days until we were towed free. There was some talk of an investigation then, but everyone was too busy with the operations on the island. I persuaded a Navy photographer to take pictures of the ship while she was broached. I have those pictures now." Phillip paused to let the significance

19

of this bit of strategy go to work. "The captain made life hell for all of us. And, well—"

"He seemed particularly rough on you," Bruner supplied sardonically.

"The captain was a nervous man," Phillip said.

"I've met Captain Pratt," Bruner said, expecting Phillip to be upset by this information.

He wasn't. He replied blandly, "Then you are aware of his eccentricities." Phillip went on without waiting for an answer. "During the next three weeks everyone watched the captain make a monkey of me. He assigned me to jobs ordinarily given to enlisted men—messenger duty, chart correction, and the like. On several occasions he left the table when I came into the wardroom. He made frequent remarks about certain officers not being gentlemen. For a while I was amused."

"But why should you complain about doing the work assigned to enlisted men when you've said you didn't mind working with the crew?"

"Sir, whose side are you on?" Phillip's voice was swift and venomous, causing Bruner's eyes to widen with amazement.

"Yours, of course," Bruner said. "I'm merely trying to show you how the prosecution will look at your side of the case. And you are certainly giving me every reason to believe you are guilty of insubordination." Bruner smiled pleasantly. "But go on."

"The spark that touched off the whole thing came the night before we left for Saipan for repairs. The officers were shooting dice in the wardroom. I stopped to try my luck. By the time I went on watch at midnight, I had seventy dollars of the captain's money and about the same amount from the other officers. I'll admit that it gave me a great deal of pleasure to take it."

"So we have the charge of gambling to add to your crimes?"

"I hope the officers who investigate me have had sea duty," Phillip replied dryly. "Gambling may be forbidden on naval vessels, but there isn't a ship afloat that doesn't offer a choice of

20

dice, poker, and blackjack from the chain locker to the ward-room."

"They'll be salty, I assure you. Go on."

"Around zero two thirty we had a red alert. In keeping with the captain's orders of the preceding week, I had the messenger on duty call him to the bridge."

"Didn't you read the captain's night order book?"

"Captain Pratt didn't keep one," Phillip replied.

"Captain Pratt told me while he was here yesterday that he had given orders to be called only in case of an actual air raid," Bruner said, looking at Phillip closely.

"If I was given such an order," Phillip said evenly, "I don't remember it. I don't think he gave it to me."

It was a lie, but he knew that his word in this small matter was as good as the captain's, as there had been no witness to the scene. Morally his conscience did not rebel at this falsehood, since the whole ridiculous affair rested on half-truths. In any event, he would never tell Bruner the delight it gave him to break his captain out of his bunk at two thirty in the morning, to make him puff up three flights of ladder just to go down again when the alert went off five minutes after it had sounded. As far as the Navy was concerned, he was guilty; but he felt no personal guilt at all. The dice game was a lucky stroke. It put the captain in still a worse light, and Phillip realized that his future might well depend on his captain's fall from grace. Part of his defense plan included an investigation that would certainly ruin the captain if it ever came about. It was his business to see that it did. Later he would mention this to Bruner. Now he had other irons in the fire. He frowned and pitched his voice lower for his climax. One more point and he was through.

"The captain came up to the bridge. He was angry and he called me a son-of-a-bitch. I told him to apologize. He refused. I—I grabbed him by the shirt and told him to fight. He broke away from me and ran from the bridge."

"Do you object to being called a son-of-a-bitch?"

"Wouldn't you?" Phillip made no effort to conceal his contempt.

"Southerners," Bruner said. "I think I would have considered it just an expression and ignored it."

"We were all tired, sir," Phillip said, his tone revealing none of the mockery he felt. "Our nerves were raw. We had been under fire for weeks. We all did things we'd never have done under ordinary circumstances." He thought how pat these trite phrases were now.

"Did you strike Captain Pratt when he broke from you?"

"No, sir. But as he went down the ladder, I think I kicked him."

"You think you did?" Bruner's mouth worked with suppressed laughter.

"Yes, sir. My foot hit something soft that might have been the seat of his pants. He is a very fat man, and it was dark."

Phillip was not unaware of the farcical quality of his words. He deliberately built the effect up.

"In his cabin," Phillip continued innocently, "the captain ordered me placed under arrest. The officers refused. The crew could not. So he suspended me from all duty just before we sailed for Saipan without convoy. Two days out, he reinstated me to duty to navigate the ship. We were four hundred miles off course and he did not know enough celestial navigation to get us back on. Before I consented to help him out, I insisted that all information be entered in the ship's log for my defense. He did not suspend me from duty again, but he used me only in emergencies."

"You've been expecting a court martial, I see."

"On the contrary. I've collected data to save myself from one."

"At your captain's expense?"

"He deserves a GCM as much as I do."

"Well, go on."

"At Saipan, where there were no facilities for repairing our damaged hull, he tried to have me removed from the ship. The authorities laughed at him. He tried at Eniwetok, Majuro, and later Pearl. No one would touch the case. We were at Pearl six months. I worked ashore in the small boat pool rather than remain idle on board."

"Had you anyone's permission to do this?"

"No."

"The captain tells me that you were needed on board at that time."

"The captain lies. I've forty witnesses on board to prove it."

"Don't you think, Mr. Froelich, that you were hard to get along with?"

"What has that to do with it? I entered the Navy to fight a war, not to advance Captain Pratt's social position."

"Have you many friends, Mr. Froelich?"

"As many as I need."

"Is that many?"

"Lieutenant Bruner, I had the respect *and* the admiration of 90 per cent of the crew—"

"And of your fellow officers?"

"They kept their distance. I did the same."

"Sometimes one is forced to pal around with his companions to avoid friction."

Phillip made an impatient gesture with his hand.

"Well," Bruner said, leaning back in his chair again, "your facts agree with your captain's, but the approaches are a good deal different. In spite of certain comical aspects of the case, you are in serious trouble. You've admitted your guilt. A court martial board won't consider that lightly. Naturally the old school Navy man will be against you. You're a reserve and they resent you as one of a class. You've stepped out of line. They won't dwell on extenuating circumstances. All I can do is try to assure you a fair trial." The lieutenant became grave. "Don't be surprised if you are dishonorably discharged from the service for this bit of nonsense. Stranger things are happening every day. Don't expect justice. You're confronting a code, perhaps outmoded. There will be no appeal, even if you are given a prison sentence, and I am in no position to tell you that there won't be one."

"Then I'll hire a civil lawyer," Phillip said.

"No, don't do that," Bruner said, to Phillip's surprise. He explained, "You'd be doing yourself more harm than good. The Navy hates civilian interference."

Phillip did not understand this, but he said quietly, "I see."

He was remembering how proud his father had been of him the day he had been commissioned, how his father had flown East to see him graduated. Phillip thought of returning to Devereaux in disgrace. A prison sentence. Absurd. It must not happen. He had been a fool to risk his commission against the satisfaction of baiting his captain. He could see a hundred things he could have done to save himself all this embarrassment. But he was caught.

During the past year, he knew he had changed radically, but he did not understand why. All his life he had lived by reason. He had admired only that which was well ordered and logical. He had been a model of excellence in his town. The banker's boy. But suddenly it had seemed that all his virtues had deserted him and left him melancholia for his only companion. Life was tedious or horrible. He was bored or afraid. He hated everything, everyone around him. Yet he knew the war and the Navy had had little to do with this attitude. The cause went deeper. It was an ugliness inside him, a scar tissue on his brain that had suddenly begun to ache and throb until he could no longer sense anything clearly. Why else was his judgment no longer trustworthy? . . .

Bruner broke into his thoughts with, "Don't worry about all this any more than you can help. Relax. Your tests will begin tomorrow and you'll want to do your best on them."

"Tests?"

"Yes. The Navy must determine whether or not you're fit to stand trial. In the mornings you'll go through a planned

24

course of tests. Your afternoons will be free. First, a complete physical examination lasting several days. Then your IQ and accomplishment tests, and last of all, you'll be given a psychiatric examination."

For a moment the structure of Phillip's life swayed, shuddered dangerously, and slowly righted itself. He felt a modicum of his inward horror creep into his disciplined features.

"You're not afraid of such an examination?" Bruner asked too casually.

Phillip laughed nervously. "Isn't everyone? I've heard man's first terror is of learning too much about himself."

A psychiatric examination! He'd rather enter a dark room with a blind copperhead than submit himself to a psychiatrist. He understood his reasons well enough. He had much to hide from the world. First, this growing melancholia. Second, his superiority complex hid something that was terrifying. Third, the strange incident with the sailor, Stuff Manus, though, God knows, he had had nothing to do with that. Still, probed from his mind by the forcep fingers of a doctor, it might appear in any shape. Left alone, Phillip knew that he would solve his own problems as he had always done. He had a ruthless self-reliance that had never let him down. But in the hands of strangers with words and names for everything, anything might happen. And perversely enough, Bruner was now saying, "Since we'll be working closely, I think it would be wise to dispense with formalities. My name is Lee and I'll call you Phillip. Okay?"

Phillip understood the request. Bruner was smarting under his snobbish desire to isolate himself. Phillip stood up. "As you wish, sir."

"Fine," Bruner beamed. He had the hide of a rhinoceros. "And now to get you settled in officers' country, Phillip. Unfortunately we have two men to a room here. No privacy." His sarcasm was heavy-footed, but Phillip expected nothing better.

"Sir," Phillip said, "my cousin is stationed here. I've written him about my trial. He is expecting me to call him."

25

"Help yourself," Bruner smiled, indicating the telephone on his desk. "Is your cousin a Froelich or a Devereaux?"

"Neither. He is Lieutenant (j.g.) Francis Barriman in Supply."

"I know him. I can't say that you bear any resemblance."

"None, sir."

"Well, call him and we'll all have lunch at the Officers' Club." And Bruner looked at the elaborate watch on his wrist.

3

$\mathscr{A}$s a result of high fees and the staggering number of transient officers who had stopped on their way to and from the Pacific Theater, the O Club on Amphib Island was the grandest of its kind on the West Coast. The angular building squatted on a stone terrace on the city side of the island. On the terrace there were salt and fresh water pools, a private yacht anchorage, and sun chairs. Inside, the two wings were divided by a low, wide foyer, elaborately mirrored and paneled. To the left was the huge dining room with its foursome tables and steam-tabled chow line for the ensigns and lieutenants, its larger tables for lieutenant commanders and up who were served by Negro messboys in white jackets, and a long table overlooking the Sound for the admiral of the base and his guests. On the right there were the main lounge and smaller game rooms, with big chintzy chairs, low tables, potted palms, knotty pine, magazines, pool tables, slot machines, and card tables. It was big, crude, dazzling. But the bar room was the gaudiest of all. The bar, a great oval

27

affair with pink lights; blue mirrors, and white bartenders, was surrounded by gigantic wall murals of childishly executed destroyers, dive bombers, and prostitutes ogling enlisted men. The toilets were labeled "Pointers" and "Setters," a trick that Phillip had previously seen in a Chicago dive. The aim had been for risqué intimacy; the effect was a Baptist minister's setting for a bacchanal. Like other phases of the Navy, it promised one thing and delivered another.

"Do we pass inspection?" Bruner asked. He and Fiancis Barriman had been showing Phillip around prior to entering the dining room.

"Four-O," Phillip said. He was feeling better now that he was getting his bearings. Seeing his cousin again had helped his mental state, too. "It beats bamboo bars and Scotch drinking monkeys." To his surprise, his companions frowned. "I meant the kind with tails," he explained. "Every bar past Pearl has a pet ape."

The two men laughed politely. Because he had little to say to these men, he was ill at ease. He looked at Bruner who was watching him closely and wondered what the man was thinking.

Half an hour before, Lee Bruner had seen the two cousins greet each other in his office. From his impression of Phillip, Bruner had not expected back-slapping exuberance, but neither had he been in the manner prepared for the display of cold-blooded friendliness he had seen. They had shaken hands, holding each other's eyes unwaveringly like fighters expecting foul play. And as they had chatted, Bruner had had a distinct feeling that the pair hated each other completely and intelligently. Clearly they had but one feature in common: ancestors.

Bruner had met Francis Barriman at the supply depot several times, but he had never noticed him particularly until now when he appeared in low contrast to his younger, more attractive cousin. Actually there was probably two years difference in their ages, yet Francis looked ten years Phillip's senior. Always Francis had been aloof, but friendly enough in an impersonal way.

28

Snobbishness, Bruner decided, must be a family trait, the result of being the petty nobility of a small, provincial city. There was nothing aristocratic or unusual about Francis. He was nice, but dull-looking, steady, and perhaps even capable.

He was of average height, inclined to stockiness, and he wore a mustache that was beginning to gray, as was the black hair over his small, well-shaped ears. His forehead was tall and sloping, with thin brows over light-blue eyes and low cheekbones. His nose was thick and bent, turtle-like, destroying the effect of primness created by the small, thin-lipped mouth. His uniform was neat but faded. He might be a young minister, a C.P.A., or a high school English teacher. Bruner knew that he had been studying law at Harvard when the war started. He did not drink, smoke, or swear, and he looked it. But his cousin was everything Francis was not. Phillip carried many of the features of the aristocrats they obviously believed themselves to be.

He held himself proudly, chin up, belly flat, buttocks tucked in, ready to move with assurance and purpose. Unconsciously he attracted attention. Bruner had noticed officers glance in their direction and then look with interest at Phillip. Yet the boy was too self-centered to be much aware of his effect on others.

His head was fine and youthful. His hair, which badly needed cutting, was a sun-streaked, mahogany brown, curling childishly low over the brow, giving him a false look of naïveté. The dark, narrow eyes were too shrewd in expression to inspire confidence. The lips were full and dark as if his blood were thick and sluggish and there was too much of it. There was a pagan contrast in the whiteness of his uneven teeth against the false swarthiness of his skin. To Bruner, the face fell into no category, being both virile and decadent, chaste and inhumanly gross. It was a pack of contradictions.

It was easy for Bruner to understand how the boy had got into his present predicament. Lifted by the Navy from the only background he had ever known, he had clinched with everything that stood in the way of preserving his ideals. Very likely his captain, who was unquestionably a slob, had offered friendship and Phillip had spit the offer back in his face. Bruner had no sympathy for Phillip. In fact, he enjoyed the prospect of the boy's degradation. The worse it was, the better it would please him. Yes, Bruner thought as they walked toward the dining room, the cousins were vastly different. They would be interesting to watch.

As the three officers started to cross the entrance foyer, someone called, "Attention!" and everyone but Phillip snapped to a rigid attitude of respect. Phillip looked toward the door and saw a two-star admiral, flanked by a captain of the medical corps and another officer. He was amused. In the Pacific, gold braid demanded and got little such ceremony. The admiral nodded his acknowledgment and the same voice called, "As you were." The officers, about two dozen of them, relaxed and watched the admiral check his hat and purchase a chit book at the main desk. The medic and the other officer had strolled on toward the dining room.

"The captain with the admiral is Morgan," Bruner whispered. "He will be your psychiatrist. I'll introduce you."

Phillip turned insolent eyes on the two approaching officers. Captain Morgan was a tall, heavy man with a barrel chest and a porcine jowl dark with bristle. Phillip thought he would probably grunt if he were prodded in the ribs with a heel.

But suddenly his grim humor died and a tight feeling of premonition gripped his stomach. He looked at the other officer, a lieutenant commander wearing the gold shoulder aiguillettes of an admiral's aide, dreading what he knew he would see—the man with the furred jacket and the ring of the night before. Hastily he turned to engage Bruner in conversation, but Bruner had raised his hand in greeting, calling, "What's the hurry, you two?"

Both officers looked up and moved toward them. Phillip felt

30

his fingernails dig into his palm as he saw the smile of recognition on the commander's face.

Phillip had been guilty the night before of making a few absurd remarks and of passing out, but these things were not enough to cause him to face the stranger with such uneasiness. He supposed it was because Francis represented his family and Bruner his naval career, whereas the strange commander was a reminder of an undisciplined element in his personality that Phillip wanted to conceal. The worst the commander could do would be to make some remark that would require an embarrassing explanation. Still, Phillip did not relax, but watched the man with hawklike attention.

"When did you get in from Frisco, Tim?" Bruner asked the commander.

The man shot Phillip a look of conspiracy before he replied, "I flew in just a couple of hours ago, Lee."

Phillip wondered why the man should tell Bruner such a roaring lie, but because of it he relaxed a bit.

Bruner put a friendly hand on his shoulder and said, "Captain Morgan, a new charge of mine, Phillip Froelich, and this is his cousin stationed here on the base, Lieutenant Barriman."

They shook hands and Bruner was about to present them to the commander named Tim when the admiral joined them and the two juniors were introduced to him instead.

Phillip liked Admiral Marcien who was in command of Amphib Island. A slight, meticulous man with a sallow complexion as if he suffered poor health, he was well past sixty and had an intelligent, inquisitive face as if he were a connoisseur of humanity rather than a part of it. His eyes were merry, yet Phillip suspected they could be severe. He seemed to wear his elegant military furnishings with faint apology, and this pleased Phillip, too. The hand he gave was well shaped and steady as a fencer's.

"Welcome aboard, Ensign Froelich," he said, and Phillip, for once, did not find the expression absurd when it was used off-

31

ship. For a few minutes the Admiral talked to him about the Pacific and at last paid him the compliment of asking him and his companions to lunch at his table. Bruner gave Phillip a swift glance of appreciation as if to say, *Now why aren't you that nice to everyone?* Phillip smiled benignly, hardly giving Bruner a second thought. Something else far overshadowed his triumph. He had escaped meeting his companion of the night before, and somehow that was very important to him just now.

There was some jockeying for positions near the head of the table in which Phillip did not join. Of the twenty officers present, all had axes to grind. Phillip and Francis sat apart from the others. Bruner was beside the Admiral's aide. Phillip noticed the emerald again and saw the man's eyes on him. He turned to Francis and did not look back at the man again throughout the meal.

"I thought you were being discharged last month," Phillip opened the conversation with his cousin. "You've the points."

"I agreed to stay on until I go back to Harvard this fall."

Francis never missed an opportunity to refer to his Eastern education, a taunt for Phillip who had attended the free public schools of Oklahoma. Phillip in turn delivered a blow of his own, not so subtle.

"How is everyone at home? I've had no mail for three weeks." And he added with undue emphasis, "Overseas, mail takes on importance it never has here in the states." The reference was to Francis' four years' service without once going overseas or aboard a ship. When Francis turned pink, Phillip knew his barb was not lost.

"Everyone's fine," Francis said. "Fanchon took young Paul-Phillip to St. Louis for X-ray treatments. They had sore throats." Fanchon Cully was Phillip's only sister. "Mother is now in New York shopping. She asked your mother to go, but Aunt Vicky refused, naturally."

"Naturally," Phillip repeated. Each of them had injected his own brand of polite scorn for the other's mother into the word.

32

Soup was put before them and removed. The table grew noisy. For a quarter of an hour Francis related the happenings of their world, and Phillip noticed that as yet no reference had been made to the girl he was going to marry.

At last he interrupted, "And what of the Voths, and Sybel Jo?"

"Oh, yes," Francis laughed. "I knew there was something I wanted to tell you." The fake oversight was accepted as such by Phillip, but his cousin's next words hurled all the complacency from his mind. "Sybel Jo and Madame are coming out here the first of next week."

"What!" Phillip exclaimed sharply. "Who in the hell asked them?"

"Keep your voice down and don't swear. I did, naturally. It's supposed to be a surprise, but I thought you ought to know."

"That's goddamned considerate of you." Phillip's words carried down the table, filling one of those awkward conversational lulls that often trap the unwary. Immediately all eyes turned to him and he felt himself blush. He clenched his teeth until his jaw ached. Someone down the table tittered and suddenly the conversation was resumed as unexpectedly as it had been dropped. Almost inarticulate with rage, Phillip whispered hoarsely, "You clod! You know the one thing I don't want is for Father to find out about my court martial. Sybel Jo and her loud-mouthed stepmother will make it common gossip an hour after they get home. Or maybe you've already spread the glad news!"

Their eyes swung together and locked. Francis' wavered first.

"I don't have to take that from you, Phillip."

"The devil you don't!" Phillip lashed. "You asked that pair out here. You can wire them to cancel the trip."

"I will not. Sybel Jo is your fiancée."

"I'd better not have to wire them," Phillip said and Francis was routed.

"I didn't really invite her. I just wrote her the approximate date of your arrival. It was really her idea."

33

"Bullshit! Sybel Jo never had an idea of her own in her life. You cooked this up so that Madame could do your dirty work. Well, they are not coming!"

"I'm afraid they are, Phillip. They are on their way. Right now they're in Chicago. They'll arrive here Monday morning." And Francis added insult to injury before he claimed the round. "Remember, Phillip, you aren't married to Sybel Jo, yet."

For a few minutes Phillip had to make himself remain at the table. He wanted violent action—a long flesh-shivering swim toward exhaustion, a long delicious-feeling blow to Francis' ugly little nose. During the past agonizing months, Phillip had kept alive one determination: to solve this problem alone; and one hope: that his father and his town would never learn of his predicament. His cousin's move was a clever one, but not entirely unexpected. Ethically unable to inform on Phillip, Francis was delivering his weapon into reliable hands. Madame Voth, Phillip's prospective mother-in-law, would make the court martial number one topic of conversation around every supper table in Devereaux. Phillip could see his father shaking his head solemnly, hear his hammering questions already: *Why . . . ? But why . . . ? Couldn't you have . . . ? But why . . . ?*

He moved uneasily in his chair and looked at the chicken à la king in his plate. He looked at Francis eating the mess as if he liked it. Silently Phillip swore, "One day, dear cousin, one glorious day, I'll break you so completely that you can't crawl!"

In the beginning, when Oklahoma was still The Indian Nations, old Phillip Eugene Devereaux (whom the family still referred to as Grandfather Dev) had founded a bank and a town. With the discovery of oil, he had founded an empire. But since he had fathered no son to succeed him, he had divided his estate equally among his two daughters and his best friend, Felix Mehl, a naturalized German immigrant. This split had been the beginning of a struggle that might last for generations. Immediately the two sons-in-law, Phillip's and Francis' fathers, had moved in to

34

do battle for control of the bank, the nucleus of a fortune that amounted to about ten millions.

Julius Froelich had won the contest by winning the support of Felix Mehl, who during the following years had acted as a stabilizing element for the family. But the Froelich branch had prospered outside the bank. The Barriman branch now had nothing but its original third of the bank, which actually represented only about a half of the great estate. Julius Froelich's second—and perhaps most insulting—victory had been the election of his son-in-law, Paul Cully, into the number two position at the bank, the position Tony Barriman considered his own. At the same time, Julius had offered to buy Tony out. As a result, the two families had not spoken socially for almost seven years. Undoubtedly the present generation belonged to the Froelichs. Now each family was preparing its bid for the coming generation in the person of its male heir.

Phillip was the townspeople's choice, and in Devereaux this was no small factor. Although Phillip stood to inherit only one-half of one-third along with his sister, Fanchon, while Francis would inherit an entire third, Phillip had many points in his favor. There was now "the Froelich money" that people had started talking about in the thirties. Phillip was locally educated, the friend of most of the people in the city and county. He was admired, even venerated a little, because he bore a striking resemblance to his grandfather, Old Phillip. People expected great things of him. The scandal of a court martial could do him no good. A prison sentence might easily wreck his future in Devereaux.

Francis was "the Barriman boy," Roman Catholic, educated in the fancy schools of the East since he was eight. He commanded no real respect from anyone. If he took over the bank, it would dwindle into mediocrity. The Barrimans were snobs, spending most of their time in Boston, Washington, or New Orleans, where they had invested a fortune in schemes to advance their social position. To everyone's delight, they had lost everything and were now compelled to live in Oklahoma on their dividends from the bank. The Froelichs, like Old Phillip, were popular leaders, feeding their harvests cautiously back into Oklahoma enterprises. They were as solid and familiar as the earth they owned. Phillip had always considered himself a worthy heir to his parents' and his grandfather's position. His generation was his problem; Francis was his enemy. He was intensely proud of his obligation.

Once more, sitting at the Admiral's table, Phillip felt the wolves of disaster circle him: Bruner, whom he did not trust; the brutish Captain Morgan with his fat fingers ready to plunge into his troubled brain and bring forth a monstrosity; Francis, a rotten twig on a bad limb of the family tree; Madame Voth and his fiancée, Sybel Jo; even the strange commander of the night before. Yet somehow he had to conquer them all and fulfill his father's faith in him. He felt that his very soul was being tried. This was his first crisis, the first step in the gigantic task of gathering up the scattered parts of Grandfather Dev's empire. Yet he was glad for the challenge.

Once more he went over his weapons. Money. His personal savings account stood at twenty-three thousand, money he had saved all his life; gifts, proceeds from the sale of prize Hereford cattle he had raised, stud fees from his thoroughbred palomino stallion—in short, money that represented the hope and labor of his whole life. Now it would have to go to buy his freedom. Bruner, who he believed might nip this whole thing in the bud, would have his price. There would be other Bruners as the weeks went by. Phillip wondered how long it would be before he could ask Admiral Marcien for favors. Money would not count there, but good manners. He remembered his uncouth remark that had been overheard a few minutes ago. Perhaps he should apologize after lunch. No. Better to ignore the incident.

Tomorrow he would go into Seattle and secretly put his case before the best lawyers in the city. Then if all else failed, he'd fight through them. No appeal! That was Bruner's idea. But until that time, there were things to do. Francis had opened the attack, but the first skirmish had only begun. Perhaps Madame might be persuaded to silence. Perhaps he could defeat Francis' first scheme. He doubted it, since he hated Madame and she had no genuine love for him. Still, they hadn't seen each other for two years. Sybel Jo, his fiancée, did as her mother told her. Madame was the key. He could fight Francis only through her. But it would be well to regain his cousin's confidence. He could do more damage from the inside.

He picked up his fork, touched his food, and with quiet emotion in his voice he said, "I'm sorry, Francis. I didn't mean what I said. I've been under strain so long." He groveled harder. "I was foolish to think that I could keep all this a secret. Actually I'm glad Syb and Madame are coming out. And I'm glad you're here." He laughed a bit shakily. "I must be crazy to fight with the only member of the family who is a lawyer."

Phillip played his role with a delicate regard for detail. He toyed unconsciously with his fork, refusing to meet Francis' eyes from the depths of his great shame. The wan smile, the wistful tone, combined with his extreme youth and innocence, struck the right note of bewildered incompetency, neither too loud to sound genuine nor too soft to be misinterpreted. For once, Phillip was glad that they knew so little about each other.

"Well," Francis replied uncertainly, "I don't know much about naval court procedure. Just do what Bruner tells you."

Phillip relaxed, knowing that with practically no effort he had scored a bull's-eye. Francis sounded very paternal. Phillip wanted to howl with laughter. Instead he nodded solemnly.

"Somehow," he said, "I feel that this may be the real beginning of our friendship, Francis." And his cousin's face grew pink with embarrassed pleasure.

Bruner joined them after lunch and they strolled into the lounge for cigarettes. Phillip listened attentively to the advice of both men until he asked to be excused to pick up his bags and get himself a room. He shook hands with both men and as he was about to turn away, Bruner asked, "By the way, Phillip, do you know Tim?"

Phillip tensed. "The admiral's aide? No. Why?"

"He was asking about you at lunch. He seemed interested."

"I might have met him overseas," Phillip said doubtfully.

"He has never had Pacific duty."

"Oh." Phillip pretended to give the matter some thought and then dismiss it. "Well, I'll see you both this evening here at the club. And, Francis, I'll call you when I get a room."

"Fine."

Again they shook hands and Phillip walked toward the foyer. At the lounge entrance he turned and gave them a final friendly nod. Then, starting to round the corner, he collided violently with another officer. But for the hand that seized his arm, he would have been knocked flat. Angrily he made ready to deliver a few comments on people who round corners too closely on their left, but as he looked up, he gaped foolishly into the amused face of the man named Tim.

"Excuse me, sir," he murmured.

"Tell me, Ensign Froelich," the commander laughed, "is everyone in the Navy guilty of getting in your way?"

"I don't know what you mean, sir," Phillip said coldly, waiting for the hand to release him. "If you'll excuse me."

"Of course," the man said, his sibilant voice growing harsh.

Stiffly they walked past each other. Phillip did not look back at Francis and Bruner, but he knew they had observed the scene.

"Damn!" he muttered. "If it isn't one stupid thing, it's another."

4

❖·❖·❖·❖·❖·❖·

*H*e had no difficulty in finding his room in bachelor officers'
quarters. Fortunately he found it unoccupied. At least he could
expect some privacy. But it was a depressing, ugly square with
two of everything—bureaus, desks, beds—all painted an enervat-
ing gray. The air was musty and his head ached from the frustration of the interview with Bruner and his scene with Francis. He
threw the windows open and put his bags on the bed to unpack.

They were handsome bags, rawhide, silk-lined, gifts from his
godparents, Uncle Felix and Aunt Minna, the year he went off
to college. He unpacked the handmade French linen shirts, gifts
from his sister, his dress blue uniforms of English cloth tailored
by his brother-in-law's tailor in Boston, custom-made shoes, a
robe of stiff brown silk, silk socks, linen handkerchiefs, and his
writing case of morocco. He put solid ivory brushes and cuff
links of chased antique gold on the bureau, possessions of
Grandfather Dev, purchased in Paris forty years ago. Everything
he possessed reminded him of that which he would one day

inherit. Yet expensive as his belongings were, there was little that was effeminate about them—no fluff, no excessive color, no "fairy"-like scents. They had the beauty of quality—his family's investment of dollars to show their love for him. Out of place as they were in the Navy, and a source of constant worry lest they be ruined or stolen, they nevertheless served a subtle purpose. They were visible reminders of his past and future, surrounding him like a nest of cotton wool, choking out the present entirely.

He made a list of his laundry and put it outside the door. Then he smoked a cigarette, wished he had some brandy, tried to write a letter to his mother but dictated a telegram over the pay telephone in the corridor instead, and at last started wandering unseeingly about the hideous room, feeling the familiar lethargy of melancholia steal over him. His bowels tightened with loathing for himself.

For many months he had felt near to death. He imagined it moved at his side. He waited for the event that would release him from this void. He did not fear it, but at times the waste of it depressed him. All his life, his father had trained him to be the material leader of their town. The time was approaching for him to marry and take over some responsibility. He accepted this calmly; he believed he looked forward to it, for he was well aware of his capability. The peculiar nature of the wealth Phillip planned to govern was that it was medievally elemental. It lay about him in objects he could touch. It involved no tricky financial strategy with entities he could not see. Any businessman of ability could control it—his Grandfather Dev had seen to that. He knew these comforting things and oftentimes he longed to flee back to bury his senses in the minor turmoils of local politics.

But he was not entirely foolish. He had read enough of the machinations of the diseased mind to know that he was suffering from something that might easily destroy him. No normal man was beset with melancholia, emotional frigidity, or the

40

homosexual symbolism that he found in himself. If only these things were something he could see Returning to Devereaux now might destroy him, or it might cure him of his phobias. Dimly he realized that his entry into the Navy had brought these shadowy things to light. He wanted to fight them successfully, but he wanted to do it alone. He hated the thought of a psychiatrist. If he were too weak to solve his own problems, he was too weak to deserve the right to live; so he fought with himself blindly, savagely. Until lately, he had sometimes felt that he was winning, if slowly. But if he lost his fight—and now he believed he might lose it—he must go quickly. One minute he would be alive, aware. The next he would be dead. The break must be clean, smooth, sharp.

At the approach of melancholia he had usually stripped naked, if his ship was in one of the island ports, and plunged over the side to swim hard for an hour, stopping only when he was dangerously near exhaustion. Fatalistically he had feared neither shark nor barracuda, and because no one understood him, he had earned a reputation for bravery among the men he commanded. If the ship was under way at the time of an attack, he turned to any manual labor at hand, chipping paint scale or stripping and servicing the twenty-millimeter antiaircraft guns —a feat he could do faster and better than any man aboard. He would not allow himself to think. Only a fool would sit idly by, helping his mind spiral downward into a miasma of half-truths. He lived for the day when he could free himself of the Navy and select his own master. While waiting, he broke himself physically and thereby drugged himself mentally. Worst of all, he drew further into himself. Whereas once he had only mild contempt for humanity, he was now approaching the point of loathing it. In rare lucid moments, he was so struck with his selfishness that his blood chilled with horror.

Phillip tossed his cigarette into the wastebasket—painted gray, too—and put on his hat and coat. This was a big base. He would go out and find something to interest him for the rest of

41

the afternoon, something to focus his attention on other than himself. If this failed, he'd swim all afternoon, not in the pool at the club but in the cold, blue sound. And if, when evening came, melancholia still threatened, he would go into town and pick up a woman and relieve himself in one night of many weeks of festered dreams. Or perhaps he'd stay on the base and drink himself senseless.

He left the building, left officer's country, headed for the repair docks, and gently eased himself into the stream of activity about him. Immediately he felt better. At a small boat slip, he watched sailors take a sea-slimed engine out of a LCVP. One of the men was stripped to the waist, tall, blond as a Norse god.

"Salt?" Phillip asked him.

"Naw. Points."

Phillip nodded. That the man had failed to address him as "sir" pleased him. He disliked this effete naval custom. He admired brute force and cunning as qualities of leadership among men. He grew interested in the engine's removal, but he offered no advice to the men. They began to relax and once in a while cast a speculative eye in his direction. At last they started pointing their remarks to him as if they had a desire to please him so long as he kept his distance. Finally the half-naked sailor who seemed to be in charge approached.

"Cigarette?"

"Thanks." Phillip took the offering and the sailor's light.

"New here?" the encouraged sailor asked.

"Transient." Phillip allayed the man's suspicion with one deft word. "Just moseying around," he added.

The blond nodded toward the boat. "Core struts rotted out." Then he asked, "Where you from?"

"Oklahoma."

"I had a buddy from Nowata once. Good Joe. I'm from Wisconsin."

"I knew a fellow from Madison once."

"I'm from Ishpenring. That's on the lake."

42

Two more sailors approached and one, the clown of the group, said, "Get to work, you big son-of-a-bitch." And winking, he added, "This sucker acts like he's carrying braid during the day, but on liberty it's buddy-buddy, buy me a drink, lend me a buck, gimme your woman."

Phillip laughed easily and offered the newcomers cigarettes. "Where is a good place to make liberty?" he asked.

"That's according to what you want," the jester grinned.

"I'm just in from the fleet," Phillip said evenly.

"Well, there's a couple of bars down on Fifth."

"Hell, he don't want no scud, you goddamn dope," the blond said, and to Phillip he advised, "The best pick-up place right now is The Snake Pit. Servicemen's wives out here waiting for their husbands and on the town for a night or two. Not whores. Clean stuff."

Phillip nodded again, respectfully revealing his admiration for the man's judgment. The remaining sailors had at last got the marine engine on a low-wheeled dolly and were pushing it toward the repair sheds. The blond stepped over, gave orders, and came back.

"I gotta cut new struts. Wanna come along, sir?"

"Okay." Phillip was pleased at the invitation and the belated title, now that he had earned the man's respect. They walked up the dock in silence and entered a long, medium-sized building with wide double doors at either end. It contained two shops, for through a door in the half-partition that divided the building Phillip saw tables of electrical equipment to be repaired, armatures and so on. In the end Phillip had entered, there was a wood and metal workshop. It possessed a small forge, lathes, power saws, and half a dozen open cabinets of tools. In piles, lumber and sheet metal of various lengths and thicknesses had been stacked for use.

Already rummaging through a pile of quarter- and half-inch iron, the blond sailor called, "Hey, chief, how about makin' a couple of struts?"

43

"Sure, help yourself," a short thickset man in dungarees replied, appearing through the door in the half-partition. Before he closed it, he called to two squatting men at the opposite end of the building who seemed to be cleaning parts with a wire brush over a can. "Hey, you bastards, I'm going to small stores. Be careful with that goddamn naphtha. It explodes."

"Aw, go on," one answered. "We read Dick Tracy, too."

"Go to hell," the chief returned, and to the blond sailor he said, "Keep an eye on 'em. They're liable to blow you to kingdom come." And he left the shop.

Phillip experienced an unexplainable tinge of uneasiness at the word naphtha. He had used it in chem classes a few times and he was acquainted with its deadly properties. He was also aware of the average sailor's carelessness. He had an impulse to get out of the building, but he put it down as foolish and turned to watch the blond coxswain pull a strip of iron from the heap. He carried it to a bench and marked it off carefully with chalk. Phillip liked this fellow, silent, capable, polite. It was a pleasure to see him work after listening to Bruner and Francis.

Phillip helped him adjust the piece of metal before the great upright circular saw and held it while the sailor put on goggles. He handed Phillip another pair which Phillip held to his eyes rather than take off his hat to put them on. Phillip watched the man throw the switch and saw the band saw spin into motion, its bright teeth blurring into a narrow gleaming halo about the outer edge. It was a fearful object, Phillip thought, as the sailor slowly but firmly fed the chalked line against the blade. The whirling circle screamed, its speed staggering and recovering as it bit through the iron bar. When the first chalk line was sawed, the sailor pulled the metal back and held it up for Phillip's admiration. They grinned at each other but said nothing, for their ears still rang from the high, fierce shriek of the saw.

The second line was poised before the saw when they heard the yell of terror from the two men in the other end of the building. Phillip felt the breath leave his lungs as he grabbed

44

the table for support against the impact he knew would come. He was starting to turn and face it when he heard the iron in the sailor's hand touch the whirling blade, evidently by accident, for Phillip heard the man utter a curse. Then the explosion hit them, hot as the swift blast of.a furnace and as enveloping as a feather mattress, as hard against their eyes and stomachs and lips as a hundred battering fists. Phillip felt himself driven against the wall, and he remembered the saw, that silver halo, whirling a foot or so from him before he lost consciousness.

He had been unconscious for only a few seconds, he decided, focusing his eyes on dark billowing smoke and clear pale flame before him. The pain in his neck was hot and liquid, as if marrow were pouring out of broken bone. His chin rested on his chest and he was on his back on the floor, covered with metal and lumber. For a sickening instant he thought he was trapped before the boiling wall of fire that leaped over the flattened partition toward him. But he could move, he found, and started to get to his feet. Thank God, he was near the door. Then he remembered the sailor and the saw and looked toward the now quiet table. He felt the mask of his face shatter into pieces of horror and his flesh grow cold and wet all over. The arm of the blond sailor was trapped halfway through the stopped saw by a fallen timber wedged between roof, bench, and deck. The bright metal was stained with crimson, its teeth sharp and anxious inside the mangled flesh.

The unconscious sailor, his hair gone, his flesh the color of a half-roasted pig, the ludicrous goggles awry, hung by his imprisoned arm halfway between the table and the floor. Instinctively Phillip seized the two parts of the arm at wrist and elbow and tried to pull it free. But as he caused the severed muscle to part, arteries spurted fresh streams of red over the blade. He felt his stomach heave, but he forced himself to seize the grisly thing and pull at it again and then again. A ghastly moan escaped the man's lips. The bone, half-sawed through, had not moved. The man was there to burn to death. Phillip glanced

45

over his shoulder at the fiery wall that had moved about three feet closer. He turned back and hastily examined the timber that pinned the wrist to the blade. He threw his ebbing strength against it, but it did not budge. He found a smaller plank to use as a pry against it, setting it under the base of the timber and lifting cautiously, trying to spring the heavy beam just a few inches to relieve the pressure, but the pry snapped and he fell against the wall. He rushed back, feeling the eager stab of panic.

The heat was becoming unbearable on his back. He wiped the stinging sweat from his eyes with his sleeve and brought it down slick with blood. His own, he thought dully, trying to decide what to do next to free the man. If he had some help—he ran to the door and tried to see through the thick, choking smoke that poured out around him. There was no one in sight, so he ran back to the pinioned man who would soon be dead if he weren't already. Another dull explosion, probably a can of gasoline, sounded within the flames and a spurt of fire landed on the sailor's dungarees and naked skin. Phillip beat it out with his hands, choking, crying for breath, fighting the nausea and strange weakness that seemed to be growing within him. He looked at the arm again and the widening mess of blood, trying to keep his head. It was the arm that held him. It was almost gone. If the blade had sawed another inch, the sailor would be free. The answer was clear. The arm had to go. Swaying, with unsteady hands, he seized the arm and the switch, thinking that he might be able to push the arm on through if the power were turned on. He threw the switch and cringed toward his job, but nothing happened—no answering roar of the saw. The power had been knocked out by the blast.

He was panting now. Fear and courage fought for possession of him. In sheer panic he seized the sailor's body and heaved, hoping to pull the arm off. He felt the limb give like a joint of beef, but it held. Nearly vomiting, he swayed against the dead weight of the man. Thank God, the fellow was unconscious. Phillip saw his clothes beginning to smoke. His neck and hands

46

felt raw. The fire was no more than eight feet away; the heat was hellish. Wildly he looked about him for a knife, for anything he could use to sever the arm. And when he saw it, a short-handled hatchet on the floor, he leaped at it as if it might disappear. For a second he balanced it in his hand, leaned over the sailor, took aim, gritted his teeth, and strucked timidly at the dirty flesh. The hatchet bounced off as if it had struck hard rubber. His timidity infuriated him. A flame of anger, clean and determined, flashed through him hotly, and snarling at the horrible thing before him, he aimed and delivered a powerful, biting blow, feeling the savage sensation of breaking bone beneath his directed force. Another blow through muscle and flesh and the spurting stump slipped free, the big sailor's body sliding down against his legs to the floor.

Quickly Phillip dropped the hatchet and seized the body to struggle with it toward the door. Once he fell, but he recovered his burden and cleared the door. He carried the sailor as far as he could and when he felt his knees buckle, he dropped with the unconscious man and immediately listened to the feeble heartbeat, his ear and cheek sticking to the burned, bloody chest. He started working quickly, making a tourniquet of his handkerchief, remembering to put it below the elbow, placing small stones against the arteries to give additional pressure, and finally with a sliver of stick, twisting the handkerchief tight. At least he had stopped the bleeding.

He became aware of the crowd forming around him. He heard their babble over the dim blast of the fire whistle that announced the disaster to the whole base. Trucks roared by; men ran about shouting excitedly. For a minute Phillip ignored them, watching the sailor; then he roused himself long enough to tell one of the crowd to call an ambulance. He was told that one was coming. Trembling, he wiped the blood from his forehead so he could see. He bent and listened to the heartbeat again. It seemed stronger. Suddenly a groan escaped the man's lips. He was coming around. For a moment Phillip thought of tying him, but

47

there was no time for that. Looking up at the circle of faces, he picked out four of the calmest.

"You," he pointed the four out. "Stand by to hold him."

The men knelt about him, each grasping an arm or leg, waiting. Phillip gripped the dirty tourniquet, dreading the scream of recognition that he knew would come, steeling himself against it. His nausea returned again, but he fought it down, trying not to think of the man before him—the man that he had maimed for life—or the piece of arm somewhere in the inferno behind him. He found himself saying inanely, "Fresh-cut alfalfa, still in the field, the hill and the spring at dusk, cattle going to the barn for milking, pausing to drink where the watercress is thick and ropy and cold, the smell of mint and creek mud mingling. . . . God! Why don't they hurry?"

There was no warning that he was fainting. He did not relax slowly, nor did his vision blur. In one instant he was aware of the heat and the blood; in the next he was aware of blinding light in his eyes. He lay on his back and people were talking in a darkness he could not penetrate. He frowned and tried to sit up. Immediately hands emerged from the gloom to hold him. Someone said, "Don't move." There was a familiar odor in the air. The hospital. Someone was bathing his arms and from the feel of the sheet under him, he knew that his clothes had been removed. Suddenly there was a sharp pain high in his scalp and the dull sensation of something stringy and resinous being pulled out of his head. He understood that he was being sewed together. He lay silent, hearing the voices, feeling the wet cloth on his skin, counting the sharp pricks of the needle and the ensuing pull that reminded him of saddle patching back home. Twice, three times, four, and the voice said, "There it is." And another voice, feminine, jovial: "Too bad we had to cut into that mop of curls." The light went off and he opened his eyes.

They were winding bandages about his head. Faces, smiling and curious, appeared, disappeared, appeared again. His brain felt languorous, but his body remained stiff. There was a sharp pain in his shoulder and the dull burn of antiseptic whose caustic odor crept over his face. He closed his eyes again, wishing he was not nude before these people, but not really caring. The feminine voice said, "Hey, cutie, don't go to sleep. I want to ask you for a date tonight." Nurses—bold, impudent. Fingers at his eye, forcing it open, forcing him to see a round pretty face with crinkling eyes and fluffy hair. He turned his head away. "You're not very appreciative." His arms were lifted and forced into sleeves. They lifted his head and tied strings at his neck. Machinery was moved over him and he was forced into uncomfortable positions. X-ray pictures. He was growing drowsy.

It was dark outside when he awoke and the lights in his room were softly shaded. He tried to move, and for a moment pain, unbelievable in its quality and completeness, enveloped every bit of his body. He felt as if he had been beaten all over with thick hickory clubs. He opened his eyes cautiously, seeing Francis and Bruner standing on either side of the bed, looking down at him grimly. For a moment he thought they were a dream, but Francis touched his hand.

"Do you feel like talking, Phillip?"

"No."

Phillip closed his eyes and heard Francis burst out softly, "But why were you down there when it happened, that's what I can't understand? Phillip, do you want me to call your parents?"

"No."

"Would you like us to come back tomorrow?"

"Yes." Phillip waited until he heard the door close before he opened his eyes. He wanted to go back to sleep, but the fog about him was beginning to clear and suddenly he felt the distinct jar of the ax in his hand and saw the bloody stump slip free. He shivered violently.

Why had he been forced to make that decision? Why did disaster dog his movements? Why was he out of harmony with

49

everything? Everything. He felt a scream swell in his chest until his throat ached with holding it back. If it got the better of him, if it escaped, he knew that his mind would snap. He tried to focus his eyes on a crack in the ceiling, but they blurred. He gripped the sides of the bed and clenched his teeth, letting the volume of sound in his throat escape in a thin stream as one lets air from a balloon.

"Uncle Felix," he panted aloud, "dear Uncle Felix. *Dies sind die Tage die. mir nicht gefallen.* Grandfather Dev, help me, hold me," and at last, words which shamed him to utter, "Pray for me." They bubbled from his mouth, the froth of madness and death.

"Would you like to sit up?"

Swiftly Phillip's eyes went to the door. At the foot of the bed, his face calm and serious, stood the lieutenant commander named Tim. Phillip had not heard the door open or the man enter. His pent-up breath escaped in a silent rush. But when he remembered the man's question, he answered, "I don't know."

The man smiled faintly and bent to the controls of the bed. He cranked Phillip's head up a bit, paused, and cranked a little more. It felt wonderful, releasing him from the feeling that he was helpless.

"Thank you," Phillip said.

"Now how about turning over on your side awhile?"

"I don't know again. I'm too sore to try."

"Perhaps if I helped."

The man put his hat on the table, leaned over Phillip, slid his hands under the boy's shoulders, lifted him easily, held him with one arm while he made the pillows horizontal, and then, with a minimum of pain, eased him back so that he rested on his side.

"Thanks again."

The man pulled a chair close and sat down so that Phillip could see him. "Now that you're helpless, perhaps you'll let me introduce myself." He smiled. "I'm Tim Danelaw."

50

"How do you do, sir?"

"Quite well, young fellow. But the question is: how are you doing?" The man's eyes twinkled with subdued humor.

"Not so good, sir."

"Fate has given you the back of her hand again."

Phillip smiled. "That she has."

"Like a cigarette?"

"Please."

Tim Danelaw gave him one from a dull metal case and lighted it. They smoked in silence while he studied the boy frankly. At last he said, "Tomorrow morning you'll be questioned by the base security officer. They'll want to know why you were in the machine shop when you had no business there. They'll want to know everything about the sailor you carried to safety. When they got the fire out, they found, among other things, a small ax." He let the smoke cloud his narrow, thoughtful eyes a moment. "The explosion was on the other side of the building. Naphtha, a careless cigarette. You can't be connected with that. But what they will want to know is what happened before you got out of there. In your present delicate position—the court martial I mean—there can't be any loose ends. Understand?"

Phillip nodded, his eyes so wide he felt them ache.

"As it stands now, some fool may decide that the sailor should have remained in the fire. Naval investigations are clumsy affairs. Suppose you tell me why you were there so you'll know what you're going to say in the morning."

"The sailor?" Phillip asked. "What of him?"

"He died late this evening . . ." he answered quietly. "No. Not from the loss of blood. Concussion. A clot formed in the brain."

"Oh." Phillip took this information into his mind carefully, as if he were undecided where to lay it.

Danelaw stood up. "How about a rubdown?" he asked. "As a Scandinavian, I should be an expert."

Phillip did not answer, but he did not protest when the man

51

put him on his stomach and untied his nightshirt. Nor did he think it strange that the man knew his way around a hospital. He shivered at the first icy touch of alcohol against his skin, but he soon relaxed under the hypnotic rhythm of the man's slow fingers. And he started to talk. In hard disjointed phrases beginning with the strange restlessness in his room, Phillip described the scenes he had passed through. Finally he paused, breathing shortly with the horror of his words. He swallowed and went on breathlessly, "It took three blows. If he had been conscious . . . if he had screamed. . . . Then I carried him outside . . . that's all."

The powerful fingers continued to massage as if their purpose was to transfuse strength into him. When the man answered, his voice was low, filled with the drama he had heard. "You acted very bravely. Many would have faltered." The massage ended and his nightshirt was retied. "Feel better?"

"Much, thanks; and mentally, too."

"It always helps to put fear into words," Danelaw said. "And speaking of fear, one more question. Why are you afraid of me?"

Phillip, growing sleepy again, looked at the face above him and smiled. "I'm not afraid of you, sir, but of myself."

Through the windows the sound of footsteps and distant laughter from the street crept into the room, breaking the silence that followed. Danelaw crossed the room and turned off the light. He approached the bed.

"At the risk of being misunderstood," he said softly. He leaned over the bed and put his lips briefly to Phillip's forehead. "Good night. Sleep well."

"Good night, sir."

The room was dark and a fog laden breeze moved the curtains sluggishly. For the first time in months Phillip felt a flow of happiness within him. He felt warm, secure, desirous of sleeping soundly.

5

◇•◇•◇•◇•◇•◇•

*H*e was kept at the hospital five days. On the morning after the accident, he waited with some impatience for the base security officer to arrive. He wanted to tell his story for the last time and forget it, for he considered it neither noble nor brave. He had acted under pressure and fortunately he had not lost his head. His fainting had ruined any glory he might have found in the episode. Fainting he regarded as unmasculine. The stitches in his scalp were irrelevant.

But the security officer did not arrive. Instead, at 0830 Francis and Bruner came in. They were innocently cheerful and sat down for a long talk about everything but what was on their minds. Francis did not burst out this time but sat quietly discussing the legal procedure of Phillip's approaching trial with a ghoulish interest in possible repercussions. At 0900 he started glancing first at the door and then at Phillip. By 0930 he had traded his interest in the door for an interest in the ship's chronometer that ticked pleasantly over the small desk, filling in the increasing gaps in their ragged conversation. And as Francis' uneasiness increased, Phillip's impatience died for now Phillip knew that because of the unexpected interview of the preceding night there would be no questioning. The contrast between the selfish secrecy of Francis and Bruner, and the friendly consideration of Timothy Danelaw strengthened something cold-blooded and cruel in Phillip. He could appreciate Francis' hatred for him, for he returned it; but Bruner was beyond all reason. Beyond reason, too, but by another standard, was this man Danelaw. At last, to Phillip's relief, the unwelcome pair departed, leaving him alone to analyze the problems before him, the first of which was Timothy Danelaw.

Was the obvious explanation the only reason for the man's interest in him? Homosexuality was no stranger to the Navy or to Phillip. Many years ago, and without too many serious qualms, Phillip had admitted to himself that certain men found him more than interesting. He looked upon this fact as a potential weapon which he might better use to his own advantage rather than have it used against him—so long as it was confined to those limits within which he had been reared. Many men had sought his friendship; he had granted it to few, partly because he was aware of this element in his personality, but more because he found that most men did not inhabit the rarefied atmosphere of his lofty ambitions. He cultivated snobbishness as a shield against those he did not want to know. Assiduously he avoided persons, places, and events that suggested any possibility of erotic trouble. He was engaged to be married to a girl who would contribute to his material wealth and who was capable of bearing him sound, sturdy children. That she was beautiful was a bit of luck, for sexual pleasure, his Baptist father had taught him, was an element of marriage and confined to marriage by the decent, civilized people of the earth.

Physically, Phillip dominated himself. He was simply a splendid young animal, comparable by a stretch of imagination to a half-grown cougar, sleek and tawny in appearance. The muscles

54

of his arms and legs rose slowly from bone, swelled trimly, and slid into the contour of his body. His chest, deep with muscle about each vestigial nipple, sloped gently to abdomen and the incredibly hard lines of narrow pelvic organization. Other individual features—lean, lower ribs, an almost triangular face, steady eyes, and his own peculiar gliding movements—gave him the half-hungry air of a young cat. His body was the result of irregular but vigorous exercise and a stoical moderation of desire.

Mentally the boy was apt. If his reasoning was more concrete than abstract, it was because of his training. That he was temporarily off balance did not ordinarily bother him greatly, for given a chance to retreat from a world he disliked rather than misconceived, he was certain he could develop into a good citizen, doing a great deal more to further his community than most he would meet. He was completely practical. From his first years, he had worked in the bank after school and on the farms over weekends, doing the most menial tasks; and he had devoted his summers to jobs his father approved—ranch hand at the family property on the Kansas line, and later a roustabout in the oil fields that lay on family property. But always he had worked for his father, the severest boss of all, learning the various needs of the three industries the family fortune rested upon —land, cattle, and oil. He had joined every farm and fraternal organization that his father had selected for him—4-H, Demolays, and finally the Junior Chamber of Commerce—but never as an ordinary member, always as a future leader.

Intellectually he had twice been forced to decide between fool and businessman, his father's terms, and his father had made his selection. Phillip had dreamed two dreams. At the age of eight he had wanted to become a pianist; at thirteen he had wanted a career in the diplomatic corps. And he had continued to drive the tractor, bale the hay, ride the fences, dig out the leaks in the oil lines. In the winter he went to school and justified his father's theories on child rearing by making more perfect marks than imperfect ones. Phillip had set out early creating

55

the third Devereaux legend, a legend he believed he believed in.

Now he thought of Timothy Danelaw either timidly or morosely but as frankly as he knew how. Danelaw was an unorthodox man. In Bruner's conversation a few minutes before, Phillip had been surprised to learn that Danelaw was only thirty-three years old (he had guessed him to be almost forty), only ten years Phillip's senior. The name Danelaw, which had at first seemed familiar, Bruner had explained, too. The man was a member of the Milwaukee family that brewed the famous Danelaw beer, "The Ale of Vikings—There's a Skoal in Every Stein." Phillip had drunk it during his midshipman days. He had preferred Budweiser. Francis had said that the man was married to a woman with the formidable title of "Bitch of Queen Anne Hill," and that the couple lived in some artist's showplace in the city. The man was painter, traveler, and something of a dilettante, though Phillip thought that the term had died with the last century. The sound of these accomplishments stuck crossways in his mind. They sounded right for the man who had driven him up to Seattle, but wrong for the man who had aided him last night. He remembered the man's hands, lifting his aching shoulders, massaging his hot, stiff back; the drowsy voice, asking for and receiving confidence. It had not occurred to him to be suspicious. Of course, he had been drugged. Still, had Francis or Bruner asked for the same information, he would not have given it. And when Danelaw had turned off the light . . . *At the risk of being misunderstood . . . Bonne nuit. . . .*

Suddenly Phillip realized that the man had spoken French to him, that he had replied in French, the transition having been so smooth he had not realized that it had taken place. Yet how had the man known that he spoke the language? He tried to reconstruct the rest of the conversation, but it had blurred. He remembered only the last part clearly. Why had the man kissed him? No longer doped, Phillip did not like the idea. Again, it was unmasculine. Yet last night it had been the farewell gesture

56

of a man to his favorite younger brother. It had been rather Biblical in its flavor. He thought of Joseph and the young Benjamin. And in the man there seemed to be some strange, ancient quality. Or perhaps it was universal, rather in time with all time.

Phillip never kissed other men, except his Uncle Felix on birthdays to show his appreciation for the old man's handsome gifts, but that was an outgrowth of his babyhood, a custom his godfather insisted on keeping alive. And always, he kissed Felix' sister, Aunt Minna, too. But whatever Danelaw's motive, the practice was not desirable. Certainly Phillip owed the man a debt and he must show his gratitude. He must call at his office one day, express his thanks, and thus end the matter.

But he could not end his thoughts of the man abruptly. Dimly Phillip realized that in some way there were counterparts, the man possessing a strength that ran to decadence, the boy a decadence that yearned to be strong. Phillip was completely unaware of the nature of these factors he had just admitted into his conscious mind. In one compartment he had placed living tissue. Immediately above it, ready to break through, an acid.

Timothy Danelaw would not be called extremely handsome by any popular advertising standard, unless it was his size, a thing that slightly repulsed Phillip. He had the massive head and frame of his ancestors. Already his black hair was thinning at the temples, giving his brow an even broader appearance. His heavy brows and dark eyes were well spaced, but his nose was large and rather bulbous, diving to a sharp triangle of cartilage over the full, bluntly shaped lips. His mouth was wide, and he had a trick of holding one side practically immobile as he spoke, causing a deep line to appear on the opposite side as if he were half-smiling. The heavy jaw inclined to fleshiness about the throat. Against Phillip's cold-blooded passionlessness, he appeared more sensual than he was.

Despite the unwholesome connotation of his actions, nothing could have been more natural than Tim's interest in the boy he had picked up at the cafe. To Phillip, the man seemed obvious; but crafty as Phillip was, he still thought as the average man of his class thought.

He did not know that as flag secretary, an outline of his case must reach Danelaw's desk before he could even be arraigned for trial. Nor did he know that in the performance of his duties, Danelaw was often forced to give a great deal of his personal energies. In the selfish world about him, Tim was an unique man. There was nothing lofty in his generosity. He devoted himself to the job at hand because he had nothing better to do, and by delving into the chaos of amphibious affairs, he escaped the searing boredom of pettiness that surrounded him. Like many servicemen, the war had placed his personal life in a bell jar. Unlike most of these men, he directed his faculties against a snarl of problems of such proportion and character that they could never be completely solved. He was that curious combination of philosopher and executive found often enough in history books and rarely in the mundane course of living. Personally he was ambitionless; that was the crux of his personality. Twice in his life he had abandoned his Olympian calm, and twice he had faced disaster squarely; once in the guise of suicide; again, and more horrible, in the disintegration of self-respect. He felt in each case the fault had been his own, and he was determined to add nothing more to his list of crimes against humanity. Had Phillip known this, he would have regarded the man with a great deal less alarm.

All his life, Tim Danelaw had been alone. As one of the few legitimate heirs of an American fortune, he had been used by his Viennese mother, with whom he lived, to dislodge more dollars for her infamous Riviera affairs. Her friends, average boors of the era, called her "Dolly," and she had been one of those international pierrettes that helped to make the twenties fabulous. She had been murdered when Tim was eleven, and he had been summoned to Chicago to meet his father and his

58

great Aunt Cathinka with whom he was to live. That was in 1924. He remembered the scene well.

Cold, gray sheets of rain whipped in off Lake Michigan against the tall windows. There was a blue parrot in the room and a fire. Silently he kissed his aunt, a large woman with puffy white hair, a silver-embroidered gown, and an ebony cane. His father, a ponderous irritable man, continued to gaze out of the windows, ignoring his son. Tim, tall, self-contained for his years, quiet and shabbily dressed, waited for someone to speak. At last, after a few remarks in English, which Tim did not understand well, his aunt asked him what he wanted to do. Tim replied, in French, 'hat since she had the money, it was hardly up to him.

Turning abruptly, his father had ordered him to address his Aunt Cathinka in English or Danish. Tim realized that the old lady did not speak French and that his father had sneeringly included Danish to put him in his place. But his dollar-wise mother had looked far into their future and had gone to the trouble of having her son taught more than the rudiments of his ancestors' language in the hope of placing her pry even closer to the family treasury. So young Tim, in Danish, asked his aunt which language she would prefer. The effect of this *coup de main* won him a friend, for the old dame was enchanted with him. She remained so the rest of her life.

He was sent to a nearby military school so he might visit her frequently. In school he was called "brilliant, an excellent sportsman and leader." He demanded and received solitude. He longed for Europe constantly. So his aunt engaged a young couple, Sam and Dootie Richards, who taught music in a junior college, to take Tim to Europe for three months every summer. They were the nearest approach to parents he ever had. They made him happy because it was advantageous to do so. In Europe they inevitably went to Northern Italy, Milano, Venezia, Turino, Firenze. So when he was graduated at fifteen, he announced that he wanted to study painting. His father's cable from Africa read: "Hell no!" He entered a prep school, the first leg of his study of architectural engineering. But when his father was killed two years later in an arctic hunting expedition, he returned to live with his Aunt Cathinka. A year later he had her permission to study painting in Italy and eventually to take his place among the masters. It took him two years to realize that he would never rival them, much less outdistance them. Philosophically, he changed his ambitions to hobbies and sailed for Egypt, a new setting, a new frame of mind. He was twenty, with a faint suspicion that his interest in life was gone. In a few months he returned to Europe and played. And then he met a man named Jardine.

Jardine was a doctor from the University of Glasgow, on his way to the Orient to experiment with a new cholera drug on which he had been working. Tim went along as a laboratory assistant. The next four years were the most important of Tim's life. He matured under many influences: the East with its wretchedness and its understanding of human nature; hard work; failure; defeat; the war in China; and his first friendship with its elusive demands that soon became all too apparent as something else; and at last the death of his friend. He sailed for the States determined to study medicine. Instead he had married his wife. This was the man whose interest Phillip had unconsciously aroused.

All afternoon Phillip waited for Danelaw to call, but he did not come that day or the following days that Phillip remained in the hospital. He was puzzled, a little disappointed, a little glad. However, on his second day he had a caller, a plain pleasant-mannered little man in gray carrying a neat black brief case. Phillip, sitting by the window, arose stiffly and shook hands when the man introduced himself.

"Lieutenant Commander Danelaw asked me to call on you. I am his legal representative in Seattle. He thought you might want to talk with me."

Phillip nodded and they sat down. Phillip asked the man a

few questions and when the answers seemed satisfactory, he began to discuss his court martial. Once more Danelaw had guessed his desires and sent his own legal adviser to him. For two hours they talked, and when the little man left, Phillip felt much better.

Once more an old fact was brought sharply before him: that in all organizations, particularly those that profess to represent the people equally, the strong rule the weak, the wise the dull, the wealthy the poor. Once more Danelaw had interfered; once more Phillip had made a step toward peace of mind. Yet, perversely enough, Phillip grew more certain of the man's motives. Conceivably Danelaw would do him a series of favors—perhaps even dispell the court martial by certain pressures—and expect Phillip to surrender himself.

Phillip smiled faintly. All obligation he felt to the man melted. Anyone he could outguess he could not respect. He would play along until he was free. The break would be gentle and considerate, for it would be bad strategy to incur the wrath of a powerful man. Yes, the break must be gentle, he mused, but firm.

On the fifth day, his last in the hospital, he received three letters, his first mail in a month. It should have been a joyous occasion.

6

⟡•⟡•⟡•⟡•⟡•⟡

$\mathcal{M}$y dear son,

"Your father and I are happy that you are once more in the United States and near one of the family again. I hope that you and Francis have grown up sufficiently to enjoy, or tolerate, each other's company. We are quite well now that your father has recovered from another severe attack of indigestion. Fanchon left for St. Louis today for the last of young Paul-Phillip's treatments. We're all saying that you won't recognize your nephew when you return. Franchon sends her 'most gracious love to her civilization-starved brother,' and says that she hopes 'that Madame Voth has kept Sybel Jo on ice for you.' There are times when your sister shows the poorest possible taste in getting to the roots of truth.

"And having mentioned the Voths, I am giving you warning, though you must know by now, that Sybel Jo and her mother will arrive in Seattle Monday morning for a week's visit. The idea is theirs and it does seem odd to all of us here. You won't

62

find either of them changed, unfortunately. Sybel Jo was out the other evening with the Leversen girl to tell me of the trip. After her account of it, she asked me if there was something I wanted to send to you." Here Phillip smiled, half in embarrassment for the girl he planned to marry, half in sympathy with his mother's amusement. "She is bringing you a riding crop." His smile became a guffaw as he thought of his mother's twinkling blue eyes and her serious face as she had written this. The Voths' ingratiating friendliness had always been a source of hilarity among his mother, sister, and himself. That his mother was sending him something as useless as a riding crop, to the girl's complete artlessness, struck him as funny. Later the three of them would howl about it.

"Though it is June, Uncle Felix and Aunt Minna have delayed going to the farm because of the unseasonably cold weather we're having this year. Aunt Minna's diligent work has at last been rewarded. The Catholic diocese will have a new church when materials are again available. The poor old dear wept when she told me the other afternoon, and I must confess I was close to tears, too. She is more of a saint than ever. The sweaters and gloves she has knitted, the nursing she has done to prove her loyalty to our country, as if anyone would accuse her of sympathizing with the Nazis. And her concern for your Uncle Felix was really pathetic, and all because he fought for Germany during the First War. As your Grandfather Dev so aptly put it once, 'Minna's life is devoted to Jesus Christ and Felix Mehl, but there's some confusion in her mind as to which of the two is her brother.' But for Felix, she would have been a nun fifty years ago.

"As for Uncle Felix, he is less active than when you saw him two years ago. He mutters to himself in German that these are the days that do not please him. He is longing to see you and speaks constantly of 'small Felop' when he is here. Lately he walks out to your grandfather's grave when the evenings are

63

mild. He tells us he takes a constitutional, but Paul and your father learned of his destination quite by accident.

"Devereaux is much the same. Luckily we were not close to a service base, so the few small changes here have been wrought by those who travel. I've kept a list of casualties for you so that you may make your condolence calls as soon as you like.

"Your father, who will write tonight, will ask you to come home on leave. Use your own judgment. I feel you will prefer to wait and return when you can stay. He will send you a small check for the Voths' hotel expenses. I am sending you what you will need. Your father has a happier idea of the cost of travel these days. So this check is, as always, *entre nous*.

Your loving mother,
Victoria Froelich."

Phillip looked at the pale-yellow check, a gentle nostalgia threatening to sweep over him. She had sent him three times the amount he would need. Grimly he opened the second envelope bearing the name of a famous Chicago hotel, and read:

"My darling Phil." He was surprised his fiancée hadn't spelled the word "dahling" and he wondered again if he would have to create a scene before she learned that he hated any contraction of his name.

"Just the briefest note to tell you of your surprise. We just might be at the depot in Seattle Monday morning. We, Madame and I, decided a long time ago to see you the moment you got back. Madame calls it a pre-honeymoon for us, so on Monday don't forget to be surprised.

"Devereaux is such a hole. Madame and I both agree, and we did need a change of scene. USO tours are over and Madame is glad not to be chaperoning me. I wish they weren't. Over I mean. We tried to get plane reservations but there wasn't time. Madame offered the man a bonus and I offered to sing to him, but there just wasn't any. So we plod on by train.

64

"Chicago is loaded with celebrities. There are three movie stars here at the hotel. Think of it! And I bought a new dress, white tulle, simply fathoms in the skirt and a tight bodice that ends here and leaves me bare on top. It has a spray of silk hollyhocks on the skirt, but I'm thinking of taking them off. It's a dream and Madame says you're sure to like it. I feel sixteen instead of nineteen in it. Please have somewhere really yummy to go so I can wear it and drive all the boys simply wild."

Phillip's jaw tightened as he read it through to the end to see if beneath all the froth there was anything important. There wasn't. He dropped it into the wastebasket. Deliberately he fought down the thoughts that threatened to burst forth in a good round solid oath. This was the girl he planned to marry in the fall.

He left the third letter on the desk for five minutes trying to decide whether to tear it up without reading it or to open it. It was from Stuff Manus, the sailor who had carried his bags for him the night he left his ship. While he decided, he dressed to leave the hospital. When he was ready to leave the room, he took up the letter and with resignation tore the flap open, expecting a flood of recriminations.

"Dear Mr. Froelich," the cramped childish hand began, "the boys left aboard are fine and wishing all the luck to you. The captain's wife arrived from Iowa yesterday and visited the ship. Holy Moses! No wonder the captain never could give an order." This brought a smile to Phillip's lips.

"What I'm writing about is this. Last night a Commander Danelaw came aboard with a four-striper. I had the gangway and he stood around a while and shot the breeze with some of the deck apes and me while the captain that was with him went below to talk to Captain Pratt. Then this commander starts asking about you and the trouble you're in. Naturally everyone clams up, thinking maybe he's looking for dirt, so he left with the four-striper a few minutes later. When I was relieved at 2000, I got into my blues to go in town for some beer and this Danelaw is waiting on the dock alone in a big black Lincoln. He drives me into town and we have a couple of brews, then he starts giving me some facts. I don't know how he found out so much, but he knows plenty about you, from your folks right up to now. Maybe I'm fouled up, but I got to liking the guy and to thinking that he's on your side, so I told him about the captain and the ship from the time you came aboard until we hit the States. I'm giving all this to you as fast as I can so if I've made a mistake, you'll not be going into anything blind.

"This Danelaw is either a straight guy or a damned smooth operator. He said he wasn't directly interested in the case, but he knows too much about it for that to be true. Still I'll stake money that he isn't a phony. He's funny but he makes sense. I hope I haven't got you in hot water.

"Well, that's about all except I'm getting a transfer to a carrier on the East Coast and there's a rumor on deck that the captain is going to get that investigation after all. Well, so long for now, your shipmate, Stuff. P.S. I didn't say anything about that night we hit the storm out of Pearl. Someday I hope you'll let me explain."

Phillip held the letter a moment, staring out the window at the white clouds above the sparkling sound. Danelaw interfering on his behalf with Base Security. Danelaw offering his own legal counselor. Danelaw with a four-striper promoting an investigation that would ruin his ex-captain but perhaps save Phillip's commission. He nodded thoughtfully, seeing the pattern of these events.

Stuff's attitude was surprising in several ways. It was amazing that the cautious sailor had talked. Whatever else Phillip had to think about Stuff, he had to give him credit for excellent judgment. After all, he once would have trusted his life with the sailor.

66

Stuff Manus, boatswain's mate, regular Navy man with eight years of sea duty, had entered the Navy at sixteen rather than his home state's reformatory as a petty thief. He was a man with an eighth-grade education and a knowledge of the waterfront. His story was harsh, sordid, typical. The Navy had transformed him from a hoodlum into a man. Innately decent, Stuff had appreciated the security, regulation, cleanliness, and self-respect about him. He had become so completely a Navy man that little of his former life was evident.

From Phillip's first day aboard he had found a friend in the big, silent boatswain's mate. Stuff hated the ship's captain because he was sloven, lazy, and stupid—in short, not the Navy's standard for either officer or gentleman. But to Stuff, Phillip personified this standard and something more—a quality that derives from family rather than Annapolis. From the first hectic days of squaring the ship away, the sailor sought the young officer out on every occasion. From their divergent backgrounds, they met on common footing. Stripped to shorts, they worked side by side, each a leader in his own right, neither jealous of the other's power. Quickly they realized that, cleared of the supercargo of gold braid aboard, they could run the ship very efficiently. In a manner they became conspirators, making themselves necessary, taking power from the captain that the other officers were too lazy or timid to take. And when they had time to relax, they came to each other naturally to relax and plan together. The captain's accusation was right. Phillip was unofficerlike. He preferred the conversation of an uneducated enlisted man to that of any of his golden equals.

Stuff could tell a good yarn and Phillip could appreciate one. So Stuff talked about Shanghai, Calcutta, Manila. He had abandoned ship on a carrier and had had a DE knocked out from under him. And as he talked, he saw the fire of excitement leap from his words into the officer's eyes. He had much to offer Phillip, and Phillip was ready to accept. There were informal lessons in seamanship and gunnery. Seeing how the boy absorbed naval customs and admired the ancient rites of seafaring men, Stuff felt the challenge to give more and more of his knowledge. He also felt an urge to protect him. This embarrassed the sailor until he realized that Phillip's attraction was the appeal of all young, immature animals. But Stuff was never guilty of violating that supercilious distance between officer and man. Their confidence in each other grew.

For his part of the bargain, Phillip talked cattle and ranching, because Stuff shared the universal, primitive dream of all city dwellers—land of his own to stretch on, acres of it. Stuff revealed that he had planned to buy a ranch in the southwestern part of Texas just before the war started. But when his buddy from Texas died on Tulagi, he had abandoned the scheme. Now Phillip set the man to dreaming again by discussing general farming problems, methods of increasing purity percentage in scrub herds, the barest requirements for starting a small ranch, the ratio of acres of feed and grass per head to bring a herd through the winter in fair condition, the advantage of this or that legume, irrigation, soil fertility. When Stuff showed him a San Francisco bank balance, which in all truth owed more to the man's ability as a gambler than his monthly earnings, Phillip suddenly grew interested. He decided that anyone who could save that much money in the Navy deserved his interest.

On his own ground with a pencil, Phillip was shrewd. In his idle time he worked on a plan to start a small ranch. From his wealth of training, he drew facts and tricks that made his father glow with paternal pride. He wrote to Oklahoma and Texas for information and co-ordinated the figures, converting pre- to post-war costs and profits. When the project was done, it was a complete folder on the operation of a small ranch, as concise as a geometric theorem, beginning with initial costs including mortgages and loans, necessary equipment, implements, and machinery, first outlay for buildings, ranch and general farming stock, and continuing through proposed actions in the event of possible failures. Phillip was so proud of it he sent it to his

68

father and received a few minor corrections and a complacent okay. The sailor was tongue-tied at his good fortune.

At the same time other ideas had been taking root in the young banker's mind. Among them, Stuff's prospect as a financial risk, for he knew that the man would need a good-sized loan before he could get anywhere. It was instinctive for Phillip to judge all men as his father judged those who came into the bank seeking money—from the grimy sharecropper, battered straw hat in hand, seeking twenty dollars on his part-Jersey heifer fresh come January, to the business-suited owner of the local peanut mill, seeking thousands for expansion. And Phillip had recognized in Stuff that type of individual so important to landowners, the overseer. It was through men like Stuff—simple, loyal, energetic—that families like Phillip's controlled and enlarged their fortunes. In Phillip's mind the sailor was already a satellite. He wrote his father and received another qualified pat on the head.

Meanwhile the state of affairs aboard ship grew worse. By the time the ship shoved off for Guam, Phillip was eating alone in the wardroom and sleeping during the day to avoid the insidious manner of his captain. And without leave or any audible appreciation, he started taking the ship over at night, doing all the necessary navigating. It was a strange situation. During the day he was a pariah, relieved of all duty. At night he was the commanding officer by no authority but his own, taking the con at 2200 and returning the ship to an officer at 0600 the next morning for the captain to run as he pleased. Only in the amphibious forces could it have happened. His constant companion on watch was Stuff Manus. They kept the ship on course for eight hours and plotted the course for the next sixteen. The captain relaxed.

Another idea took shape. Phillip learned that Stuff wanted a high school diploma. At Guam he procured the necessary application blanks, textbooks, and examinations issued by the Armed Forces Institute. He wrote to his old principal at Devereaux

High School (on whose home his father held a first mortgage) and received approval for the plan he had worked out to "graduate" Stuff from a school he had never seen. With a long-standing loathing for his own stultifying education, he calmly dictated the answers to the questions that Stuff was supposed to answer. He diagrammed sentences, explained the muscular system by which a snake moves, discussed the Hohenzollern versus the Romanov dynasties, and found a hundred unknown quantities by the proper algebraic formulae. In short, he did the things that Stuff had proved he did not need to do in order to earn a living. He invented officers to witness the examinations, forged their names, and finally, when Stuff's diploma arrived, expressed his delight at having sold American education a small bill of goods. He was giving generously of something for which he had no earthly use, and when the time came to be paid, he figured that he would reap about a hundred to one. He was making Stuff his friend, tying him to a family he had not yet met and could never know. Julius Froelich would have approved this exercise in the purchase of capital stock.

Then, quite unconsciously, he made his first mistake. On watch, standing on the windy black bridge of the cavorting ship or sitting on a ready ammunition box, swaying with the lulling roll of the sea, looking up at the glittering, velvet-black sky, Phillip relaxed his mental vigil and talked of his home, his family, and his dreams. Even if he could have seen Stuff's face, he would not have recognized the expression in his fine eyes. His ambitions were too bright to let him see anything so ineffectual as affection.

Phillip had no concrete indication of the growing emotional attachment in his new friend until one day, there it was. At first he was a little nauseated and then, worse still, amused. He had read enough on the subject, from Freud through Proust, Gide, and Mann to Sinclair Lewis, to understand what it was. He even examined the case at hand a bit.

Physically Stuff might dominate him. Mentally the balance

70

would be restored. Emotionally Phillip knew he could be cold-blooded as a snake, and he was sure that Stuff would never violate the trust he had placed in him. He felt so safe that he indulged in a little private laughter at the absurd situations his cruel sense of humor called up before him. Perhaps Stuff sensed his amusement and drew away from him at a loss for words. Often Phillip caught him blushing and addressing his remarks to the horizon that enclosed them like the pale rim of a great shallow bowl.

A week out of Pearl they hit a storm. At midnight Phillip left the bridge to inspect the shoring over the hole in their side. Stuff went with him, cursing the captain who had just had him into the wardroom for a dressing-down over some triviality that he had failed to attend to. They fought their way down the careening deck, getting soaked to the skin every time the ship took a header. Phillip loved the challenge of the storm, the danger that dared them to live. He wanted to hurl oaths back into the yawning maw of the sea. The wild nature of the night possessed him for a moment. Turning to Stuff, hoping to make him feel it too and perhaps shake him free of his petty anger, he laughed, the sound singing out weirdly between the screaming rushes of wind.

Stuff stepped behind a protecting bulkhead and shouted, "What's wrong, sir?"

Phillip, still laughing, put his face to the man's and shouted, "You're amusing, Stuff." The wind screamed again and a roll of the ship ground his mouth against the sailor's ear. "Here the gigantic ocean is doing its best to frighten us and you go stomping around, cursing because of what one little fat man has said to you." But the wind sucked up most of his words; so he shouted, "You're funny!"

He could not see Stuff's face, but somehow he knew that it was not smiling in understanding. Nor did he know whether or not it was the pitch of the ship that threw him against the man, but in an instant he felt himself seized by the wrists and pinned between the sailor and the cold steel bulkhead.

"Funny am I?" shouted Stuff. "Let's see how funny you think this is!"

Phillip felt for the first time the strength of Stuff's body. The arms, hard and rigid as timbers, the chest and thighs, heavy against him and hot with an animal vitality that Phillip could feel through their wet clothes. For a moment he was shocked, then terrified for the first time since he had been in the Navy. He felt Stuff's firm mouth on his own, the man's tongue forcing itself into him. Phillip lunged and struggled to free himself from the face, harsh with beard, that pinned his head brutally against the bulkhead—from the tongue that continued to search and explore, to taunt and invite until Phillip felt his stomach heave and he knew he must vomit. Then, to free himself, he bit down hard. Immediately the face retreated and Phillip felt himself free for an instant before the sailor struck him across the mouth. The blow sent Phillip to his knees and Stuff was beside him instantly, holding him close, pouring apologies into his ear. There was the taste of blood in his mouth, his own or Stuff's.

At last, when he could talk again, Phillip rose and said, his voice clogged with emotion, "Get away from me!" And afraid that the order would not be obeyed, Phillip stumbled backward into the darkness.

For the rest of the night he walked the deck thinking. His trust had been betrayed and he had no recourse. His captain would welcome such an incident to use against him. His tiger riding had brought him to this and he must continue in the role he had assumed until he was free of the ship. Deliberately he skirted the real issues of the incident and as a result fell into one of the worst states of melancholia he had ever known. The weeks that followed were well nigh unbearable. He was eaten from within and without. Stuff's constant apologetic presence and the double role Phillip enacted for himself and the crew was

72

the hardest he had ever assumed. At sea, eyes are sharp. But he had come through at last. He had escaped and settled the issue of the sailor in his mind. Characteristically he shouldered most of the blame, reminding himself that he was responsible for all things that happened to him. But one question still remained. Why had the man attacked him? Neither of them was homosexual. Never once had he permitted Stuff to discuss the subject, though the sailor had brought it up frequently enough in their conversations. Perhaps if they had discussed it rationally—but that was absurd! How could anything so irrational be treated rationally?

Phillip sighed and passed his fingers over his eyes to brush away the panorama that had unfolded before him. He had settled that score long ago. Stuff no longer troubled him. But was another problem, a greater one, arising in Timothy Danelaw? And when he had solved that, would there be another, and another? Of himself he had nothing to give to any man, or even if he had, he would never permit himself to give it. One became degenerate or one didn't, as he chose. He would marry and live the good life of his father and his Grandfather Dev. That was his destiny. A fault ceased to be a fault in Phillip when he realized he had it, for automatically he set about making himself perfect.

Slowly he tore the sailor's letter to bits and dropped it into the basket. Then he crossed to the desk and found the sleeping tablet prescription the doctor had given him and left the room. He closed the door and walked down the long white corridor to the dispensary. His mind was still dazed, unable to clear itself of thought. He reached the barred window at the end of the hall and handed the paper through to the pharmacist's mate inside. The man looked at it and took down a large brown bottle of pills, shook out two of them, and dropped them into a small envelope.

"Enough there in that bottle to give the whole damned base

rigor mortis," the sailor observed. Phillip became interested in the bottle.

"Are they really so deadly?" he asked.

"Deadly?" the sailor repeated. "Half a dozen of these would lay you out stiffer than a—"

The phone rang and the sailor turned away to answer it. "Yes, sir." Pause. "He hasn't picked it up yet, sir." Pause. "Well, I can lock up and bring it up." Pause. "Not at all, sir."

"If you'd like," Phillip heard himself say, "I'll stay here for you, if you won't be gone too long."

"Oh, it's just on the next floor, sir," the sailor said. "It won't take a minute. Just come around through that door there."

Phillip went through the door and found himself on the opposite side of the barred window. The sailor took a box from the refrigerator and started out. "Don't be long," Phillip called.

"No, sir. Just a minute."

Phillip nodded. Very calmly he went to the table, picked up the brown bottle of tablets, poured about two dozen into his hand, and slid them into his pocket. He held the bottle up judiciously a moment and then poured out another two dozen which he deposited with the others. Then he set the bottle down, carefully smearing his fingerprints as he released it, and turned away, pretending to examine a beaker of blue liquid over a Bunsen burner nearby. The sailor returned, sealed the two pills into the little envelope, and handed it to Phillip.

"Thanks very much for standing by for me, sir."

"You're welcome." Phillip walked to the door and opened it.

"Goodbye," the sailor said.

Phillip turned briefly and smiled. "Goodbye."

7

◆•◇•◆•◇•◆•◇•◆

*E*arly the next morning Phillip and Francis met at the main gate of the base and went into Seattle to meet Sybel Jo and her mother. They were silent in the swift power launch that took them to the mainland, but in the taxi, moving through the gray deserted streets, Phillip said, "Strange. Their coming is against my interests but I'm rather anxious to see them."

"Sybel Jo is your fiancée," Francis said.

"Oh, that," Phillip shrugged, glancing at his cousin's sick face. "Tell me, Francis, do you really love her or do you just hate to see me get her father's support?"

"That was nasty, Phillip."

"It amuses me to be nasty around you. I like to show you what you really are under your Harvard exterior," Phillip chuckled.

"Must you start a fight before they arrive?"

"I'll stop before train time." Phillip smiled pleasantly and at Francis' look of hatred, he added, "Why don't you poison me?"

"Oh, shut up."

75

"Why don't you shut me up? I'm just out of the hospital. And by the way, I was sorry to disappoint you and Bruner the other morning. You were obviously expecting to witness my questioning by the base security officer. Terribly sorry to have spoiled your fun."

"Don't gloat. We know how you got off that. You're making a mistake asking Danelaw to intervene for you. His reputation isn't too savory in some quarters."

Phillip felt surprise, but he asked smoothly, "My, my, and how did you learn that?"

"Bruner inquired at Headquarters."

"A pretty picture that," Phillip snarled. "Big ass Bruner stalking in, demanding as my counsel why I haven't been accused of sabotage and murder yet! You're just not smart, Francis."

"Bruner told me about Danelaw's asking for all the data on your case, too," Francis shot back, "so you're not putting anything over on us. If you won't take Bruner's aid, then you'll get his rancor. You don't think Danelaw gives a hoot about you, do you? He's out to embarrass Lee Bruner and he's using you as a cat's paw."

The cab stopped before Union Station. Phillip paid and the cousins glanced at their watches as they hurried into the huge drab waiting room and down the steps to the train that was already coming to a stop.

"There she is!" Phillip shouted from the steps and broke into a run. "Syb! Honey! Down here!"

The very pretty girl in the small pink-flowered bonnet and short fur cape saw him and waved before starting down the steps on very long shapely legs and extremely high heels. On the bottom step of the train Phillip caught her close in his arms and gave her the stagiest kiss he could muster, determined to prove by her standards how happy he was to see her. He kissed her until he was sure she was breathless and then exclaimed for all to hear, "Syb! My God, but I'm glad to see you. I was afraid Francis would forget to write you the date of my arrival. And

76

Madame! Still the handsomest woman in Oklahoma. Come on down here and let me kiss you, too! Beautiful, just beautiful, both of you."

His one consoling thought was that his mother and sister were not witnessing his gushing banality. And his guests, simple people that they were, were narrow-eyed with pleasure at his flattery. He kissed the hard-faced woman of some thirty-odd years and turned back to Sybel Jo, whispering against her mouth, "I'm so glad you're here, so glad."

"Lover man, let me go," the girl cried, holding him tighter.

"My God! That accent. Where have you been this time? Let me guess." Everyone laughed, aware of the girl's love of pretending to be from someplace, as she put it.

"Phil, you're a rogue!"

"That does it. You've been to Boston."

"People from Boston don't sound like that."

"How right you are, darling."

"I just got back from New Aw-lins."

"And now you're a Creole belle."

"Phil, I just hate you at times."

"Prove it," he grinned, kissing her.

"But you're yummy most of the time and I think I'm going to cry."

He laughed, giving her his handkerchief and tucking her head beneath his chin to let her sniffle and blow while he made what he supposed to be comical, loverlike faces to her mother who was beaming her delight on them. At last the girl was able to shake hands with Francis. They walked back toward the station, everyone talking at once about the trip, home, and a dozen other topics.

To understand Phillip's fiancée entailed first understanding her formidable stepmother. "Madame" Voth, as plain Roxie Cook from the cotton gin district, had been the scandal of Devereaux in 1926, the year she graduated from high school and got a job as teller in Joe Voth's City National Bank (across the

77

street from the Devereaux National). She had married Joe Voth scarcely a year after his first wife's funeral. People said that Roxie had "hurt" Joe, meaning that his bank had suffered, but then no bank could have hoped to compete with the Devereaux National in those days.

In 1924 people had said that Devereaux didn't need a second bank and looked toward their first citizen and founder, Old Phillip, for approval. His bank had expanded with the town, freezing out competition in 1912 and 1917. Depositors ignored the upstarts, and old Phillip had a line on every piece of property worth having a line on within a radius of twenty miles. But the wise old man, seeing farther into the future than his subjects, had quietly given the Eastern Banking chain a smile of encouragement from the sanctity of the already powerful Oklahoma Banker's Association. There were certain schemes and developments he wanted to see tried for it was time for the town to make some substantial growth now that its boom days were safely in the past. The old man did not care to be the sole loser in these new ventures. And he wisely acknowledged that Eastern capital was the real source of the state's wealth. Without it, Oklahoma's oil, gas, coal, and cattle would never have been developed. As yet, the state hadn't enough native millionaires to stand alone. So under Old Phillip's benevolent guidance the big chain established a satellite across the street, making sure that the new building did not surpass the old, nor their president appear anything nearly so grand as the old man. The situation had the faint odor of a diplomatic love nest even to the average Devereaunian. They watched Old Phillip for a sign as to how to react to this new rival. He gave it on that first hot August Sunday after the new president and his wife moved to town. The next afternoon the *Devereaux Democrat* reported: "Our first citizen, accompanied by his two daughters and their families, called on the newcomers and took tea on the back veranda where it was cooler." On the following Sunday, the

78

Voths dined with the Antony Barrimans and attended evening vespers. The Voths were established.

A week later, Mrs. Joe Voth, daughter of a Pennsylvania stockholder in the chain, died giving birth to a daughter, Sybel Jo. "The terrible heat," everyone said, adding that the poor lady hadn't looked any too strong in the first place.

The following June, Roxie Cook, as the seventeen year old, second Mrs. Voth, made her bid to be accepted as one of the first matrons of Devereaux. Then, as now, Roxie was typical of a species of womanhood found in the Texas and Oklahoma oil-fields, Phillip had often thought. She was a big-boned woman, amply fleshed and handsome-headed. Her prototypes were fond of marrying oil-field workers rather than farmers, ranchers, or businessmen. They weren't particularly clever or shrewd; they didn't need to be. They were—Phillip weighed the word carefully—easy-looking. That was it. Big and easy.

He'd seen big women all his life, German farm girls, Polish serving women, great Negro laundresses with buttocks that couldn't be squeezed into a No. 3 wash tub, but he had never ceased to marvel at the fine solidity of these oil-field wives. He admired them as he might admire an exhibit of prize brood mares. Their long, coarse mane of hair, their fine wide eyes and plump, painted cheeks, quick kindly smiles denoting even tempers, their big shoulders and bouncy breasts, gently bulging stomachs and meaty loins and hocks, and their legs—long, sturdy, but shapely and capable-looking. Usually they wore few clothes, no hats, stockings or gloves when they came to town to shop. They jarred along the hot sidewalks on their battered high heels, smiling, sweating, perhaps swearing at a kid or two— a joy for every male to behold.

At thirty they started thickening, but they did not lose the knack of pleasing their husbands, whose instincts to roam they had thoroughly sapped. These women were seldom found in divorce courts, and they always seemed to give humanity two or three children as healthy and strong as any to be found. Phillip

79

liked oil people, modern gypsies that they were, but he did not like Madame Voth.

Roxie was different from her sisterhood. She was ambitious. She hated her beginnings in the gin district and she wanted what Joe Voth represented—money and respectability. Joe was her easy target. No one understood Joe, but Phillip thought he did because he knew that if he ever fell in love, he'd go through hell just as Joe had gone through hell for Madame. Once Phillip's mother had made the indiscreet but apt observation that "women of that sort seem to have a way that enchants men." So Madame became the first enchantress in Phillip's world. He had come to hate her only when he realized that she stood in the way of his ambitions.

She had earned the title of "Madame" in her tortuous social climb. Just after her marriage she had joined a French club of ex-high school students, most of whom were of the best families and unmarried. It was the only social organization she could enter at the time. At these meetings she was addressed in the French fashion as "Madame." The good matrons of the city, learning of this, snickered over their cards and crocheting. Having never been to France, they pronounced the word "madum" and associated it with the keepers of whorehouses—which went well with their conception of the new Mrs. Voth.

At a Christmas dance that year, one of the bolder ladies had addressed her by the derisive title before an expectant audience of twenty or thirty conspirators.

Roxie, shrewdly divining the situation, had boldly carried the bomb back into enemy territory and exploded it there by crying artlessly, "How kind of you! All my real friends call me that. But your pronunciation is wrong. The accent is on the *last* syllable and spoken as the word 'dam!' " The retort had carried the evening in her favor. Devereaunians, particularly the men full of Christmas punch, capitulated, bestowing upon the newcomer the most gracious title in town. Gradually she was accepted as the real head of the Voth household. A few still deplored that

80

she was ruining Sybel Jo and her husband, but out of respect for Joe, they were courteous to his wife. Everyone knew that Joe loved Madame hopelessly and that she didn't give a rap for him.

Madame loved money and she was fond of week-long trips to Houston, Chicago, and Los Angeles to spend it. There were usually four or five of these trips a year. At the beginning of each season she would go off unaccompanied "to buy clothes and get some new air in my lungs," as she said. But Harry Kasendick, barbershop wit at the Hotel Devereaunian, suggested to the mayor one day that it wasn't only new air in her lungs she went after. As a result, Joe Voth had very quietly succeeded in having Harry run out of town. But despite such outbreaks, Madame's position had grown stronger each year. Joe Voth was now a very rich man from wise investment of his first wife's money. And Sybel Jo's marriage to the heir of the Froelich family would be Madame's last victory. From obscurity, she would have attained the social peak of her world.

In the cab outside, Phillip gave the address of the hotel. He sat between the women while Francis occupied the jump seat.

"I've got you a suite," Phillip said. "Three rooms. Enough?"

"Fine. Neither Sybel Jo nor I can abide sleeping any way but alone." Then Madame smiled. "Of course, Sybel Jo has a lot to learn." Sybel Jo looked coy and Phillip laughed to show he had understood the implication. Madame continued, "I don't see why you two don't get married out here and I'll go back to Oklahoma and leave you to your honeymoon."

Phillip, aware of Madame's ability as a meddler, pretended not to hear her. He touched a small seed pearl pendant on a fragile gold chain below the hollow of Sybel Jo's throat. It was a small fleur-de-lis.

"That's nice," he whispered. "I like it."

"You should. You gave it to me Christmas before last." The girl laughed gaily, knowing that Phillip let his sister do his shopping.

"I was overseas and Fanchon—" he began.

81

"Don't explain," Sybel Jo laughed. "Fan told me all about it."

"Then what did I give you last Christmas?" he asked her boldly.

"An evening barrette of pearls to match this." She touched the pendant. "It was from Cartier's, Phil, and I just loved it."

"And what in the deuce is an evening barrette?"

"A thingey to hold my hair back."

"Oh," he grinned down at her. "Love me?"

"Uh-huh. You love me?"

"Like sin," Phillip replied, and they wrinkled noses at each other.

It was a heartless role for Phillip. He was fond of the girl but that was all. He would never respect her as an equal, but he might love her as he would love the children she would bear him. He would be clever enough to make her happy so long as she never crossed him, and there seemed little danger of that after Madame's severe domination. As the girl had little spirit, her stepmother constantly urged her to be brighter or gayer or more aggressive. The result was a desperate, pathetic effort to please. As his wife, Phillip knew that she would change, though she would still be dominated. His mother and sister would set her on a more natural plane, persuading her to be quiet and dignified, simple and gracious, as they were.

She was a slender, fawn-like creature of wistful face and great expressive eyes. Her hair, gleaming black, fell abundantly over her shoulders, giving her a piquant, ultra-feminine look as if she throve on cherishing. Phillip liked her for this and felt the desire to protect her. Her arms and shoulders were graceful if a bit thin, and her hands were delicate as his mother's Meissen figurines. She had their same exquisite coloring, too. Her breasts were small and hard; he could cover them completely with his hands. She was wide through the hips. Childbearing would likely be easy. He hoped so for her sake, for he wanted a large family— a desire inherited from his father.

Politely Madame asked Francis if he were returning to Harvard in the fall, and Francis proudly said that he was.

"I'm not going back to school ever," Sybel Jo said. She had had a year at Hockaday. "Neither is Phillip. We're going to be married instead."

"I've been trying to persuade Sybel Jo to be married out here," Madame said again. "You've been separated so long and all of us could escape the fuss of a church wedding."

Phillip could guess how much Madame wanted to escape any social fuss. She had probably made her mind to a bit of meddling. Mentally he dragged up his guns ready to defeat her when the time came.

"Here's the hotel," he said as the car swerved to the curb. "I hope the coffee shop is open. I'm starved."

He was puzzled by Madame's desire to change his wedding plans. What glory would she reap from a quiet ceremony in Seattle where no one could see her parade? Or did the cause go deeper than glory? Was something wrong at home? Phillip, reared with the idea that his life belonged to the public, knew that he would be married in the largest church in town before as many townspeople as could crowd into the structure. Since he was the future first citizen, the ceremony did not belong to him but to his community. Madame's schemes were fantastic.

He checked in at the desk for them and sent for their luggage while Francis took them into the dining room. He joined them and they ordered breakfast. He took his fiancée's hand and asked after his family, feeling certain that neither the girl nor her mother knew any more about them than the average citizen, which was nothing of importance. But the question pleased both women and they told him what they knew. To his amusement Sybel Jo, wreathed in sweet smiles, produced from her purse the riding crop his mother had mentioned. He took the soft braided quirt he had once carried at horse shows and looked delighted and surprised at once. Sybel Jo, he thought, looked rather like a spaniel who had just retrieved a stick. How Fan

83

and his mother would laugh when he described this to them. Madame beamed and Francis looked puzzled, suspecting the cruel trick his unholy relatives had perpetrated on the girl.

"I thought Mother had forgotten," Phillip exclaimed, fondling the object. "How kind of you to bother with it." He made no explanation as to why he needed a quirt when he had neither mount nor clothes out here. But then no one thought to ask.

Madame launched into a description of the horrors of a trip from Chicago, and Sybel Jo babbled about her career as a USO singer.

"I just loved every minute of it," she sighed. "I really didn't know I could sing until Madame had me audition with Miss Green. You remember her, Phil—the dancing teacher over the Megland Hardware. The Rotarians sponsored us and we did a performance every weekend for six months. Once we went to Texas for twelve days and did thirty shows. Madame was pooped."

The word hit Phillip in the face. He could swear like an outraged pimp, but even slang from Sybel Jo annoyed him.

"What kind of numbers did you sing?"

"Oh, commercial stuff mostly. You know. Moon spoon. But the band was really gone and I was strictly in the groove."

"Oh."

Now it was Francis' turn to be amused. They changed the subject at once and again Madame urged an immediate wedding.

"I'm afraid that's out of the question," Phillip said. "If we married now, Sybel Jo might have to spend her honeymoon in jail. I'm awaiting a court martial."

While the others sat dead silent, Phillip outlined his case. Breakfast was forgotten.

When he finished, Madame said, "But you might be acquitted. The whole thing sounds ridiculous."

"Unfortunately Francis and his friend Bruner don't agree."

"Don't you have a lawyer?"

"The Navy doesn't like civil lawyers in their courts. We

84

thought it would hurt Phillip to retain one," Francis said primly.

"That's silly," Madame said flatly. "You get one right away, Phillip."

"Actually," Phillip said, grinning at Francis' red face, "I've engaged the best law firm in the city. In the event I'm convicted they'll fight from the outside."

"Good," Madame agreed. "Your father will handle this."

"But that's just it," Francis prepared to pounce. "Phillip doesn't want his father or anyone to know. He didn't even want you folks to come out here."

"Excuse me, Francis," Phillip said, "I'm telling this." And to Madame he said, "You understand why I'm keeping it a secret, don't you?" Their eyes met across the table. She nodded. Phillip smiled guilelessly. "Francis was afraid you might do a little friendly gossiping at home and give the whole thing away, but I told him he needn't worry about you. After all, your interests are my interests, aren't they? We even stand together against Francis now." He laughed pleasantly and gave Francis a long, friendly look.

"Well, heaven knows, I never gossip." Madame glared at Francis.

"Of course you don't. Francis just isn't clever at times."

"And I wouldn't breathe it to a soul," Sybel Jo protested.

"It's sure to get around," Francis blundered.

"Only if you want it to, Francis," Phillip pointed out. "If I have to, I'll tell Father, but I think I can beat this by myself, one way or another."

Madame nodded her approval and yawned. "Shall we go?" she asked. "I'm going to sleep all day."

"Me, too," Sybel Jo said. She had played a minor role in Phillip's scene, but now she entered again, trailing her clouds of glamour. "What are we doing tonight, Phil?"

"Surprise," Phillip grinned. "Like you surprised me. But you'd better wear that new dress you wrote me about because this occasion is really a big one and you've got to be the prettiest girl there."

"A party?" she squealed, her eyes sparkling with excitement.

"Much nicer, huger, drunker, gayer than any party you've ever seen. The admiral is saying goodbye to the war and everything is full-dress."

"I'm just mad about Seattle already!" the girl sighed, and they all laughed at her childlike delight.

The cousins left them at the elevator and went outside to get a cab. On the way, Phillip said thoughtfully, "You know, Francis, you may win our little fracas, but frankly I wouldn't give a cent for your chances. You're bucking nature, and cats always land on their feet."

"God! If only you knew how disgusting you are!"

"Tell me, Francis, after seeing Sybel Jo again, is your heart broken yet, or again?"

Francis, thoroughly baited by now, swung in front of Phillip and stopped. For a moment Phillip thought his cousin would strike him. He tensed himself and crouched, cocking his fist for one sharp swift blow to the solar plexus in retaliation. But waiting for the blow that did not come, Phillip saw the anger die slowly out of his cousin's face. Phillip gave a soft snort of contempt and brutally pushed the man out of his way.

"You coward," Phillip gritted. "No wonder Grandfather Dev wouldn't allow you to bear his name!"

8

The Admiral's reception, which was to be held at the Officers' Club on the island, had a dual purpose: to introduce the new admiral from California who was relieving Admiral Marcien in August and to act as the first full-dress affair since the war's end. It was to be followed by what the invitation called a Monte Carlo night of dancing and gambling for the guests. The guest list, Phillip learned, included all the important rank of the Seattle area and many civilian dignitaries. He had been surprised when his invitation arrived, but supposed it came from Danelaw. Francis said that they had Bruner to thank for the favor.

The cousins called for their guests at the hotel early, for they planned to dine in the city rather than at the club. Sybel Jo met them at the door of the suite looking misty as a fresh fall of dew. She had not exaggerated the yardage of silk tulle or the décolletage of her gown. She seemed to drift rather than walk in the voluminous wispy skirts, while her tight bodice fit snugly over her waist and compact little breasts. Her throat, shoulders,

87

and arms seemed very white and very naked. Her long hair was brushed back and caught at the nape by the barrette of pearls. She wore the little pendant and short white gloves. She looked rather quaint and extremely lovely. Phillip felt proud of her as he kissed her and said, "I like that."

"Madame said you would," Sybel Jo chirped. "I think it's super-gooey." Sybel Jo's idea of fashion was sequins from Hollywood.

"That means she likes it, too, Phillip," Madame laughed, coming from her bedroom. Wearing the first Mrs. Voth's diamonds that had aroused so much comment in Devereaux, she looked quite handsome in her gown of stiff turquoise lace.

They dined at a private club in which Francis had a serviceman's membership, and they were all very gay and companionable. Even Phillip, who usually disliked such functions, looked forward to the evening after his third Martini. The women were delighted with everything—the view, the food, the wine. Almost reluctantly they left their table to go on to the reception.

Only one thing marred Phillip's pleasure. In the taxi—they had decided to take two in order not to muss Sybel Jo—Phillip took the girl in his arms and kissed her tenderly, feeling and giving the promise of his love. When he released her, she whispered, "Phil, let's not wait. Let's get married now. I want to."

A cold knot of anger tightened inside him. He knew Madame had told her to say this. He answered evenly, "You, too, Syb?"

"But it's a wonderful idea."

"It's idiotic. What about my family and Devereaux?"

"Oh, damn Devereaux!"

"Don't ever say that again!" Phillip's voice was so steely that she drew away from him, afraid.

But her good humor was restored instantly when she saw the gaudily lighted club entrance on Amphib Island. Undoubtedly she saw herself attending a Hollywood "preem." Her responsiveness to such trivialities amused Phillip. And at the noisy spectacle of the people around the gaming tables in the main lounge, she could scarcely contain her glee.

"Phil, it's just super," she cried, holding his arm. She took a deep breath as if the whole atmosphere exuded some perfume.

"It does beat the Bible Belt all to the devil," he laughed. This remark got a laugh of appreciation from Madame coming up behind them.

They checked their wraps and entered the lounge, almost too late to travel down the long irregular reception line of officers and their bosomy, orchid-bedecked wives. Phillip, his lovely fiancée on his arm, led the way, performing the necessary introductions while Francis brought up the rear. Phillip had an easy charming air of naïve dignity that his sister had helped him perfect for these occasions. He knew that he and Sybel Jo were attracting a good deal of comment, and this made him very proud. They were a handsome couple and he knew it. He was always pleased when he was excelling.

As they progressed, Phillip found that his impending trial and his part in the explosion had given him some notoriety. Many showed an inclination to keep them for an exchange of pleasantries, but he preferred to remain aloof. It was hard for him to forget his hatred for this organization that had toppled him from security into a limbo of stupidity and fear. Once more, Phillip felt the magnetism of his own personality before an audience. He nodded slightly, spoke with assurance, smiled down fondly on Sybel Jo as he presented her, displayed friendly interest in every ravening bitch he met, and all the while thought his own thoughts. Sybel Jo's appearance on his arm could do him only good.

Toward the last of the line he saw Tim Danelaw and quickly averted his eyes. He conquered the half-smile on his lips, relishing the thought of the expression that would be on the man's face when he met Sybel Jo. If there was one thing that would cool this man's growing interest, Phillip suspected, it would be the presence of a pretty and adored fiancée. He had little desire

89

to hurt Danelaw, but he was beginning to see the solution of a very ticklish problem.

He moved on slowly, apparently unaware of the Commander until he stood before him. And then he said with quiet pride, "Commander Danelaw, my fiancée, Miss Voth."

Briefly their eyes met in the second before Phillip spoke, and the look between them was so intimate, that Phillip felt his face color swiftly. Sybel Jo, eyeing the magnificent gold aiguillettes and probably ascribing to them more importance than they deserved, smiled and extended her hand.

"Miss Voth," Tim Danelaw said, bending slightly over her hand in a fashion that was genuinely graceful, "you're even lovelier than your fiancé deserves." His manner was so courtly, so full of an old-world punctilio, that both Sybel Jo and Phillip were captivated. Phillip, wondering why the man had completely succeeded in upsetting his expectations, continued with the introductions.

"Madame Voth, Commander Danelaw. You know my cousin, Francis."

They shook hands and Tim turned to a slight woman beside him, whom Phillip now noticed for the first time.

"My wife, Mrs. Danelaw," Tim said. "Ensign Froelich from Oklahoma, the lad I mentioned to you, my dear."

Phillip found himself staring at one of the most beautiful and unusual women he had ever seen—small, blonde, fresh as a girl yet sophisticated, too. Without knowing it, Phillip relaxed and a lazy glow of pleasure stole over him. He was reminded of strong afternoon light on old marble back home. He felt like an oaf as an exciting thought occurred to him: *Here is a woman I could love, a woman I could make a fool of myself over.* And as the woman put forth her hand, he had an impression of amused eyes the color of gray-green jade. In that instant Tim Danelaw had retreated to Mars. But Phillip's lovely impression vanished with the woman's first words.

"So this is the man who told his C.O. to go to hell. Hello,

Phillip. We're going to be good friends and iconoclasts together."

It was the dash of cold water in his face. The hypnotic torpor of her beauty slid away and he looked down at her coldly. He nodded and turned to Sybel Jo who was round-eyed with admiration of Mrs. Danelaw. Phillip could have smacked her for paying the woman such an extravagant compliment. He felt that it made them look provincial and inexperienced. He covered Sybel Jo's hand on his arm, an indication of his protection. Both Danelaws smiled faintly at the gesture.

In a group of beautiful women Pat Danelaw would have been startling. In this crowd she was outrageously fascinating. She was taller than Sybel Jo and their figures were exact opposites, Pat's breasts being full and deeply molded, her hips slender and rigid with youth. Her skin was the color of honey and her hair was the rich warm gold of sunlit wheat straw, gleaming wet from sudden summer showers. It was cut in a boyish pompadour, brushed back into a loose-fitting cap over her long, softly rounded head. Her brows, arching naturally, were dark; and her eyes were set well under the deep porch of her brow. She had a small delicately flared nose and full wide lips. Her clothes were dramatic in their simplicity—a white, sleeveless dinner suit with severely straight lines from throat to hip where the jacket ended. The close-fitting skirt continued the lines to the ankle, displaying her fine long legs. She wore a necklace of heavy yellow gold links, and she carried a white fur stole over her arms. The effect was that of a modern ivory and gold Pallas Athene, Phillip had thought at first. Now he decided she was a trifle overdone. He remembered what Bruner had said about her to Francis in his hospital room:

"The usual slut of breeding these days. Little money, less family. A model and singer in some supper club before she married Tim. Professional beauty. It colors everything she does. Married Tim so her relatives could get jobs in Danelaw Brewing. Interested in arty people, but knows nothing of art. Gives open

91

house cocktail slaughters to every visiting celebrity. Knows everyone in the Carmel, Taos, and Mexico City art colonies. Would
like to be unfaithful to Tim but doesn't dare; he would probably
beat her to death or kick her out without a cent at the first
suspicion. A strange couple."

Pat Danelaw was asking him, "Have you a table?" And when
Phillip admitted that he hadn't, she said, "Then the four of you
will join our party. We've lots of room."

Phillip, resentful of her authority, was about to decline when
Sybel Jo, who guessed his purpose, said, "We'd love to, Mrs.
Danelaw."

"Heavens, call me Pat. We'll be through with this mess in a
few minutes. Or would you prefer to go on ahead?"

"We'll wait," Phillip said stiffly and continued down the line
in something of a daze. He had suffered two shocks. He had
expected Danelaw to be dazzled or embarrassed or both by
Sybel Jo. He had been neither. Then he had presented his wife,
a woman that Phillip had felt he could love but now actually
disliked. She was beautiful but she was artificial, inane, common.

He barely heard Sybel Jo tell Madame, "Did you notice that
stole she was wearing? White mink!" And to him she was saying,
"Phil, aren't they simply gorgeous?"

"Who?"

"Pat and Tim, of course."

"So it's Pat and Tim already?"

"You're so Victorian," she laughed. "This is 1946."

"We are dated," Phillip said dryly.

But Sybel Jo was off on other flights about Pat's clothes and
jewelry, speculating who had created them. She calmed down,
however, when the Danelaws appeared and led them to their
table just off the bar, a huge affair that already had a dozen
people around it, handsome friendly men and women, hand-
picked by their hostess, Phillip suspected. After the introductions, Phillip and Sybel Jo found themselves between the Danelaws, while Francis and Madame were near Bruner and Morgan

92

at the other end. Phillip knew that his case would be thoroughly hashed by that foursome before the end of the evening.

He looked around the dining room. It had been fairly well converted into a night club by the simple use of screens and candlelight. There were ice buckets around the crowded tables and the sound of good-natured laughter mingling with smooth music from the bandstand beyond the crowded dance floor. After his first sip of champagne Phillip asked Sybel Jo to dance, for he was becoming intensely aware of the combined interest of Tim and Pat Danelaw. They left the table and went to the dance floor where Sybel Jo snuggled her face into his neck— probably smearing his collar with lip rouge, he thought. They danced in silence because he liked it that way. Once he glanced back at the table and found his host and hostess leaning close, talking, watching them. Phillip pretended not to notice Pat's friendly smile of recognition. If he was rude, he reminded himself that he had not invited himself to their party.

"When is the wedding?" Pat asked when they returned to the table.

"Late in the fall," Phillip said, "or during the holidays. Then, if we go to Rio, we'll enjoy it."

"Rio in season," Pat exclaimed. "You'll love it. Won't they, Tim?"

"Undoubtedly."

"Have you any friends there?"

"No." And Phillip added dryly, "Thank God."

"But of course," Pat laughed. "This is a honeymoon. I was about to tell you to look up some wonderful people."

"You're very kind, but—"

"But, Phil," Sybel Jo put in, "we won't be alone all the time."

This brought a shout of laughter from everyone who had been listening to them. Again Phillip felt very provincial, a new experience for him and one he didn't like at all. Nor did he appreciate Pat's suave way of extricating him from his embarrassment.

93

"Shall we try our luck?" she asked, rising. "I'm a rotten gambler—to Timmie's sorrow."

Phillip went along with Tim and bought fifty dollars' worth of chips and then joined the women at one of the roulette tables. To get around the Navy's rules against gambling, the club had nothing but small chips at the main tables and all profits went back into the club fund; but this was obviously a formality, for already Phillip had noticed some rather steep poker tables nearby. He dropped the chips into Sybel Jo's bag and let her do the playing. She gambled with erratic, amateurish hunches and usually lost. Pat, however, who said that it was her black night, played some unknown numerology that Phillip amused himself by trying to figure out. Her system, he guessed, was stupidly simple or femininely complicated. He finally decided it was the latter, since the numbers *two* and *nine* figured conspicuously, but with no logical sequence.

In a few minutes they were joined by Madame, Francis, and Captain Morgan. Pat suggested they try their luck at poker, but Sybel Jo opposed this because she knew nothing of the game. So she decided to stay with Francis and her mother while Phillip went with the Danelaws. Morgan seemed to be backing Madame, and before Phillip left, he gave Francis three twenties, which his cousin accepted without comment. Only Tim caught the exchange.

The three bought their chips at the table, Pat sitting beside her husband, Phillip across the table. As usual, Phillip paid no one the slightest bit of attention while he gambled. His first hands were rotten and he began to lose his hope that he might win back what Sybel Jo would certainly lose. He even had a vision of the evening costing him three or four hundred dollars, and he decided once and for all he hated gambling. Reared by his father's strict principles, he considered gambling a vice, but in the Navy he had gambled often to escape boredom. He seldom lost money. He sat patiently waiting for his luck to break, knowing that with some luck his ability would carry him

94

well above the average. In the sixth hand he threw away a pair of jacks that would have taken a pot. He was cold with fury because Pat laughed at him. After that he became a bit reckless, losing consistently, and Pat started to needle him, asking him if all Oklahomans were rotten gamblers.

Then it hit him—the feeling that he was going to win—as he picked up his first two cards, a black deuce and a five. But he discarded grimly and then bet cautiously. Pat, raising the table dangerously, said, "I've always heard that cowboys were card sharks. Aren't you a cowboy, Phillip?"

Phillip pretended to quietly lose his temper. Glaring at her, he raised her a trifle. She glanced at Tim, who smiled at her, and raised again. Phillip, like an enraged youngster, stiffened and with a hand that trembled slightly, tossed more chips on the pile. Pat was delighted. Everyone else checked, and twice more each of them raised. Then Phillip, quickly surveying the pot and calculating he'd just about break even no matter what Sybel Jo was losing, took out his wallet and laid a fifty on the pile with his last chips.

"It's going to cost you that to see what I've got, Mrs. Danelaw," he said.

Too late Pat realized she might have walked into a trap of her own making, but she answered coolly, "No woman could refuse such a bargain."

She put her money next to his and put her cards down—three queens. Phillip smiled and spread down a straight flush of spades. Pat's eyes held admiration, recognizing at last his attitude of unreasonable pique as crude but effective strategy.

"Speaking for the cowboys of my state, Mrs. Danelaw, we thank you," Phillip smiled.

Tim and the others laughed but Pat said, "Don't laugh, Phillip. Lucky at cards, you know, unlucky—"

"Eros and I are on excellent terms, m'am. Shall we join the others?"

95

"By all means," Tim answered. "I think Pat is thoroughly crushed."

Captain Morgan, the psychiatrist, was backing Madame to the hilt, they found when they returned to the roulette table, and Sybel Jo was growing tired of continually losing.

"I guess Madame has all the luck in our family," she said. "I'm as bad as Daddy." Silently Phillip agreed.

But he was noticing something else. Madame and Morgan were fairly devouring each other with their eyes. *Shades of the Roaring Twenties*, Phillip thought, *you can practically smell the odor already. Joe Voth will sprout his horns again within the week.* He'd often wondered about Madame's amorous conquests, and now, looking at the piglike psychiatrist, he was disgusted. He hoped the others wouldn't notice the precious pair.

At the table again, Phillip politely asked Pat to dance and followed her to the crowded floor. He noticed that his arm was slightly unsteady as he put it around her. She stepped close to him.

"You dance, too," she murmured. "Amazing, rural education these days."

"The delight of every middle-aged matron in Oklahoma," Phillip returned. "I knew you'd enjoy my dancing."

"An excellent riposte. Why don't you call me Pat?"

"I prefer to wait before I'm intimate. Look before I leap."

"Are you capable of intimacy?"

"Do you want proof?" he asked, tightening his arm.

"Later. After you've had a chance to look."

Phillip was amused and a little pleased at her obvious approach. He felt her lithe body and legs move against him, her arm close about his neck, and now he was aware of her perfume.

"Let's go outside," she said.

He stopped dancing and led her out on the terrace. They walked to the balustrade where it was dark and they could see the brilliant view of Seattle across the water. He slipped his arm under hers and bent his head. Her response was complete,

96

and his lips moved from hers to her cheek and temple as he murmured, "Sweet." She moved his lips back to hers. She was so obvious she was comical. . . . *The Bitch of Queen Anne Hill. Married to a gentleman with wings.* . . . He smiled wryly.

"Just like the movies. You're Grable, Hayworth, and Turner all rolled into one. Tell me, are all women alike, or are there decent ones roaming the earth yet?"

She stepped back, her face white in the reflected light. Phillip released her and turned toward the city.

"Then why did you kiss me?"

"A variety of reasons. Number one, I know a push-over when I see one."

"You're even worse than I've heard. You're a boor."

"I could call you something a good deal more descriptive in four letters," Phillip chuckled softly, delighted to return her insults.

"Tim would beat you to a pulp if I told him that."

"Really?" Phillip drawled. "I'll tell you what you do, Mrs. Danelaw. You run in and tell him and I'll wait for him here. All right?"

"I feel sorry for you," she replied scornfully.

"Oh, everyone does, but I go my way, winning poker pots, kissing ladies, doing as I damned please. Well, run along and make your scene. Or at least slap my face so I'll have an excuse for picking up my fiancée and leaving your charming company."

She was silent a moment. "Why do you hate everyone, Phillip? Is it this GCM? I could ask Tim to help you."

"And what is your price for such a favor?"

"What do you think?"

"My dear lady, as another man's wife you're snake eyes, no good."

"Phillip, what's the purpose of this pose? Do you think you're making yourself irresistible to women by being rude to them?"

"And before I ask you why your sudden illogical interest in Sybel Jo and me, I'll explain my attitude. You and the crowd you represent have nothing I want. I don't understand your fancy world or your morals or anything else about you. I am a hick in your eyes, but in my town you'd be just as out of place as I am at your table. But in Oklahoma we wouldn't be rude to you. So far as you're concerned, you're lovely and desirable and I'm a human being. But you cost too much and I can get what I need a lot cheaper."

"In Sybel Jo?" Pat asked cuttingly.

"That remark was my caliber. You're slipping." He took out a cigarette and lighted it.

"May I have one?" Pat asked.

"Oh, sure." Phillip lighted it for her and flipped the match into the water.

Pat's voice was no longer flippant when she spoke again. "I see now that I made a mistake with you. Now I'm going to be honest. My interest in you is because of Tim, not myself."

Phillip felt his muscles tighten, but he said casually, "Now there's a novel approach."

Pat ignored his remark and continued, "Tim is an artist, a painter of some promise, but he has the idea that he is no good, so he gave art up to study medicine. Naturally I want him to continue painting. The other day he made a sketch of you. It's good and I think he might ask you to sit for him if it weren't for the court martial and your friends from Oklahoma."

"I see," Phillip said. "In other words, you want my services as a model. Then why didn't he ask me instead of sending you out here oozing with romance intent on luring me into immortality on canvas?"

"It isn't his idea. It's mine."

"Whosever it is, the answer is no. I'm no model. If you're ready we'll go back so I can say my polite goodbyes and clear out of here."

"You're angry about this other," Pat said. "Let me apologize."

"Mrs. Danelaw, when you were using the whip I didn't

98

cringe. You'll keep my respect if you don't grovel now." And he led her to the door.

At their table he did not bother to sit down but held Sybel Jo's chair while she got shakily to her feet. He was surprised to see that she was tight. He spoke briefly to Francis, said his good-byes, and holding the girl firmly by the arm, piloted her outside to a cab.

Bewildered, drunk, and petulant, Sybel Jo was silent for a while, shrinking into her corner away from him until he fished out one of his father's favorite cigars and lighted it. Phillip preferred cigarettes, but he had made up his mind to smoke cigars and he was breaking himself in gradually.

"Must you smoke that nasty thing?" Sybel Jo said. She was close to tears.

"You'll get used to them."

"Then why didn't we stay at the club?" she asked incoherently.

"Because your gorgeous lady in white mink wanted to play house behind your and her husband's back. Lovely people you choose to admire."

"You mean . . ."

"Exactly. So come off your high horse."

Sybel Jo brightened considerably. "And you didn't want to?" she asked suspiciously.

"Hell, no!"

"You preferred me to her?"

"Hell, yes!" He studied the end of his cigar to hide the amusement he felt dawning in his eyes.

Sybel Jo sighed and said somewhat proudly, "She's very beautiful and she must have loads of men admiring her all the time."

Phillip choked back the laughter that threatened to explode. It was typical of this girl to miss the moral issue involved, and her stupid observations were not entirely due to the liquor she had consumed.

99

"You look cute with a cigar, Phil," she said, giving him her hand.

"I'll bet you would, too," Phillip returned her banter. "Want one?"

"Silly!" She snuggled close for the rest of the way to the hotel.

At the desk he got her key and took her upstairs. He unlocked the door and followed the reeling girl inside and flipped on the light. She was a good deal drunker than he had thought at first. He was glad that they had left the club when they did. He tossed his hat on the chair and took the little cape from her shoulders. She put her arms about his neck and lifted her face to be kissed. He kissed her gently and found her lips parted. He felt her fingers stroking the short, stiff hair at the back of his neck and he kissed her again, keeping his head for an instant before the sweetness of her plunged him into a warm, exciting darkness. His arm went farther around her and his hand closed over one of her small breasts. He caressed it lightly as she pressed it closer into his palm. His desire for her spread through him as quickly as fire flashes through fur. He knew that if he wanted her this moment she was his without marriage, without promise. She was brushing her lips back and forth against his, murmuring half-intelligibly, "Yes, yes, yes, yes," like a litany. Then as his hand dropped swiftly to explore, she pushed a fingertip into his ear and giggled softly. The action—one of the oldest in the world, he supposed—sobered him at once. He straightened slowly, looking at her with new eyes. As he released her, her eyes opened, very blue.

"Your mother," he whispered hoarsely. "She'll return any minute."

"Madame?" Sybel Jo smirked. "Madame doesn't care."

A picture rose in Phillip's mind: a picture of three girls from a USO troupe he had seen in an O Club overseas once—three girls and a group of drunken men pawing them like a pack of sex-crazed apes. Could he include his girl in that category? Certainly she had not been so lax two years ago. A tiny flicker of

100

doubt suddenly ignited the anger in his mind, and he held her away from him by her thin bare shoulders. Her head lolled forward drunkenly.

"Sybel Jo! Answer me!"

He shook her harshly, but she pushed against him weakly and then sagged toward him. She had passed out. He held her propped against him a moment and stared down at the top of her dark head, seeing only the pearls nestling into the silky beauty of it. Fan's words in his mother's letter: *I hope Madame has kept her on ice for you.* Was it a tip, a warning of information to come once he was home? He knew how obscure his sister could be at times. His mother's own words: *the roots of truth.*

Slowly he picked the sleeping girl up and carried her to the couch and put her down. Her mouth had opened grotesquely, destroying all semblance of beauty. He stared at her.

Why was she willing to give herself unconditionally? Why, except to give herself an advantage? Why was Madame anxious to see them married? Why had they rushed out to see him unless dire emergency had prompted the action? How close had he been to starting the life of cuckoldry her father lived? If a trap existed, where were the teeth? Who the quarry?

Always he had supposed that this girl would be a virgin until he took her the first night of their marriage. Not that he prized virginity. He preferred experience and he had known both. He could forgive incontinence in any woman—in fact, he was rather proud of his broad-minded attitude on this subject. If her love was real, inescapable, he would not condemn. But he would damn the culprit unconditionally if she were so lacking in imagination that she could not conceal her error. For Phillip, living in the secrecy imposed by living all his life in the public eye, believed that many evils, if cleverly concealed, did a minimum of harm. Take Madame, for instance. Everyone suspected her of infidelity, but no one could prove anything. Result? Complete marital bliss in her home. And now if Sybel Jo had been indiscreet with some soldier or sailor in her USO career, he was willing to make the best of the situation. After all, he was marrying this girl for her father's support in gaining possession of his family's bank. And as a pawn, Sybel Jo had certain rights that another prospective wife would not have—rights that he would gradually deprive her of in the years to come, but rights just the same. His love for her was a secondary thing; her father's money was of first importance. If there was to be a child, it must be disposed of before he married her. An abortion, an institution for orphans—anything. He would forgive her this error if it were corrected before their marriage. But if his first-born was not his, he knew that he could kill her.

He turned away, forcing himself to relax. He had been brought to his senses in time. Now nothing could force him to marry her until later. This was the first of June. Plenty of time to learn the truth before they were married. He sat down to wait for Madame to return and to arrange his thoughts and plans. He had a long while to do so, for Madame was finding Captain Morgan a most interesting man. Phillip went into the bedroom, got a blanket, and covered the sleeping girl on the couch.

"You poor little kid," he murmured looking down at her. "What in the hell did you ever do to deserve a gang of sons-of-bitches like us?"

As he paused outside the hotel entrance to look for a cab, he was surprised to hear someone call his name. Frowning but amused, he turned to recognize Pat Danelaw sitting in the Lincoln cabriolet parked next the curb. He went to her, opened the door, and got inside.

"Sybel Jo must need a long bedtime story," she observed.

"Passed out cold," Phillip replied indifferently. He watched the woman with secret curiosity. "Are you alone?"

"Yes."

"Waiting for an escort home?" he asked stiffly.

She smiled. "No. Just waiting for an escort."

"You don't mince words."

102

"Not when I know what I want."

"What about your husband?" Phillip broke the silence that deepened about them.

She shook her head once and said, "You."

She put a warm hand on his wrist. The slight pressure made him restless, unsure of himself. But at last he covered it with his.

"Where?" he asked.

"I've found the hotel convenient on occasion."

He smiled. Her frankness pleased him. If she'd been coy, he'd have been disgusted.

"I'll get a room," he said, moving to open the car door.

"I've already done so," she said, "with champagne."

Phillip's smile became a chuckle. "Lady, you've got a customer." He reached for her but she put a hand against his shoulder.

"Let's not waste time down here," she said. "Come up in ten minutes. Number ten-seventeen."

Still holding his eyes with hers she opened the door and got out. Then with a toss of her head she walked quickly inside, her heels clicking lightly against the pavement. Phillip watched her go, admiring her hips and the amazingly long lithe legs so well revealed by her tight skirt. When she was gone, he lighted a cigarette, smoked it impatiently, and got out of the car. Carefully he looked up and down the deserted street before he went inside to the elevators.

The door was unlocked. She stood at the window with a glass in her hand. Another glass stood on the table. She indicated it with a quick gesture. "Wine?"

'I've had enough," Phillip said, still standing with his hand on the knob. A persistent silence threatened them for a moment. "One question, lady," Phillip said softly. "Why?"

"Why?" Pat said. "Do you think this is a trap?"

"Perhaps."

"Then look around. The bath, the closet—don't forget under the bed."

Phillip did not move. "Okay, lady, I trust you."

"So you are a gambler after all?"

"Hell, no. I'm just hard up."

"There's such a thing as overdoing this frank twist."

"I asked you a question," Phillip repeated. "Why? Why should you, a respectably married woman, open up to me whom you've known a few hours?"

"Are you trying to embarrass me or flatter yourself?" Pat asked. "Isn't it enough that this is as it is?"

Phillip studied her a moment, trying to fathom her half-sneering, half-anxious attitude. He saw her body, the smooth bare arms emerging from the white fur stole which she still carried as if she were not sure of staying with him.

"What are you thinking?" she demanded suddenly, setting her glass down on the window sill so hard that wine sloshed over her hand.

"I'm remembering," Phillip smiled at her tenseness. "I'm remembering the way you felt against me when we danced at the club."

She relaxed and her puzzling attitude returned. She crossed the room and turned the dial of a small radio on the nondescript metal bureau.

Phillip went to her and took her in his arms, not to dance but to hold, to caress with trembling hands. He found her zipper and freed her of her tight jacket. He slipped it down from her shoulders and tossed it and the furs on the bed. She stood before him, naked from the waist. Lifting her arms, she unfastened the gold chain at her neck. Her full breasts strained up at him, reminding him of Sybel Jo asleep in the same building. He covered them with his hands.

"Pat," he whispered, his voice catching.

"Hush!" she protested, touching his face. "Hush."

He lay on his back relaxing, conscious of her moist weight upon him, conscious of her lips and breath on his neck. The fur stole was warm against his feet. It was all wrong, he thought, all of it all wrong, but he did not know why. The first time had been the fury of an animal. He had been incapable of thought, of reflection. But again and again he had become aware that something was wrong. It was with her, not with him. She did not want him—at least she told herself she didn't. She was acting a role. She did not desire him nor need him—not as he needed her. She was worse than a whore. She was probably acting from boredom or some neurotic urge he could never hope to understand, rather than from any necessity he could appreciate. Yet she had wanted to please him and she had known the tricks of the trade. He could not deny that. . . . He rubbed his eyes with the heels of his hands as if to erase the thought. Abruptly he pushed her aside and swung his legs over the side of the bed.

"What's wrong?" Her voice had something of the warm darkness in it.

"God damn you," he said evenly through clenched teeth. "God damn your rotten little soul."

"What's wrong with you?" she asked nervously, getting to her knees and switching on the reading lamp at her side. Her hair was charmingly mussed, her body still struck him with its firm sweetness. They glared at each other in the pinkish half-light. "Tell me! What is it?"

Deliberately he turned his back on her and started pulling on his undershirt. Immediately she was out of bed, before him, holding him desperately by his arms.

"Phillip, what's wrong with you?"

For a moment Phillip debated the wisdom of telling her the trick he was using to draw from her the motive of her behavior. He had sensed that he would learn nothing from her if he merely asked her.

"You're false, Pat," he said, freeing himself and reaching for his shorts. "I feel as if I need a bath. You're a good lay, but you're an abomination. You act from a sense of evil, not from a sense of—" *Decency* was not the word he wanted.

The woman's anxiety vanished as he faltered. She turned away laughing and picked up her bag and took a comb from it. Standing before the mirror, her chin high, she combed her short curly hair back into its soft pompadour.

"So I'm the scarlet beast, eh, Phillip?" Her laughter was rich and young. "You're a jewel, my child, a real jewel." She put away the comb and retouched her lips. "Shall I drive you back to the base?"

"Is that included in the cover charge?"

"You've got it all wrong, darling. I'm paying the bills. How does it feel to be on the market?"

But he did not rise to her bait. He was puzzled by her nonchalance. Still one question nagged him and at last it escaped his lips.

"But why?"

She gave him a quick glance before she said crisply, "Let's just put it down to curiosity. Oh, yes, in case your pride as a man is suffering, you're quite adequate but a trifle young. You'll improve with age, I'm sure."

"Coming from a connoisseur of—" Phillip began, but he made a gesture of disgust. "What's the use. You win."

"Thanks. Usually they aren't smart enough to admit it."

"What is the grudge you have against the male sex," Phillip asked.

"No grudge," Pat said. "Help me with this zipper, please." She presented her bodice to him. "Thanks."

But Phillip knew she was lying. By his pretense of anger he had come close to her secret. And of her secret he knew two things: that in some way it was concerned with her husband; and that one day, he, Phillip, would know that secret.

9

Early the next morning Phillip took the first of a long series of pre-court martial examinations that faced him. Sleepily he reported to Sick Bay at 0700 and spent the entire day alternately dressing and undressing. Like the mills of the gods, the Navy missed nothing once it was set in motion. With combined persistence and luck he finished his physical exam by 1730 that evening, and the results were gratifying. Physically he was abnormally perfect, but then he had known that for years. The first hurdle was behind him, cleanly taken. Tomorrow he would start his accomplishment and IQ tests. They would take nine or ten mornings. His afternoons would be free in order to allow him to relax. Then he would face the psychiatrist. As always, the thought brought up a sickening tremor of uncertainty from within him. He longed desperately to be found capable of standing trial, to defend his actions as a normal man before a board of his superiors. For lately, growing more familiar with the problems he faced, his confidence had grown. But to be dismissed from the Navy without a trial, labeled a freak or an inadequate personality, would be the most humiliating blow of all.

His relation with Bruner was near the breaking point. He didn't care. Like Francis, Bruner was to be scorned, a victim of his life, not an administrator of it. Danelaw was too elusive as yet to be accepted in any role; so Phillip depended on his own talents and the Seattle lawyers he had retained to pull him through. And concerning Danelaw, a strange thing had happened in his mind. Instead of despising the man because he had had his wife, Phillip had grown intensely curious about him. In him lay the answer to his wife's puzzling behavior on the previous night. Pat was a whore, no better and no worse than a million of her sisters. As such, her individual attraction that had at first disturbed him no longer presented a menace to his mental freedom. His only interest in her now lay in her motive for throwing herself at him. Once he knew that, he could despise her completely.

While in the hospital, he had asked for and received books on naval law and procedure. He had saturated himself with facts. When he faced the board of five admirals, he intended to face them with confidence in himself, not as a weakling dependent upon Danelaw or a man like Bruner.

Sybel Jo's presence in Seattle, along with other minor annoyances, was not really important now that his mind was made up as to the course he must follow with her. He would simply refuse to marry her and in a week she would be gone. Now he concentrated on retaining his commission.

He hurried to his room that evening, stripped, washed his hands and face, and rubbed his body clean with a cold towel—a trick he had learned overseas where all showers were of sea water. As a result of such bathing, his skin, rich in its own oils, gleamed smooth like a surface of hand-rubbed mahogany—all save the startling white strip of flesh that had been protected by his shorts, which had been the uniform of the day overseas. Now the trim band of ivory looked like a saddle mark, he thought with amusement. He dressed quickly, brushed his hair cautiously over the wound on his scalp, and whistling an air from *Tannhäuser*, went to pick up Francis who had the tickets for the ballet they were attending that night.

At Francis' suggestion when the four of them left the hotel, they decided to dine at Cappy's, a place famous for its sea food. The food was superb and they lingered at the table talking of home. Phillip, drowsily content with cigar and coffee before him, relaxed and listened to the others, throwing in questions from time to time more to keep the talk going than from a desire for any real information. That would be supplied in good time by his family, who understood the significance of city and county affairs. With some amusement Phillip decided that ninety per cent of the gossip he was hearing was actually worthless. Who cared if so-and-so's boy had attained the ephemeral rank of colonel in the Air Force? Back in Devereaux he would be so-and-so's boy again in six weeks, living in the fading glow of his brief splendor while selling washing machines in his papa's appliance shop. No. These three missed the real significance of his community. Not once had they mentioned the certain rise in the price of beef, wheat, cotton, and oil. They were the setters. They would inherit their wealth; and if it grew, it would be from luck, not hardheaded management.

Once Madame brought up their marriage, and Phillip, prepared for the sally, advanced his court martial as a final, effective check against her future arguments. They left the restaurant for the ballet at last, Sybel Jo saying, "I hope we don't run into the Danelaws. I half-promised them we'd come to dinner at their house tonight."

"They don't count," Phillip said easily. "Don't worry about it."

"I thought they were lovely people," Madame said. Phillip looked at Sybel Jo and smiled. She winked. Last night was their secret, though the girl remembered little after she left the club. When Madame had come in at last, she had looked at the girl

109

on the couch calculatingly before asking Phillip, "Have you been here long?" To which Phillip had answered gravely, "Not long enough, Madame." She had understood.

They arrived at the theater only a few minutes before the first curtain and settled themselves quickly to enjoy the performance. Phillip was no balletomane. Modern ballet left him unmoved with its angular pantomime and grimacing faces. But for ballet in the classical tradition he had an unusual receptiveness, a feeling tied obscurely to something in his past. Uneducated to the subtleties of the dance, he appreciated the ballet most as a part of the opera. On his two trips to New York, and in San Francisco, he had attended every possible performance of the opera. Standing four hours at the Metropolitan in New York had not cooled his ardor. Opera was one of the few aesthetic joys in his life. This was due to his musical education and to his knowledge of two other languages besides English. He had a fair mastery of French and the piano, a sketchy acquaintance with the violin and German. To Phillip, all this—together with the interest in Latin and Greek fostered in him once by his Grandfather Dev and later by his Uncle Felix—was delightful though useless knowledge. His father, of course, scorned it.

The ballet made him think of his grandfather, who had spent half of his years on the Continent of Europe. The love of opera was Uncle Felix' contribution. Once his godparent had taken him to the fair in San Francisco to spend the most glorious three weeks of his life. And of all his impressions of that trip the most thrilling was that of his Uncle Felix erect in an opera box beside him while he heard Wagner for the first time from a stage, having it explained to him as the old man leaned over to whisper in his ear. But those thrills belonged to youth. Now he was mature and his destiny lay before him. Still, one could enjoy the ballet occasionally and yet become a fine businessman.

With the first notes of the Chopin overture the curtains parted, revealing a dim, shadowy pastoral setting for posing,

110

gauzily clad coryphees who rose slowly to dance the first somber measures of Fokine's masterpiece. With no effort Phillip became immediately absorbed in the picture before him. Its mood and appeal were unique in his practical world. To him it was a world of its own, surviving the memories of a Europe that had existed long ago; a history-book world of effete dynasties and unbelievably gory wars, of exquisite diplomacy and barbaric crudity, of sophisticated philosophies and naïve superstitions; a world composed of France, Napoleon's still grieving whore; Germany of Prussian blood and iron, strudel, and bock beer; Italy with the Borgias ruling from the papal throne; Austria with her Vienna so chic that she called Paris "hicktown"; czarist Russia of the egg-like jewels and egg-like intellects; and, last of all, Victorian England, detached and aloof, the conscience of a naughty continent. This was what Phillip saw in the abstract patterns the dancers created. It was a world that Phillip might have felt more at ease in than in the present, for it set much store on class, beauty, and leisure. Phillip's present world—when he allowed himself to admit it—demanded too much and in return gave too little. Nowadays the student of music, for instance, played Chopin to keep his fingers supple to create the unheard of noise of some damned Russian that Chopin wouldn't have pissed on. But these were dangerous thoughts to allow in the mind: There was nothing to be gained in revering the past. One appreciated it and forgot it and made the best of what was at hand. So Phillip watched the nocturne, mazurka, *pas de deux*, and the lilting waltz, and with the final curtain dutifully returned to the present and a Sybel Jo who was sound asleep, her hand trustingly in his.

For a moment he was exasperated; then remembering how little interest one of her accomplishments could have in the ballet, he chuckled, called the attention of Madame and Francis to his sleeping beauty, and roguishly bent his head and kissed the palm of the girl's hand. She smiled, sighed, and as if sensing something amiss, opened her eyes to their laughter.

"I'd like to know what you were dreaming," Phillip said.

"It was all about you," the girl said coyly.

"I hope so."

As Madame was clamoring to go out for a cigarette, they joined the audience and moved slowly toward the foyer outside. Phillip produced cigarettes but found he had no matches.

"Just a minute, I'll borrow a light." He walked toward a man with a lighter a few steps away.

"Phillip! Phillip Froelich," a cool voice called. "Over here."

He turned to see Pat Danelaw standing with her husband, Bruner, and Morgan. Phillip nodded stiffly in their direction and turned his back on them, but the damage was done. Madame and Francis were already moving toward them. Sybel Jo followed. Phillip let them go while he got his light. Then, because there was nothing else to do, he went to join them.

"I say, Phillip," Pat asked with some mimicry of his accent, "are we being snubbed?"

"Why, no, Mrs. Danelaw. Can you think of a reason why you should be?"

Tim Danelaw smiled at the thrust.

"Only that your fiancée promised to bring you to dinner tonight."

"Sybel Jo didn't know that we had plans for this evening."

Once more Pat was strikingly groomed in white. The gown was of stiff, brocaded silk, simply cut to reveal her long beautiful lines. Tonight she wore one piece of jewelry, an emerald on a white metal chain at her throat. Instinctively Phillip glanced at her husband's hand, for he was sure that the stone was the one he had seen him wear. Once more he was struck by the stone's uncommon beauty. Now it brought out the fine color of a woman's eyes, whereas once it had drawn flattering attention to her husband's hands. In the strong light over them, it seemed to smolder with intense chemical fires as it moved upon her flesh. Phillip found his eyes returning to it with embarrassing frequence. He stood apart from them and smoked in silence,

112

hating the people he could not accept, making little attempt to conceal it.

Pat babbled, "Wasn't the Chopin sticky? I felt as if I'd eaten candy on an empty stomach." To Phillip's disgust everyone agreed with her. She turned to him and asked sweetly, "Didn't you think so, Phillip?"

"I liked it," he said flatly. "But then I have a strong stomach." The implication reached even Sybel Jo.

Tim Danelaw chuckled. "My dear, you've met your match at last." And giving Phillip a mock salute, he said, "You'd better be careful, young fellow, or my wife will murder you for revenge."

Phillip shrugged. He was bewildered by these people. If any man had made the same remark to Sybel Jo, he would have moved swiftly even though he got his face beaten to a pulp for it. A man was supposed to protect his wife as he did his property. The Danelaws were impossible.

"Oh, I don't mind Phillip," Pat said airily. "He's like a dog —what he doesn't understand frightens him, so he barks."

Phillip felt his face turn scarlet. His hands tingled with the desire to slap the bitch flat.

"If you will excuse us," he said softly, his lips felt moldy with hatred as the words slid past them. He took Sybel Jo's arm and said to his cousin, "Are you coming, Francis?" But Francis' eyes were alight with pleasure at the scene, and immediately Phillip knew that he had no ally there. Their group had fallen into a deadly pool of quiet in the midst of the noise around them.

"No," Francis said, "I'm staying here."

"Then stay and rot, you bastard," Phillip said. "You're in your element. Come, Syb!"

"Phillip!" It was Madame. She stepped in front of him, her face working with fury that puzzled Phillip for a moment. "I've never seen such a display of childishness in my life," she said. "Your father is right. Handling you is like handling a bull with

113

a pitchfork. I forbid Sybel Jo to go with you until you apologize to your cousin and to Mrs. Danelaw and her guests."

With the quiet cunning of a trapped animal, Phillip stood his ground watchfully, looking for an opening to escape. He understood Madame's motives in facing him publicly and on such a minor issue. If a quarrel developed over this, it could be settled. Piqued at his refusal to marry in Seattle, anxious to attract the attention of Morgan to herself, she was offering Phillip his first ultimatum. He could tell them all to go to hell and win the least important round, or he could give in and weaken Madame for the important issue. Too, he must not lose the Voth support, and to embarrass Madame now would be to set her against him in the future. With every fiber he longed to turn on his heel and walk out of their lives forever; and, clearly enough, that is what they expected him to do, for in each face there was a different degree of triumph. That is, all but one. Tim Danelaw's eyes were inscrutable.

Phillip took his time before he answered. Above all, he remembered his ambitions and the ambitions of the Froelich family. There was nothing to prevent Sybel Jo marrying Francis except the fact that she did not love him, and Phillip knew how unimportant Sybel Jo's desires were. There was but one course to follow just now. These people were not his people. He could bow before them, for they didn't count. He would be bowing for his father, his mother, Fanchon, and himself. So, playing the role to the hilt, he reached for Sybel Jo's hand and smiled down at her a bit wryly.

"For you, darling," he whispered, yet loud enough for the others to hear. She smiled radiantly but vacuously, and he lifted his head and said, "Of course, Madame." He almost smiled at the relief that shattered the harshness of her face. And to the others he said, "At home, when we rope calves for branding, they run until they hit the end of the rope. Then they are usually flipped on the ground so hard they're stunned for a while. That's about the way I feel now." He smiled a little and lifted

114

his head. "Please accept my apologies." He took the few steps that separated him from Francis and extended his hand. But he could not prevent his lip from curling the least bit as he said, "I'm sorry I lost my temper, Francis." His cousin took his hand silently. Phillip turned and looked once more at the faces surrounding him, anxious to stamp each one in his mind for future reference. Undoubtedly he would find some of them helpless before he died.

"Well," Pat said, "now that custom no longer topples—"

"My dear," Tim Danelaw's voice was as lazy as a purr, but it had a strange effect on his wife. She seemed to stiffen and falter. The man continued, "I'm sorry, you were saying?"

"Why, I was just going to ask everyone out to the house after the performance," Pat said quietly. "We're entertaining the ballet cast." She looked at Madame. Because it was natural for her to do so, Madame shot a questioning look to Phillip. He noticed and smiled.

"We'd be delighted, Mrs. Danelaw," he said.

"Oh, please call me Pat. Everyone does."

"I think it's time for the curtain," Phillip said easily, glancing at the crowd going back into the theater. "We'll meet you after the performance."

The two groups moved apart, Phillip's unusually silent. Now that Madame had her victory, she obviously didn't know how to use it. Phillip was a thorn in her flesh. His swift decision before he apologized had been right. Madame would have been stronger if she had lost the tilt.

As they reached their seats, she said nervously, "If you'd rather not go, Phillip—"

"That's entirely up to you, Madame," he said with sincere consideration, thereby upsetting her still further.

"Well, then we'll go." But it was a question rather than a statement.

"Fine," Phillip agreed.

10

•◇•◇•◇•◇•◇•

*F*or their stay in Seattle the Danelaws had rented a ten-room house on two levels. It belonged to some artist that everyone in their crowd seemed to know as "The Mason." Phillip gathered he was still overseas with the Army, and from the taste he had displayed in building and decorating, Phillip hoped the man stayed there.

The modernistic building perched apart from its neighbors on an almost sheer bluff and commanded an impressive view of the city, the harbor, and the mountains to the north and east. But the line of everything inside and out seemed wrong—an abrupt attempt at some ideal that didn't quite come off. The room Phillip's party entered, a combined living and dining room, was an enormous polygon of a dozen irregular sides. To Phillip, unused to modern architecture, the walls looked as if they had been blasted and set back by a lunatic. Madame, exchanging glances of appreciation with her stepdaughter, whispered knowingly, "Functional." Phillip remembered that so was a bowel movement.

116

The room was a welter of washed-out pastels and freak hues that jarred against his eyes—magenta and amethyst, lime and ice-blue, chartreuse and brick. There must be harmony somewhere, Phillip thought, but it escaped him both in color and contour. The furniture looked like packing cases on legs, or exaggerated nursery blocks. A great square coffee table especially irritated him. Its legs seemed to be three boomerangs. On a bleached wood chest against a glass wall there was a collection of primitive idols, the only natural objects in the ugly, brassy room. But the chandelier was the crowning horror, floating overhead in wrought iron—a fish, a trumpet, and three instruments for drawing teeth. The thing was designed to reflect the moods of a fast, hard, brittle people.

Already there were twenty-odd guests at the bar and buffet, dancing or talking, each of them, civilian and serviceman alike, acting as if he were the host in this place. If the Danelaws had a servant problem, they were doing well enough with three Filipino boys who tended bar and buffet. Every few minutes the door opened to admit another cabful of guests, more civilians in evening clothes that might be anything from industrialists to janitors, and of course the ballet cast, women with too much muscle and men with too little.

Francis and Bruner headed for the bar. Madame and Morgan were making progress in the terrace doorway, and Sybel Jo had gone to meet the ballet crowd with Pat and collect autographs to show back in Devereaux. Phillip shrugged. He sought a solitary chair and with the first copy of the *New York Times* he'd seen in two years flatly refused several offers of companionship. That is, he refused all but Pat's.

"Come along, darling—" she patted his cheek despite Sybel Jo—"I'm going to show you Tim's paintings, the ones you think don't exist."

"I haven't demanded proof," Phillip said.

"Of course you haven't. But you're going to see them anyway. There are only five, so they can't bore you long."

Reluctantly Phillip put aside the paper and allowed Pat to lead him through the noisy room as she collected others for the private showing. Ascending the broad, shallow stairway to the open mezzanine along the top of the first floor, she explained, "These are some of Tim's best works. He had them sent out from Chicago last year. He works on a canvas spasmodically for years and then throws it away because he's lost the original idea somewhere along the way. That's why he has so few canvases to show for his career. Timmie, you do the showing, please."

Tim nodded and opened one of the doors for them to enter. He followed them in and started setting up an easel in the middle of the room to catch the best light. Phillip, prepared to show polite interest, glanced around the pleasantly cluttered masculine room, which was evidently Tim's sleeping quarters. There was fishing tackle piled on a table of books and painting supplies. On the wall there was a collection of magnificent fencing foils and daggers, their grips inlaid with colored stones. Phillip would have preferred examining them to the man's artistic efforts, but he turned back to look at the first of the pictures Tim was setting in place. Suddenly the mundane "Very nice" he was preparing to utter died on his lips.

It was a nocturnal landscape illuminated by a preternatural light, ghoulish, foreboding—the setting for a feast of grave robbers. For a few moments Phillip, like the others, stood at rapt attention before the aura of evil that the canvas held. But any concrete evidence of evil was not to be seen. Every object was extremely ordinary, if slightly blurred. Then it came to Phillip that the effect must be in the color. He could not describe it, for his knowledge of painting was negligible. But he looked at Tim Danelaw, realizing for the first time that he might well be in the presence of a great painter, even a great man. Tim stood apart waiting, neither coy nor proud. His manner was entirely impersonal, as if the painting belonged to someone else.

The others were beginning to murmur comments, and Phillip

118

was happy to hear that they were as much at a loss for words as he had been. Strangely enough, it was Sybel Jo who came closest to the truth with the homespun verdict, "It looks creepy."

Tim set the next canvas into place—a head. Once more Phillip had the strange feeling that he was seeing through the exterior into the very spirit of the subject. Without knowing why he sensed immediately that the old man depicted was both lecherous and sanctimonious. Yet the features were aggravatingly commonplace. The mood seemed to come from the color again, the flesh, the eyes, the mouth and hair. But now he saw something else. The same blurred aspect of the first canvas was present here, too, but here the blur was actual distortion. The comments of the others were lyrical this time.

The third canvas was a nude, a young woman, madonna-like in her serene beauty. The hair fell over the shoulders, golden as wheat; the eyes were as clear as jade. It was Pat, painted as she should be, as she might have been once. And then Phillip realized that no one had yet recognized the subject. The long hair, the soft warmth of the features, the nudity had duped them.

Pat was saying, "And to think, Tim wants to destroy it."

This was greeted with a chorus of "But why?" "How could he?" and "Oh, no!" But Phillip could understand the man's desire. Tim wanted to destroy a past, not a picture. Pat had already destroyed the ideal.

In a half-voice Pat said to him, "You're very silent. What do you think of it?"

And to his surprise Phillip heard himself answer, "He must have loved you very much."

Pat's consternation was only slightly greater than his. She looked at him as if he had tried to insult her.

Tim, who had moved near just in time to catch Phillip's remark, said, "Not one person in fifty makes the transition. Why did you?"

"I don't know. It's your wife as she should be, I think." And

119

he blushed at the tactlessness of his words. The artist studied Phillip with new concentration.

There was another landscape and a still life, but Phillip was too upset to do more than glance at them.

Pat had snapped back to her cool caustic self once more and was saying to the others, "And now, just one more. A whimsey in black and white that Tim just finished. Actually it is a cartoon."

"Perhaps you'd better not," Tim said uncertainly.

"Why not? He just took a crack at me, didn't he?" she said, looking at Phillip. Already she had crossed the room and pulled a drawing board from a cabinet. She set it on the easel and stepped back, temporarily blocking Phillip's view.

There was a titter of laughter and Madame gasped, "Why it looks like Phillip!"

Remembering Pat's words of the night before, Phillip moved forward and looked at the thing on the drawing board.

It was a chiaroscuro of heavy masses of black against the dead white of the paper. And though it was nothing human, it did look like him. It was devilishly clever, and after his first shock he found himself smiling, too, unaware of the eyes on him.

The image was a man masquerading as a cat, or—more accurately—a great jungle cat masquerading as a man. The thing seemed to be relaxing on a shelf of rock, one blunt black paw that looked strangely like a hand hanging over the edge. Lazily it regarded its audience with narrow, appraising eyes that were Phillip's, its slightly pointed ears, located at the side rather than on top of the head, erect to catch the first hint of danger. It had long drooping whiskers. But something—perhaps it was an element in the triangular shape of the face—caught the fundamental appearance of Phillip. The artist in a playful mood had described him as no one else had bothered or dared to do. Instead of being angry, Phillip was delighted. He studied the wide anthropoid angles of the chest, the limbs that were half-human in shape but leonine in position, and the fur that covered them.

120

The final touch was the long black tail that curved up over the belly like the closed fan of an idle woman. Phillip smiled broadly at the faun, a cross between man and cat rather than man and goat.

"Very amusing," he said, turning to Tim. "I congratulate you."

"Amusing?" Madame said. "If you looked like that, we'd shudder."

"Of all the unpredictable people, " Pat murmured.

"But that's just it," Phillip said. "I don't look like that. It's all in the suggestion." And to Tim he said with enthusiasm, "Now I understand your pictures. Your techinque is simply your power for distorting subjects—a distortion that is perceptible yet acceptable. The basic outline is always true and faithful, but the content is vaguely pushed out of place." He turned to the canvases propped against the wall. "For instance, this line in the head here. It's no line at all, but a shadow. It's impossible, but it looks right somehow. Your color is important, too. There's a touch of green in your black here, and purple in the red of these lips. The entire effect is a sort of off-center balance. One wrong move and the whole thing falls apart. As an artist, Commander Danelaw, you pack a powerful left and a very delicate right."

"Tim!" Pat exclaimed, "he's charming. You can't let him get away."

Tim gave a little nod of approval. "You aren't angry then?"

"Because of the caricature? Not at all. I'd like to buy it."

This made the man ill at ease. "It has no value," he began, "either artistic or decorative, but if you want it—"

"Wait, Phillip," Pat interrupted. "Tim gave it to me when I saw it. If you want it you can have it if you sit for a portrait which will also be mine when it is completed."

Phillip frowned. "I'm sorry. The court martial—"

"That isn't for weeks. Tim works rapidly. A few nights after work is all he needs. And if necessary he can paint you in jail."

121

"But I want my evenings free," Phillip hedged, looking at Sybel Jo.

"She'd love to come out here, wouldn't you, Syb?"

"Oh, yes," Sybel Jo agreed enthusiastically.

"You see. You haven't a leg to stand on—"

"But perhaps your husband doesn't want to paint the portrait."

"Tim wants to or he'd never have bothered with the sketch."

"Well. . . ." Phillip continued to flounder, wanting the sketch but not enough to sit to the man hour after hour for it. He glanced at Tim who seemed totally unconcerned as to his decision.

"Then it's all settled," Pat said grandly. "And it's up to you, Syb, to get him out here tomorrow night for the first session."

The others took her at her word and forgot the episode, collecting before the canvases to talk. But Phillip felt as if he had been left in the middle of a ring of fire. He had been talked into a situation he did not want, could not understand or intelligently shape to his own ends. The thought of being an artist's model for a price was degrading to him. He was no pauper, nor did he consider himself handsome enough for an artist to want for any purpose. Like most of the men of his class, he considered art effeminate, the most damning adjective in his vocabulary.

He glanced at Tim for some hint, found none in the impassive features, and dropped his eyes. The two men stood before the easel alone. The others had retreated like a tide of words. Phillip's brain swarmed with words he wanted to say, but his lips were stiff. He gnawed the inside of his cheek nervously a few seconds, glanced up at Tim again, and made a move to join the others. But Tim's voice stopped him.

"Shall we go outside for a while?" he asked, indicating the double doors opening on a shallow balcony at the other end of the room.

Silently they crossed the room and Tim stepped aside to allow Phillip to go out first. Then he pulled the doors shut after

122

them and joined the boy at the balcony rail. They stood in darkness above several couples dancing on the terrace below. Music reached them indistinctly.

It was the third time Phillip and Tim had been alone, and each of them was intensely aware of the fact. On the first occasion Phillip had been drunk; on the second, under the influence of narcotics. Now he was sober. He knew that he might expect anything, but he also knew that this was the logical time for declaration and clarification of purpose, even though he dreaded such a possibility because he felt inadequate and unable to act reasonably in the presence of this strange man. A continuous flicker of excitement like heat lightning played within him, causing the muscles of his arms to grow increasingly tense and his hands on the cold iron rail to tremble with concentration. Tim spoke first, making a sweeping gesture with his cigarette over the horizon.

"It's eloquent, isn't it? The entire world on stage."

Silently Phillip looked at the magnificent scene. Far below their cliff lay the city and the harbor. In the center of the velvety water, Amphib Island, a patternless brooch of yellow diamonds. And far away, lifting herself through moonlight and a flying scud of rain cloud, sat Rainier, cold, massive, thrilling in her mysterious beauty. For many minutes they were quiet and Phillip's agitation increased. . . .

At last Tim said in his impersonal tone, "I've had two occasions to admire you tonight, young fellow. First, when you backed down before your future mother-in-law and my wife. A man is always wise to avoid issues with a woman. Because they seldom act from reason, a man must come off second best. For a moment I was worried, but I see now I shouldn't have been." He ground out his cigarette against the rail. "The second time was just now when you put your finger on the real elements of my painting technique. Few critics could have done better."

He was silent awhile, expecting Phillip to speak, but Phillip

123

was still tongue-tied with his consideration of other questions that lay between them.

And as if Tim realized this, he said, "I'll tell you what let's do. Let's just consider everything said and go on from there, shall we?"

"All of what?" Phillip's voice caught with his excitement.

"All those things you want to say to me and don't quite dare: the base security officer that didn't question you, my lawyer's unbidden but very welcome visit, your ex-captain's approaching investigation for incompetency, and the other things."

"How did you know I knew about them?" Phillip asked with surprise.

"I had no desire to keep them from you," Tim said. "And I know, too, that you've been wondering about my motives."

"I have."

"And what have you decided?"

"My decision doesn't make sense."

"Except to an adolescent?"

"Perhaps I am wrong. I seem to make only mistakes lately."

"And what is your opinion on that score?" Tim asked with interest.

"Fate, I guess. An astrologer would say my star is in descent."

"And perhaps he would be right. We constantly pass into and out of states of being as we develop. Few people even recognize them. Fewer learn to master them."

"I like that." Phillip turned to look at the man and found his eyes on him. "It helps somehow. Gide speaks of lyrical states of creation."

"So you're familiar with Gide?"

"Not very. *The Counterfeiters*, *The Immoralist*, *Lafcadio*."

"And *Corydon*?"

"Yes." And Phillip added, "My frandfather met Gide once in Paris."

"And he spoke to you of him?"

"No. He died when I was a child." They were silent for several

124

minutes while Phillip exhausted his train of thought and said, "Back to the present, sir. I want you to know that I'm grateful for all the things you've done for me."

"They were in the cause of justice."

"I—I want to say other things but I'm not clever with words."

"You're thinking of my wife," Tim supplied. "You want to say that she means nothing to you despite her rather obvious advances. I know that. And then you're trying to say that you'd rather not sit for this portrait. You don't have to."

"But I'd be ungrateful if I didn't."

"Gratitude can be a scar. We'll call it off."

"No, I'd rather sit to you, if you can accept my motives."

"You like to feel you earn your living."

"I always have. I always will. And I do want the cat sketch for my sister. We're very close. She would understand it, I think." Phillip smiled, thinking of Fanchon's pleasure. They were silent again and Phillip felt certain hard peaks of uncertainty in his mind grow soft and crumble. "There's one more thing," he said.

"I know," the older man answered. "The knottiest problem of all. You want to talk of you and me and what is between us."

"Yes." Phillip's breath grew short as he waited.

"You're safe, Phillip. Despite the questionable appearance of my actions of the past days, there is no cause for alarm. We've both too much to lose to risk—tilting with windmills."

"That's what I wanted to hear. Now everything is—" Phillip made a short, smoothing gesture with his hand. And from the excess of his relief, he said, "I wish we were friends. That is, if you can see anything in me that would make you want my friendship. The picture must be pretty horrible."

"The picture, as you call it, isn't finished," Tim said. "And I see a great number of admirable things in you. Your friendship would be a worthy possession. I accept."

"And you're the person I feared the most," Phillip mused.

With a sharp click the doors behind them opened and Pat's

125

caroling voice said, "Oh, there you are. Tim, be a lamb and go inside. Bruner and Mike Mallory are in the same crowd and you know that whenever they argue there's a scene. Break it up, will you, lamb?"

"Of course."

As Tim left, Phillip turned back to the view with annoyance. He wanted their conversation to go on. It was the first soothing, sensible thing that had happened to him since he had arrived in Seattle. Now he had to put up with Pat. Leaning on the rail beside him, she pointed to a couple in a dark corner below, close in embrace.

"They look cozy, don't they?"

Phillip looked down and then back to the majestic mountain.

"You don't approve of that, do you, Phillip?"

"Oh, my God, do we have to go into that again? You've had your victory. You've seen me crawl before your friends."

"But I want you to crawl to me alone," Pat said candidly.

"Heaven forgive me for finding fault with Syb," he muttered.

"Why *are* you marrying her?" Pat asked. "Money?"

"The Froelichs are a good deal richer than the Voths," Phillip said tersely. "I love her very much."

"But she doesn't love you. She thinks she does."

"No? Sybel Jo will love the man she marries. I'll see to it."

"You know, you fascinate me, Phillip."

"I'm not flattered."

"I wish you'd trust me. I'm not what you think I am."

"Why do you act like what I think you are?"

"Because everyone expects me to."

"Then get away from everyone."

"But these people are fun. They laugh and love easily."

"Very human of them."

"Which you aren't. You're the personification of five per cent interest. You're a snob, and with your temper, you're easily baited."

"Who told you that?"

126

"Tim. You amuse him. He was telling the Admiral the other evening that you are in the final formative stage, just before your character jells for good. That's why he wants to paint you."

"I hope he finds what he wants."

"You don't like him either, do you?"

"Don't you ever do anything but ask personal questions? Let's go."

"No. Wait a moment, Phillip, please." Her hand touched his imploringly. There was a new tone in her voice, low, unhappy. She looked up at him uncertainly. Phillip was puzzled. "This is something I've said to few people," she said. "I'm not happy. I hate this crowd as much as you do, but I tolerate them because Tim likes people around him. He feeds on them like a vulture."

"Tim?" Phillip said scornfully. "Come now, Mrs. Danelaw."

"I know it sounds unbelievable, but it's true. I suppose it's my fault for not being able to please him. You'll learn about him soon enough. He'll take what he wants of you for his picture, which won't be pretty, and toss the rest of you away. It happens to everyone who knows him. I've been married to him four years now. I was twenty and naïve." Phillip suddenly remembered the madonna-like portrait. "He was rich and handsome, considerate and interesting. I thought I loved him very much. And then, too, I was modeling and being pawed by every dolt in New York. So I married him—and learned that he wasn't a very nice person."

Phillip frowned. She could be telling the truth.

"If I found someone, Phillip, someone sincere and gentle, some—"

"They aren't so rare," Phillip interrupted, not wanting to hear what he knew she was about to say. "And if it's so bad, why don't you do something about it?"

"I am," she said, her voice shaking. "I'm divorcing him in the fall."

"What?" Phillip stiffened, wondering why this bit of information should bring such a violent reaction. And from the doorway, Tim's smooth voice reached them.

"In September, to be exact. Pat is leaving for Reno in August."

In the semi-darkness, the man's face was its usual benign mask.

11

*P*hillip sat on the edge of his bed, teeth chattering with cold, sweating with fear. In one hand he held the deadly sleeping pills he had stolen; in the other, a snapshot of his grandfather. By his watch it was three hours past midnight.

He had had a dream. He remembered that clearly. A dream of a slaughter house in which there had been marvelous machines for dismembering human corpses, cleaver-like instruments that cut the white limbs at the wrist, elbow, and shoulder with quick, solid blows. He had watched the operation with a minimum of horror. Then his companion had recognized one of the victims being fed into the machine and had called his attention to its identity. And here the dream became vague. He could not remember whether the corpse had been his Grandfather Dev and his companion Tim Danelaw, or vice versa. The important thing was that sometime between the dream and the time he awoke he had got out of bed, found the sleeping tablets, and found himself a glass of water.

He stared at the snapshot in the moonlight again. Faintly he

129

could make out the two familiar outlines of himself at the age of eight, and his Grandfather Dev, kneeling on the lawn at home. He carried the snapshot with him always, a reminder of his grandparent, and his childhood which were gone, never to be retrieved. But what had Danelaw to do with this? He would not accept the obvious explanation, for he was not willing to admit the seriousness of his malady.

Phillip dropped the pills on the nightstand and pulled the bedclothes around him. When he was warmer, he poured himself some brandy, studied it a moment, and decided not to drink it. He needed to think.

For the past week, since the night of the ballet when he had rammed the outer limits of his selfish desires and had prudently fallen back to formulate new strategy, the Danelaws had taken complete charge of his life. In the mornings he took his accomplishment tests, the results of which had been excellent. To his amusement two of the IQ tests had given him the rating of genius. However, there was one dark spot which had shown up in the personality series. On a masculinity-femininity scale he was barely across the border in the right direction. The questions, designed with a time limit, had to be answered reflectively. He supposed that in racing through them, one inadvertently gave a clear picture of his tastes. Phillip did not delude himself over the importance of these tests to men like Bruner.

His afternoons, which were supposed to be free, usually contained the most hectic hours of his day. He spent them with Sybel Jo, Madame, and Pat. They drove out to the island, picked him up, and carried him off to some of Pat's friends' places to swim, sail, or play cards. Phillip had been looking forward to the end of the week when Madame and Sybel Jo would leave for Oklahoma, but Pat had persuaded them to stay another week—not that much persuasion was needed—and Phillip's hopes had plunged. Madame had evidently made up her mind

130

to return home minus her stepdaughter. Phillip was equally determined to outwait her.

Pat was playing a strange role. She seemed to be trying to learn Phillip's world. She managed to be near him constantly, alone or with his guests. She encouraged all of them to talk about Oklahoma. She was a shrewd listener, a subtle questioner, and Phillip began to suspect her of several plans. But was she stupid enough to suppose that she could fit into his world or he into hers? Conceivably she might be a rich woman after Reno, and lately she was presenting another side of her personality, gentler, graver, more appealing, but she was wasting her time. He knew he could never succeed Tim. Yet beneath her sophistication, Pat was exciting. He loved to hold her in his arms when they danced, to feel her passionate lips and body against his when the opportunity presented itself—and she saw to it that opportunities were frequent. But he was afraid of her, afraid of what she could do to him if she ever secured a hold on him. His love for Sybel Jo would never rise to a level of any intensity. Pat could make herself an obsession, one that would take years to break, years that he must devote to the bank. He did not trust her. He remembered her words too clearly in the hotel room. She had a secret, something she desperately wanted of him, and he was determined to find out what it was. So they played a game, his skill against her endurance—a game that she was winning.

Guessing that he did not intend to marry his fiancée in Seattle, she joined forces with Madame in urging him to do so. She was bent on forcing him to a decision of some kind—a decision that would somehow benefit her. And as usual, Phillip found the female mind too complicated to follow. Yes, Pat was exciting, but she was also a continual source of annoyance.

He had two sources of consolation, however. The first was the letters from his family. His father's were stern and demanding of him. Fanchon's were casual, presenting always two sides of each question, leaving the decisions to him, yet knowing

131

which one he would take. But from his mother's letters he drew a quiet determination to carry out his ambitions. Victoria Froelich was decidedly a rare woman. He read her letters religiously, saving them to reread when the circus of people in which he was living became too uproarious. And often he smiled over an imagined situation, one made of pure dreams. He imagined this crowd suddenly transplanted to Devereaux, confronting him as one of his clan, and his eyes clouded with pleasure at the thought of the results. Madame fleeing as usual from his mother. Pat crossing blades with Fanchon and being deftly hacked to pieces by his sister's dry wisdom. Francis, Sybel Jo, Bruner, Morgan—all sliding to the bottom of the heap where they belonged. But it was too fanciful. Phillip was a prisoner in an enemy camp. All he could do was wait for deliverance, and patience was decidedly not his strongest virtue. As yet he had been spared the ordeal of informing his family of his predicament. He still hoped to win his battle and their admiration alone.

His second source of consolation was an equivocal one: Tim Danelaw. Their friendship had progressed rapidly. Phillip had an enthusiastic inclination to admiration, and Tim's strange talk and facile wit delighted the boy after a two-year diet of cultural K rations. He loved good talk, excellent food and wine, and as Tim's model he had them all. Yet he did not understand him at all. The strangest element about the man was that he seemed to sense Phillip's thoughts sometimes before he thought them. The boy never uttered a sentence without the exasperating feeling that if he stopped abruptly in the middle of it, Tim could finish it for him just as he had planned.

During their conversation on the balcony after the exhibition of the cat sketch, Phillip's scorn had simply turned about-face to become admiration. Tim had made his position clear. He had given his word that he would attempt no degrading alliance, and instinctively Phillip knew that the man was not a liar. Freed

132

of this primary concern, he had steadily warmed toward the man while the portrait was being painted.

It was going to be a gigantic affair, life-size if the measurements of the new canvas were an indication. Phillip had seen nothing of the painting yet, nor had anyone. Tim's habit was to display only finished work; so when they left the room after each sitting, he locked the door.

At the first sitting, Phillip had been self-conscious, assuming various attitudes while naked before the man. But the pose was quickly decided upon and with a faint smile Tim told him that in the future he might wear his shorts while sitting—in the event that someone popped in on them. After the first hour, Phillip relaxed.

The sessions were not trying. Tim, it seemed, made only infrequent reference to his model. He urged Phillip to move about often, read, listen to records, and even talk as much as he wanted. Painting as he did, Tim drew his qualities from the mind of the model rather than the physique. He sketched a great deal on a pad from every possible view—angles that could not possibly show on canvas.

When Phillip asked about this, he explained that one must understand the subject in three dimensions to paint it in two. Then he went on, "All artistic creation can be divided into two categories, the necessary and the fine. The first, or body and background of the piece, is usually ignored by the layman. The last, or the fine, is the finishing touches that the artist is known and praised for. That's why good critics are as scarce as good artists. Concentration on the wrong things. But then we're all guilty of it. And by the way, if you're ever troubled over the term *artistic creation*, don't think of it only as a process of building, but also as a process of selection. It helps."

It was an example of the offhand comments that produced an almost chemical reaction in Phillip's mind, releasing all sorts of hidden elements into activity. And being curious as a young ostrich, the boy's interest was always sharp during these hours.

133

He realized that it was good for him, too, lifting him out of himself.

Once as Tim was sketching his profile, the artist looked up and exclaimed, "There it is! I'm surprised it escaped me so long."

"What?" Phillip asked as the artist went to search for a book.

"Did you ever hear of Donatello?" Tim asked.

"Yes. He cast some doors during the Renaissance, didn't he?"

"That was Ghiberti. But the period is the same." He selected a book and turned through it. "Donatello was a sculptor. One of his finest statues is a *St. George*. The head is particularly good, catching a certain beauty of youth and courage in arms that is rare. For centuries critics have referred to the marvelous appearance of movement within the marble. Here, look at this. It's a picture of the profile of the head." He gave Phillip the book and picked up his sketch pad and held the two close. "You see? The profiles are the same. I recognized the familiarity the first time I saw you, but I didn't put the two together until now. Look." With his pencil he pointed. "The same cap of hair over the head, the position of the ear and the eye in the skull, the almost unbroken line of the brow and nose." He drew a line on his sketch from the lobe of the ear to the tip of the nose. "You see. The top part of each skull is over twice as large as the lower, making the lower seem weak until you consider the piece as a whole, and particularly the hard line of the jaw. The throat and neck are exactly alike. In profile you have the same sharp purity of line, the same clean planes and angles of the *St. George*." He looked down at Phillip and smiled. "However," he said, "full-view, you resemble anything but a saint. The cat portrait does you justice there."

Phillip laughed, studying the book as Tim returned to the easel. "It's strange that you sketched me as a cat," he said.

"Why? Lots of people resemble animals. You resemble a cat."

"I've always liked them. Suppose I've picked up a characteristic here and there?"

134

"Hardly," Tim chuckled. "You love horses, too, but you certainly don't look like a palomino stallion."

"How did you know that?" Phillip felt as if he were setting a trap.

"I think Francis mentioned that you owned some mounts."

"Oh." Phillip was curiously let down.

It was the first time Phillip had spoken of his family. Thoroughly aware of the mistake he had made with Stuff Manus, he did so with some doubt. For a time he had tried to draw parallels from his experience with the sailor in an effort to avoid any similar crisis. It did not take him long, however, to recognize that there were no parallels in the two situations, for the men concerned were antipodes. With Stuff he had been the leader and up to a point he had set the pace. With Tim he was the follower. He learned that his wisest course of action was to trust himself completely to the older man's judgment. But even this course was not without its puzzling moments.

"Tell me, Tim," Phillip once asked, "is Proust right when he says that art can console one for the loss of living?"

"What are you referring to?"

"In *The Captive* he says that there is in art a more profound reality in which the real personality finds an expression not offered by life."

"I suppose there is such a reality, if the artist is intent on revealing truth. But Proust couldn't let well enough alone. He was continually probing himself."

"Is that wrong?" Phillip asked, relaxing with a cigarette.

Tim smiled. "For a man, yes. For an artist, no."

"And what is truth?" Phillip asked, aware of the nature of his question.

"That lies within the mind of each man. To know it, one must first discover it in the basic patterns of life around him."

"And what are they?"

Tim looked up from his canvas. "Maybe they are the virtues. Charity, consideration, tolerance in opposition to greed, envy."

135

"In what do you believe, Tim?"

"That's hard to say on such short acquaintance," Tim said. "Some complex system of domination and sublimation, I suppose—" he smiled slyly and gave Phillip an oblique glance— "perhaps that complete selfishness makes for a generous personality."

"Then why am I not a generous man?" Phillip laughed.

"To quote Carlyle, who seems to be your philosophical rock, you haven't transcended the necessary levels yet."

"How did you know that?" Phillip was pleased with the turn of conversation, for though he was still afraid of the man, this was the opportunity he had wanted to declare himself on certain points that he suspected might be in the man's mind.

"Your friend the sailor didn't forget the lessons you taught him. Quite a votary you have there."

"Stuff puzzled me," Phillip began. "We became friends too easily. I respected him too soon. More important, I liked him. I think he kept me from going berserk a couple of times." Tim painted on, undisturbed. "Then one day I was aware of something else. I even remember how I noticed it. We were tearing down a twenty-millimeter together and the sea was heavy. He stepped behind me to give me a hand. We were stripped to the waist and we touched. I thought nothing of it until the barrel was in and I looked up and found Stuff blushing." Uncertain that he had made himself clear, Phillip asked, "Do you understand what I mean?"

Without looking up, Tim said, frowning over the paint a bit, "You suspected him of a homosexual interest because of one incident."

"And others later," Phillip added defensively. "I was shocked and amused. I guess I should have discussed it, pointing out that the unnatural, all-male society in which we lived had germinated such emotions. I might have prevented what happened later if I had."

"And what did happen later?" Tim's fingers gripped his brush.

136

"The inevitable pass in my direction. We were alone on deck one night and—" Phillip's voice stopped abruptly as he saw Tim's face. Instinctively Phillip's hand went to the freshly healed wound on his shoulder as if to protect it from danger, wondering what he had said to offend so deeply. The man's face was transparent at last, revealing hate and rage that chilled the boy's blood.

"And?" Tim asked tightly.

"And nothing," Phillip replied shakily. "We had a fight."

To Phillip's amazement, Tim's face cleared instantly. "You must have looked like the climax of 'Virtue Rewarded,'" Tim laughed, turning his back on Phillip.

Phillip did not like the tone of the remark at all, but he was so overwhelmed with relief that he was not interested in learning the complexity of Tim's anger, nor was he ready to accept the simple explanation that confronted him. He was a coward on this point. But the incident stood alone. From then on, they kept their observations on safer, more impersonal levels. Soon the portrait would reach the stage where Phillip was no longer needed. After that he might relax, but until that time he must move cautiously.

Huddled in the bedclothes, he looked at his watch again. Four o'clock. It was useless to try to sleep. At nine the Danelaws and Sybel Jo were picking him up to fly to Canada for the weekend. It was not a good idea, he thought, and he blamed Madame for allowing the girl to go unchaperoned. But Madame was attending a house party somewhere out of Seattle. He was certain that Morgan would be there, too, though she had not mentioned the fact. She had little regard for her stepdaughter these days, he noticed. Probably she thought that the worst that could happen to her would be the best in the long run.

Phillip got to his feet and started dressing. He'd go for a long walk, maybe even over to Seattle. There was no point in brooding in his room.

137

12

ensive from the dream he had had and worried over his approaching interview with Morgan on Monday morning, Phillip met the Danelaws and Sybel Jo at the Ferry Building and tossed his bag into the back of the car. Another guest had joined the party at the last minute—Mike Mallory, a young lieutenant who worked for Tim. Phillip had met him at the Danelaws' several times. He had a round Irish face and a matching wit, hailed from University Avenue in the Bronx where he had a wife and four youngsters, and seemed to have that unusual knack of liking everyone he met. He was a happy addition, Phillip decided, getting in by Sybel Jo.

"Boy, what's wrong with you?" Mike asked in his typical direct manner. "You look like forty days of rain."

"I'm in love," Phillip said. "Morning, Syb." He kissed her.

"Phil, aren't you excited? I am. I've never been to Canada."

Softly Phillip closed the doors on any serious thoughts he might have had and prepared to make himself as agreeable as possible on the stage that Sybel Jo and Pat occupied.

138

"What's the name of this place we're going to?" he asked.

"It's called Fleurs du Mal Cove," Pat said from the front seat.

"What does that mean, Phil?"

"*Fleurs du mal?* 'Flowers of evil,' I think."

"You'll see why when we get there," Pat said. "It's up in the Georgia Straits just off Vancouver Island and British Columbia. The Mason built it. You should have known The Mason, Phillip, if you think my arty crowd is a gang of characters. He tops everyone I've ever seen. He was mad about Tim once. That's how we got his house. He won't charge us a cent of rent." Pat laughed gaily. At the wheel, Tim seemed unperturbed. Phillip glanced uneasily at Sybel Jo, but she was as innocent as ever. He could have kicked Pat's tail but she continued, "Before the war he used to throw fabulous orgies up there, hiring priceless entertainers—sort of like the old New Orleans circuses. You know about them, don't you, Phillip?"

"I've heard of them," he said, hating her foul, modern talk.

But when Mike asked him what they were, Phillip, for some reason he could never explain, replied coarsely, "Groups of degenerates hired by tourists during Mardi Gras to put on exhibitionistic shows. Usually a Negro man, a white woman and a Negro one, and sometimes even children. They did tricks," he said flatly. "One of the most famous groups was a quartet of high-yellow boys who sang spirituals. However, I think such entertainment has virtually disappeared from the Vieux Carre now."

"Jesus!" Mike said hoarsely. "Why can't the old country keep its filth?"

Pat's eyes met Phillip's in a hard, knowing look which he returned unflinchingly. She'd started this. He had finished it once and for all. As for Sybel Jo, the whole thing was over her head.

They parked the car at the airport and went aboard the big commercial airliner. One hour later they were disembarking in Vancouver and going through the Custom's gate. A taxi sped them through the Canadian city to the waterfront where a seaplane was awaiting them, moored at the end of a floating ramp. To Phillip all this was another example of the smooth, powerful efficiency of money.

The pilot, whose business was catering to American hunters, stood by, waiting to assist them aboard. He was a smiling, lantern-jawed, carrot-haired Englishman who shook hands solemnly all around before asking Tim if he'd like "to take 'er off." Tim agreed and they all got into the cabin where boxes of food and beer were stored. They fastened their belts and at exactly 1000, with Tim at the stick of the dual controls, the trim, powerful little ship left the water with a sharp upward spring and slowly swung into the sun on their right in its climb for monotonous flight. The city and the great Lion's Gate Bridge disappeared rapidly and very soon the tiny hamlets became fewer, too. Pat pointed out a few of the landmarks below them during the next hour and a half over green forest carpets and the azure-blue waters of the Strait, Texada Island, Powell River, Lung, where the highway and civilization seemed to end together, and at last the islands around Toba Inlet.

Once Tim said something to the pilot beside him and the man nodded and unfastened his belt. He motioned for Phillip to exchange places with him. When the exchange was affected, Tim asked against the roar of the motor, "Want to take it awhile?"

Phillip nodded, immensely pleased. He supposed, as he took the controls, that Francis or Sybel Jo had mentioned that he had his private license and was working on his commercial rating when the war started. It was the first time he had flown a plane in three years, but he had forgotten few of his lessons. The seaplane was heavier and slower than the trainer he had been used to, but he adapted himself quickly. He made a few climbing turns to two thousand feet and, pointing to two points of land, executed a figure his instructor had called "eights on pylons," in which the tip of the wing is kept constantly on a fixed point

140

in the center of each loop of the eight. When he finished, he checked his altimeter and found he had lost no altitude; so he did a 720-degree turn. Tim smiled his admiration, and Phillip lost his altitude in a series of complete power-on stalls, much to Sybel Jo's discomfort, he learned later when they landed. Then Phillip went back to his seat, grateful for Tim's consideration. It was such things as handling a plane again that made a civilian of a serviceman, Phillip thought—little things that no one thought of, much.

At last the plane started down and they had their first glimpse of Fleurs du Mal Cove. Pat explained that the spot had been named by some romantic trapper because of the strange rock formations in the center of the cove. These round flat rocks that projected just above the blue water were arranged like the centers and petals of two huge simple flowers such as a child might draw. But undoubtedly because of their bone-whiteness and the fact that they seemed to spring from the mysterious floor of the sea, the trapper had called them evil.

They looked down to where Pat pointed and saw two thin, curving necks of land, a long and a short one arranged so that with a bit of imagination one could see the shape of a long, bony left hand reaching for a highball glass. On the high fingertips stood the cabin; while on the thumbnail, which was much lower, there was a floating jetty with a small boat. A path of white stone connected the two points, and well within the clutching grasp were the two crude flowers.

The plane dropped gull-like and hit the water roughly. For a moment Phillip thought they would somersault and he seized Sybel Jo's hand protectively. But the engines roared and they taxied smoothly toward the jetty. He looked up to meet Pat's derisive eyes.

"Tim's a good pilot," she said, "but playful at times."

As Phillip stepped from the plane, any doubts he might have had of the weekend vanished in the vast pure swatches of water, the sky, and the tree-fragrant air about him. He didn't bother to help unload the plane, but stood and looked reverently at the cabin high on the cliff. *Mother of God*, he thought, *and some artist had orgies here.*

"Rather lifts you, doesn't it?" Pat said at his elbow.

"That's the word, all right," he answered.

He shouldered one of the boxes and picked up a bag for the steep climb to the cabin as the plane with its carrot-topped pilot taxied into the cove for its take-off. It would be back late to-morrow afternoon. Meanwhile they were four hours by water and fifteen miles by land to any outpost. The feeling was exhilarating.

They decided to swim before lunch. For an hour they plowed through the cold salt water between jetty and the rock forma-tions until a shifting tide made the sport dangerous. Then they lay in the hot sunshine and feasted on sandwiches and beer. Even Sybel Jo was ravenous. Later, while the men slept on the jetty, she and Pat went up to the cabin for a nap. Phillip, who said he felt like a constrictor that had just devoured a small deer on an empty stomach, took his cigar for a hike.

"If that thing makes you ill, try to fall on it when you pass out," Tim called. "Forest fires." Phillip gave a friendly wave.

He headed inland where Tim said there was a trout stream that held their suppers. The country did something good to him. It actually seemed to ease the tension in his mind as exercise, liquor, or letters from home had never done. Trees, earth, clouds, sun, and wind—these were Phillip's first love, bequeathed him from his French peasant ancestors. Bringing him here for the weekend just before he came to grips with the psychiatrist had been the best thing Tim Danelaw had done for him yet.

Deliberately Phillip purged his mind of thought, determined to let Nature administer her tonic under fair conditions. So he walked and climbed, his mind and body free, projected into the vastness and eternity that held him so carelessly. He found the stream and caught a glimpse of some of the speckled beauties lying in the still pools along the bank. It was an amazing coun-

142

try and he decided he had never appreciated Canada until now. Hearing someone relate vacation experiences and seeing all this had nothing in common.

At last he started back, retracing his steps with no difficulty. He arrived at the jetty to find Tim and Mike awake and talking over new bottles of beer. Mike handed him one as he sat down.

"Are you the same kid that left Seattle with us this morning?" he said.

"Does it show?" Phillip asked.

"You look like a new penny."

"I feel like one, too. Canada has everything for my money."

Tim smiled at them lazily, his chest with its deep, broken line rising and falling slowly as he breathed. They were silent for a while as they drank. Mike broke the silence at last.

"Look, kid, would you like a little advice, the kind I'd give to my punk brothers?"

"If you've something on your mind, let's have it."

"Okay. You've given me permission," Mike said. "Lay off Miss Blue Eyes up there." He jerked his head toward the cabin. "She's a nice girl, but not for you."

"What do you mean?" Phillip would not let himself look at Tim.

"Well," Mike drew a long breath, "you're heading for trouble. For a wise sprout, you can be dense at times. I'm married to a woman, a pretty little thing but awfully dumb. Sort of like your girl friend. But here's the difference. I know where I stand with her now; I'll know fifteen years from now. My life doesn't begin and end in bed in the third position. Nor does hers. If she gets too frantic and I'm tired, she gets pregnant because that's the way she wants it. The beauty of Irish Catholic rearing. But take you and Miss Blue Eyes. Now you live upstairs." He tapped his ear. "That's apparent even to a dope like me. But that isn't good enough for her. One of these days she's going to find out she's got enough woman for about five men, and she isn't going to be willing to give it all to maternal instincts. I've seen it

143

happen plenty of times in my thirty-six years. Life's sort of raw in New York because we're all crowded up together."

"Is this your way of saying that I'm not man enough to keep up my end of a marriage?" Phillip asked stiffly.

"Oh, come off it, kid. I'm trying to give you a hand." His voice softened. "Either a guy wants a lot of love, or a little. And if you marry this girl, you aren't going to have much time for anything else."

Crude as he was, Mike was making sense. The boy picked at the colored label on his beer bottle thoughtfully for a moment.

"No," he mused, "she isn't like Madame."

"Ha!" Mike said quickly, "so you've thought of that angle, too. . . . Now answer me another question. Are you really in love with her?"

"I think so. I—"

"Hell, man, at your age you don't think about love, you do something about it. How about it, Tim? You're getting ready to call your marriage quits after a four-year try. What do you think?"

Tim's voice was low. "You're doing the talking, Mike. This is your idea. Phillip may be marrying for reasons we don't know."

"Sure," Mike said lightly, catching the hint. "Sure, kid. I'm all fouled up. Let's forget it. Okay?" Phillip nodded with relief. "Think I'll go for a swim," Mike said, standing up and clapping Phillip on the shoulder before walking to the edge of the jetty.

"Make it a short one," Tim said. "We're going to have to go fishing in a little while or starve tonight."

"Righto," Mike said, plunging into the water and starting a lazy crawl toward the rocks now standing slimy green above the cove. Phillip and Tim sat statue-like in the thick atmosphere between them.

"One more word of that free advice, Phillip, before we close the subject: Pat isn't the answer you seek, either. I know."

They spent the rest of the afternoon at the stream where Pat taught Phillip and Sybel Jo the art of casting. In no time they

144

caught all the trout they needed. An hour before sunset they started back, and the three men took an ax to cut the necessary supply of logs for the night's campfire. They had decided to cook supper near the jetty instead of up in the cabin. By dark they had a roaring fire, plenty of wood, and the appetites of beasts. The women did the cooking, Pat being the defter of the two. Sybel Jo complained of the heat of the fire, the chill of the night, the lack of utensils, her hunger, and her sunburn. Until she was fed, she was definitely a cranky child.

Supper was glorious. Trout, rashers of Canadian bacon, potatoes and eggs roasted in the coals—all eaten with the fingers—and, of course, more beer. Afterward Phillip helped Pat wash up and carry everything back up to the cabin. Then silently they returned to the fire where the others, their faces ruddy in the flickering glow, leaned contentedly against logs and stretched their feet to the heat. Pat knelt at Tim's head and touched his hair.

"Want my lap?" she asked.

"Uh-huh," he said. "But not in this position. I'll turn over."

Only Sybel did not smile. She came to stand in front of Phillip, and he put his arms around her while she snuggled close.

"Why doesn't someone go up to the cabin and get the radio?" she said.

"You're standing," Tim replied, taking one of the cigarettes Pat was lighting. He looked very comfortable with his head in her lap.

"Not a radio out here," Pat protested. "I want to forget cities. With all these stars and the firelight, I want something unsophisticated."

"The average radio program seems to be in that category," Tim said.

"You know what I mean. There's an old guitar in the cabin."

"Phillip can play it," Sybel Jo said enthusiastically. "He used to play for the ranch hands. Daddy was telling us about it."

"Hush," Phillip said, squeezing her against him.

145

"Wouldn't you know it?" Pat gurgled. "Phillip *is* a cowboy; Stetson, boots, and woolly chaps. Sing to me about the doggies, Phillip."

"It's *dōgies*, not *doggies*," Phillip said darkly, but grinning all the same. "A fine American you are."

"All right," Pat said. "It's up to you."

"Sybel Jo was joking. I don't know anything about guitars."

"Oh, now don't be modest," Mike said sarcastically, grinning widely.

"Phillip does know how to play the guitar," Sybel Jo said defiantly. "I heard Daddy tell about it when he came back from the ranch that summer." And breaking away from Phillip, she said, "I'll get it."

"Bring the radio, too," Mike yelled after her, "or I'll drown myself!"

Freed of Sybel Jo, Phillip dived for Mike and landed on his chest. "Now, you Irish mutt," he laughed, "I'll teach you some manners."

It was strange behavior for Phillip, even though he was in high spirits. They wrestled for a while until Mike threw his leg into the fire and gave a yelp of pain.

When they settled down, Pat asked, "Have you a lot of land in Oklahoma, Phillip?"

"Probably about a million acres," Mike said, ruefully examining the spot on his leg where all the hair had been singed off. "For *Grapes of Wrath* characters they're doing all right from what Barriman has said."

"We're the Oakies with the tractors who stayed," Phillip grinned. "Around home we have some farm land but up on the Kansas line the bank owns several large tracts of grazing land. Limestone grass," he added, as if he were used to supplying this information.

"You really have ranches in Oklahoma?" Pat asked.

"Well, it's all under fence, but it takes all day to ride it horseback."

146

Pat raised her eyebrows in appreciation. "You always speak of the bank instead of your family. Why?"

"It's simple. The bank is the reservoir that keeps us from seeking our level as individuals. Without it, the Froelichs and the Barrimans and the Mehls would be ordinary people—some of us white trash in ten years."

"But don't you get tired of supporting these bad elements?"

"Part of the responsibility of money," Phillip said philosophically. "I've yet to hear of a family that didn't have its drones. Then there's the ratio of numbers to income in these days of huge taxes. French practicality rearing its ugly head again."

"You speak of yourself as French, but Froelich is German."

"My father. I think of myself as mongrel, which is what I am. My great-grandfather was a French peasant immigrant. His wife was a quarter-breed Indian woman from the Creek Nation. The Creeks, upon freeing their black slaves, intermarried with them. Draw your own conclusions about the blood in my veins."

"Why on earth should you tell us that?"

"Mostly to chagrin Francis," Phillip chuckled. "Unlike my cousin, I have nothing to conceal. My Grandfather Dev married into one of the oldest, most decadent families in New Orleans. Francis likes to play up his aristocratic Creole background. . . . Aristocrats!" There was gloomy contempt in his voice. "They contributed no constructive thing to what we are today. We are what we are because Grandfather Dev had the ability to get what he wanted and the wisdom to hold it." But before he could go on, Sybel Jo came running down the path.

"I'm back," she panted.

"And you ran every step of the way on you all's little old feet," Mike said with a fair imitation of her accent. Even she had to laugh. She handed the guitar to Phillip.

"You asked for this," Phillip said ominously. He was greeted by a curious silence. He thought they were probably waiting for the worst. He started tuning the instrument as best he could, taking his time, playing simple chords, letting them fall against

147

the noise of the fire or sink slowly into the black walls of the night that pressed in around them. He looked at the people around the fire, different now that they had spent a few hours out of their ugly little circles. Their shiny faces and grime-caked hands were familiar to him. He felt closer to all of them than he would have thought possible. By pretending a little, he was back home on a summer night during wheat harvest among the farm hands with whom he had worked fifteen hard hours in the fields. Men who were now silent, well fed, and cool, content to smoke, drowse, talk, or listen to one of their number sing a few songs before turning in. There, life held no complexities. The earth and its fruits did their thinking for them. In Phillip's mind past and present merged. Sybel Jo leaned her shoulder against his. Phillip relaxed, touched the strings lightly with the simple rhythm of hoofbeats, and in a soft low-pitched voice sang the well-known words of a ballad familiar to every American who had ever listened to a radio.

The effect was good—even better than he had calculated. His voice, untrained as it was, blended perfectly into the sentimental mood, pointed it upward to even greater sentimentality. The smell of charring wood, the chill sea air, the uncertain light, the full bellies and tired muscles, and the straightforward words of a ballad-maker, telling the tale of a hard but gentle world. It was a scene to etch dreams against. And as he began the second chorus, Phillip was surprised to hear Tim's baritone and Mike's tenor join him.

When the song was ended, Pat applauded. "Bravo. Let's have more. Lots more. Where on earth did you ever learn to do all that?"

"I heard Carl Sandburg once," Phillip said.

So Phillip sang more songs—some that he had to hum because he had forgotten the words, but it did not matter. Ballads with titles such as "The Streets of Laredo," "Blood in the Saddle," "The Roving Gambler"; songs that were sung by farm young-sters at Grange parties or 4-H steak fries; songs that each year

148

fewer people knew and appreciated. And he was amused that such obviously sentimental ballads could attract the sophisticated Danelaws. Perhaps this was one of the basic patterns Tim had talked about several days ago. These people, who wouldn't know a stallion from a gelding, were caught in the simple appeal of the lives of the uneducated men among whom he had lived all his life. Here, away from their ultra settings, their ultra passions, lips parted, gazing into the fire, remote in their private dreams, he liked them. He could understand them now—their open, unguarded minds. And because he felt they were ready for it, he played his favorite ballad, a tale of unvarnished sentimentality, "The Little Mohee." When he finished, he put the guitar aside. There was no protest, no comment. In a moment one of them would break through this mood and set them all to laughing, but not now, he thought, not now.

Glancing contentedly at Sybel Jo, he was surprised to find her eyes fastened across the fire in avid fascination. Quickly he followed their direction and saw what it was. Tim's head was still in Pat's lap, her hands resting gently on his face. But now Mike, on his back too, had put his head on Tim's stomach, and Tim's arm was across the man's chest. Somehow it was more than camaraderie; it was shocking, intimate, indecent. Phillip would not have been more embarrassed if he'd looked up to find the three of them embracing each other without regard to sex. And Phillip knew that he was not alone in this feeling, for unconsciously Sybel Jo had called his attention to it. Yet the trio was unaware of the consternation they were causing.

Roughly Phillip pulled Sybel Jo to him and kissed her to keep her from seeing this spectacle rather than from any desire to kiss her. Immediately she put her arms around his shoulders and leaned back against his knees. He watched her eyes close slowly as she turned her head slightly, fitting her mouth closer into his, and he knew that the picture in her mind was fading. His lips opened hers softly and touched the smooth warmth of her teeth. For a moment his head spun with the flickerings of emo-

149

tion. But the fire would not catch. He tried again, but with no success. It wasn't there, the feeling he sought, and he would not force a substitution. Yet within the girl he felt the thing he could not arouse within himself. Her mouth clung and her body tensed under his hands.

Gently he released himself and held her face against his throat until she could recover her poise. And when he raised his eyes across the fire again, he found the trio sitting up, staring at him like an audience in a theater absorbed in the dramatic conflict unfolding before them. Only Tim's face did he remember, and the expression he saw there he did not dare define.

13

❖❖*❖*❖*❖*❖*

*T*he first session of his psychiatric examination was set for 1000 Monday morning. Sunday night, after he had returned from Canada, he had taken a sleeping tablet to insure a peaceful night and set his alarm for 0930, which would give him just enough time to get to Morgan's office per schedule. He didn't want time to think. He felt he had done enough of that. This was H-hour. He wanted to throw himself into the struggle headlong, to fight instinctively from here on out until he had won or lost. But before the alarm had rung, a hand on his shoulder roused him from deep sleep.

"Mr. Froelich, Mr. Bruner wants you in his office right away."

It was a colored steward bending over him. For a moment panic swept him. What in the devil had gone wrong now? What new torture had that SOB devised? But Phillip answered calmly, "Very well."

The steward left the room. Phillip sat up mechanically and shut off the alarm. A few minutes before eight. God damn that

151

man's guts anyway. If this were some trivial thing, he'd beat the man senseless one day if he had to wait years to do it. He got up, washed in icy water, and dressed. Ten minutes later he stood before his counsel.

"Yes, sir?" Phillip asked coldly.

"Sit down, Phillip," Bruner smiled pleasantly. Phillip ground his teeth but took the indicated chair. "I take it you're all set to meet the psychiatrist." Phillip nodded stiffly. "Phillip, I've been wanting to have a serious talk with you for a long time." Phillip lifted his shoulders slightly. "For your own good," Bruner assured him. He paused. "I don't enjoy your trust, do I?"

"Few people do, sir."

"Why?"

"I've no idea," Phillip said quietly.

"Well," Bruner smiled unctuously, "perhaps I understand you better than you think. You're overwrought because of the trouble you're in. You must not be too concerned over the loss of your commission. I've really no right to tell you this," his voice grew softer, "but pressure can be brought to dispel this whole thing, you know." Phillip tensed as he waited to hear if the man would name an actual amount. Bruner went on cautiously, "You understand, a matter as delicate as this is never brought out in the open." He paused again.

"How much?" Phillip asked.

"You misunderstand," Bruner said with some indignation. He got to his feet. "It wasn't money I was referring to."

"What then?"

"Well, your confidence, your friendship. Those things that cause people to help each other," Bruner floundered, and added pompously, "There are some of us here on the base who genuinely want to help you, strange as that may seem."

Phillip knew that Bruner wanted money from him. That the man bothered to deny the fact had surprised him a little. Perhaps he wanted to be coaxed, Phillip decided, so he changed his tactics. "I've been half crazy these past days," he said with

152

downcast eyes. "If there was someone I could trust— Francis and Madame are the logical ones but they are in no position to help." He gripped his fingers hard and watched them turn dark red. At length he burst out, "I'd do anything to get out of this mess!"

He heard Bruner walk to the window and turn. "Anything, Phillip?"

The mocking quality in the man's voice caused Phillip to look up. "Well, almost anything," he admitted reluctantly. Bruner was smiling at him knowingly. "Is there a way out?" Phillip asked at last.

Bruner walked back to the desk, his eyes holding him closely. "I thought you'd already found it."

"What do you mean?" Phillip kept his voice free of belligerency.

"Phillip, I hesitate to say any more for fear of offending you."

Completely baffled, Phillip let his guard down still more. "I have been hasty," he admitted, "too hasty with everyone lately. Please speak frankly, Lee." He brought the man's name out with a fair show of ease.

"Phillip, there is some talk around the base about you and the Danelaws."

"Do you think they would help me?" Phillip asked, more comfortable now that he had identified the direction in which Bruner was moving.

"They might, if one understood their motives."

"I see," Phillip answered for want of something more noncommittal.

"For instance, what are your relations with Mrs. Danelaw?"

Sensing they were still in the preliminaries, Phillip decided to play along. He said, "She has indicated that she is willing to be more than just friendly."

"And you?"

"I am still, just friendly," Phillip said with a hint of a smile.

"I see." Bruner walked back to the window. Though Phillip

153

half suspected what the man was leading up to, Bruner's next question jarred him thoroughly with its bluntness. "Phillip, has anyone here on the base approached you with propositions of a homosexual nature?"

Phillip's front of confidence vanished. "Certainly not!" he snapped. "Don't you think I would report such a thing to the Provost Marshal if it had happened?"

"Well, as Pat says, you are unpredictable at times," Bruner hedged.

"Only to foolish women like Mrs. Danelaw," he returned cuttingly.

"I thought you might try to—"

"No such proposal has been made, Lieutenant Bruner."

"I should have known," Bruner said, toying with his watch. "Is that all, sir?"

"Not quite." Bruner paused dramatically. "Your case is dropped."

Phillip looked at the man blankly for a moment.

"Aren't you going to say anything?" Bruner wanted to know. "You aren't having a court martial. You're free, reinstated to active duty as of last Thursday, according to the directive. You haven't a spot on your record, not even a letter of reprimand. Do you understand?" Bruner was watching him closely, fathoming his innocence.

"I'm confused, sir," Phillip answered slowly. "Why?"

"Do you mean to say you don't know that Tim Danelaw asked for all the data on your case—a most unusual procedure—and that Admiral Marcien has recommended that your case be dropped, citing a temporary shortage of qualified officers as his only reason?" Bruner's voice was only faintly sarcastic as he asked, "Haven't you seen Tim lately?"

The questions were designed to cow him into some half-confession to save himself, he realized, but his mind, working furiously, told him one thing: that he was free—free of Bruner, too, thank God!

154

Phillip answered with dignity, "I spent the weekend in Canada with the Danelaws. You know that."

"And Tim didn't mention all this?" Bruner was skeptical.

"No."

Bruner took a deep breath. "Very well." He became businesslike with the papers on his desk. "Here are your temporary additional duty orders. You are hereby assigned to duty with The
Flag until your discharge from the Navy in August." He held
out the papers.

"The Flag!" Phillip could not conceal his surprise. "But I'm
not capable of doing work for Admiral Marcien."

"I know," Bruner said with satisfaction. "That's why this
whole affair looks so—" Phillip knew that he had started to say
suspicious—"strange." Phillip took the papers and glanced at
them.

"You see," Bruner continued, "that you're to report to Danelaw at 0900, just one hour before you were to have met the
psychiatrist. Quite a close call, I'd say."

"Would you, sir?" Phillip smiled. "And what should I be
afraid of disclosing to a psychiatrist?" Phillip stared at Bruner
until the man turned a dull red; then he said, "Good morning,
sir." He turned abruptly and left the office.

He had terminated an interview with a superior. This was an
insult, a breach of protocol, but it was a slight gesture in comparison to the wild, turbulent emotions that were rampant in
Phillip's mind. He stepped outside the building and took a deep
breath, held it, building it up to a crescendo, a savage yell of
triumph he could never utter. The morning about him was a
sparkling thing, just climbing out of the aching blue Sound,
fresh and laughing from its morning bath. The wet streets
gleamed like molten tar and the grass was a poisonous green
beneath the gauzy shawl of diamonds and pearls caught by a
golden sun, warm enough to thaw even the chilly Rainier. And
Phillip, shying instinctively from such strong emotion, started
for the nearest telephone to share his news with Sybel Jo.

"Syb?" His voice shook with happiness. "The GCM is over! I'm free!"

"Oh, Phil," the half-conscious girl wailed. "Did you wake me up just for that? Pat told me about it up at the cove."

"You knew about it?" Phillip asked incredulously.

"Ummm. It was to be a surprise. May I go back to sleep now?"

"Of course," he whispered, staring at the dark rough surface of the wall before him. He felt like sagging, as if he had been punched unexpectedly in the stomach.

"Night, darlin'." The receiver clicked in his ear.

"Well," he said at last, "I asked for it." He squared his shoulders and glanced at his watch. He had enough time to shave before he reported in to Tim. Smiling a bit disdainfully at himself, he walked briskly back to his room.

Atop the Admiral's quarters a dark-blue flag supporting two white stars snapped smartly in the breeze. It was a symbol of the neat, plain offices inside the building. Everyone, Phillip noticed, sailors and officers alike, seemed busy and cheerful, yet there was a minimum of sound in the big reception pen. He asked for Tim and was taken to his office immediately. The sailor knocked and opened the door for him with a friendly smile.

Tim was hunched over his desk. When he saw Phillip, he laid aside the manila folder he was reading and stood up. He was wearing heavy-rimmed glasses which gave him the owlish appearance of a student. This amused Phillip. It seemed somehow foreign to the other aspects of his nature. Tim put the glasses on the desk.

"You didn't waste time getting over here," he observed.

"Would you have—in my boots?" Phillip asked.

"I think I might have run the other way—in your boots."

"The idea presented itself," Phillip said. They laughed and shook hands. "Thanks, Tim." They stood looking at each other.

"You're welcome, Phillip." Phillip released his hand and

156

looked around the office. It was severely naked of anything but the most necessary articles—desk, chairs, file cabinets, hat tree. Suddenly Phillip was ill at ease. Sensing it, Tim said, "Have you any questions before I shove off? You've come at a busy time. We're going down to Frisco again the day after tomorrow. I'm spending today with the Admiral checking details in Seattle prior to the trip, but I've a few minutes before I have to go."

"Yes, I've some questions," Phillip began with a frown. "Sybel Jo knew about the court martial being called off. Why?"

"Did you ever know a woman to hold her tongue? I guess Pat told her. She knew about it from the first when we called Washington. We didn't want to tell you until it was a certainty. No point in building hopes."

"Bruner was pretty mad about it," Phillip said. "I know he hates me, but why does he hate you so much?"

"It dates back to a black market affair in Salerno. Too long to go into right now. What did he say?"

"He asked me if anyone had approached me with homosexual proposals."

Tim laughed. He tapped his knuckles against his desk a few times thoughtfully. "I'll tell you about Bruner some day. Perhaps this evening. Pat's giving you a victory dinner, you know."

"Isn't that grave dancing, rather?" Phillip asked.

"Perhaps," Tim smiled. "But there's one question you haven't asked. I thought it would be the first. You haven't asked me why I've engineered all this."

Phillip lifted a shoulder delicately and looked away. "I'm not as dumb as Mike thinks I am," he said simply. "In your position I'd have done the same thing, I suppose."

"That's a good deal more understanding than I'd hoped for, Phillip."

"I know. But now that all this ridiculous folderol is over, perhaps I can show you a better side of my nature. There's only one thing bothering me: I haven't any idea of what work I can do here."

157

"Frankly, neither have I. But we had to give Washington some reason for the request. This seemed the logical spot under the conditions. We'll find something to keep you busy for the next ten weeks. There's plenty of work. The question is: can you do it? You are inexperienced."

"Or immature."

"Let's have it my way this time. By the way, would you like the day off? Tomorrow I'll be around to show you the ropes."

Phillip smiled. "No, thanks. I'll stick around and get in everyone's way. Besides, if I see Madame she may rush me off to the nearest justice of the peace now that I'm out of marrying excuses."

"If I had as many kettles of fish as you, I'd give up," Tim said. "But since you're going to be around, here's something you can work on." He picked up the folder he had been studying. "This is some fool's incomprehensible ideas on all the movie equipment in our entire area. As bases close, we have to see that such equipment is gathered together and stored or turned over to surplus property. We gave the job to some dolt over in Supply a month ago. He waits around until he is discharged and at the last minute gathers up a lot of odds and ends and turns them in as a report. Result? Fouled up for fair. Now we have to gather, sort, compile, and have something definite to show in Frisco on the subject in two days. I'll let you worry with it today. By tonight you'll wish you were back with your own little court martial. You can use my desk today. There's the telephone and the base directory. My yeoman is outside. Mike's down the hall, but he'll fry you if you blunder in .with anything but a cup of coffee. In other words, here's your haystack. I have to meet the Admiral." He handed Phillip the folder and picked up his hat. "Oh, yes," he grinned, "it's a pleasure to have you aboard, a real pleasure."

"After all this," Phillip indicated the file, "that's an insult."

"I'll see you out at the house tonight," Tim said.

"Until tonight," Phillip repeated.

158

With a parting glance, Tim was gone. Phillip continued to look at the door for a moment. A strange man, but strangely on the level, as Stuff Manus had guessed. Phillip owed him a great debt and he wanted to pay it. There was one way to prove it— his only way. He took off his coat and sat down to read the folder through. Fouled up was hardly adequate, he decided. Some of the basic correspondence, requesting instructions, was dated ten months before. Phillip lighted a cigar and dug into Bureau regulations and directives on movie equipment. The stack was two inches thick, most of it of no consequence or rescinded by later directives. At least Tim's comparison to a haystack was correct.

Two hours and another cigar later, Phillip called in the yeoman and they went over the material together, giving and taking information, diagraming on paper, planning toward some order out of chaos. He was beginning to appreciate the enormity of an admiral's task and marvel that the fragile-looking, immaculate Marcien still had time for social functions. If the movie equipment was any indication of the work the Admiral's staff did, then it was merely a trouble-shooting outfit for those problems that were too big for the departments to handle.

At 1200 the yeoman and he had sandwiches and coffee in the office. Then Phillip spent an hour on the phone, demanding information from indifferent department heads, doggedly running down leads to the Lake Union Movie Exchange (which might have been operated by Martian immigrants from the responses they gave), the Welfare and Recreation Department at Piers 90 and 91, and even the supply and storage warehouses over in Bremerton, where he checked available storage and transportation throughout the area. He had one advantage. All sources opened smoothly to the salutation, "Admiral Marcien's offices, we want . . ."

Meanwhile the yeoman was typing out a condensation of inventories, a tedious task with countless revisions. Actually it

159

was not only dull work but nerve-racking. But Phillip, taught to spend tedious hours in the bank at home, did not mind it particularly. He worked with one purpose: to justify Danelaw's kindness to him. He could lose himself in the maze before him for minutes at a time and still retain enough perspective to come out with something. Then, too, his father had taught him that enough unimportant details, piled high enough, usually made a structure worth studying.

He went into the outer offices and the file rooms, explained to anyone who would listen what he was doing and what he wanted. Movie equipment was freak property. No one would claim it. So for a while he probed alone, always courteous but determined, while the office personnel noticed, nodded approval, and started dropping by with pertinent data and suggestions he might use—a list of post-war bases and ships operating out of the area that would need equipment, a half-forgotten letter telling of transfer of certain equipment, the name of a man who might know about the disposition of spare parts for Bell and Howell projectors. Their reserve toward the new officer melted rapidly as they realized that he was as anxious to do his job as they.

By 1600 he had his first real grip on the problem in the form of a condensed report. The yeoman asked to leave and Phillip let him go, taking over the typewriter himself. He had located half the missing equipment by accident (a remarkable feat in itself); had listed in categories according to make and size all projectors on hand (which seemed to be the most important factor); had prepared a list of possible outlets for sale, storage, or reassignment; had drawn up a bibliography of his various sources of information; and finally had indicated a rough program of action, plus alternatives. As a labor by one who was supposed to be inexperienced, it was good, revealing many things about its author, none more clearly than a capable mind and a passion for thoroughness. He finished typing the final page,

160

stapled the whole thing together, and lighted a cigarette with a sigh of contentment. An ambitious task, a good day's work. He could look himself in the eye the next time he shaved.

"Are you still here?" Tim stood in the doorway.

"Hello." Phillip glanced at his watch. "Great Scott! 1900."

"How's the movie equipment? Problem solved?" Tim crossed the room to unload his brief case at the desk.

"By no means. But here's the start."

Tim took the folder and started reading it, wrinkling his forehead with approval. He sat down and continued to read, turning the pages with thick, blunt fingers, finally only scanning the last part. When he looked up, his eyes were seriously appraising.

"Who helped you?" he asked at last.

"Your yeoman and everyone I asked, practically."

"I mean who planned it for you? Mike?"

"No. I haven't seen him all day. Is something wrong with it?"

"It's fine. I couldn't have done better in the same length of time. Your approach is a bit too direct for the Navy and you're certainly unorthodox in method at times, but your work is concise enough for anyone to understand. The Admiral is going to be pleased with you, and needless to say, I'm very pleased." Phillip dropped his eyes in embarrassed pleasure. "It's amazing the distance between the outposts of the human mind," Tim continued thoughtfully. "I expected you to play around an hour or so and shove off for the day." Then, realizing how uncomfortable his flattery was making the boy, he tossed the report aside. "But the working day is over. I'm afraid we've missed your party. Do you mind?"

"I'm delighted," Phillip replied.

"Pat will be furious with both of us."

"But she's your wife," Phillip smiled.

"Ah, don't I know," Tim sighed. "I'll run you over to your quarters so you can change. We'll make our entrance together."

"For protection?" Phillip asked mischievously.

161

"Wait until you're contemplating your first divorce, my lad."
Instantly Phillip's face fell.

"I'm sorry," Tim murmured. "I must have been asleep to have said that. Come. We'll drop by the club for a quick one."

"Sure, Tim. I can use one right now."

14

There was nothing unusual about the guests, manners, conversation, or liquor at Pat's victory dinner—unless it was that everyone was drinking champagne spiked with brandy to distinguish this party from the rest that she gave. Phillip, recognizing most of the weary, animated faces, wondered how Pat kept from being bored to insanity by these intellectual and artistic would-be's. Her statement that she tolerated them for Tim's sake was absurd, of course. But privately Phillip suspected that she surrounded herself by this menage to protect herself from a husband she did not love. When she was free, he hoped she would change. As she was now, he rather pitied her.

When he and Tim arrived, they were surrounded immediately, champagne pressed upon them, and toasts proposed this way and that. Maliciously Phillip insisted on drinking "to the splendid support of my sterling counsel, Mister Bruner," and that gentleman responded with a skull-like grin from the bar. Madame wanted to toast her Captain Morgan, though Phillip thought of a more appropriate verb for the operation. For several days now, Phillip had suspected that the pair was the laughing stock of this vicious little clique. As usual, Sybel Jo suspected nothing. Tonight Madame was a study in tipsy, belligerent friendliness to Phillip. He was expecting some attack from her, and it wasn't long in coming.

"Now Phillip and Sybel Jo can be married immediately," Madame announced. Phillip shot Tim a knowing glance, and Tim nodded.

Pat, who had seen the exchange, lifted her glass. "To the happy couple. May the event be felicitous, and soon."

"Just a moment," Tim's voice halted them. "Have you told them, Phillip?"

"Not yet." Phillip concealed his ignorance of Tim's intent.

"Then I shall," Tim said easily. "Phillip will have to wait a few days to get married, I'm afraid. The Admiral is taking him to San Francisco with us instead of Mike."

"Ohhhh." Sybel Jo sounded wounded. Madame looked it. Mike came forward beaming.

"That's right. I'm holding down the fort while the Admiral is gone." He said this as if it were a triumph, clapping Phillip on the shoulder. "Sorry, fellow. Seniority, you know." The three conspirators couldn't have been more convincing if they'd rehearsed the act.

"Sure," Phillip said, bearing up bravely. "I understand."

"But Phillip can't go to Frisco," Pat said with authority. "He's not qualified. One day in the office and then a conference. Absurd!"

"Not really, Pat," Mike laughed. "All I ever do is hang on to half a dozen brief cases and hand in the right papers as needed. I can teach Phillip that routine in half an hour."

This seemed to settle the question. Mike's intervention had made the whole thing authentic. A very grateful Phillip was safe for a few days more. By then he would find another excuse now that he had Tim and Mike on his side. Among them

164

they'd find the right stall. The guests drifted away from them and Mike gave Phillip a sly wink.

"All right, Phillip," Tim said, "to the salt mines with you. The portrait is waiting."

"Do you have to tonight?" Sybel Jo pouted. "They're having a simply gorgeous movie in the playroom and I wanted us to see it together. It's about an opera star who gives up her career for a man—"

"Sorry, Syb, but the portrait is your idea. Remember?'

"I suppose so. Well, I'll see you later."

"Bye. Enjoy the movie."

Upstairs, the door closed, Phillip and Tim looked at each other and broke into uproarious laughter.

"Who says it isn't a man's world?" Phillip gasped.

Slowly he removed his clothes and tossed them on the bed. Before he walked to the dais where he posed, he stretched his arms high over his head, flexing every muscle up and down his body. "Golly, but I'm tired," he said.

Through the haze of his cigarette Tim watched the lithe, rippling muscles of the boy's splendid body, flesh that revealed the necessity of living rather than any storehouse of brute strength which came from the blind grubbing of athletes. He saw the white cups beneath the arms, the lean ribs, the ridiculously narrow waist and hips, the smooth down-covered columns of the legs, the high white arches of the feet, and above everything else the graceful, straining, uplifted arms that framed a relaxed sensual face. Tim turned away and started to mix paint on the palette. When he glanced back at the boy, he was sitting, his eyes momentarily closed. Tim walked to the bureau and from the top drawer he took an object and brought it to Phillip.

"Here. I'll give you something to play with." He grinned. "This may keep you awake for a while."

"Sometimes you treat me like a child," Phillip said, opening his eyes.

"It amuses me to do so, but I'll stop if it annoys you."

165

Phillip did not answer but looked up curiously and took from Tim's hand the ring he had noticed the man wearing on the night they met.

"But I thought that Pat—"

"I saw you look at her necklace the other evening and then at my hand. They are twin stones. I bought them in China several years ago from a thief, a ghoul who had plundered a bombed city. The price was so low I couldn't resist temptation."

"I can't blame you," Phillip murmured, studying the beautiful green and gold bauble. "I could rob a corpse for this too, almost."

Tim laughed good-naturedly as he started to paint. "I had the ring made in India just before I left the Orient. A Chicago jeweler made the necklace. It was Pat's wedding gift."

"They must be very valuable," Phillip said shrewdly.

"They are. Not as twin stones particularly. They are well matched, but the color is constant and the cutting is very clear if crude. They are as flawless as any you'll find."

"There are symbols engraved inside the band. What do they mean?"

"Some gem of oriental philosophy that goes, 'He who looks upon beauty at will can never be betrayed.' Pat says it's sticky. Her term."

"She doesn't like Chopin either. What's wrong with women anyway?"

Tim's laughter was low. Absorbed in the magnificent stone, Phillip barely noticed. As he turned it, its fire ran the entire gamut of greens.

"It's unbelievable," he mused gravely. "Looking into it, it seems to actually grow in proportion. It holds animal eyes at night caught in sudden strong light, magnolia leaves after a spring rain, or silent jungle walls that conceal cockatoos and enemy guns, or the color of moldy velvet loomed two centuries ago for an idiot king, or algae-slimed pools high in the moun-

166

tains and deep in the forest—all the beauties and all the horrors of all the worlds that ever existed."

He paused and glanced up self-consciously to find Tim standing over him. The man's face was transformed into a mask of tenderness and anger. With a finger, Tim tilted the boy's face roughly.

"What are you?" he asked softly, but he expected no answer. "By your actions you're a stoic, at best an aesthete. But at times, when you forget yourself, you might be a mystic, or a sensualist."

"I don't know what you mean," Phillip said uncomfortably.

"No. I suppose you don't yet." He removed his finger from the boy's chin and turned away. "Get dressed. We're finished." He put his brush down and scraped the palette clean. The silence became heavy. Bewildered by the sinister change in his friend, Phillip put the ring on the table and got into his clothes.

"Aren't you going to finish the portrait?"

"No. I was wrong about it. It's going to be a daub."

Phillip was afraid to protest. "We could go to the movie."

"We could but we won't. We're going for a walk instead."

They left the room, went downstairs through the silent house and out into the still, wet darkness, each extremely conscious of the other. At last Phillip asked timidly, "Have I offended you, Tim? Something I've said? I'm clumsy with words."

"Offend me? No. Bewilder—destroy, perhaps—but not offend."

For an instant Phillip, anxiously searching the man's face which was turned against a rising fragment of moon, glimpsed a melancholy there that caused his breath to catch with surprise.

"Then what is it?"

"This is it." Tim's voice was strained in an attempt to be calm. "I'm beginning to see you differently than when I started to paint you. I've sensed the change for several days. As a result, I've decided to destroy your portrait. It can't have two effects."

"Is it so bad then?"

"It might have been my best if I had finished it in time."

167

"Have I changed so much?" Phillip asked.

"You? No, Phillip. It is I who've changed." Tim was silent a moment. At last he said hollowly, "Once I told you that you were safe with me. I was wrong. You aren't."

"You dare to say that?" Phillip asked, "With Pat and Sybel Jo—"

"I dare," Tim answered harshly, "because it's true. A moment ago, watching you with the ring, I could have outraged our friendship. It's no fault of yours nor can you say it is mine. Unconsciously you have been offering me a challenge from the moment we looked at each other in that dirty little roadside cafe, and unconsciously I've wanted that challenge despite what we have told ourselves. And now I know that I am going to accept it, for better or for worse. . . . But you, what of you?" Tim paused.

Vaguely Phillip was aware that the moonlight was cold.

Receiving no answer, Tim continued, "I thought I understood your sailor friend. Out of the barrenness of his life he saw the glitter of your dreams and wanted to make them his, too. He acted in the only way he knew and he didn't deserve the treatment you gave him, but then you couldn't see past the first wall of convention. I thought I understood your splendid beauty, the paradox of your mind. I thought I was above the appeal of them. I am not, though I would never force you as the sailor did." His voice became softer, lower, as he continued, "I want you, Phillip, just as he did. It isn't a sudden desire of no foundation, but one of swift and quiet growth. Constantly seeing in you wonderful, unexpected facets of character; your gallant, hopeless struggle with forces you can't hope to conquer; and above all, seeing the hurt little boy you are beneath all your bluff—the gentle, lonely kindliness where others can see only bad manners. That was why I helped you when no one else would: not because I was interested in seeing justice done. I was sorry for you. But now . . . Phillip . . . *je t'adore.*"

For several moments they stood silently apart, looking at each

168

other. In spite of the outrage he knew he had to feel, Phillip was deeply moved. It was a tender speech of loveliness and longing, filled with an appreciation of the elements involved in their situation. It was not the gibberish of a fool proclaiming "love is all." But on the other hand, reason told him, it might be the clever approach of a veritable devil.

Phillip half turned away. "Don't say that," he said. "What can a man know of adoration for another man? I want your friendship and your respect but not that—" Phillip's voice caught in his throat—"because it is indecent, and ugly, and diseased, and perverted."

"Do you believe me capable of indecency, ugliness, disease, perversion?"

"No. I—I—don't know what I believe. Until now I believed that between us there was something such as you have suggested. But now, confronted with it, I know it isn't really there. One can't do such things and then forget them. It's inside you forever. I like you, Tim. I admire you, though I don't understand you. And I believe you are sincere. The portrait is to blame. Remove the cause and you remove the evil, and it must be evil."

"All of love isn't gratification, Phillip. Even you, who've nailed your emotions and instincts into a prison—you have loved."

"Don't use that word. *Desire, passion*— anything but that."

"As you wish, but do you think that facing homosexuality twice within two months, as you have done, is merely coincidental?"

It was a telling blow. Phillip made a swift movement toward the house, but Tim was quicker. With sure hands he held the boy's shoulders.

"You can't run away forever, Phillip. Do you think I would force you to face this now if I thought you could outlive it? I am thinking of you in five, ten, perhaps twenty years, when you've more to lose and less with which to fight. The time to fight is now and here— not later and in a place where you may be preyed upon by unscrupulous elements. Fight me with words, reason, threats—any weapon you may possess—but do me, and yourself, the honor of telling the truth."

Slowly Phillip relaxed and his mind grew calm. His eyes found Tim's again. There was a growing beauty in the tremulous air about them, and the drowsiness Phillip had spoken of earlier in the evening came to him again from Tim's voice, Tim's face, his hands.

"I will listen," Phillip said at last.

Tim's hands gripped him harder as he spoke quietly. "Then, tonight . . . when the others are gone . . . my club . . . in town . . . you know it . . . here . . . the key."

The words were half-demand, half-question, and Phillip's answer came as slight as suggested movement in the towering trees about them. Thus they stood, suddenly fearful of the contact they had completed, already sensitive to the nature of the approaching unknown, until a cloud dragged itself across the moon. Then, of one accord, they returned to the house.

15

◆◇◆◇◆◇◆

*I*nside the door they noticed two things: the guests had left the movie early and were wandering about the lower floor, and the door to Tim's room on the mezzanine stood ajar. Swiftly their eyes met with understanding. "I forgot to lock it," Tim said.

In their agitation upon leaving, neither had noticed the error. They crossed the room and mounted the stairs three at a time. Already they could hear the voices of the intruders. "Simply wonderful." "All the nobility of a ruptured satyr," another laughed drunkenly. "He's done it this time for sure," came Mike's voice.

They burst into the room together. The others, grouped before the easel, glanced up uneasily, but greeted the artist and model with a chorus of extravagant comments.

"Phil," Sybel Jo said ecstatically, "Pat's so lucky. I wish it was ours. You're just out of this world!" She seized his hand and pulled him toward the mysterious canvas.

171

"So *this* is what you've been up to," Bruner croaked knowingly.

Phillip, his excitement increasing with each step, ignored them all until he confronted the woman standing before the others. Then he was aware of one tense face, one pair of brutal eyes, one trembling mouth. Pat. He smiled uncertainly, but her expression did not alter. At last he knew her secret. At last he knew how much she hated him and why. To her, he was the successful rival for her husband's love. The thought sickened him.

Almost timidly he stepped before the unfinished portrait and cringed away from the painted thing staring back at him. It was as if he had stepped before a mirror in the midst of a nightmare. He felt his eyes widen, his lips curl with disgust. The emotion Tim had spoken of a few minutes before leaped at him from every inch of the canvas. But more important than Tim's evident love was his cruel homage to truth. He had resisted emotion long enough to give the observer a portrait of Phillip as he actually was, created by a man intent on destroying a god with every brush stroke, every meticulously executed detail. The result was a chilling masterpiece of terror— a boy-man tottering on the narrow ledge between disaster and mediocrity. Phillip knew that Pat had sensed this just as Sybel Jo had felt only the first thrill of a remarkable painting.

Tim had caught him in one of those brooding, unreal settings he alone seemed capable of seeing, painting as was his custom with a hand conditioned to tragedy. There was a beach of ancient, sea-ravaged gray behind which lay a lead and green sea in that curious calm that is already impregnated with approaching storm. Bloated thunderheads tore the sun to pieces. The nude figure—which was undeniably Phillip but a Phillip only Tim had seen—half-crouched in this ghastly setting, its long, coltish legs partially drawn up under its emaciated, warped body. From the expression on its face, one knew it had just glanced over its shoulder at the pressing storm and turned back to face the artist. It appeared to laugh, yet the terrible mouth might emit either laughter or a crazed jumble of hysterical screams. The eyes heightened the terrifying effect. In contrast to the nostrils, whitely pinched in fear of passion, were the living warm tones of hair caught for the last time by doomed, watery sunlight.

The fingers clawed at the damp sand before it, each muscle visibly distended as if the beastly thing had been frozen in the act of springing to its feet. Nearby lay a crude little boat with a broken sail. It was the only obvious symbol in the whole scene, put there, Phillip knew, to mislead the unwary. Distorted by Tim's satanic brush, the expression of the whole face held drunken, animal-like challenge, insane despair, and hilarious, bacchic invitation. *This*, Phillip thought, *is the Antichrist, damned not as an individual, but for containing the very essence of corruption.* It fascinated him even though he knew that in merely studying the decadently beautiful thing he was willfully approaching the rim of self-destruction closer than ever before.

He felt a strong sense of personal defeat—an idea that he was not only helpless before, but useless to, humanity. Death was preferable to this, this innocence before him. It was the extreme youth of the thing, heightened by the broken toy, that hurt him and made him feel outraged pity for it. It was as if he were about to witness its torture. Above all, it brought back one long-forgotten scene from his childhood.

He was a child again, sitting on his mother's lap fresh from his after-lunch bath. She was reading him to sleep. The room was dim and her breast was warm and fragrant against him. The book was old with highly colored illustrations. He was growing so drowsy he no longer played with her little embroidering scissors, but held them in lax fingers. The story ended: "And they lived happily in the great, turreted castle forever after." "Next one, please," he said mechanically for the third time, certain that the page would turn and the soothing voice would go on until he was oblivious to everything. He glanced at the book to

173

see what the next story would be and stiffened with stubborn dislike. "No. Not that one. I don't want that one!"

But his mother had laughed and started to read the hideous story of the little lost babes who were left in the forest by cruel robbers to die of hunger and cold. The voice went on recounting the untold agonies and finally the end, when the children clasped each other close and lay down to die. The birds had covered them with leaves. Phillip, feeling mounting outrage for such inhumanity and frustration at not being able to prevent it, poked his fingers deep into his ears to shut out the hateful words.

Then he remembered that his mother had been called from the room. Thoroughly awake now, he held the book and stared at the illustration of the dead babies being covered with leaves by their bird friends. His head ached with chagrin. He tried to cry for the children, but no tears would come. After minutes of growing despair, when it seemed his forehead would burst open, he had suddenly flung the book on the chair seat and using the little scissors in his hand as a dagger he had stabbed the colored picture savagely many times, whispering, "I hate you, you grunt!"

Suddenly his mother had stood over him and the damaged book. His anger had retreated so quickly it had left him hiccuping loudly in the ensuing silence. She had talked to him then, but he could never remember what she had said. He only knew he had done mischief because of her persistence in making him hear the story he hated. He knew he had not cried, even when she had spanked him. That was very important. He had not slept that afternoon, and later in the garden he had leaned his aching head against the smooth, violet-colored trunk of the big peach tree. On the bark, jellylike lumps of clear amber resin had congealed and started to harden. (Once his father had told him that it might be poisonous.) He had gathered a fistful of the substance and stuffed it into his mouth. He had chewed the bitter mess a few times and swallowed it. Now he was vindi-

174

cated. Now he would die. Now the little lost babes in the woods would be his friends again. Of course he had been horribly sick in the lower pasture later on, but no one had ever known, not even Fanchon, to whom he told everything.

This was the scene Tim's painting brought to mind as he stood before it. It had been a rare incident in his life, one in which emotion had ruled him. He could not pity; he could only hate.

"Phillip! Hey, boy, snap out of it." Mike's voice reached him as Sybel Jo took both his hands in hers.

"Phil, hon, isn't it just terrifying? I wish it was ours."

Phillip looked down at the girl. He thought of his promise to Tim. Mediocrity or disaster. Now there was no doubt which it must be. He laughed, knowing the others were waiting for his comment.

"I think I prefer the cat sketch," he said. "More human."

Everyone laughed. The note was struck. Turning to Tim but avoiding his eyes, he said, "Congratulations. My first verdict still goes. You have a delicate right and a very powerful left." There was more laughter and Sybel Jo, twisting her hands into his, discovered the key which he had forgotten until now.

"What's this, Phil?"

"This? Oh, it's something that belongs to Commander Dane-law. I think he dropped it downstairs." And holding it out, he dropped it into the man's reluctant hand. Then, turning to his fiancée, he said, "I'm very tired, Syb. Do you mind going now?"

"Not at all, Phil. And, honey, you were lucky, not going to that atrocious movie. We called it off half-way through. You know that new star with the kind of thin face, well, she was in it and—"

"Good night," Phillip called from the doorway. Silently he blessed Sybel Jo for everything she represented. With her he was safe. The emotional stress Tim had created within him had been destroyed quite accidentally by its author. But Phillip did not know that violent emotion when curbed is comparable to a dying pendulum, turning upon itself again and again, eating into its own momentum until it rests quietly, waiting for the familiar hand to set it once more in motion.

16

◇◇*◇*◇*◇*

$\mathcal{T}$he Admiral's plane was dropping swiftly. Far below, Phillip could make out the two bridges that linked San Francisco with Oakland and Marrin County. Almost directly beneath them were Treasure and Mare Islands, to the left the air field where they would land in a few minutes. Phillip felt a thrill of anticipation when he looked down on the city his Uncle Felix had taught him to love so well. Tonight he'd dine in town. The feast of a glutton: beluga caviar with chopped egg and onion, Chianti (if they still had it), oysters Rockefeller or perhaps a shrimp supreme, and then a lobster with French fries or maybe a curried chicken with chutney; and later something really festive, a fresh peach tart, baked Alaska, or one of those farcical creations in ice cream followed by a Café Diable. Then, if he could still move, and he was sure he would be able to do so, there might be a good show in town, something on the road from Broadway. It was the kind of indulgence he felt he needed after three weeks of Sybel Jo, the GCM, and Pat's crowd.

He looked at the three men around him preparing to land: Admiral Marcien, with whom he had talked most of the way down; Tim Danelaw, who had treated him with strange impersonal courtesy these past thirty-odd hours since they had stood before the portrait; and Lee Bruner, who had come along, as Mike put it, because it didn't cost anything and because the Admiral was a generous man. Back in the plane the three enlisted men with the files were preparing to land, too. There was some good-natured confusion among them, low-voiced argument over who was to take this or that. Though they would not be in the conference room, they would be as busy as anyone else in the party.

Phillip had spent one whole day with Mike, going over the material to be covered. And he realized the very best he could do to grasp the situation before the board of admirals would result in the sketchiest knowledge of that which was to be decided. The burden of this lack of knowledge would fall on Tim, who seemed content enough to take the responsibility of Phillip's job in addition to his own. An important factor seemed to be that the Admiral liked Phillip. Impressed with the report on the movie material, he had readily agreed to Phillip's coming along. All the way down from Seattle he had talked with the boy about a hundred subjects: horse shows, the State Department, Indians, Iwo Jima, oil, and so on. Thoughtfully he selected topics in Phillip's realm, and wisely Phillip gave his comments a modest impersonal flavor, while still employing his native cleverness, enthusiasm, and hard-headed practicality in his observations. To Tim's delight and Bruner's annoyance the two had got on famously. It was quite a step for Phillip—from the brink of discharge into the graces of an admiral. Rightfully enough, he acknowledged Tim as the patron who had executed this reversal of fortune. But since the episode surrounding the portrait, he had refused to attack the problem Tim presented. Had it not been for the accidental unveiling, Phillip knew that his life might now be moving in another direction. And here lay

178

the point that kept him from facing his problem: he could not feel anger or disgust for the man. He knew some change had been wrought in his personality, but he was afraid to learn what it was.

Cars awaited them on the field—one for the enlisted men, the other for the Admiral, Tim, and Phillip. Bruner was going in to San Francisco with their bags to secure their reservations, for only the Admiral would remain on the base that night. The Admiral's car moved out on the bridge and over the bay, turning down a long ramp to the naval base. There they had breakfast with their host, the admiral who had called the meeting, and another party of officers called up from San Diego. At 0745, without fanfare, they were in the conference room ready to go to work.

It was fascinating business from the first for Phillip. The purpose of the meeting was to complete arrangements for the dispersal and storing of certain amphibious vessels and their equipment throughout the three naval districts pending the next emergency when such instruments would be needed again. Phillip, wide-eyed as an urchin, missed nothing. From San Diego there was a party of nine; San Francisco was represented by five officers. Admiral Marcien was accompanied by Tim. Phillip was too modest to pretend that he counted. The decisions of these men would have far-reaching effects, for in their hands a part of their nation's security rested. Actually it was a grim game over a gigantic board covered with graphs, charts, and statistics Phillip could only vaguely comprehend. Each of the three districts had its own ideas and had done its own planning, and, of course, had its ax to grind. Now they worked to fuse the plans.

Phillip sat quietly beside Tim, listening, destined to say nothing, occasionally finding this or that file as Tim requested it. Tim and the Admiral were the enigma of the group, Phillip quickly discovered. While the others talked, the two men listened calmly, breaking in with infrequent comments. And

179

as the others talked, their eyes constantly sought the pair for support or approval. When the time for decision on each point arrived, it was Tim who rose and explained their argument briefly, lucidly, yet always politely. The Admiral spoke only when it seemed that the opposition of sheer gold braid would ride his aide down. And Phillip realized with no small admiration that the pair was well-nigh unbeatable. Together they worked as one, commanding the respect of everyone. This was the result of years of co-ordinated planning in Africa, Sicily, Italy, and at Amphib Island.

And Phillip's respect for the Navy grew by leaps. As an officer aboard a landing ship, his grasp of the Navy had been meager. Now he was having his first view in perspective and it was exhilarating. It left him feeling painfully inadequate, but anxious to grow in understanding until he commanded the respect of Tim and the Admiral. He began to appreciate the term "naval career." By no means was it retiring as a captain after twenty years of moving a vessel from harbor to harbor, but something a great deal vaster and more noble, a chance to shape the destiny and policies of one's nation. These men—all but Tim— were engaged in the business of waging wars, and as such, they were admirable to the boy. They planned campaigns and fought them, and now they were putting their equipment away until it was needed again.

It was time for lunch before Phillip realized that hours had slipped by and that it was time for still another lesson in naval strategy—this time social politics, which appealed to him a good deal less than the morning's business. At table he found himself seated between two other minor aides. One, an Annapolis man graduated too late to participate in the war, talked to Phillip of Japan with ill-concealed envy. The other, a j. g., invited him to a dance at Vallejo that night, but Phillip declined. Their conversation was filled with references to the Navy circles in which they moved. They accepted Phillip as one of their world and told him how lucky he was to be starting with Marcien. Danelaw appeared to be something of a mystery to them, but they were enthusiastic in discussing his tactics at this and other conferences. They had even heard of Pat. When they questioned Phillip about the Danelaws, Phillip had to admit with some embarrassment that he knew nothing of them. How could he tell these men what he knew of Tim? Here, Phillip realized, was an important factor in understanding his own problem with this man. Here was the first of two levels on which Tim lived, or perhaps it was the first of two faces he presented—one to the world, the other to Phillip and those he loved. The thought jarred Phillip, who in his ideal concepts of honesty tried to shape all things so that he need present but one face. Tim's solution was easier, but was it honorable?

They adjourned again and worked all afternoon. It was more of the same business, and though some of the others seemed to grow restless as the hours wore on, Phillip did not once grow weary of it. When they finished, it was dark outside. The Admiral looked as exhausted as Phillip felt, but Tim still looked fresh as they all rose and shook hands preparatory to leaving. In the corridor the Admiral spoke with Tim a few minutes and then left with the two other admirals. Tim came over to Phillip.

"We'll leave for Seattle at o8oo in the morning if there isn't fog. We can go in town to the hotel now."

"Do you mean it's all over?" Phillip asked, a bit disappointed.

"We'll clear up the details by correspondence," Tim said with a smile. "You liked today, didn't you?"

"Yes. I think I like the Navy, at last."

"It's all a matter of understanding it, like everything else."

They took a cab into the city and up to their hotel on Knob Hill. They rode in silence. Some of Phillip's old caution returned at Tim's first sign of friendliness. He could not help it. They picked up their keys at the desk and entered the elevator together.

"Do you know the city, or would you rather dine with me tonight?"

Still on the edge of suspicion, Phillip read more into the question than was really there. He answered too quickly, "I know it well enough." And he added apologetically, "I planned to call some friends over at the University in Berkeley."

"I see," Tim answered, coolness edging his voice. The elevator paused at his floor. "Goodnight. I'll see you in the morning."

Phillip, suddenly conscious of a strange disgust with himself, went up to his room, showered, shaved again, changed clothes, and went downstairs. He took a cab to a restaurant where his Uncle Felix had taken him several years ago. It was nearby, but he was not familiar enough with the streets to walk the distance. He was half-way there before he realized he had forgotten to turn his key in at the desk. He was completely absorbed in thought. Once more Tim Danelaw had crowded everything else from his mind.

In the restaurant he was given a secluded table. He ordered his gluttonous meal and devoted himself hungrily to the caviar —wet, shining, sooty black, its bitter salt tang awakening other memories—and to the wine that was like the thoughtless kiss of a happy child. For a while his mind freed itself of Tim, but soon it was back to the same topic. He thought of the inbred nobility of the man, the strength and wisdom apparent in everything he did. Unholy as he might be, already he had figured tremendously in Phillip's life. Could he blithely ignore his future without a showdown of some kind? Until now, he had hoped to slide by these next ten weeks without any unpleasantness.

Perhaps it was the food, or the day that had passed, or gratitude for his unexpected freedom, or merely his nature, but when the meal was over, Phillip knew what he would do. Taking a cab back to the hotel, he went immediately to Tim's floor and, drawing a deep ragged breath, knocked at the door. Tim, in shirt sleeves, opened it.

"So you received my message?" Tim said.

"What message?"

182

"The one I called down to the desk." Tim looked at him narrowly as he entered the room. "I thought I'd assemble some of this data for the yeomen and I left word for you to drop in if you got back in time."

"It doesn't matter. I'm here. Shall we go to work?"

"No," Tim said thoughtfully, "no, perhaps we've done enough today." He crossed the room to a tray on the table. "Drink?" He poured two brandies and added soda. "Couldn't you reach your friends?"

"There weren't any friends. I wanted to be alone a while."

"Then why did you come back?"

Phillip made a helpless gesture with his hands. "Tim, I don't fancy living with the idea of what I may become, as you said, in five, ten, or twenty years."

Tim nodded. "And what is the answer to that?"

"You have the answer. . . . Now. . . . Here."

"I see. Are you drunk?"

Phillip shot him a scornful glance. "Tim, you compared yourself to Stuff once. You can't do that. I could never respect the sailor—except as I respect some other men—because I knew that I could ride over him in a fair fight. But not you. I don't know why, but I can't fight you intelligently. I don't understand you—how you guess my thoughts before they occur to me. Usually men fall into one category—at the most, two. They are lawyers, contractors, doctors, bankers. One expects a certain standard of behavior of them. I've lived in a man's world all my life. I know them well. But you—artist, medico, dilettante, executive. What are you? I respect you. I admire you, though I should despise you. But until I know you, I may not be able to live peacefully with mere admiration. Always my mind will tend toward an over-appreciation. It will swing to the promise I made you two nights ago, and from that it will jump to this desire to see you in a flattering light. I rather imagine that half of this problem of homosexuality amounts to an over-appreciation on the part of its victims. Do you see what I'm driving toward?"

183

"Not clearly. Go on," Tim said calmly, swirling his glass.

"There is something discolored in my personality, something that drives me in that inverted direction. You sensed it the first time you saw me. You saw it again at lunch with the Admiral the next day, and again in the hospital. That first night at your place you brought it out in the open and said I was safe. Then night before last you asked for a promise, which I gave you."

"And then broke when you saw the portrait. Do you know why?"

"I think so. For the first time in my life I saw myself as a savage instead of the drummer boy of civilization. I've had the idea presented to me before, but never so—forcefully. I broke my promise because I was afraid; I ran away to preserve myself as I am. Does that make sense?"

"Excellent sense. Go on."

"You showed me two destinies. Maybe they are the same. Mediocrity and disaster. Is that right?"

Tim nodded.

"I preferred mediocrity. I still do. But how can I accept one without a knowledge of the other?" He paused, watching Tim closely, trying to calm himself.

"Go on," Tim said brutally.

"You offered me a challenge for the challenge you said I had unconsciously offered you. You took it a step forward by putting it into words, by saying you were ready to accept it, for better or for worse. . . . Well, now I am ready, too. If your philosophy, or whatever it is, makes sense, now is your chance to prove it."

"And do you think it makes sense?" Tim asked harshly.

"I think it is vile. It can be disguised with words and emotion, but beneath any surface you put on it, it is as corrupt as anything on earth. This is your chance and mine to stand free of each other for the rest of our lives. Once you said I would have to stop running and fight. Now I am ready."

Tim drew on his cigarette and put it out. He put down his glass.

184

"So you're ready to gamble with disaster, as you call it. Suppose you lose. What then? Are you really willing to accept the consequences? Do you even understand them?"

For a moment Phillip wavered. Then his chin came up slightly.

"I don't think I will lose, Tim," he said softly.

"And what of those in Seattle?"

"Let Seattle take care of its own problems. This is San Francisco."

"You speak of vileness very glibly," Tim answered tightly. "If only you knew how vile—" But seeing the beginning of triumph on Phillip's face, he did not finish the thought. "You want me to back down now, don't you? To leave you free to go on with your life as it is, lulled with another half-victory?"

For a moment they studied each other as two duelists, their first salutations over, their blades in thirsty readiness.

And Tim said, "The victory is yours, Phillip. I make it an easy one for you so that it may serve you the longer. Once more you stand head and shoulders above everything else on the field." He smiled wryly and walked back to his desk where the only light in the room burned.

Phillip's shoulders sagged and his lips twisted with puzzled words. He had overplayed his hand. Tim had merely withdrawn. He had not fought. Nothing was settled.

"I—Tim, I—"

"No?" Tim asked mockingly. "You don't want your victory?" He turned slowly on the boy. "It carries no spoils, does it, Phillip? No pain, no suffering, nothing to make you feel superior. It's hollow this way, isn't it? I was wrong about you, Phillip. You're no savage. You're a beast endowed with a bit of reason. You *are* a cat, bringing down what you want, ripping out that with which you would fill your belly and leaving the rest to carrion hunters. I'm damned if I'll give you that satisfaction!" With difficulty he brought himself under control and said, "What did you expect me to do after you pranced in here

185

liquored to the gills to fling down your precious challenge? Turn off the lights, turn on the soft music, take you in my arms and fondle you as I would a woman!" Tim laughed, mimicking Phillip's tone perfectly, "Now I'm ready for you, Tim. Here I am. Seduce me. And let me show you what a fool you are." Tim's voice plunged. "Do you think that you, tonight, and the boy I spoke to the other night are the same?" Suddenly his voice grew quiet. "I think you'd better go to your room, Phillip. And you are right. Now we can stand free of each other for the rest of our lives."

But the boy did not move. He stood trembling by the tall open window, half feeling the fog, half-conscious of the noises of the traffic far below. He steadied his glass with both hands and looked down into it. He had never been so ashamed of himself in his life. But he forced himself to speak.

"All right, Tim. I'll go. As usual, I've rushed into a situation—" a vague hint of irony touched his lips—"and as usual there isn't an angel in sight. There is no victory for me. There will never be so far as you're concerned. It's all yours."

He had not heard the man cross the room but when Tim's hands touched him, he looked up into the face above him, kindly once more.

"I was unnecessarily harsh, Phillip," Tim said gently. "Forget what has been said. Would you like to give me a hand with this work for the Admiral?"

"If you want. But first, answer me one question: What's wrong? Why do I spoil everything I touch?"

Tim smiled sadly. "It's a very common fault these days, Phillip," he said simply, "you have no heart."

"And how do I go about having one?"

"You'll have to figure that out for yourself, I'm afraid."

"Are you sorry for having helped me so far?" Phillip asked.

"Sorry? I don't know. At any rate I'm glad it stopped here."

"But don't you see," Phillip burst out, "it hasn't stopped here

186

for me? It's worse than ever. You've destroyed my reason for living. I don't want it to stop here."

"Then prove it." Tim's voice was almost lost in a flare of noise from the street below.

"But how can I—" The man's expression stopped him. Phillip recognized one of the major decisions of his life. He was outclassed on every point. He could run away, or he could make the best of the one situation he could not alter.

Tim took the glass from him and put it on a console nearby. Phillip's gaze wavered and dropped until it rested on the man's hand still on his arm. The boy touched it uncertainly, then lifted it, and, bending his head, pressed the palm against his lips, feeling the warm cushion of flesh, the tips of the blunt curving fingers brush his cheek lightly. It was a gesture of humility, containing the core of his pride. And the small harsh sound that escaped his lips was as if swift sharp pain had struck him.

"Are you very afraid, Phillip?"

"Very afraid," he whispered.

There was silence between them and Tim moved away, back into the dim room as if giving him a chance to change his mind. Phillip followed him with his eyes, seeing him pause and turn to look back. The atmosphere had changed. Between them there was now only the inevitable. Slowly strength concentrated in Phillip's muscles, yet a gentleness pervaded him, too. His body felt hard and clean; only his chest moved. His mind, so filled with his precious ideas of a few minutes ago, now felt like a quantity of broken glass. The portrait was becoming reality.

He saw Tim approach and stop before him and gently brush his hair back from where it had fallen over his forehead. His touch was comradely, fatherly, and Phillip shuddered slightly. In the shadows of his face, Tim's eyes glittered like onyx. Then Tim's hands, the jaws of a vise, gripped his waist, lifted him from the floor, higher and higher until he floated over the pavement hundreds of feet below. If, in the seconds to come, his body went plummeting down through the fog-laden air, he would feel no fear, for Phillip knew that at last his years were justified—that the first cycle of his personality was at last completing itself, releasing him to other cycles to be lived. With this moment some distorted thing frozen into his boyhood began to melt. To live on without this relief would be hideous. So, with his hands on Tim's forearms, he steadied himself and waited. He understood Tim's action in lifting him now. The man was declaring himself in a rite as primitive as tribal mankind. He was making his bid for dominance and the responsibilities and privileges it carried. Phillip could offer no feat of strength to surpass or equal it, and relative values did not exist at this time. This was an exhibition of power that Phillip could understand. By it one would lead; one must follow. This was right, but—more important—it was indisputable. Then Phillip felt himself being lowered into a world of incredible satisfaction.

PART

2

❖•◈•◈•◈•◈•◈•❖

Oklahoma

Summer—1946

17

All through the night Phillip dreamed; short, strange dreams, untinged with reality. Once he stood over a gaping scar in the earth, a deep fissure in which many elements of the world bubbled like chemicals in an irregular test tube, each separate, all on the point of fusing their molten bodies of cobalt, sulphur, blood-carmine, and tangerine. This dream was brief and elusive. Another was longer, more persistent, more damning in its content.

He found himself submerged in a vast world of water, a pleasant, half-familiar world of sight and sound and liquid impression that pressed all about him. It had the vital animal warmth of new milk, caressing the flesh and nostrils with intimate, mysterious sensation. He moved in it, breathed it, floated in it, one infinitesimal part of it, the modicum in a transparent universe. Lifting his arms high, he rose upward languorously—a brilliant, tropical merman—paused, jackknifed, dived downward, ending naturally in a dancer's arabesque, his arms so, his legs so, touch-

191

ing nothing, being held by that which loved him, his parent, his playmate, the great god Ocean in which he lived.

Something touched his neck relaxing a tension of muscle there. He looked down. Seaweed. Drowsily he watched it retreat and then creep toward him again and slyly touch his little privates. Far away, his oceanic protector watched, chuckled with thunderous glee. Phillip's eyes narrowed as he smiled wisely and guided the seaweed up to his navel and held it, an easy prisoner. His protector roared with pleasure at such youthful impudence. He lay on his side and moved his shoulders so that he alternately touched the seaweed with each brown nipple. So engrossed in his play was he that he was unaware of the storm that had been shaken loose by his protector's mirth. He feared no thing, for this was nothing. Eternity in an instant, a vast concept of bliss that existed forever and not at all, all at once. He was a child amusing himself. His parent lover petted him with a constant pressure like a gigantic pulsebeat through the liquid about him, finding its counterpart beating inside his small ears. It was the boy's first happiness in many years, and the satisfaction he took from it was monstrous enough to destroy him. This was the zenith and nadir of his life, destined to remain a dark jewel caught deep in the mud of his mind.

Once he had walked a levee of the Mississippi on a cold Louisiana morning just after daybreak. It was the morning after he had discovered his love for his cousin, Anne. He was fifteen. He had walked the grim levee after a sleepless night, the ice floes from lands he had never seen moving at his side. He had felt eternity then, in the gray light and the gray river. Suddenly, overcome with his thoughts, he had stopped and stared out over the swollen river, jagged with dirty ice. Two parallels had met in his mind and merged. From Anne's arms he could have given himself to the river. But a hunter approaching from downriver had interrupted his reverie. That had been melancholy happiness, capable of being measured in various ways. His present joy was boundless, timeless, emotionless.

192

Phillip awoke. For a moment he refused to give up his exquisite relaxation enough to open his eyes. Nor did he attempt sleep again. He simply waited for the decision to arise to come of its own accord. His body was exhausted, drained of all energy, as if he had walked for hours in deep snow. Yet he felt curiously light rather than dull or heavy. His mind was stiff, for the impressions recently burned there had started scabbing over like new cattle brands.

Reluctantly he became aware of sounds, a streetcar grinding down Knob Hill, a faint blunt sound from the bay telling him that the fog of the night had remained and that they would be delayed in taking off for the north, a splash of water that would be Tim shaving, and then Tim's voice, ripping through the cobwebs of lethargy to actually touch him.

"Are you awake?" He spoke French, using a sobriquet of the previous night that made Phillip blush with remembering.

"Don't you know?" Phillip asked, cautiously opening an eye to see Tim regarding him from the mirror in the bath. Tim's face was covered with lather and he wore the trousers of his pajamas. His back was smooth and dark.

"Yes, I know," the man smiled, his teeth less white than the shaving cream. "From now on, any question I ask you will be superfluous."

"I feel the same way," Phillip murmured, opening the other eye. As Tim cut a long brown swath down his cheek, Phillip pulled one of the pillows to him and hugged it close with his knees. Tim nicked his chin and immediately blood dripped into the water.

"You get up," he said sternly.

"You come back to bed." Phillip smiled narrowly.

"You're lascivious!"

"You're scared!" Phillip argued.

At last, with an effort, Phillip got up on one elbow. His lids drooped and his lips formed sounds clumsily. "Do I smell coffee?"

193

"In the other room. Breakfast will be up in a few minutes. I thought you might need the coffee to get out of bed."

"Right now I need a robe." Phillip yawned.

"Like a fan dancer needs plus fours," Tim grinned.

Phillip dropped his chin and shot him a mischievous glance. He stood up and tied Tim's pajama top around his middle by the arms, took a deep breath, shook his head, and started into the next room. Tim took up his razor. "Little devil," he muttered, hearing Phillip pour coffee and turn on the radio. As its sound drowned Phillip's movements, Tim's mind swung back to his thoughts before the boy had awakened.

He was trapped. He stared at his image in the mirror and repeated the fact. He had known it from the second he had touched the boy the night before and felt the spasm of pain as Phillip had relinquished command of his life. But one does not inspect damage in the midst of a night storm. Now, at last, he had an idea of how hopeless their predicament was. As Phillip would insist on doing, Tim took the blame for their actions. He felt he had deliberately fostered the event without sufficient excuse. But there had been much tragedy in his world and, often enough, little incentive for living and working. Tim loved the boy as nothing else in his life. In comparison to Phillip, Tim's wife had cast but a silhouette upon the screen of his senses.

Considered alone, not from the standpoint of past causes or present significance or future repercussions—and that was the way it must be considered at first—their relationship was now perfect. For Tim (who could accept this fact and live with it) believed that anyone attempting to explain or justify it, was, in addition to being a coward, defeated before he began. Still, in a few minutes he had to face Phillip with some explanation, some justification, some logical program of future conduct in the most hostile world the boy had yet faced. Still later, when Phillip had accepted what he could of the situation, he would have to do battle for its right to be recognized against greater,

194

more powerful elements. It would be then that Tim could be of the most use to him. Now, however, the aspects of their problem confronted Tim. In a sense they were old fears in new guises.

In the first place their relationship was too perfect. It had been lifted past all barriers to its zenith and stayed there, transplanted from the dregs of impulse to rare heights of emotion. Such flawlessness could only inspire doubt in a man of Tim's experience. He had found a young man, so vibrant from the stimulation of the world that he had seemed about to snap from it. Moved by a desire to help him, Tim had become enamored of him. Ten hours ago that had seemed no insurmountable problem.

The one thing Tim had been half-afraid and half-hopeful of finding in Phillip was the timidity of inexperience. Squeamishness would not have surprised him, and a genuine loathing for homosexual practices would have signaled an immediate retreat from the inflexible complications such affairs inevitably carry. But rather than a reluctance in the boy, Tim had found a fervor of passion that, once released, consumed all restraints swiftly, completely. Tim had sensed this quality in Phillip, but until it was actually revealed, he had not believed it possible. The boy's knowledge was timeless if not limitless, showing the same quick readiness for humor as solemnity, as each had been indicated. He had the uncanny ability to evaluate each second, to confine or set free passion that was rare in one so young and so addicted to conventional living. Nor had there been any tendency to lose balance either in utter indifference or at the outer limits of desire. Never before had Tim been so captivated by an experience.

Never one to retreat because he knew the contours of fear, Tim nevertheless found a recurring desire to stop, to turn back and search for something he had overlooked. Tim had examined himself years ago, and more recently he had studied Phillip as thoroughly as he could with the facts he had obtained. He had found faults, but now they seemed so immaterial to the situation at hand that they deserved only the most perfunctory of glances. This chilling apprehension was the result of something else—something he had not yet discovered.

The second aspect had to do with Phillip himself and the responsibility Tim felt for him now that their futures were fused. It would be impossible for either to travel utterly alone again. Phillip had completed the rapid growth of adolescence and had already started fulfilling the slower process of growing sound with maturity. He was like a comparative graph—too long on some subjects, pitifully short on others. Tim felt that he could divine what the boy needed. Tutoring him would be a delight, for he stood at the threshold of real intellectual activity, if those underdeveloped portions of his personality did not hold him down too long and too often. Already he had discovered a little of the sublimity of thought and, happily, he had never slipped off into idle dreaming. What Phillip became would depend on his next five or ten years and the influences about him. But he must have the opportunity to take his time and work things out for himself. Tim knew that he could, and he would give him this opportunity. Doubtlessly Sybel Jo, demanding and disillusioning, would ruin him. Phillip's marriage to her would serve him worse than a dozen homosexual affairs. Whereas the affairs would give his mind no relief, the life of a respectable brahmin would lull him into eventual inactivity.

Phillip was made to respond to stimuli with the best he had in him. Given stimulus of a type, he might easily leave his traces in more than one world. He was an ordinary man, aware of his ordinary qualities; and a more driving combination cannot exist under proper conditions. Such a man would work to project his background rather than himself. The brotherhood was often mistaken for genius, for it included zealots and martyrs, Napoleons and Christs. Phillip, for example, could shrug his shoulders at the teachings of his church, yet he could not see above the

196

false morality of his class. Tim had lived too long to regard morals or ethics as anything but abstractions. Keen at perceiving foibles, he believed that he could help Phillip do the same, sorting and discarding ideas until he had worked out a satisfactory personal philosophy that consisted of no philosophy at all. If Tim could teach the boy one thing, behavior in the presence of fear, he would know that his influence had been beneficial. If he could show him that every problem has a solution, every unknown a denominator, for the patient man, his influence could not be questioned. But was he capable of putting his feelings aside long enough to help him?

The third aspect was consideration for himself. Like Phillip, Tim was intensely individualistic. He functioned best alone, on his own resources. And by the same token that was Phillip's, Tim's own strength was the only thing that could defeat him. He was a man who used the world sparingly and gave to it generously without keeping accounts. As a result he was an esteemed inhabitant. He lived his life quietly, waiting to find something worth while to ask for, to fight for if necessary. And now Phillip had touched that spring within him. With each second that tripped over the face of his watch, new desires awakened to break his placid lack of attachment to the world about him.

But more disturbing than this was the strange delight at discovering the parallels in his and Phillip's characters. They were alike—so much alike, in fact, that at times he felt they had practiced the narrower rites of Narcissus rather than those of homosexuality. It was as if in exploring each other, each of them discovered something of himself he had not yet learned to love. Tim had a horror of love of oneself. He saw a serpent devouring its tail from hunger, digesting itself to its own destruction. If he were ever to desert Phillip, it would be because he found too much of himself in the boy. But that was a strange thought for a happy man. He pushed it aside.

He washed his face and reached for his robe when he heard over the voice on the radio in the next room a knock on the outer door and Phillip call, "Come in."

Realizing that the boy was expecting a waiter with breakfast, Tim called, "You'd better let me answer that!"

But he was too late. As Tim reached the sitting room, the outer door swung open and Lee Bruner stepped inside. Tim saw the crafty eyes appraise the absurd pajama top about Phillip's middle, and the indescribable look on the lad's face as he stood staring at the intruder, a coffee cup half-way to his lips.

"Well! Excuse me," Bruner bared his short teeth in a smile. "I just stopped by to see when we are taking off."

"When the fog lifts," Tim snapped. "I left you a note last night."

"So you did," Bruner said with mock consternation. "Perhaps I wanted to talk to Phillip and couldn't find him in his room."

"See him at the airport," Tim said, starting toward the man.

"By all means," Bruner said hastily backing out the door. But before it closed, they heard him laugh. To Tim it had the vague rustling sound of blackmail money—a good deal of it, he thought grimly.

He turned to Phillip, who still held the cup. The gaily colored pajamas broke the straight clean line of him. His anxious eyes held a question. And knowing that he could not hope to answer it at this time, Tim saw everything between them crumble away, leaving them to stand like isolated peaks of hatred. This was why he had been afraid of their perfection. Now he realized that a thing so easily created is just as easily destroyed.

"Phillip. . . ." But he could find no words to counteract the poison he knew now flooded the boy's mind. He grasped the hot shoulders to comfort him, but Phillip shrank back as if he were loathsome.

"Don't touch me!"

Phillip set the cup on the table and went to the window where his clothes still lay in a disorderly heap. Swiftly he picked them

198

up and put them on. Miserably Tim watched him, knowing that until the keen edge of the boy's humiliation was gone, no one would be able to approach him. At last he turned away, unable to bear the sight of his friend's suffering any longer. He heard the door close at last, and he knew that Phillip had gone to face his own private hell. Mechanically he turned and picked up the pajama coat and took it into the bedroom to put it into his suitcase.

18

Tim was the only person in Phillip's present circle of acquaintances who would not have condemned the boy for what he had done, and Phillip would not trust him. Instead the boy concerned himself with the effect knowledge of his indulgence would have on Madame, Sybel Jo, Francis, Pat, and—most of all—his family and Devereaux. He had little idea of what to expect once Bruner talked, except that the total sum would be catastrophic, ending in his ruin. He hadn't thought of those back in Oklahoma for days. Perhaps that was his trouble. He had lost sight of his ambitions for this, this—his mind stalled completely searching for words.

He sat in the Seattle-bound plane, sunk in a very apparent mood of shock. It seemed that they had been flying for days instead of hours. Once he had closed his eyes, but he had opened them immediately when out of the darkness had come Lee Bruner's delighted, sneering face. So he stared out of the porthole, worrying over the details of the events that awaited him.

He was dimly aware of the plane, the clouds, the earth far below. His mind accepted the fact that the Admiral had given
him a puzzled look at the airport, that Bruner wore the expression of a dutiful child on Christmas morning, and that Tim
Danelaw was watching him like a hawk while trying to keep up
a half-hearted conversation with the Admiral. But these things
were not important.

He did not recall the night that had passed, the new vista of
his life that had been opened for him, that phase of his personality so stunning in its pain and ecstasy. He could only think
of how he would appear to everyone once the truth was out.
That was the thing he must prevent. Unlike Tim, he did not
think of buying Bruner's silence. He preferred the thought of
luring the man to the Sound and drowning him, unlikely as that
prospect might be. He turned abruptly from that train of
thought, knowing it was wrong rather than caring why it was
wrong. He did not think of asking Tim for aid. This was his
problem. Nor did he blame Tim for what had happened. He had
gone to him in complete awareness.

Gradually his thoughts began to settle and his persistent, painful thinking cleared the issue down to its basic features. He
faced the question of keeping a man silent. Bruner had no proof
for what he suspected, and the man would recognize this. So
Phillip considered how and where Bruner would strike first. If
Tim were to be the first victim, Bruner might approach the
Admiral. That was unlikely, however, for it would take irrev-
ocable proof to discredit Tim in that man's eyes. Pat would be
a better bet—Pat who was about to start divorce proceedings.
Phillip quailed before the imagined newspaper articles. There
had been something like that in Texas a few years ago. It had
been in every Southwestern newspaper for a fortnight. His
family would never forgive him such a scandal. But if Bruner
chose him for the first victim, to whom would he go? Francis?
That was likely, but more logically he would threaten to reveal
his suspicions to Madame, for Bruner, Phillip was certain, had

guessed how desperately a marriage to Sybel Jo was needed. And to Madame, suspicions were far more terrible than facts. She was angry with Phillip for putting her off about Sybel Jo. With what Lee Bruner would tell her she could easily withdraw all her support.

The only possible answer was at once apparent. He had to marry Sybel Jo as quickly as possible. Once she was securely in the family, Madame would have to make the best of keeping her mouth shut. This would mean a change in Phillip's plans. No wedding in the fall. His parents would be disappointed; Fanchon might despise him for being weak until she knew the circumstances, and he certainly intended to tell her everything. She was closer to him than anyone else and she would understand him. He could count on that.

Of Sybel Jo he thought little. She was a pawn in the game. He had no qualms over the shadowy part of his nature he was concealing from her. It would be foolish to try to explain anything to her. Why confuse her and jeopardize his chance with her when ignorance was her natural, blissful state? Then, too, he attached much less significance to their affair than Tim did. Eventually he would surmount it. He had found only one thing he could not surmount—his father. And in comparison to his father, Tim was a minor woe. . . . His father. . . . He shivered and tensed himself for the coming struggle with Bruner.

As the plane approached the naval air station outside Seattle, Phillip gave Bruner a cold stare of challenge. Immediately the man's face sobered. Phillip felt himself regaining ascendancy. Tim Danelaw caught the challenge, too, and relaxed for the first time on the long flight up the coast. The boy was recovering from the shock Bruner had given him. Tim felt a strange surge of pride, for he knew Phillip was about to make some move, wise or foolish. He would have to keep an eye on him for the next few hours.

They landed and drove back to the base for lunch. To Tim's chagrin, Phillip asked to be excused. The Admiral, aware that

202

the boy's fiancée was in town, agreed, and Phillip left them at the club. He went immediately to the telephones in the foyer and called Sybel Jo's hotel room. There was no answer. He glanced at his watch. She might be lunching, or shopping, or attending a movie. She didn't expect him back until tonight. He called again and received no answer.

He passed his hand over his eyes. He was weak from lack of food and sleep, yet he didn't dare take the time to eat until all this was settled. For a moment he debated taking a cab into town. Suppose Bruner called while he was on his way in and told Madame enough to arouse her suspicions. He couldn't risk that. He'd stay by the telephone and call at three-minute intervals for the next hour. If they hadn't answered by then, he'd go into town and wait for them in the lobby. It did not occur to him that perhaps he was putting too much emphasis on this point.

"My God, have you been to a wake?" a voice said at his ear.

"What?" Phillip looked up to see Mike.

"You look like hell, kid. Didn't you shave this morning?"

"I must have forgotten," Phillip said, touching his chin. Mike nodded knowing that Phillip never forgot such things.

"If you're any indication of the things they're doing in Frisco these days, I'm asking for a leave," Mike observed with interest. Suddenly Phillip's flesh had gone from feverish to icy cold. It must have reflected on his face, for Mike said, "Why don't you go to your room and clean up? I'll come along."

"No. I'm making a call. The Admiral is in the dining room if you want to talk to him and Tim."

"There's a phone at the BOQ, or had you forgotten that, too? And I'd rather talk to you, since you took my place on the trip." He glanced at Phillip. "Have you any liquor in your room?"

"Some brandy," Phillip answered weakly.

"Then come along. You need a drink."

They did not talk on the short walk to Phillip's room. In the corridor Phillip called the hotel again and got no answer. They

203

entered his room and Mike handed him the brandy. He drank from the bottle and it hit his empty stomach like a shot of acid. He grimaced, but by the time he had removed his shirt and run water into the basin to shave, he had begun to feel better—perhaps a bit high. He bent over to wet his face, but as he straightened up, the mirror before him suddenly twisted to the side and started revolving slowly before him. He clutched the basin desperately and closed his eyes. But the tighter he gripped, the more rapidly it slipped from his grasp. He felt himself losing consciousness rapidly and turned to make a try for the chair. Mike, an interested observer, guided him to the bed and let him lie down. The room was rolling like a destroyer in rough weather.

"If I didn't know better," Mike said mildly, "I'd say you were pregnant. Now take my wife. About three months along she starts—"

"Oh, shut up," Phillip groaned, waving off the glass of water Mike offered him. Once more he was icy. His teeth chattered and he huddled gratefully under the blanket that Mike threw over him. For five minutes he was very sick. But at last the feeling ebbed as quickly as it had come and he sat up cautiously, then stood and walked to the window. He lighted a cigarette and the misty ache behind his eyes retreated. But the illness had left him horribly depressed. He tossed the cigarette out the window and returned to the basin, using a cloth to dampen his face this time. Shaving was an ordeal, but he brought it off. He began to feel well enough to notice Mike.

"That has never happened to me before," Phillip laughed uncertainly.

"I'll just bet it hasn't."

Phillip glanced at him quickly and knew that somehow he had learned of what had happened in San Francisco. "You've seen Tim," he said.

"In the dining room at the club," Mike nodded. "He asked me to have a look-see."

"What did he tell you?" Phillip demanded.

204

"Nothing," Mike said easily, and Phillip almost relaxed until he continued, "He didn't have to. I've been around Tim three years. I know him well and I admire him. . . . Want to tell me all about it?"

Phillip put the razor down with a slam. "Look, Mike—"

"No, you look, you goddamn little snob," Mike said, standing to face him. "Take this mess and jam it up your tail for all I care, but get this straight: everyone who tries to give you a hand isn't out to rook you. Frankly I think you deserve everything that's coming to you, but Tim Danelaw doesn't, and I like him as much as I hate your kind! In fact, my little friend, so far as you and I are concerned, I wouldn't piss on you if you were afire!"

The attack from Mike, a man he had barely bothered to notice, made Phillip realize what he meant to this mouthy Irishman. He was a stumbling block.

"Hell, I know what happened in Frisco," Mike continued. "I've seen it coming since the first time I saw you two together. Evidently Bruner saw it coming, too, from what Tim said, and it will cost him plenty. You're strictly bad news!"

"It may not cost him so much," Phillip interrupted quickly.

"What are you going to do?"

"Marry Sybel Jo as soon as possible."

"And how will that help?"

"Then it boils down to my word against Bruner's. Do you think anyone would believe a story Bruner might tell if I had just been married?"

"Some might."

"Then they'd believe anything," Phillip said brusquely, "because I'll act the role of bridegroom so well no one will doubt me."

"You could do it, too," Mike sneered.

"Never mind the compliments. I've a call to make."

"Just a moment. What about Tim Danelaw?"

"What about him?" Phillip asked blankly. "He'll take care of himself."

"Is it possible you don't realize what you've done?"

"It isn't what I've done but what I'm going to do that's important."

"Exactly. You're out to save your own skin. Once more you've been the naughty little boy. You were just being mischievous when you kicked your captain in the pants making a beach head. Endangering the lives of fifty men didn't matter. You had your pride. So Tim understands, comes to the rescue, and sets you up higher than you've ever been in the Navy without even slapping your little hansies. And you, wonderful glowing you, take it all like the young prince accepting homage from the citizenry. Do you think Tim helped you because he helps everyone? He did not! His judgment is respected, sought after on this base. He's worth a hundred stupid little Phillip (spelled with two *l*'s) Froelichs (pronounced *Froy-lick*), Oakie empires and all. So why did he help you? I'll tell you, though I'll never understand it. He sees something in you that no one else sees—something that restores his faith in a race of human beings he has seen with their pants down too damn long. Do you know why he's going to earn a degree in medicine when he gets out of this outfit?" Mike was growing a bit hysterical. "He wants to find a cure for cholera to save the lives of a lot of Asiatic scum that would as soon be dead as alive. And do you know why? He doesn't give a hang about them, but because some guy he liked wanted to find the cure and blew his brains out, Tim feels responsible for him and now he's going to finish the work. And the ironic part is that he has picked you as his inspiration! So he hasn't told you. He doesn't dare because you'd fly off some moral handle because you're not big enough to do otherwise. You haven't transcended it. Ha, Ha, Ha. That's a laugh. It's like a tumble bug trying to take a load up the Tower of Pisa!"

"And what would you have me do?" Phillip asked quietly, "be his *mome* the rest of my life?"

206

"You could do a lot worse, sonny," Mike shouted. "But if I were having anything, I'd have him tell you to go square to hell!"

"I'm no homosexual," Phillip said defensively.

"Oh, yeah? You might fool some of your hick friends by charging around making fists at everyone, but you haven't fooled Tim, Bruner, or me. Every guy has some of it sometime. If it happens when he's twelve and he gets over it, he's called normal. At any other time he gets another name, depending on who's doing the calling. That's all, chum. Now go call your Southern belle—or go to Tim and give him a chance to handle Bruner in his own way and, incidentally, to restore his faith in you."

Phillip finished putting on his shirt, tucked in the tail, and picked up his coat. He was not angry, but he was stinging from Mike's contempt. If he had needed a final argument for doing as he planned, this was it. Phillip could be led, but he couldn't be driven.

At last, when he was ready to go, Mike asked, "Well?"

"Well, what?" Phillip asked coldly.

"What are you going to do?"

"I'm marrying as soon as the state permits. Goodbye."

"Wait a minute."

But Phillip closed the door and walked rapidly down the corridor to the telephones. Thirty minutes had elapsed since he had tried to reach Sybel Jo, and this time she answered.

"Syb? Phillip. We're back early."

"Darling, I know. Lee Bruner just called." Phillip's stomach gave a sickening plunge. "I've missed you, lover, and I'm—"

"What did Bruner want?"

"Cocktails at five here at the hotel. Madame's having a session with the beautician downstairs. Bruner said he had something important."

"Can I come in?"

"Yes, of course, but why?"

"Let's just say that I love you. Is that reason enough?"

"Ummmmmm. Just hold on to that thought until you get here."

"I'll take the next boat. Bye."

On the way in, Phillip began to suspect Bruner's plan. Probably Tim was the target. Phillip was to be the cat's-paw. Bruner would build up as much gossip as possible around him and then use this as pressure against Tim through Pat—that is if he could persuade Pat to join forces with him. And why shouldn't she? Fortunately Phillip could still act to save them both.

He planned a little episode for Sybel Jo's benefit and worked on the idea until he arrived at the hotel. She was waiting for him in the lobby, radiant in a simple white dress. He kissed her despite the observers and guided her outside.

"Where are we going, Phil?"

"Surprise."

He took her to the Smith Tower, which he had heard was a popular tourist point. In a rather rickety elevator they went to the top where there was an observation platform with a view of the city. He paid the admission and took her outside on the ledge, enclosed by thick iron bars to prevent accidents and suicidal leaps. The day was still and calm and the city seemed far below them.

"The tallest building west of the Rockies," Phillip explained.

"Love it," the girl said, her blue eyes scarcely leaving Phillip's face, her slender hands clutching his tightly. She was so glad to see him that for a moment Phillip thought that she might actually be in love with him. More likely Madame had been giving her orders to bring him in or else. Well, this would settle Madame's problem and give Sybel Jo a little peace, he thought.

"Look," he said, "there's Amphib Island, and over there is Pat's house."

"We're going up there tonight," Sybel Jo said doubtfully.

"Fine," Phillip answered to her surprise.

"Do you really want to go?" she marveled.

"Anything to make you happy." He smiled down at her,

208

touching the soft curve of her cheek with the back of his fingers. To his consternation she burst into tears. He held her gently as he might hold his nephew who had awakened from his nap in a cranky mood. He petted her, urging her to talk.

"Phil, everything's so messed up," she sobbed.

"You mean Madame?" Phillip supplied, stroking her head. The girl nodded.

"She wants us to marry out here?"

Again a nod.

"And if we don't, what then?"

"She wants me to marry Francis," Sybel Jo said.

"What?" Phillip said unbelievingly.

She repeated the statement.

"Syb, is there some reason for this haste? Something you should tell me?" His voice was gentle, persuading her to confidence. It was a genuine attitude, for he was sorry for her.

She shook her head. "It's just Madame. All my life—"

"Forget it, Syb. When we're married it will be different."

She lifted her face and he took his handkerchief and dabbed her eyes before he kissed her tenderly. Sorrowfully Phillip saw what his life with this girl would be. She would be his child, never his wife.

"You're very lovely, Syb, and I love you very much."

She smiled. "You seem so different today," she said.

"I'm happy." He pointed to a cloud low over the Sound. "I'm on top of that. Want to come up?" She nodded enthusiastically, ready to play games. "All right," he said. "All set?" She put her arm around his waist as if in preparation for a leap. "Syb, will you marry me? Now? As soon as I can get the license? Please say yes."

Her incredulous gasp brought another flood of tears, but she managed to put her arms around his neck and say, "Phillip! Oh, darling, yes, yes, yes!"

He held her to him a long while, and since he could not make his mind blank, he vowed that he would try to make her as happy as he could. He supposed that was what all men thought on these occasions.

Sybel Jo sighed. "Phil, let's go tell Madame."

He was touched at her innocence. "All right. We can work out the details there."

When Lee Bruner arrived at five, Phillip had the pleasure of seeing his face melt like wax as Madame blurted out the good news. Wryly he offered Phillip congratulations and they were accepted with condescension. They talked for a while and at last decided to go out to the Danelaws' for cocktails, since they were going out later in the evening. Phillip said that he and Lee would have to change clothes so Madame told them to run along and Phillip not to come back to the hotel for them but to meet them up at the house. They were very jovial and Phillip went out with his hand on Bruner's shoulder. But when the door closed, he removed his hand quickly as if he had accidentally put it into filth. While they waited for the elevator, Phillip could not resist the temptation to needle Bruner enough to try to learn his plans for the future.

"Nice afternoon, isn't it?" he began. "Much nicer than Frisco."

"Somehow I thought you preferred Frisco's climate," Bruner said.

"Sometimes I do," Phillip smiled, studying his nails elaborately. "I'm a man of many moods."

"And many tastes," Bruner sneered.

"That's right," Phillip said, meeting his eyes. "But no taste for blackmail, you gat-toothed jackal, particularly when there is no truth in it."

"I wouldn't be too sure about that," Bruner said, reddening.

"I would. In fact I dare you to make any accusations where I can hear them. I'd love to stomp the shit out of you."

The elevator slid open smoothly before them, and deliberately Phillip stepped in front of Bruner as they entered.

210

19

◆◇◆◇◆◇◆◇◆

*P*hillip was the last to arrive at the Danelaws'. He had had a letter from Fanchon in his room and he had lingered over it, debating the wisdom of writing her everything. He had finally decided not to do so, but to wait until he could explain in person. Fan deserved something more than half explanations for he loved her dearly.

As Phillip stepped through the door at the Danelaws' he was met with a shout of congratulations. Sybel Jo came to hang on his arm as he shook hands all around. He was gay as he accepted the jarringly uncouth jokes on planned parenthood, and told everyone that the ceremony would be a quiet one within the next three days and that they had made no plans, which was certainly the case. No, he had no idea where he and Sybel Jo would live until he was discharged. They would probably move to a hotel in town. No, there would be no wedding trip at this time. Later they'd go to Quebec, New York, or South America. Sybel Jo said that she would love to go to Southern California for a month, but Phillip made up his mind that they'd go back to Oklahoma before he spent four weeks staring at movie stars. As for the ring, he planned to buy an inexpensive one until they returned home where he would have a loop made of some of his mother's stones. That was the arrangement she had made for Fan. He could expect the same consideration. *A beautiful start we're off to,* he thought grimly. *One we'll probably never get over.*

He looked over the crowd. Madame was glowing over her coup. She'd make an ass of herself in Devereaux, too. His family didn't deserve that. Lee Bruner was looking sullen by himself in a corner, probably brooding on new plans. Francis had been a surprise. The first to congratulate Phillip, he had welcomed Sybel Jo as a cousin and then let his hand rest briefly on Phillip's shoulder in a comradely manner. Phillip felt that the gesture was genuine, not calculated for the benefit of the others. He felt some pity for Francis, for the man was aware that this alliance, if anything, would guarantee Phillip's future presidency of the bank. Undoubtedly Francis was a gentleman. Phillip responded accordingly chatting with him ten minutes and feeling no urge at all to lose his temper.

Pat was enthusiastic about the approaching marriage and agreed to attend Sybel Jo at the ceremony. Phillip would have preferred another arrangement, for that meant Tim would be there, too. But he couldn't have everything his way yet. The idea of Tim and all the unspoken thoughts between them gave him an uneasy feeling. It was rather like planning to be married while kneeling in a morgue. But he had made a definite stand. Safety lay in carrying it out. The night in San Francisco floated free of the coherent bulk of his life. Steadfastly he refused to think of it. And even if their story was told, it would be of little consequence. Only the words might seem strong for a while, and Phillip would erase them by his future conduct. Still, because of the afternoon's scene with Mike, Phillip was suffering something near a stricken conscience so far as Tim was con-

212

cerned. Tim was the only person in the room who had said nothing to him and this made him sad. Later in the evening, when the atmosphere had grown thicker and drunker and Phillip saw the man go out on the terrace alone, he followed him and found him standing at the cliff, staring out over the glittering city. Once again it was very quiet and the house seemed far away. Tim glanced at him and then looked away.

Phillip spoke softly, "I'm sorry, Tim. I wish it might have been another way."

"The groom usually regrets his impulsiveness after the ceremony."

"I wasn't speaking of my marriage."

"I was."

"In that case, I'm doing what I feel is necessary to save myself and you. After all, I'm saving you a good deal of money."

"Is that all you think of—money?"

"Yes."

"I see that it's impossible to insult an honest man." He turned to Phillip. "I suppose you feel you're forestalling some grave disaster?"

"I won't wait until my back is to a wall to start fighting."

"But do you realize what you're storing up for yourself? Your motives will come out. Madame will have a powerful weapon over you."

"Do you think that Bruner will talk now?"

"I do. If you'd ever learn to respect your enemies—"

"How did you know?" Phillip remembered the scene before the elevator.

"I know you. Remember?"

"I suppose I treated Bruner foolishly."

"The whole thing is foolish. Why don't you call it off?"

"Don't interfere," Phillip said quickly and added, "please."

"Please?" Tim said, irony in his voice.

"I want to get along with you, Tim. We'll be working together. . . ."

"And you want to be friends until you leave?"

"No. We can't be friends, not after San Francisco."

"Then what do you want?"

"Indifference. Treat me as any other officer."

"That won't be easy. Three months of indifference, knowing that when you leave—Phillip, don't go through with this marriage now. Later you'll be free and so will I. These situations are ephemeral. But if you break them suddenly, they take on significance. I've seen them before. They are dangerous to people like us. Wait until you can face Sybel Jo with a life you can call your own. It isn't yours now. It's mine, and no matter what you tell yourself, it will be mine until—"

"Don't," Phillip said. "It sounds so damned—well, so damned adolescent here, in this setting."

Phillip was completely miserable as Tim turned from him. The word *adolescent* had obviously hurt Tim deeply.

Suddenly they both heard a voice upstairs call, "Madame? Oh, there you are." They turned quickly to see a figure in white leave the shallow balcony above them and enter the bedroom. It was but a fleeting glimpse, yet both of them knew that it had been Madame.

"She was standing there while we were talking," Phillip whispered. He felt Tim's brutal, steadying fingers on his wrist.

"Careful, youngster. You aren't flying off on another tangent this time." They stood in silence, reconstructing the damning sentences they had uttered. With Bruner's suspicions and now this, Madame would believe anything.

Phillip's mind raced two thousand miles back to Oklahoma. He visualized the news of his broken engagement, Madame's vicious stories, Francis to back her up. A drop of perspiration fell from his armpit. His mother, his father; their outrage, humiliation. Fanchon facing her friends; her husband, Paul Cully, still an outsider because of his Boston Background, facing the customers at the bank. Jesus H. Christ! There would be no end to the damage. At last Phillip knew that he had gone as far as he

214

could go alone. Now was the time for family advice. He had to talk with his mother or Fanchon. His father would be a last resort. They must be warned of his predicament to protect themselves. The telephone, he thought quickly and immediately discarded the thought as the last possible alternative. He could hardly call Fanchon and blurt out the truth, not with telephone operators who eavesdropped and relayed juicy stories to their friends. If he could approach either Fanchon or his mother gently and reveal the idea in a proper setting of words, something might be worked out.

"Tim, I've an idea," he said. "Listen to this." Rapidly he sketched his plan and ended with, "Can you get me a week's leave?"

Tim was silent. Phillip had made no mention of anyone's welfare but his own, but then that was no more than the man had expected.

"How will you explain your absence to Madame?" he asked.

"We'll say that at the last minute the Admiral decided to send me East with you. You leave tomorrow for New York and Washington, don't you?"

"Yes," Tim said reluctantly.

"And no one ever sees you off at the airport. Suppose I left for Oklahoma tonight. Tomorrow, before you leave Seattle, you could leave a message for Sybel Jo, explaining that I was going with you. You could pretend the message came from me. You'll be away a week. I'll be back in Seattle the same day you are. All I need is one day at home to explain things. While you're in D. C., you can send a few telegrams in my name. If I'm lucky, no one here need know that I was in Devereaux. When Madame does find out, I'll say I flew down from Chicago and then flew back to Chicago."

"But Madame is suspicious of us now. Won't it look worse for you if you suddenly go East with me?"

"I don't think so. She won't do anything until she has a showdown with me, and by that time, I'll have seen my family."

It was a clumsy, impulsive plan, pregnant with a dozen mishaps, yet if anyone could bring it off, it would be Phillip, Tim thought. The boy seemed to have extraordinary luck, almost an aura of good fortune, as if he were the particular favorite of an earth-loving god. Tim thought of the Admiral and knew that it would be unlikely that the man would object to the plan if he were told that Phillip needed a quiet week to straighten out certain matters at home.

Something else was of greater importance to him just now. Old questions concerning Phillip rose in his mind, questions that had puzzled him since he had known the lad. What manner of family life had produced him? What kind of parents could he have that he could blithely tell them that he had just had a homosexual affair and that he was sorry and, please, could he now be forgiven? Fanchon, Uncle Felix, Grandfather Dev —which was responsible for this little monster he had come to love. Or perhaps at last Phillip was guessing wrong. He could be heading straight for a lot of trouble, trouble that would awaken him to the actual state of affairs around him. If this were true, he would need a friend. Tim's trip East was an excuse to let him make certain property arrangements against Pat's divorce proceedings. Traveling alone, he could easily swing down to Oklahoma just at the right time to catch Phillip in dire family straits. All in all, it wasn't a bad plan. He studied the boy a moment longer, his narrow eyes, sharp jutting chin, tense as a headsman awaiting the signal to raise the ax.

"If the Devil ever dies," Tim muttered, but he did not finish the adage. "There's a plane for Chicago tonight."

"I want to go by train. It will take two or three days—time to plan exactly what I'll say. A plane would give me too much time at home. I don't want or need it."

Tim nodded. "I'll call the yeoman on duty and have him fix you up some leave papers. I'll bring them to you. When can you get a train?"

216

"I don't know. I'll take Syb to the hotel now, go to the base and pack. Shall I meet you at the base or the depot?"

"The base. I'll drive you in." Tim added, "You're taking this coolly enough." He saw Phillip's teeth flash dimly.

"I'm thinking of tomorrow."

"It hasn't occurred to you, I suppose, to stay here and face your problem alone, decently?"

"Why should I act decently before a sow like Madame?" Phillip demanded hotly. "The only way to beat Madame's kind is to outbeast them."

Tim laughed. The boy's enthusiasm for the job ahead had suddenly given the possible tragedy a farcical flavor.

"We're wasting time," Phillip snorted. "You call the yeoman and I'll get Syb." He started for the doorway, hissing over his shoulder, "Hurry!"

Tim Danelaw watched the boy until he had disappeared. He shook his head again. What would happen if that sly, evil little brain were forced into happier channels? He knew that if such a thing were ever to happen, it would be up to him to accomplish it. He alone occupied this unique position in the boy's hagiology. And he understood the two methods he might use in shaping Phillip. He could make the boy act from the deep consideration for humanity that he took pains to ignore, or he could break him so thoroughly that nothing of his old self remained, and from the chaos he could reconstruct the personality he wanted. But Tim had work to do. If he caused Phillip to miss a train, he would never be forgiven.

Of one thing he was certain: Phillip was approaching a point where he must fly to pieces. Strain was apparent in everything he did now. And someone would be standing by. Phillip, despite his desire for independence, could not move alone. For Phillip's sake and for his own, Tim was determined to reap the benefit of the boy's metamorphosis.

20

❖❖❖❖❖❖

*I*t took Phillip seventy hours to reach Devereaux via Chicago and Kansas City. His plans had been perfected a few hours out of Seattle, and he had spent at least half his time cursing himself for not allowing Tim to get him plane reservations. He had gone over his speeches to his mother (he had selected her as the wisest, strongest, most sympathetic ally) a dozen times. He had rehearsed the attitudes, pauses, and expressions, as well as the words, that would swing her completely to his side in the shortest time. If she responded as he planned, his father would need to know nothing. He had even drawn a diagram of the situation, marking every possibility. Seeing the thing in black and white had a good effect on him. He had a passion for maps and graphs inherited from his father, who often said he could get more usable knowledge from a table of percentages than from a day's conversation with the average informed man. So, when the train pulled into the low white stucco depot of the town his grandfather had founded, Phillip, radiating tremors of confidence, anxiety, and pure joy, was the first to alight.

It was Sunday morning and Phillip considered this an omen of impending good luck. The station was deserted. Everyone would be in church at this hour—everyone but his mother, if he remembered her habits correctly. The good lady developed headaches on at least fifty Sunday mornings every year, and mournfully sent her husband off to do the week's praying alone —a chore he undertook with stoical pleasure. Victoria Froelich was a humane woman, Phillip thought with pride. Reared in the spectacular tradition of the Popes, she loathed the plain interiors of Protestant churches and, though she now professed the Baptist faith, she seldom passed between the great granite pillars on Sixth Avenue. Victoria would be at home enjoying her coffee in bed on this glorious late spring morning.

Phillip stopped in the station long enough to telephone her and thus alleviate the shock of his sudden appearance. Then he took a taxi, since he knew that Oliver, the chauffeur, would have driven his father to church. Eagerly he drank in the details of the small city as he was driven through the wide tree-shaded streets. Already he felt better. Perhaps half his trouble in the Navy had been the fact that he had been away from the things he loved too long.

Three women awaited him on the wide stone gallery of the house: his mother in a flowered dressing gown; Goldie, the Negro cook, a study in gleaming black and white; and his mother's best friend Georgie Parks, who often came to sit with Victoria during her Sunday headaches and to escape the frightful odor and noise of hellfire and singing sinners. Georgie Parks's presence was another piece of luck, for as Madame's foremost enemy, she fitted into Phillip's plans.

He left his bag and coat in the taxi (in Devereaux all hack drivers took care of luggage) and ran up the steps to catch his mother in his arms. For several moments there were the usual tears, muffled kisses, and incoherent cries of happy welcome. But when the two released each other, Phillip turned and planted a kiss firmly on Georgie's round, astonished mouth.

219

"Why, Phillip!" she twittered with delighted frustration only women past fifty seemed to know. He grinned and kissed her again.

"That," said Phillip, "is for your lovely charming daughter Gretel. I hope she's not married, because I want to deliver it in person."

Georgie shot his mother a pleased but puzzled look and laughed, "Vickie, I think you've reared a sailor in spite of yourself."

They laughed as Phillip turned to Goldie, who was beaming shyly at him. Instinctively Phillip knew what she was feeling. He sensed the anxious moments she had just lived, standing beside his mother, wondering how he would receive her, steeling herself not to care if he failed to kiss her as he had always done when he came home from college. Phillip knew that she was realizing that two years had passed, that strange influences had come to bear on him, that he was no longer a little boy. What he had done thoughtlessly once might be distasteful to him now. And Goldie, always conscious that her color was an abomination in the eyes of whites, had prepared herself for the worst, yet had been brave enough to come out on the porch to meet him. Now she stood waiting for his decision, a decision Phillip wanted to tell her he had made on the day she had presented his fifth-birthday cake trimmed with sugar animals like a merry-go-round. Instead he put his arms around her and whispered "Goldie! This is the best of all."

He kissed her cheek that smelled of toilet soap and received her kiss on his. She was too overcome to do more than gulp. Her love and gratitude touched him more deeply than his mother's joy. Goldie and Oliver, natives of New Orleans, had been brought to Oklahoma by Phillip's grandfather shortly before his death. This made them dear to him. They had fed and chauffeured the family for nineteen years. They had a son, Courtney, two years older than Phillip, a college graduate and

220

now an officer in the Army. Phillip asked after him and learned that he was doing well.

This small colored family, living behind the strong Froelich arm, enjoyed an unique position in this Southern town, perhaps even in this border state. They were accorded all the privileges offered any white—a principle Old Phillip had believed in fiercely. The old man's treatment of them had been his answer to the senseless expression: "A nigger's all right in a nigger's place." Phillip admired his grandfather's position in this matter, and he hoped to uphold and carry it further during his lifetime.

Old Phillip had, of course, been criticized for his treatment of Negroes and for many other things, including his stand against the poll tax, his generous gifts to Catholic and Jewish organizations, and his outspoken admiration for the New Deal. He had been a peculiar rich man, and a deadly one. But the Negro issue had taught the town its real respect for the banker.

The story was this: Ephram Jones had been a wealthy contractor from St. Louis, arriving in Devereaux to enjoy the old man's patronage, make a good deal of money and become the city's mayor. But there had been trouble. No one knew what it was, but for weeks the two men did not speak. Then, at a city council meeting one night, Jones had proposed to pass an ordinance prohibiting Negroes from being in the business district after sundown—a direct blow at Devereaux authority. Hearing of the proposed measure in time, Old Phillip had appeared at the meeting like a slight, avenging angel and taken Jones to task so shrewdly that the man had slapped him across the mouth. Old Phillip had left the meeting, white-faced with rage, to start a campaign of vengeance that was to last eight years.

He had ruined Jones in Devereaux in a year. Jones had moved to Tulsa. Old Phillip had followed. There had been a property lawsuit. Jones had gone to Dallas. Old Phillip had followed. By now oil men had spotted the jinx on the contractor. There had been insurance trouble in Dallas and Jones had suffered a tremendous loss because of the negligence of a secretary, who some were foolhardy enough to say was in the pay of Old Phillip. The situation grew so intolerable that Jones had committed suicide. Oklahoma newspapers had referred to him as a fraud. Then Old Phillip had bought and foreclosed the mortgage on the remaining Jones possessions, thereby reducing the man's widow to penury. She had died soon after—the last scene in a drama of personal devastation that left the average Devereaunian mute when faced with the possible displeasure of such a man. Of course, Old Phillip was dead, but the town had changed little during the Froelichs' time, and there was now a Young Phillip, as much like his grandfather as two peas in a pod.

With one arm still about Goldie and the other about his mother, Phillip waited for Georgie Parks to say her goodbyes and leave. She made her speeches down the steps to the waiting taxi.

"Tell Gretel I'll be by this afternoon," Phillip called.

"She'll be delighted," Georgie chirped, seeing the event in the society column.

As the taxi drove away, Phillip went inside with his mother and Goldie. The servant was saying in her well-remembered drawl, "If we'd known you were coming, we'd have had dove for lunch. Oliver shot some and we've kept them in deep freeze for you all this time."

"I should have wired," Phillip apologized.

"That's all right," Goldie promised, "we'll have them tomorrow."

"That's a promise." Phillip pinched her ear playfully. "Now how about some really good coffee?"

"Sure good to have you home, honey," she said, going down the hall.

He turned to his mother and their eyes met shrewdly, seriously. "The library?" he asked.

She nodded and he opened the door for her. They went to

222

the fire that had driven the morning chill from the room and stretched their fingers to it. He did not waste time looking about the familiar room. He could do that later when he pretended to be interested in his father's ponderous talk.

"I'm in a bit of trouble," he said.

"I know," Victoria replied calmly. "I've sensed it in your letters of the past year." She smiled fleetingly and indicated a chair. "We'd better get as far into it as possible before your father arrives." She glanced at the ornate Sèvres clock across the room.

"First . . ." Phillip began, taking out a cigarette. Then he flushed, remembering where he was, but his mother nodded her approval. It was only his father who had forbidden him to smoke. "Has Sybel Jo gotten herself into a situation with a man?"

"Do you mean is she *enciente?*" she asked, and he loved her for using the French term. "I don't think so. But we can ask Fan. Why?"

"I'm going to marry her in Seattle."

"Phillip!" His mother's blue eyes were wide with disapproval.

So Phillip started with the trouble overseas, telling about his captain, of the proposed GCM and Seattle, giving the reason for his escape as his captain's loss of command because of incompetency. He did not mention Tim Danelaw. Instead he lied to protect the man, though he did not fully understand why. It was as if an invisible bond held over all else. Later the truth could be told when he had more time, perhaps to his mother, certainly to Fanchon, but not now. He painted Bruner as black as he dared without arousing his mother's suspicions of his honesty. At last he arrived at the most dangerous part of his story, and he paused to gnaw his lip.

"One of the men with whom I have been working is—peculiar." He shot a calculating glance across the fire. Victoria stared at him blankly. This was going to be harder than he had thought. He moved uncomfortably in his chair. "Mother, you know about Harry who works at Lee's?"

223

"You mean the man who crochets?"

"Yes." A flicker of amusement touched Phillip's lips. "He isn't the only one of his kind."

"I've suspected as much at times," Victoria said dryly.

"There is a name for them and some of them are in the Armed Forces. Their personalities are inverted. They are called homosexuals."

To his extreme horror, his mother broke into a peal of laughter.

"Now what have I said that's so funny?" he demanded with annoyance.

"You've said nothing funny, Phillip," she said, serious at once. "It's just that twenty years ago someone else explained homosexuality to me sitting in that same chair." Immediately Phillip thought of his grandfather. But his mother continued, "And your Aunt Minna was almost as uncomfortable as you are now."

"Aunt Minna!" Phillip would have put any other person in that chair before Uncle Felix' saintly sister.

His mother was saying, "But we're concerned with the present. You'd better continue."

"I was decent to the fellow. I had no right to abuse him. Bruner, my Navy counsel, was unhappy over the way I'd failed to co-operate with him. He was angry because I did not offer him money to get myself free of the court martial. He even asked me if the man had made overtures. Bruner is a vicious meddler, a blackmailer. Then a few days later, Madame overheard a conversation between the man in question and myself. I was discussing tolerance with a good deal of frankness. You know how the woman's mind is hinged on filth. Anxious to see me marry Sybel Jo, she might use such an incident against me if they are really desperate for a marriage and if I refuse to co-operate. So it may mean my marrying Sybel Jo or else losing her to Francis or any one else who is available." He paused and smashed his fist against the palm of his hand. "Damn that meddling jane, anyway!"

224

"Tell me about this conversation Mrs. Voth heard," his mother said.

"Actually it was nothing that hadn't been said a dozen times before in that house where we are guests. Sybel Jo and Madame prefer this ultra arty crowd. They aren't our kind of people —too much money, too little common sense; hence they play at living."

Victoria nodded judiciously at this supreme indictment.

He continued, "I might have been drunk, loose-tongued. I was discussing tolerance with undue levity. You can guess what I said. There are circles in which everything is discussed. Madame hasn't grasped that fact yet. The conversation, coupled with Bruner's ideas, is liable to come out as anything. But one thing is apparent: Sybel Jo has to get married, and if she doesn't marry me, there has to be a reason, one that will sound good when Madame tells it."

Coffee arrived and they were served silently, Goldie guessing that an event of importance was being discussed.

When she left Victoria said, "Have you told me everything of importance?"

"Everything," Phillip replied promptly.

Victoria thought a moment before she delivered her decision. "You've always had a knack for getting into trouble, Phillip. It isn't exactly blundering; it's as if you attract incidents. I've noticed it since you were a child, and always you come out of these situations ahead of everyone else. That, if nothing else, gives me faith in you. Eventually you'll learn patience. Now, you're young—only twenty-three, isn't it? This Captain Pratt. Really, Phillip, you could have had the man's head on a salver, but you've done well enough, retaining your commission with no marks against it. And you're quite right about keeping it a secret, especially from your father." She studied the translucent porcelain cup in her hand a moment.

"The bank is your future and Sybel Jo is your problem. We'll give you some support in gaining the bank, of course, but to take it when you want it, you must do all the work. Therefore, do what you think best about the girl. As I understand it, you feel there is danger of a very unpleasant scandal which we'll have to fight by ignoring it or spreading counterscandal if it comes."

"That's right. Madame will carry Francis, but I will continue to be the town's shining example," he said. "That evens things up pretty well. But if I don't marry, there must be a logical reason. If you gave out a few discreet hints to your ladies' organizations, that might do the trick. Confide in Georgie Parks. Madame's behavior with Captain Morgan would be an extra touch. Then for the next few months I'll see a good deal of Gretel. Georgie will do the rest. The town will believe the worst about Madame and there will be so much confusion that it will all blow over."

"But that leaves you without the Voth money. And Francis has more power than you," his mother pointed out.

"I've been thinking on that score, too," Phillip nodded. "There must be other marriages I could make in Tulsa, Oklahoma City, or Dallas. Fan knows them and she despises Sybel Jo enough to welcome the challenge. And I'm not exactly a scarecrow."

Victoria studied him as she put her coffee aside. "Not a pretty picture, is it?"

"God knows I hate this finagling as much as anyone!"

"I wasn't criticizing you," his mother explained swiftly. "But I was wondering if you were being bothered with scruples yet?"

"I'm only twenty-three." Phillip's tone was cynical.

"And you're using your head," his mother said a trifle too soothingly, Phillip thought. "But don't worry about the scandal. If it comes, I'll deal with it. Naturally you were right to confide in me in plenty of time. That leaves you free to devote yourself to Sybel Jo if you decide that is the solution. Do you think you can marry her?"

"Yes."

"Then that's that. Our little problem may not be so big, after

226

all." Victoria rose and came to stand beside her son's chair. He took her hand, kissed it, and held it to his cheek as he stared into the fire. Smiling, she stroked his hair, lingering over each harsh, silky curl as it crept beneath her fingers. "You're more like your grandfather than ever, Phillip," she said softly. "He would approve of you wholeheartedly—your impulsiveness, your will to succeed. I'll be glad when you're home again to stay and your real education begins. No more temper then; no more impatience."

"You're a wonderful lady," he said contentedly. "One more ounce of love for you and I'd have a terrific Oedipus complex."

His mother's laughter was warm and free of indignation. "You flatter me, Phillip, I'm no beauty any more."

"You've a good deal more of the genuine article than most."

"Just an old-fashioned girl you're looking for," she said playfully.

"Just an old-fashioned rich girl," he corrected.

"The bank still means so much to you?"

"It means everything, as always." The mother and son were silent again for a while, deep in this perfect accord, their haven of safety within the family. "Francis made a remark the other day that upset me," Phillip said. "I goaded it out of him and I think he regretted it immediately. He said something about Uncle Tony's retiring, turning over his third of the bank to Francis."

"Your Uncle Tony has already informed us of that fact." Victoria sighed. "We can't see how that will further their interest unless they're planning to sell, and it doesn't matter who owns the interest then. Your father, Fanchon, and Paul have discussed it with me at some length. We've done very well during the war years, as you'll see this afternoon when your father shows you the figures. Tony made some money, too, but it's safe to say they've spent it. Your Aunt Marie buys all her clothes in New York now. Then that house in New Orleans. Rumor has it that it has cost them two hundred thousand. Tony and

227

Marie are such fools. Tony talks of investing with some of the family down there, and that indicates a sale of their holdings here. Fanchon heard that Anne's uncle wouldn't consider Tony even as a stockholder."

"Hooray for Anne's uncle. By the way, how is Anne?"

"Fine. She received confirmation that her husband is dead. She is taking it well enough. Fanchon asked her up in the fall."

"Is she coming?"

"Yes." Victoria smiled significantly. "You'll be home then."

"Why couldn't she have Sybel Jo's money?" Phillip mused.

"She is your cousin, Phillip."

"But how many times removed?"

"She's staunch Catholic."

"Anne is staunch nothing—unless it's woman." Abruptly Phillip changed the topic. "So the unholy Barrimans plan to sell us down the river?"

"As soon as Uncle Felix is gone."

Phillip sat up with alarm. "Is there danger of that soon?"

"Yes. His heart. He is so brave about it."

"And he still plans to divide his interest between Fan, Francis, Aunt Minna, and me," Phillip said. "And with his death, Francis and Uncle Tony apply the pressure. The last bulwark between the fool Barrimans and Grandfather Dev. God! What a finish for Devereaux!"

"Don't!" Victoria suddenly started to cry. Phillip looked at her with amazement. It was the first time in his life he had ever seen his mother cry. He stood quickly to hold her close, comforting her with words and kisses. But he was thinking of his Uncle Felix. Slowly his eyes blurred as he saw his last link with another world, the only world he had ever really loved, begin to disappear.

228

21

❖❖❖❖❖❖❖

$\mathcal{T}$im Danelaw was acutely aware of Phillip's dilemma. He was unwilling to let the boy run erratically before confused and half-formed ideas. After three days in the East, the man had made another aggressive move in Phillip's direction. It proved to be even wiser than he had imagined. Flying to Oklahoma City, he had called Phillip's mother and received an invitation to visit the Froelichs. Danelaw's explanation had been logical enough to arouse no suspicion. He had said he was at the naval air base just out of the city on business and that as Phillip's immediate superior, he had learned that Phillip could fly back to Seattle via naval transportation, thereby giving him two extra days at home. This news had earned him the invitation which he had promptly accepted. By taking a private plane to a town nearby, Tim was able to board the same train that had brought Phillip into Devereaux twenty-four hours earlier. He arrived on Monday morning.

Having been no nearer Oklahoma than a Steinbeck description, Tim Danelaw was prepared for a near desert with unpainted shanties, barefoot slatterns, and dry dusty heat. On the train he learned that in the southern part of the state there are low mountains and that June, on occasion, could be unseasonably wet and cold, which seemed to be the case this year.

As the train neared Devereaux, he saw stands of pine timber on the smooth, worn hills, small green fields caught in the many elbows of clear, meandering streams, herds of stocky, white-faced cattle, and the oil wells that helped to make the state famous. He felt excitement rise in him at being close to Phillip's beginnings.

The train slowed at the outskirts of the city and came to a stop at the white stucco station. Tim tipped the porter and took his bag. The station was invitingly clean, the air from the mountains fresh and sharp. The concrete underfoot, painted white and freshly hosed down, ended in beds of blooming flowers, tended by a gardener in white coveralls. Everything shouted of city beautification clubs and fat factory pay rolls, he thought. It reminded him of certain tourist spots along the New England Seaboard. Farther back, there were gigantic elms with whitewashed trunks, and still farther the first buildings of the business district, freshly painted and cheerful-looking in the morning sunshine. There were no billboards or newsstands with jarring colors to break the serene monotony of cleanliness. Instead there was a spacious, hospitable air about Phillip's home town that Tim found delightful.

"Commander Danelaw?" The drawl was flat and lazy. Tim looked down at a small Negro man who grinned pinkly while nervously turning a chauffeur's cap in his umber fingers.

"Yes," Tim answered, wondering if the foolish, persistent grin never left the man's face.

The grin grew even wider. "Miz Froelich and Miz Cully in the car."

He reached for Tim's bag and turned to march solemnly off down the platform. Tim followed, noting the erect childish bearing and the trim sky-blue uniform. Two women stood beside a shining black sedan parked in the wide circular drive. The older, about fifty-five, smiled and lifted her chin slightly in a manner that reminded Tim of Phillip. She gave him her ungloved hand.

"Commander Danelaw, I'm Phillip's mother. I'm delighted to welcome you to his home. Unfortunately he was with his father in the country when your call came. He'll be in soon." Her voice carried real sincerity and a warmth that invited trust. She turned to the younger woman, who was possibly thirty or thirty-five. "Phillip's sister, Fanchon, Mrs. Cully."

Fanchon Cully extended her hand and repeated that it was a pleasure to welcome him, though her tone held a slight reserve not present in her mother's. While he thanked them, Tim studied the two women carefully, already searching for signs of Phillip.

Victoria Froelich presented a dual impression: genuineness and dowdiness. Her furs and jewels were too dated and lavish to be anything but real. She wore a scarf of a dozen sables, fitted into a style from the twenties, probably purchased at the height of a new fortune when European pelts were more plentiful and somehow more beautiful. The stones in her ears and the one on her finger were all large sapphires set in dark, carved silver and encircled by seed pearls. Once more the style was of a quarter-century past. Their color was only slightly bluer than the woman's eyes. Instinctively Tim knew that she had not dressed for the occasion, but that these were a part of her normal attire.

Yet destroying the effect, or perhaps heightening it, the rest of her clothes looked mussy. Her wool dress was a youthful pink with blue flowers at the shoulder, and on her graying blonde hair, which was done in an impatient upsweep, she wore a Watteau type bonnet with too much pink tulle and too many cabbage roses. Her high heels looked uncomfortable, for she was a short plump woman. However, only serene happiness showed from her round chinny face. She was an attractive matron.

231

Fanchon Cully was still youthfully attractive. She was slight and olive-skinned, with the same lithe feline lines of her brother. Her eyes were a velvet-brown and slanted coquettishly, so that their sharp perception was at first hidden from the casual observer. She wore a polo coat severely belted in at the waist, but flaring to the knee. Beneath it she wore crisp white linen and a simple necklace of delicately colored coral that emphasized her dark coloring. Like Phillip, she had a good smile, but she seemed a bit reluctant to use it.

Oliver opened the door for them and, still grinning, took his place at the wheel to drive away.

Mrs. Froelich said, "We're all very grateful to you for Phillip's extra days, Commander Danelaw. You'll be a surprise when he gets home, and a welcome one, since he will very likely put you to work helping to prepare for his birthday party tonight."

Tim was puzzled. Phillip's birth date was in February.

"When Phillip was away at college, he used to call home before week ends to learn' what tasks awaited him. Based on this knowledge, he selected his guests from his fraternity brothers according to their ability to work: the harder the job, the brawnier the guests."

They laughed politely and Tim asked, "How old will he be?"

"Oh, Phillip isn't having a birthday. He was twenty-three in February, but this is his twenty-first birthday we're celebrating tonight—a coming-of-age party that should have taken place two years ago while he was overseas. We hold open house at the hotel in town for those townspeople who want to congratulate him."

"Rather a debut," Fanchon observed, giving Tim a sly glance.

He chuckled, noticing in these women's accents that same careful way of speaking that the Navy had dulled in Phillip. Already he realized that Fan was accepting him as an equal in age and society and that Mrs. Froelich had somehow put him in the category of her son's fraternity brothers—stations he knew he did not deserve. It was also apparent by the way they gave their exaggerated attention to everything he said that they knew absolutely nothing of him and were at a loss as to how to receive him. So when they politely asked where he was from, he talked freely, giving them the keys they sought. Yet he had to be cautious until he knew what Phillip had said of the events in Seattle that had brought him home. He explained that both he and his wife called Chicago home, but that he had been born in France.

"Then you're the artist who sent me the cat sketch," Fanchon exclaimed, "the man who speaks French and German to Phillip. You are indeed welcome. If Phillip needs anything, it is polish."

There were respect and appraisal in the woman's eyes that made Tim more uncomfortable. But by that time, the car was rolling sedately into the great park-like town square and Mrs. Froelich was pointing out the courthouse, the city hall, the Hotel Devereaunian where the belated party would take place, the newspaper building, their bank, and the Voths'.

"You've met Sybel Jo," Fanchon said, "and I suppose you know that they're planning to marry out there." She sounded slightly disgusted and Tim chanced a shot in the dark.

"I understood that nothing was settled as yet."

He saw mother and daughter exchange swift glances of approval and regard him with increased cordiality. Somehow he had made himself some allies. He wondered what the unpredictable Phillip had told his family.

Meanwhile the car had halted for a red light and the two women were busy acknowledging the nodded greetings of the people crossing the street in front of them. Some women waved to them; and when men respectfully touched their hats, both women smiled and nodded gravely. The car, its grinning chauffeur, and its passengers were well known, and the honor accorded these women was received with appreciation and returned with respect. Tim began to realize what Phillip's family was to this town.

233

As the car moved slowly around the square, Mrs. Froelich indicated a tall slender shaft of white marble with a plaque.

"A memorial to Phillip's grandfather, erected by the townspeople."

Tim read: PHILLIP EUGENE DEVEREAUX, *Founder and Benefactor.*

When they left the square, the women turned to him with friendliness and asked about Phillip's present duties. And as Tim talked, the atmosphere became almost cozy.

"The Admiral is happy to have Phillip on the staff, even for a few months," Tim said. "He has an unusual ability for planning."

"His father will be proud to hear that." Mrs. Froelich sounded pleased.

By the time they reached the Froelich house, Tim knew he had easily won the qualified friendship of two of the boy's family, but a friendship which would vanish with the first suspicious word he uttered. He felt that he was beginning to understand this world that Phillip called his, a world of harsh convention despite its varnish of kindliness and decency, a world in which the boy would never be happy until he saw it in perspective as both his mother and sister saw it now.

Out of town, the terrain dropped gradually, the elm-arched road skirting the rim of a great oval valley for several miles. At last, leaving the concrete highway, they turned into a short lane of white crushed shell that ended before a pair of iron gates so delicately wrought that Tim half expected them to swing gently in the breeze that tossed the trees overhead.

"We live just beyond the gates," Mrs. Froelich said ambiguously.

Tim looked ahead respectfully and his eyes narrowed with appreciation. From the center of thick green meadows and lawns a mile away rose a square, solid mansion of gray stone in the tasteful majesty of simple architecture. It had a strange half-familiar appeal.

234

Oliver stopped the car, opened the gates, drove through, and then closed them before continuing between the immaculately trimmed hedges of boxwood. (Of all things, in Oklahoma, Tim thought.) Its spice-like odor, hot and moist, came in the windows to remind him of England. Yet the atmosphere was as Continental and American as it was English. Suddenly he was aware of the women watching him. He blushed.

"Don't be embarrassed, Commander Danelaw," Mrs. Froelich said. "Everyone is surprised. We're so often taken for barbarians out here that this house is our greatest pride."

"To say it is beautiful is hardly adequate," Tim answered. "It is so well co-ordinated with the landscape that it seems to grow out of the earth."

"My father would have appreciated that compliment," she said. "He built it in an era that erected a welter of bastard palaces for bastard princes, as he used to say." Tim laughed, thinking that Phillip had inherited a great deal of his grandfather's virile wit. "As a matter of fact," Mrs. Froelich continued, "the house did grow out of the earth. Every timber and stone came from the surrounding mountains. He had to develop his own quarries and sawmills to get what he wanted, but he never doubted that it was worth it. We were very colorful in those days with our boom town and new wealth—adults with Aladdin's lamp. Of course, everyone built a house. But all the imported granite and marble displeased my father. He used to say he wanted a house as large and as plain as the earth it sat on, yet something elegant and full of promise to express the hidden richness of the land. No styles suited him, so he designed his own. No turrets, pillars, gingerbread, or gargoyles; and above all, no money was to be wasted. He was the son of an immigrant peasant. He did not forget it."

Tim was struck by the irony of this statement, for it seemed to him that not only had the builder forgotten his humble beginnings, but in constructing this fortress, he had made an issue of it, perhaps with the idea of enslaving the countryside.

235

He suppressed his smile and found Fanchon's merry eyes on him. She gave him a surreptitious wink.

The car was crossing the bottom of a shallow ravine that seemed to put the house on a knoll in the center of the green valley, a knoll that had been converted into brilliantly flowering semi-formal gardens. Already they were passing low tree borders of magnolia, roses, and oleander, all trimmed, all putting forth their individual cloying odors into the heavy air. Tim preferred the clean delicate odors of the alfalfa and clover meadowland they had just left. Halfway up the hill the house appeared again and at closer range. Tim was pleased to see that it was neither so large nor so grim as it had first seemed.

"Is it old?" he asked.

"It was begun in 1900 and completed in 1909. That makes it thirty-seven, doesn't it? But it looks more like three hundred."

It did. The three-storied rectangular house was constructed of uniform blocks of stone, each beautifully faced and beveled. This one detail gave it the sleek look of a chateau. On three sides of the first floor there was a wide stone gallery, its outer wall a series of spaced arches supported by short stone columns that rose at intervals along the low balustrade. This gave a delicate, base-like effect to the second and third stories, lifting their banks of slender windows encased in carved stone and steel against the blue and green of sky and hills. The mansion looked rural, cool, remote, and—strangely—both monastic and frivolous. It was a home of people who possessed the simple culture of those who live close to the earth and who are wise enough to love it—a rare example of new wealth directed into channels of taste instead of spread in all directions to soon disappear.

It was this background Tim had sensed in Phillip—something more than just clean American youth, some elusive quality that was mystical, feudal, perhaps sinister, yet basically wholesome. All this was in the boy's manner, the way he carried his head, held himself; the unconscious air of superiority and self-confidence he radiated. Tim had seen its effect on others as well as

236

felt it himself. Few were immune to it. He had watched men suddenly become dignified, choose their words, hang on Phillip's words, and pay him court. This background explained much about the boy.

The car stopped before the entrance and Mrs. Froelich directed the chauffeur to put his bag in Phillip's rooms, explaining to Tim, "Last night Phillip and Oliver painted all the guest room baths. I'm afraid you'll have to share Phillip's quarters until they are dry."

Tim said he wouldn't mind and they crossed the spacious gallery and entered the house, which seemed as agreeable as it had promised to be. He noticed that the wall in which the door was set was perhaps eight feet thick. It was a key to the solidity of the structure. A middle-aged Negro woman met them in the hall, took Mrs. Froelich's furs, and told her mistress that coffee awaited them in the library.

The hall they had entered ran the entire width of the house, separating it into wings. It was of gray stone and black walnut paneling. But for the few shrewd touches, the most important being a solid wall of windows the width of the hall at the far end, it might have been gloomy. This ingenious device, Tim saw, extended from ground to roof of the mansion, admitting the bright morning sunlight that gave warmth and cheerfulness to the long cathedral-like interior. He studied the bank of windows with interest. It was a lacework of steel and small hand-blown panes of glass such as were used centuries ago. Each slightly curved pane gave the interior a splendid iridescent unreality that Tim was to find constantly shifting with each passing hour. No matter when he was to look at the windows, he was to see something unusual in color and pattern. It was a gigantic toy, designed to delight those who appreciate the wry and distorted in the world about them. There was a stairway before the windows, of plain gray stone without banister or ornament. It climbed half its length to a narrow entresol and then divided into two flights that climbed the rest of the way in opposite

237

directions along the walls. Down the center of the stairway and stretching to the main entrance was a burgundy rug. Along the hall itself high-backed chairs were spaced between the heavy walnut doors on either side. Once more the effect was somehow sarcastically impure, defying immediate judgment. Tim was beginning to appreciate this ancestor architect of Phillip's.

They entered the library to be met by the inviting odors of wood fire and coffee with chicory. It was a large carelessly furnished room and definitely gaudy. Paneled completely in walnut, carpeted with Saruk, its furnishings were worth a small fortune. There was a pair of magnificent breakfront bookcases filled with Meissen bric-a-brac and leather-bound volumes, a delicate Sheraton writing desk, buhl commodes holding crystal vases of buff and brown iris, and period chairs upholstered in velvet and Trapunto. Everything was very expensive, comfortable, and dusty. Tim smiled. The old peasant had not been able to contain himself after all. If this room was any indication of the rest of the house, he had splurged in the grandest manner.

"I had thought Phillip would be home by now," Mrs. Froelich said, pouring coffee from the ornate service before her, "since there are hours of work before everything is ready in town." She handed him his coffee.

Fan, her legs stretched comfortably toward the fire, had been quiet since they entered, but now she began to talk in a low intimate voice that seemed designed to set him right on certain points during his visit.

"You'll probably find us rather peculiar, Commander Danelaw," she said. "Everyone does. At first we may appear to be altogether feudal, concerned with ourselves and our town. But we don't worship ancestors, or money, any more than the average family." She gave him a slow smile. "Phillip is the fair-haired one here. Everyone expects him to follow in his grandfather's footsteps. We aren't aristocrats. We are aloof because the townspeople expect us to be so. We are their figurehead by circumstance and choice. It continues or ends with Phillip." Their eyes

238

met and Tim fancied he heard her saying: *Don't disrupt him from his schedule.* But she continued pleasantly enough, "That's Grandfather Dev there." She indicated the painting above the mantel. Tim studied it closely, surprised he had not noticed it before. The physical resemblance to Phillip was amazing. Here, Tim suspected, was the touchstone to Phillip's personality.

The technique of the artist wasn't bad, but the conception was fanciful. The brown hair curled low over the forehead; the eyes were almond-shaped and could never have slanted in such a manner in a Caucasian face. The lips and nostrils were chiseled too thin to be alive. Thus the whole face had the voluptuous decadence of an eighteenth-century court favorite. Yet conceivably the artist could have painted it so by design. Tim studied the long plump hands whose nails were oval and pointed. The effect was intentional, he decided.

"Who was the artist?" he asked.

"Some young unknown in Paris, wasn't it, Mother?"

"No. Uncle Felix said it was painted at Cannes after the war."

"Did you study in France?" Fanchon asked Tim.

"Italy. I didn't care for the impressionist schools." Tim looked at the women before him carefully. "However that was almost a decade ago. Now I can hardly call myself a painter since my interest has been in medical science for the past years. From the Navy I'm returning to Europe to take my degree."

This information brought the calculated reaction. There was noticeable approval on both faces, and Victoria went so far as to give a nod. To these practical people the arts were fine, but medicine—ah, there was something with a future for a man of ambition. Tim took still another step to set these proud ladies at ease, this time on the most important issue of all, finance.

"I'm surprised," he said, "that you haven't connected my name with our product. I believe it is sold in this part of the country."

For a moment they looked puzzled until Fanchon's face

239

brightened. "The Ale of Vikings." She smiled. "I knew the name was familiar."

Thus they were assured he had no designs on their money through Phillip. He knew that it was a necessary point to make. He could have let Phillip do it, but he preferred to do it himself.

Through the half-open windows, they heard a car crunch to a stop. "That must be Phillip now," Victoria said.

Tim rose and stood with his back to the fireplace. He was nervous. Phillip was sure to label his presence with ulterior motives, and he would be right. Tim felt Fanchon's sharp eyes on him. Silence fell over the room as they heard a step in the hall. The door opened wider and Phillip stood before them, his smile fleeing before his surprise.

22

♦•◇•◇•◇•◇•◇•

*H*e was wearing civilian clothes: a dark-green shirt, brown slacks and riding boots, and a soft suede jacket. He looked young and buoyant as if infinite change had taken place within him since he had left Seattle. At last he seemed to fit into a set of surroundings, Tim noted. This point had long been a source of annoyance. Always the boy moved free of everyone and everything with a pitiable elusiveness, as if he sensed he did not belong in the world of men. But here in his mansion—and it was his—he was at home.

Seeing Tim, Phillip involuntarily dropped his chin and looked at him with catlike indecision. For a moment Tim thought he would give their situation away, but the boy caught the eyes of the women on him. Immediately his smile returned as he came forward with his light step.

"Tim," he cried enthusiastically enough to deceive anyone, "this *is* a surprise. Welcome to Oklahoma!"

Phillip gave him his hand and grasped Tim's arm with the

other. While Tim repeated the story he had given the women as to why he was here, he marveled at the boy's knack for trickery. If his mother and sister were attentive to his conduct, they probably believed that Tim was Phillip's best friend, that he was the most welcome guest in the world at this moment. They chatted awhile and Phillip repeated his thanks for the extra days of leave.

Then, anticipating her son's desire to speak with his guest alone, Victoria said, "I've put Commander Danelaw in with you, Phillip, because of the baths. Would you show him your rooms?"

"Certainly," Phillip replied.

As they reached the door, Victoria said, "You might show him the rest of the house, Phillip. He has been admiring it. You'll have time before your father arrives."

But as the door closed behind them, Phillip's cordiality vanished and he demanded anxiously, "What's wrong in Seattle?"

"Nothing," Tim answered. "I left D.C. early to meet your family. That's all."

Phillip relaxed and studied him a moment. "Then you're welcome."

"Somehow," Tim smiled, "I thought I wouldn't be."

"On the contrary," Phillip said complacently. "You are in my territory now, Tim, and *I* make the rules here."

"My presence hasn't upset your plans then?"

"No. But I will have a deuce of a time explaining you to Fan. She's jumpy with curiosity over what's been going on in Seattle. I was hoping to escape her by leaving tonight. Now I'll have to face her before I had planned to. But," he added lightly, "I'll manage it." He glanced up and down the hall shimmering with color against shadow. "What will it be first, your room or the grand tour?"

"The tour, please," Tim said with exaggerated docility.

"Oh, come now," Phillip grinned, starting down the hall. "I'm not that formidable." He opened the first heavy door. "The

242

music room," he said, following Tim inside. "We have concerts here. I play the violin and piano in addition to a mean guitar." He made a little bow. "I've been boring audiences of select Oakies since I was seven. Tonight you'll see what I mean." He indicated a painting on the far wall. "An early Picasso. My grandfather bought it in Paris. The harp there and the piano came from France, too, by way of New Orleans. Grandfather Dev's wife played them. I suspect she was as boring a musician as I am. Francis venerates the old lady's memory. Fan and I are delighted that she expired before our time."

Tim gave the boy a quick glance and found the eyes dancing with mischief in his solemn face. They left the glitteringly gorgeous room.

"Father's study," Phillip explained, opening a door on a darkened musty room. "As gloomy as the head of the house himself, Fan says."

Tim did not care for his host's flippancy. It smacked of something a good deal more vicious than he wanted to find in Phillip. And suddenly he realized that Phillip was behaving so because he was ashamed. Undoubtedly he thought that Tim was laughing at all this ostentation.

"You know," Tim said, leaning comfortably against a door, "I'm beginning to suspect your grandfather of being a rare man."

"What do you mean?" Phillip asked cautiously.

"This house. Architecturally it's sound enough to last centuries, yet it has grace and perfect landscaping. It's rather unique."

"Do you like it?"

"I do. It has a personality that reflects the country and designer."

"I've always loved it," Phillip admitted shyly. "But then I've never had good taste in such things. Most people think it's heterogeneous."

"Perhaps," Tim said, "but then isn't the land it rests on, too?"

Phillip's satirical mood vanished and in showing the rest of the house, he was by turns reverent, clever, and jocular, but always sincere. Tim, congratulating himself at having averted possible unpleasantness, grew interested in the unfolding panorama of wealth and its strange effect on Phillip. It was plain to Tim now that the young man worshipped his grandfather as other men worship their gods. The boy could not utter three sentences in a row without mentioning him. It was apparent that before Phillip could progress, he must be freed of this self-imposed slavery. For the first time, Tim had a concrete glimpse of the problem he faced with the boy.

The tour continued—the great salon, the little salon, the guest dining room, the family dining room. The house was a showplace of French Provincial and Louis furniture, mirrors, chandeliers, carved plaster, brocade paneling, cabinets of ivory figurines inlaid with rich colored stones, and the delicate pastel shades of Meissen, spode, and Sèvres. There were broad mahogany surfaces that smoldered in the morning sun like beds of dying coals, and huge sideboards of ornate silver and etched crystal. Everywhere there were flowers—not a few, but quantities of them—filling the rooms with a dozen odors, simple or languorous. Everything seemed to have a story which Phillip related with a keen interest and quiet pride, revealing the cultural poverty of his own Puritan upbringing in this house of luxury. Tim was amazed at certain contrasts in the boy's life. From rooms containing several fortunes in the world's luxuries, he had gone to attend a public school. Arising from a meal served on a king's furnishings, he went into the fields to put in his day of grimy labor like the commonest hireling of his family. And Tim could only suspect the purpose behind the pattern that became clearer with every passing minute. For the second time, Tim looked deep into Phillip's past, this time seeing clearly the sources of his pride, bitterness, thwarted dreams, and consuming ambitions; and in understanding him, Tim was drawn to him more than ever.

Phillip took him into the kitchen to inspect the great wood-burning range, explained that the family preferred the flavor of food prepared over pungent hickory fires. And while they were there, Phillip formally introduced him to Goldie and Oliver. As they were leaving, Phillip stuck his finger into the mixing bowl Goldie held in the crook of her arm. She smacked him on the bottom before he could get out the door.

They strolled out on the wide stone gallery, sheltered and warm in the full sunshine, where an outdoor table of wrought iron and glass was already being set for lunch by a young colored girl who looked up and smiled as they went by. The temperature must have risen ten degrees in the past hour, Tim noticed, and Phillip explained that once the southern sun got over the mountains, the valley caught and held the heat, but that when the sun set, cold air poured down from the hills, making the nights pleasant. At last the conversation turned to Phillip's reason for returning.

"I take it your defense is ready," Tim said.

Phillip smiled. "The first nasty rumor and Madame is a very dead duck."

"What did you invent for your family?"

"I talked only with Mother. She told Fan and will tell Father if that becomes necessary. I explained about the court martial, since Madame and Francis will tell that, but I gave Captain Pratt's loss of command as the reason I escaped it. About this other business, I first explained why both Madame and Bruner have cause to hate me. Then I concocted this story: after arriving at the base, I found I was sharing a room with a man suspected of homosexuality. Bruner, a blackmailer, may try to extort money from me. Madame, angry because I won't marry Sybel Jo immediately, might try to discredit me in favor of my cousin. So, if a situation arises here, the lewdest possible stories will circulate about Madame and Morgan. At the same time everyone will mysteriously learn that Sybel Jo is pregnant by an unknown man and that she was rushed to Seattle in an attempt to rope

245

me. All this comes out, of course, only if I do not marry the girl. Monstrous, isn't it?" Phillip asked coldly.

Tim shrugged at his bravado. "But isn't your story a bit fictitious to be believed?"

"Yes and no. Mother and the town will believe it; Mother because she prefers it to the truth, the town because they dislike Madame and think of us as next to the Almighty. But Fanchon will have the truth eventually. Not that I mind that, for Fan and I love each other. The important thing right now is that I didn't mention the name *Danelaw*. And now that you are here, that is real fortune."

"But why didn't you?"

"I don't know," Phillip said slowly. "Gratitude perhaps or—"

"Or what?"

"Or what happened in San Francisco," Phillip forced himself to say. He pulled a leaf of ivy and bit off its stem. Then studying the bit of green with elaborate interest, he said, "There is something between us now, something that has to be talked out and decided upon. I thought it could be ignored. It can't. Part of my brain tells me one thing, another part tells me another. I hesitate to do or say anything until I'm straight." He paused and looked up at Tim. "I know you came down here expecting to find me in a nasty jam with my family. I suppose you felt responsible for me and were prepared to give me still more assistance. I won't ignore that as I won't ignore your kindness in the past. I will make restitution if you'll tell me how—that is, in any way but one. I'm glad you're here, Tim. You'll understand me better and I'll have a chance to talk to you from the dominant position. We will reach a decision. And Fan will come to know you so that when I tell her the truth one day she may understand my actions the better. But now, sometime within the next two days, we will talk. Needless to say, any ambiguous action on your part in this house will do your argument unlimited harm." Briefly Phillip's eyes grew unyielding. "The episode in San Francisco will not be repeated, no matter what either of

246

us may want in a thoughtless moment. We will confine ourselves to reason, not emotion. Is that agreeable?"

"Quite," Tim answered. "Your honesty is commendable. As always, I shall respect your desires."

Phillip turned to open a doorway nearby. "This is the conservatory. My grandfather was a fancier of flowers. So are Mother and Father. Fan and I will be, too, when we turn fifty, I suppose."

Tim walked into the hot glass house and watched Phillip slide the glass walls one behind the other until the room was completely open to the garden outside. Then the boy slid the glassed roof back by pressing buttons on a panel near the door.

"Those are camellias there," he said, indicating several trees. "Gardenias over there. Here are the orchids."

They approached a large glass case in the center of the room which was equipped with heat bulbs, a ventilating and a sprinkling system. Phillip checked the thermometer and turned out several of the lights. Inside the huge case among rich green ferns, several hundred plants were attached to upright rotting tree trunks or arranged in pots on the shelves around the case. Many were in blossom, ranging from pure white through all the yellows, reds, purples, and mauves to something very near black. There were single flowers the size of a man's two hands that seemed to have faces, and there were delicate sprays of many blossoms, looking like a swarm of butterflies as they moved in the slight breeze created by fans inside.

"It's like something out of Wilde's weirdest passages, isn't it? As Fan says, all it needs is a corpse sticking out of an ant hill, or a sex-crazed cobra." The two men glanced at each other and smiled.

"It does have an atmosphere," Tim agreed.

Phillip opened the door and stepped inside the case to turn a plant so that the blossom might be seen better. The stench of mold and jungle crept out and Tim wrinkled his nose with distaste.

247

"Grandfather developed this one himself from parent plants from the Malays and Panama." He touched the flower with its magenta petals and welted brown lip. "Ugly little beast, isn't it?"

He closed the case and they turned away, Phillip leading the way out of the greenhouse. The terraced gardens rolled gently down to a girdle of trees under the hill. Phillip paused. "There are acres of them and I suppose I've crawled over every inch at least a dozen times. That's how my father spent my leisure time. I guess that's why I have so little use for flowers now." Phillip laughed suddenly. "I used to wish that a blight would descend, killing every plant within a radius of a mile. I'd really have had a job if that had happened. Actually I should be ashamed; the gardens were Grandfather's pride.

"We keep them just as he kept them and observe the customs he started. Flowers to all churches Sunday morning, the hospitals on Monday and Friday, all civic organizations, clubs, homes having sickness or death—as needed. They're distributed through the newspaper facilities which we own, too. Before the war, we kept three gardeners. Now, Mother tells me that we've been giving the boys from Lakecliff a chance to earn some extra money. Lakecliff is a farm home for orphaned boys founded by Grandfather. It's still our private charity, though now it earns its keep.

"Over there," Phillip said, "past the trees, is the prize pasture, as we call it. Our best animals from all the farms are turned in there a few weeks prior to showtime for grooming. The barn is across the creek in the trees. Down there the creek is dammed for swimming. Uncle Felix and Grandfather put up the diving board when I was four. That's why I swim well today."

Tim looked at the wide, curving dam and sparkling water between the steep breasts of hills. "Am I to meet your Uncle Felix?" he asked.

"Oh, yes. Tonight. He and Aunt Minna will probably devour you when they learn you speak German," Phillip smiled. "Today they're in Dallas, purchasing new evening clothes as a surprise for my birthday celebration. Has Mother explained the party?"

248

Tim nodded. "With Madame out of town, she thought this would be an excellent time. You'll meet Sybel Jo's father, too, but not Francis' parents. They are in New York."

They were quiet for a few minutes, standing in the colorful, cloying, strength-sapping heat, listening to the sound of bees in the flowers. Tim was no stranger to wealth, but all this staggered him when he thought of the innumerable ties between this family and their people in their city a few miles away, ties that Phillip might inherit, wanted to inherit. It was like an ancient duchy, Phillip being the heir apparent to a royal household. Tonight there would be springtime feasting and moonlight dancing in the village square to celebrate the young prince's coming of age. He thought of other American reigning families and their desire to withdraw to those rarefied circles of society and influence. This family did the opposite, plunging their heir into the middle of their subjects to gain favor. And in so doing, they stifled Phillip's personal life. Through uncertainty, they fostered in him ruthless ambition. They had taught him decency and deceit, tolerance and intolerance—many virtues that had corresponding vices. It was no wonder the boy seemed a model of duplicity, fit for no setting but this, at sword's point with everyone including himself, displaying evidences of shrewd discipline and flagrant willfulness, pagan luxury and earthy simplicity, wisdom and naïveté—all at the same time. The boy's teachers must have been a pack of raging beasts, tearing at each other for the choice bits of his brain.

Tim's eyes fell on a strange cagelike enclosure of concrete and iron bars half-hidden in the lower part of the garden. "What is that?"

"A cage for big cats," Phillip said, smiling uneasily.

"Do you mean lions and tigers?"

"You've heard of the eccentricities of the new rich. That's ours. Once it held three full-grown cheetahs. It's quite a story. Uncle Felix told it to me. I don't suppose you'd like to hear it?"

"You're joking, of course."

249

"Very well," Phillip said warmly, "here it is. Grandfather Dev spent much of his life in France and Germany from the time of his wife's death until Uncle Felix and his sister came here from Berlin. My Grandfather was an exceedingly handsome man, rich and a colorful American. He must have been very popular over there. But he excited envy as well as admiration. In this instance it was a young titled Englishman living in Paris at the time. He hated my grandfather, who was then only thirty-five or forty. He went out of his way to insult him, but always my grandfather deferred before him with beautiful courtesy. Then one evening in a fashionable salon where a famous scientist was being entertained, the young noble, finding Grandfather Dev in a group listening to the scientist, closed in, intent on making his elder ridiculous. The subject was hunting. The young man asked Grandfather Dev what game was to be found in Oklahoma in addition to peasants. This got a laugh, but Grandfather replied seriously that there were still a few buffalo, many deer, and some vicious wolves and cougars to be found in the mountains. Most plentiful, he said, were the jackrabbits. He used the English term and the young dandy translated it rather freely to everyone's amusement, though most of the crowd was in sympathy with the American. Then Grandfather explained that the jackrabbit was so fleet that greyhounds could not catch him, to which the Englishman replied that the hounds of America must be clumsy beasts indeed—as was everything else there. Whereupon my grandfather, with the sweetest smile in the world, replied that even if the hounds had been twice as facile as the young man's wit, they would have found themselves easily outdistanced. The barb was so unexpected, so cleverly delivered, that its effect was devastating. The story flashed over the crowd and the young Englishman found himself with the embarrassing sobriquet Le Jackrabbit. He was a laughingstock. But my grandfather was a kind man, too. He took the fellow under his wing during the following weeks, protecting him until the unflattering implications were forgotten. They became

250

friends. Much later the Englishman, while he was traveling in Africa, sent my grandfather a pair of cheetah cubs, the supposition being that the animals were swift enough to catch even the Oklahoma jackrabbit. The male died just before the female littered. They were quite tame and were allowed the freedom of the house. Mother remembers them well. But they screamed all night during mating season; so they were presented to a zoo."

Tim noticed the boy's animation while he told the story. Suddenly Phillip added with the swift, intense sadness of a disappointed youngster, "If Grandfather Dev had lived, my life would have been different—London, Paris, Naples, Greece, interesting people, brilliant conversation, a life with significance instead of . . ." But he caught himself in time and dropped his eyes guiltily. "Shall we go upstairs and wash for lunch? It's time for Father and Paul."

Tim nodded and they re-entered the house to climb the stone stairway before the sheer cliff of windows to the second floor.

23

◆◆◆◆◆◆

These were Grandfather's rooms," Phillip said, opening the door set deep in the spinal wall. "When I graduated from the nursery, they were given to me."

The first room, a sitting room-study, was furnished with uncluttered elegance in mahogany, impersonal gray and a brooding sage-green. It looked as though it were seldom used. The bedroom, however, was the most cheerful room Tim had seen in the house. A long low-ceilinged room with many sets of French windows standing open on a sunroof atop the first floor gallery, it was clean and inviting, a room of men who loved peaceful leisure. There was a hooked rug down the center and a fireplace at the far end. Overhead, two wide but shallow chandeliers of wrought iron and ropes of brilliants glittered dimly. Over the fireplace there was a framed dark parchment map of sixteenth-century Paris. The furniture, of mahogany again, consisted of a huge sleigh-footed bed, a serpentined-front bureau, bookcases, desk, tables, and chairs. The curtains were of thin beige silk. The walls were blue. On the whole it was comfortable, unobtrusive, retaining minor touches of the two personalities that had occupied it.

On the table there was an elaborately carved model of a Greek trireme, complete with oars. It was mounted on a block of unfinished walnut that bore the simple legend: "Phillip 1933." The mantel held three miniature replicas of famous Greek statues. In the center were the Laocoön group, on either side the Discobolus and Praxiteles' Hermes with the Infant Dionysus. On the wall were two nests of small framed photographs, each group four wide and three deep. The first were views of the Parthenon friezes; the other set, scenes from vases, entitled: "Ajax Defending the Greek Ships," "Polydamus Advising Hector To Retire from the Trench," "The Fight for the Body of Patroclus," and so on.

Phillip, going into the bath, said, "Your clothes will be in the left side of the bureau. If most of them are missing, don't be alarmed. Goldie probably carried them off to launder. She considers that her part in the current war effort."

As the door closed, Tim smiled and crossed the room to examine the trivia atop the small bookcase that evidently held Phillip's favorite volumes. First, there were two silver cups and several dozen red and blue ribbons. In the center Tim saw a framed slick photograph with a yellowed clipping in its corner. He picked it up and read: "Oklahoma Entry Wins Best Horse and Rider Event. Phillip Eugene Froelich, fourteen-year-old owner and rider of My Little Pelops, upset several traditions in Southwestern horse show annals last night when he displayed his thoroughbred golden palomino stallion before a record crowd of seven thousand spectators. Pitted against riders of twice his years and experience, the lad captivated . . ." Tim glanced at the figure proudly astride the horse. He wore dark riding clothes and carried his head disdainfully high. He had changed little in ten years.

Tim set the photograph down and looked at the well-worn books: Gibran, Santyana, Butler, Cather, Mann, Dostoievsky,

Schopenhauer, Emerson, Proust, Nietzsche, and, between a book entitled simply *Finance* and a complete Shakespeare, two novels by Gypsy Rose Lee: *The G-String Murders* and *Mother Finds a Body*. Tim chuckled, thinking of the company writers keep in the minds of their readers. Then there were a dozen volumes of ancient history, a book on horse breeding, a text copy of the *Aeneid* in Latin, a French dictionary, and a dilapidated Bible.

Phillip, returning from the bath, said, "Here, here, you'll embarrass me."

"By their libraries shall ye know them," Tim returned. He changed his shirt while Phillip put on a tie and a brown tweed coat. They went downstairs to meet the rest of the family before lunch.

There were six men in the library: Phillip's father, his brother-in-law, Sybel Jo's father, two representatives of the State Bankers' Association, and a young man with delft blue eyes, a yellow mustache, and a major's uniform. Phillip shook hands with all of them before presenting his guest. To Phillip's chagrin, the young man turned out to be a fraternity brother. They had lived in the same house for six semesters, yet Phillip had not recognized him. As Tim was presented, he was struck again by the hospitable friendliness of these people with their firm handclasps and Texas twangs.

He looked closely at Joe Voth, understanding some of Madame's restlessness the better. The man was emaciated, listless, sad-eyed. Phillip was particularly attentive to him.

Paul Cully, Fan's husband, was a personable, quick-witted man of forty. He had been a serious young student at M. I. T. when Fan had met him at a party in Boston fifteen years before. He hadn't wanted to like her particularly, but he had found her damnably attractive. He had had ambitions, but Fanchon had been without scruples. She had run him down, robbed him of his ambitions, and carried him bodily back to Oklahoma to sire her children. He worshipped her shamelessly and she returned his love wisely and well. They were very happy.

254

They had had two sons. Young Paul-Phillip, who was five, they watched with the zeal of parent eagles, Phillip had said, as their first child had died of whooping cough. It was soon evident to Tim that Paul Cully hated Oklahoma, that he still dreamed of New England and building ships. But now he was a first vice-president of a bank. It was apparent, too, that only a woman such as Fanchon could have kept him in this present state of unhappy happiness for so long. Though the man did not realize it, he had many qualities in common with his father-in-law, not the least of which were the women they had married, Tim thought.

The left side of Julius Froelich's face was slick with scar tissue —the result of an accident in the early oil fields. Yet it was not unattractive; rather it gave him the appearance of adventurousness, concealing the shallows of his intellect and the depths of his hypocrisy. He was a great, florid man of large gestures and small words that invariably referred to "God" and "man's decency," two subjects of which he knew absolutely nothing.

Julius had come out from the Pennsylvania coal mines at the turn of the century and had never returned to visit the numerous German Lutheran family of which he had been a part. If Phillip had uncles and cousins from this source, he did not know it, nor want to know it. Julius presumed that his parents believed him dead, and that made him happy. He did not remember them in a haze of sentiment, but with a terrifying grasp of their bestial poverty and cruelty. He remembered a father who whipped him with a hose and a mother whose favorite punishment for her many children was to make them kneel on shelled corn for hours and pray. Julius had kept his vow to forget his meager dirty beginnings.

In Devereaux he had first attracted the attention of Old Phillip when he had come into the bank to borrow enough money to purchase a wildcat drilling company. The loan had been negotiated at a suprisingly low interest rate for a boom town, but

255

despite this advantage, Old Phillip had been forced to foreclose to secure his money. Then the banker had done a strange thing. He had hired Julius to operate the drilling outfit, giving him a small share in the venture and a generous salary. The partnership had immediately shown profit under the banker's guidance and the laborer's execution, and Julius had started bossing other outfits for the bank. He made a few good investments at Old Phillip's advice. He was often asked to dine with the man in the fine new mansion which he inhabited alone now that his wife was dead and his two daughters were being educated in England. There was no explanation for the banker's consideraation for the uncouth young nobody with the angry red scar on his face. Julius was beginning to believe that the world was a fine place after all, when the daughters arrived home from Europe.

Abruptly the invitations to dine ceased. Only the elite were entertained in the mansion now. Because of his background, Julius had never approved of the ostentatious way of life he saw in the great house, but still he felt the insult keenly. In a few months, Marie, the older daughter, was married to the heir of the Barriman fortunes, and the couple went honeymooning to Europe. The town expected Victoria to announce her engagement, too, despite her apparent fondness for hanging around the bank and tagging her father over his farms and leases, but the town waited in vain.

Then one day when Julius stopped at the bank, he met the girl in her father's office. It was a sweltering afternoon and she had removed her coat to help her father with the books. Julius noticed the queer look she had shot her father. He noticed, too, the slight nod in return, but Julius had been too interested in Victoria's pink, plump flesh beneath the sheer stuff of her shirtwaist to give the silent communication any thought. Victoria was a very lovely woman with the high color of a summer rose, he thought poetically. She was friendly, too, inviting him to drive out to the house for iced tea. But Julius refused. He was sensitive about his disfigured face, and he felt oafish with his dirty clothes and crude manners.

A year later he had felt oafish again when he took Victoria Eugenie to wife before the disapproving society of the town. He learned later that the two sisters had had a scene in the Barriman home. Marie had declared herself outraged, it seemed, but she had been incoherent a moment later when Victoria with some candor had called her an ill-natured slut with priggish convictions and had walked out of the house.

Victoria and Julius went honeymooning in the bank. As a married woman, Victoria used her new freedom to the family's advantage. Many important things were happening at the bank —events Julius could not then pretend to grasp. Very quietly most of the Devereaux oil holdings were being sold. Old Phillip, with peasant cunning, was getting out while the structure of easy riches was intact. And just as quietly, with real foresight, the money was going into choice farms. Barrels of production were being converted into acres of production; feet of pipe were becoming head of cattle over the state and in Texas.

Too late Julius began to guess what had happened. Instead of a wife, he had taken a new employer, but a wonderful employer, he thought philosophically. Victoria loved him. Constantly she proved it in the most wanton manner. She held him up as a paragon to the public. She was demure in his presence. She praised his judgment, her own remaining like iron. Eleven months later she bore him a child, and secretly wept that it was not a son. Julius was overjoyed, but then he had never heard of the word *dynasty*.

Old Phillip made a trial trip to Europe, leaving Julius in charge of the bank. Victoria, by means of the most tactful suggestions in the world, kept the course straight and true. In three months Old Phillip was home, his eyes glinting with satisfaction as he praised his son-in-law's cautious nature, his ability to weigh and evaluate fact, to Julius' pleased bewilderment. In their bed that night, Victoria had kissed him many times, murmuring

257

against his throat that she had known he could do it. And Old Phillip had returned to Europe to stay three years, writing Julius detailed business letters, hardly bothering to answer the secret ones his daughter mailed him every Sunday night.

By the early twenties the Devereaux County oil boom was over. Old Phillip had retired for good, and business was as usual. A new figure had entered the scene. Felix Mehl, accompanied by his sister Minna, settled in the little city to take over one-third of the Old Man's wealth—to inherit on equal terms with each of the daughters. The only explanation was that Felix and Phillip were old friends. That was sufficient cause for such generosity. Once more Marie was outraged, Victoria pleased, and Julius bewildered.

Julius became president of the bank. Tony Barriman, his family fortune rapidly dwindling with the end of oil, was a vice-president hardly ever consulted. Victoria stayed at home these days with her infant son. Bank policy was settled for decades to come. The monies were soundly invested. With tender care they would grow slowly but uniformly. And without understanding why, Julius heard a good many sighs of contentment these days. The long, good life had begun for everyone but him. He still dreamed of amassing a great fortune. And why shouldn't he? He was as poor as the day he left the state of Pennsylvania.

Shrewdly Tim Danelaw looked from the stern solidity of Julius to the gentle face of Victoria and guessed the roles they had exchanged. These were Phillip's parents. He looked at the boy talking with Joe Voth and he looked at the portrait over the mantel, the almond eyes smiling down on the assemblage, and suddenly Tim knew that there was one present who would understand his love for Phillip.

"You may ring for Goldie to announce lunch, Victoria." Julius nodded imperiously. Everyone knew he ruled his house with an iron hand.

"Yes, Julius," Victoria answered dutifully. Everyone said she

258

was rather scatterbrained, as so often the wives of important men are.

Luncheon was announced and the family and guests moved out to the table overlooking the sunny gardens. They were seated, but before one snowy napkin was touched, all heads were bowed, and in his finest baritone Julius told his God that a blessing would be received upon this table, the more bountiful, the more appreciated. Tim stifled a smile and bowed his head with the others. At the "Amen," he saw that Phillip gave him an uncomfortable glance and quickly averted his eyes. Once more Tim had the impression that Phillip longed to make excuses for his family, but was too loyal to do so. Across the table, Fanchon looked boldly at him, a condescending smile for her father's customs hovering about her pretty coral lips. Paul Cully's amused eyes sought his, too, but Tim gave no answering sign of recognition or amusement. If he did, and Phillip saw it, it might do irreparable damage. So he talked solemnly with Victoria on his left.

Goldie, who had stood in the doorway with her head bowed during grace, carried a tureen of soup to Julius and he ladled it into the bowls Oliver brought him. The two servants worked with the co-ordination that comes from long experience.

From the first mouthful, Tim recognized the house for what it was. Despite the lavish, effete glitter of its many rooms, the kitchen rested solidly on earth and tradition, serving a great variety of plain, delicious food to be eaten for enjoyment as well as nourishment. It was no wonder that Phillip could dine like a glutton and drink rye highballs with ice cream, as Tim had seen him do once in Seattle, with no ill effects. With a lifetime of food such as this behind him, he had a right to the digestion of a horse, as Mike had so aptly put it. There was a baked fish, dove in casserole, cold rolled beef with vegetables—all blandly seasoned and prepared with care—steaming freshly baked breads (Tim began to understand the preference for wood fires), tall

259

glasses of milk, and finally chilled fruit in thick syrup with whipped cream.

There was a good deal of noisy talk about the table, and they all ate like famished adolescents. Yet Tim sensed in Phillip an embarrassment for all this, and he determined to say something to put the boy at ease at the first opportunity. It was nonsense for Phillip to compare his home with the menagerie that Pat kept in Seattle, yet Tim was sure that this was taking place in Phillip's mind.

Julius was saying, "Phillip, I'll want you at the bank until three."

"Yes, sir," Phillip replied quietly.

"But, Julius, you said I could have him all afternoon."

"I didn't have him all morning," Julius argued with his wife.

"Really, Julius," Victoria persisted gently. "He wants to show Commander Danelaw something of Oklahoma."

"Yes, of course," Julius said indifferently.

"Commander Danelaw is secretary to Phillip's admiral," she went on wisely. "Phillip works directly under him."

As the significance of this hit the man, he turned his heavy head toward Tim and rested large eyes on him. "I'm sure that what I had in mind can wait. By all means Phillip must show you around."

Since Julius looked as if he were going to make himself more ridiculous, his wife said hastily, "Phillip has already shown him the house." And to Tim she said, "My father's tastes were rather ornate. He was, in fact, something of a collector."

But before Tim could reply, Phillip put in drily, "We live in constant terror of an agent from Gimbels descending on us."

Fanchon and Paul laughed at his sally, but Julius demanded, "What has Gimbels to do with us?"

"Nothing," Victoria soothed. "Phillip was being witty."

"Oh."

So Victoria started giving instructions to Phillip and Fanchon concerning the afternoon's preparations for the party. Phillip

260

was to haul flowers in the pick-up, Fanchon linen and vases in the car. Tim learned that the Hotel Devereaunian, equipped as it was, was not up to catering to the Froelichs in a party mood. They would all meet with the chef and stewards at three-fifteen to check final plans. More than once, urged on by Fanchon's teasing glances, Tim was tempted to smile discreetly. But the thought of Phillip's acute humiliation stopped him.

As they left the table, Phillip asked, "When will Uncle Felix and Aunt Minna be home?"

"In time for dinner tonight," Fanchon said. "And don't you forget to admire their new clothes."

"Oh, I'll remember," Phillip said, giving Tim an oblique glance.

Tim spent the entire afternoon in his shirt sleeves driving a light Dodge truck between house and hotel, carrying crates of flowers, baskets, pottery, trellises, and even a waxing machine. This arrangement left Phillip free to stay in town and work with his mother and sister. Victoria was grateful to Tim in a motherly way, and Fanchon grew very friendly. Phillip, away from his father, relaxed again and started to clown. A stream of people came and went all afternoon to offer Phillip a premature "Welcome home and happy birthday!" Tim met them all between trips, learned their positions and connections with the family. The afternoon became a party of its own over cokes and coffee that were added to the Froelich bill. It was something of a shock to Tim to realize to what extent these good people accepted him on no other grounds than the fact that he was a guest of the family. He began to realize why Phillip was willing to marry a woman he did not love, why he could ruin a woman like Madame despite anything he did. As he felt these influences about him, doubts of his own motives grew. He questioned his right to interfere in Phillip's life.

At six-thirty Phillip found him and said, "We've delivered the last damn gladiola. Let's get out of here."

261

Tim drove the truck back to the house while Phillip relaxed in the seat beside him. "Perhaps you see what I'm fighting for now," he said.

"I think so."

"Do you think it's worth it?"

"Do you?"

"I'm beginning to wonder. Once I thought all this was everything I wanted. Now, well, it's pretty dull, isn't it?"

"It's predictable. And there are a million young men in the world who'd give anything for your life just as it stands."

"I suppose," Phillip said despondently. Then he brightened. "How about a swim instead of a shower before we dress?"

"Fine," Tim agreed, amused at Phillip's desire to evade issues.

At the house they got towels and started down the hill to the dam. They took no suits. "Father isn't around. No one else cares."

Phillip skinned out of his clothes in seconds and ran out on the diving board shouting boyishly, "Hey, Tim, watch this perfectly jolly-elegant back flip!" His sleek young body left the board, turning in a slow arc so that the setting sun flashed against the white saddle mark that broke his tanned body before it disappeared into the dark mirrored surface, throwing up a little fountain of bubbles. He appeared half a minute later, far out, his head and arms shining with water. He swam back frog-fashion. Tim watched him for a moment and then dove into the clear warm water. He stayed below until his lungs started aching; then he shot up powerfully for air. But Phillip, who had followed him on the surface, pounced as he broke the water, sending him down again with a shove of his feet on Tim's shoulders. When Tim came up, Phillip was streaking for the ladder on the dam. Tim overtook him easily and held him under for several seconds with some difficulty, for he was slippery as an otter. He tried to lock him with his legs but the boy pulled him under. They came up wrestling and shouting. Phillip's coltish antics were infectious. Suddenly Tim realized that several years

262

and much dignity had slipped from him. They were a pair of boys romping together, and Tim became aware of yet another thing: Phillip's past life had been as destitute as his own of companionship. Reluctantly they climbed out of the water at last and stood on the board toweling themselves dry, rubbing each other's backs by turn.

"My last fling, Tim," he said with a mixture of regret and cynicism. "After dinner I will have to be a man."

"Just like that?" Tim smiled.

"Just like that. Twenty-first birthday, and bang! I bloom out in calm and dignity. Or so father says."

They dressed and walked up the hill. Already the air was cool again. A breeze had sprung up from the mountains, bringing down the faint scent of pine and earth, mingling with the first cutting of alfalfa curing in the field underfoot. In the distance a cow bawled persistently for a few seconds and then was silent.

Moved by the pastoral beauty about him and by Phillip at his side, Tim said, "It has been a good day, Phillip. I want you to know that."

Their eyes met in complete accord.

"For me, too, Tim," Phillip answered. Then he looked away. "Tim . . ."

"Yes?"

"About Father at lunch—oh, to hell with it! I'm tired of making excuses!" They walked the rest of the way in silence.

24

◆•◇•◆•◇•◆•◇•◆•◇+

hey found their white uniforms, freshly pressed, laid out on the bed and their shoes, a frosty white, nearby.

"We'll probably freeze," Phillip said uncertainly, "but Mother wants to show us off in all our military glory. Do you mind, Tim?"

"Not at all."

They shaved and dressed, and as Phillip helped Tim with his aiguillettes, he glanced up at the man's image in the mirror before them.

"You know," he said thoughtfully, "you're very handsome."

"Meaning what?" Tim asked with amusement.

"I don't know," Phillip said slowly. "I think it just occurred to me. That's bad, isn't it?"

"You're a child, Phillip. Forget it." Tim laughed and glanced at his watch. "We'd better go downstairs."

"Sure." But Phillip's eyes revealed that his mind was far away.

They went below and at the open door of the large salon,

264

Phillip murmured, "Oh, oh, everyone's here; we're late and Father's furious."

As the others saw them and turned to greet them, Phillip went forward, smiling to his godparents.

"Uncle Felix, Aunt Minna, how lovely you are tonight!" His voice carried the tone he might have used to address children. He took them both in his arms at once and kissed them on the lips. The old couple were foolishly delighted at his extravagant compliments.

Felix Mehl had the kindly dignity of a very old king in his new evening clothes, with his thick, white, curly hair and still broad shoulders. He had the look of a man who has lived his life, settled his affairs in this world, and now awaits the last episode with patience. Tim smiled as Phillip had the old man turn around so he could admire the fit of his new clothes in the back. They examined the material together, discussed the price as if it was the most important topic in the world. They finished their comments in a leisurely manner and turned to give their attention to Minna, who began to model her gown for them with quaint, old-world coquettishness.

In remaining a spinster, Aunt Minna had espoused the whole world and spent her hours mothering everything in it shamelessly. She was a tiny creature with the bright expression of one of those exceedingly rare people who pray to God for what they want and who see their prayers answered. So she spread her fan and held her train to the side while she paraded sedately before her enchanted audience. The gown was of stiff pearl-gray silk with an elaborate pleated frill at the throat, wrists, and from the front of the skirt over the hips and down the train. In an accent that was still noticeable, she complained of this feature, telling Phillip that she was afraid to sit down for fear of crushing her —her— She stopped, groping for the English word.

"Your dorsal fin, Aunt Minna?" Phillip said, concealing his grin.

"Dorsal fin?" the old lady repeated in her bewildered tone as

265

the others laughed. When Phillip explained the term to her, she gave a little scream of laughter and said to her brother, "You hear, Felix? He thinks I'm a moor-maid!"

"Oh, much better than a mermaid," Phillip insisted. "A Lorelei."

She continued to laugh as she slapped him playfully on the cheek with her fan. Then Phillip, his hand on Tim's arm, brought his guest and presented him proudly to the couple. They beamed on him and took his hands and kept them as they spoke to him in German. It was evident that he had been discussed before he appeared. And when he answered them in their tongue, their delight was overwhelming. They asked him many questions, anxious to know his status and connection with their godson, for any friend of Phillip's must have a place of importance in their lives. It was a quarter of an hour before Tim greeted the rest of the family and met Phillip's five-year-old nephew who grasped his hand in wide-eyed excitement over his first dinner party. Paul-Phillip was a white sickly looking child, but possessed of the quick interest and intelligence of a sensitive nature. He asked his uncle later if there would be a hundred candles on the cake, to which Phillip threw back his head and laughed, "You put him up to saying that, Fan."

Again Tim felt himself a part of this family—friendly, natural people who ignored ceremony completely. They were noisy, they chatted with Oliver and Goldie when they were in the room, they gossiped, they criticized each other with a frankness that verged on tactlessness, and above all they made Tim feel that each of them wanted him to share in this important occasion. Tim, whose past was barren of such family life, was moved. They went in to dinner, young Paul-Phillip riding on his uncle's shoulders.

The table was decorated for the occasion with white roses. In the brilliantly lighted room it floated like a cold white and silver jewel, with its gleaming satin damask, bone china, ice-like crystal, and carved silver against the dark surrounding walls. Fan-

266

chon, standing next to Tim, took one look at the table and her smile died. Uneasily she looked at her mother and whispered, "Mother, wine?"

Victoria smiled nervously. At the same time Julius Froelich's outraged voice came from the other end of the room. "Victoria! Is this wine on *my* table?"

"Why yes, Julius. It was some of Father's. I thought he would have wanted Phillip to have it tonight to celebrate."

"This *is* a dry state," Julius thundered. "Wine will not be served in my home!"

The silence of the room beat against Tim's ears. On his arm Fanchon's hand had become a small hard fist. For an instant he saw the fire of murderous hatred flash in Victoria's eyes. Paul Cully looked foolish. Minna Mehl's lips were working as if she longed to explain everything to everyone's satisfaction. Felix stood stiff and pale. And Phillip, who had been seating his nephew on a stack of books in a chair, looked crushed. At last Victoria's voice broke the silence serenely, and in that moment Tim knew that the lady respected the rights of her puppet husband.

"I'm sorry, Julius," she said calmly, and turning to the servants, she instructed, "You may remove the glasses."

"And pour that stuff down the drain!" Julius added loudly.

No one was seated until the last wine glass was removed. Phillip's dinner party had become a wake despite the company's attempts to recapture their former gaiety. As they ate, each guest fell into spasmodic silences. The atmosphere cleared slowly, and toward the end of the meal Tim heard Phillip laugh at something his Aunt Minna said.

At last the lights were turned out and from the kitchen Goldie wheeled in her masterpiece, a great white cake of three tiers, covered with sugar scrolls, flowers, birds, and lighted candles. Amid much laughter, young Paul-Phillip gave one long gasp of disbelief and was prevented from toppling off his precarious perch only by his uncle's restraining hands. Phillip picked the youngster up by the middle and held him over the cake to help blow out the candles. They put their heads together and puffed at the flames, but the effort was too much for the little boy. To everyone's amusement, he slobbered generously over the top and side of the structure.

"You may give me that piece, Goldie," Phillip said, "because I'm going to eat this fellow anyway!" And Phillip sent the child into a delicious spasm of laughter by gnawing at the nearest ear. At last the incident of the wine seemed forgotten.

Later Goldie brought in a small tray of envelopes and boxes, Phillip's coming-of-age gifts from the family. He went to the sideboard to open them under the family's eyes.

The first and largest was from Oliver and Goldie, a leather-framed photograph of them in self-conscious finery. Phillip held it up for all to see. No one smiled and there were exclamations of "How nice!" "It's very good, isn't it?" The two servants were watching in the doorway, and Phillip went over and thanked them warmly. From his mother's envelope he then took her check for three thousand dollars to purchase his first plane. Phillip kissed her dutifully. The next box held a complete set of evening studs and links of light and dark pearls from Tiffany's. These were from Fan and Paul.

His father's envelope contained a legal-looking document which Phillip looked over carefully before saying quietly, "The first mortgage on the old Albertson home and furnishings on Eleventh Street. It falls due in November of this year. Thank you, sir." They shook hands, Julius standing for the ceremony.

"I thought you and Sybel Jo might want to live in town awhile."

"Of course, that's very considerate of you," Phillip replied.

Another box contained a wrist watch, a hopelessly expensive gadget of platinum and diamond numerals. Pinned to the lining of the box was a simple religious medal on a silver chain. This, of course, was from Aunt Minna. She helped him strap

268

the watch on and then asked eagerly, "Would you wear the medal, too, Phillip? I had it blessed specially."

"Certainly, *chérie*," he whispered, and bent his head so that she could fasten the chain about his neck and tuck it inside his tight collar. Tim, glancing at the head of the table, was surprised at the livid hatred on the face of Julius Froelich. It was the final key he needed to the man's character.

Phillip took from the tray the last flat package, and his Uncle Felix rose to say to the table, "I must ask your indulgence, and yours, Phillip, in this matter. My gift is the least valuable of all as the world values things, but to Phillip it may mean much. My gift is some of your grandfather's personal correspondence as I received it over a number of decades."

There was a respectful silence about the table as Phillip approached his godfather. "Thank you, sir," the boy said. They grasped each other's arms and kissed. It was not a hurried gesture, but one of solemn sentimentality. Minna's eyes were brimming and even Fan had no faint smile of depreciation for the two men. Tim, who knew the family only slightly, realized that a lost symbol of pride, power, and honor had reappeared once more among them.

As the two men parted, Victoria announced that coffee awaited them in the music room, and Goldie appeared to take charge of Paul-Phillip.

Across the hall they found seats, and Oliver served coffee which he brewed over a spirit lamp. Julius offered cigars from a morocco box to all the men but Phillip. The women did not smoke, though Fan looked enviously at the smokers all about her. She sat on a love seat with her husband, who covered her hand with his own on his knee. By previous arrangement, Phillip went to the open piano and began to play. The family gave him their quiet attention. If they had not been so sincere, the Victorian scene might have been ludicrous, Tim thought.

It was the first time Tim had heard Phillip play. If the boy was not brilliant, he certainly had unusual talent and a charming approach, combined with real appreciation for the music he played—selections from Bach and Schumann, Chopin and Brahms. His last selection was a rather bouncy hymn from his father's church hymnal. As it ended, he looked at his mother.

"Yes, dear," she nodded, "it's time to go."

The others rose to thank Phillip and Tim saw that it was nine o'clock, time for the party in town to start. Tim accompanied Phillip upstairs to get their hats, opening the door for him because the boy's hands were full of gifts. Phillip was unusually quiet. His face was tense and lacked color.

Inside the bedroom, he turned on Tim with a snarl. "All right, Tim. Now you can laugh!"

The attack was no surprise to Tim. He had watched its contents gather for hours. He leaned against a table behind him and wisely let the boy get it out of his mind.

"We must be very funny! Ten million dollars and we can't drink wine! We're colorful, a whole parade of heights and depths! Bach and Baptist revival hymns! We're new rich, hicks from the word *go*, but we get along fine—alone! You weren't invited here, and whatever we are, at least we aren't guilty of what you are by being in this house tonight!"

Not once did Tim allow his eyes to waver from the frantic, accusing ones of Phillip. Tim understood that if the boy had regarded him as an inferior or an equal in any way, the attack would not have occurred—that this was Phillip's way of cutting him down to size. Confronted by Phillip's negative emotions, Tim was completely at ease. Only in the presence of the gentle positive ones did Tim experience uncertainty.

Seeing that Phillip had finished, he lighted a cigarette and said softly, "I think I'd wait for a declaration of war before I started to fight, Phillip. But now that you've ripped the issue out in all its nakedness, I agree with you. Some of the things I've seen your family do today were corny as hell, others were amusing, some hypocritical. But most of them were sincere. They were doing what they believed was right. Right now, you aren't.

270

You are acting from sheer vanity. You fancy you've been hurt; so you want to hurt someone else. You're ridiculous, Phillip. Worse than that, you're cruel. You forget my loyalty to you and seize the vilest possible interpretation of my motives and hurl it at me. You're brave, Phillip, a fine example of the training you've received from your Grandfather Dev, your Uncle Felix, your mother, and Fanchon. You'll go far in Devereaux, so long as you use an ax and keep the district attorney on your pay roll." Tim paused to let this sink into the boy's mind. He was being unnecessarily harsh, but he felt he had to be. "The next step is to order me out of your house, or perhaps you'd rather go pout in a corner so your doting family can coax you back to good humor!"

"Tim!" The boy's voice broke completely. His eyes were pleading, his face mirroring his desire for respect. Instantly Tim was contrite.

"I've seen something of the world, Phillip, it's true. I've been entertained in many homes, but I've enjoyed no hospitality as I've enjoyed that which I've received here. If I'd been guilty of laughing at you, I'd deserve being told to go to hell. But I'm not guilty. Don't you see, I prefer your home because you are here."

He went to the boy and put a friendly hand on his shoulder. Phillip drew his breath in raggedly and expelled it.

"I guess I've made an ass of myself again," he said.

"No. You only wanted me to reassure you that what you really believed was true." He paused and said wryly, "And since we are speaking of presents, here is mine to you. In some ways it's far more absurd than a first mortgage when you come to realize what I hope it will always mean to you." He took his hand from his pocket and held it open to Phillip.

"It's your emerald," he said softly.

"I had it remounted for you. I thought you'd like something simple."

Phillip took it and studied the severe yellow gold mounting and the subdued depths of fire. He slipped it on his finger to

271

admire its richness against his dark skin. Then he took it off and held it out.

"I can't accept it, Tim."

"Why not?" Tim asked with real surprise.

"It's very valuable," Phillip floundered. "It must be worth several thousand dollars. And, well, I haven't earned it."

"And you have earned all the other gifts you've received tonight?"

"Yes," Phillip answered firmly, "I have."

The boy continued to hold the ring out to him, but Tim did not take it. At last he said, "Answer me one question, and if the answer is no, I'll take the ring."

Phillip nodded slowly.

"Have I never meant as much to you, or possibly more, than anyone at that table tonight?"

Phillip's eyes dropped quickly and he lowered his hand. Silently he put the ring back on his finger. "It's very beautiful," he murmured.

"There is engraving inside the new setting, too," Tim said.

"I know what it is," Phillip said huskily. In French he repeated the words that had haunted him since the night in San Francisco. And then with an effort he broke through the silence that followed, escaping the torrent of emotion that threatened them. He smiled as he looked up. "I'll have a heck of a time explaining such a gift to Fan."

"Tell her it's glass," Tim grinned. "But we'd better hurry. The others are waiting for us." They found their caps and hurried down to the cars.

272

25

❖❖❖❖❖❖❖

*P*hillip's "debut," as Fanchon called it, was in full swing when the family arrived. It was the most enthusiastic political rally Tim had ever seen. Earlier in the day he had thought that Phillip had been joking when he spoke of being governor of the state. Now Tim realized that it was no joke. The family was a popular and frequent host and the hotel was crowded with hundreds of well-wishers. There were two ballrooms in the hotel and an outdoor pavilion on the square, each with its own string band or orchestra for the dancing public. Long tables inside and out held punch, coffee, cokes, and cake. And Tim saw the method in this madness. Phillip was being groomed for a political career—probably by his father, who seemed the most ambitious of the clan.

The family took its station inside the largest ballroom: Julius (for he now headed the family), Uncle Felix, Victoria, Phillip, Aunt Minna, Fanchon, and Paul Cully. Tim, of course, stood with them. Close by, but at a distance that provided a definite symbolic break from the family, there was a longer reception line composed of presiding politicians and draggletailed hopefuls of the city and county, all seeking the vote of the people. None of the guests seemed to think this second group unusual. They filed by the family, shaking hands with everyone, including Tim, saying their flattering trifles over and over, moving on to josh the politicians about the next election. Everyone in town had turned out, from the mayor to the village idiot. The reception line was supposed to greet the guests for an hour; but it continued for four, and the file of people was still unending. They loved this sort of thing, Tim noticed.

Everyone was completely friendly to Tim and openly curious about him. In one brief lull Fanchon said, "Phillip will scalp you for stealing his glory."

"Am I?" Tim asked with amusement.

"You are. No one is willing to accept you as another naval officer. With this thingumajig on your shoulder, they are sure you must be a celebrity."

"Perhaps I should take it off," Tim laughed.

"Heavens, no! That's prestige down here. Men become senators because of such mysterious glitter."

"And who's to become a senator here?"

"Who do you think?" Fan's eyes were roguish.

"Your husband?" Tim asked playfully.

"After my death! I'm not spending my life playing hostess to a gang of corn-drinking renegades and their prostitutes."

"Then how are you going to spend it?"

"I don't know yet, but perhaps there will be a house out of Boston or some other town where they have a concert hall and a theater season and a yacht club and a good golf club." Paul had put an arm about his wife as she spoke and looked down on her tenderly. "At any rate, we'll watch our sons—and daughters, too, maybe—grow up and become nice ordinary Cullys."

Tim liked that. He thought of it while the line continued to pass, paying their respects to three generations, silently express-

274

ing their desire for three more generations of such considerate leadership.

At last the show was over. Uncle Felix and Aunt Minna were tired. When they left, Julius and Victoria went with them, telling Phillip that they were leaving the car for him. Phillip went off to dance with some of the local belles, particularly Gretel Parks, a pretty little thing who was hopelessly smitten with the boy.

Fanchon asked Tim to take her outside. They sat on the terrace and smoked awhile in silence. At last, because she expected it and had a strange right to hear it, Tim spoke of his background, his approaching divorce, his future. He found Phillip's sister easy to talk with. She displayed a rare combination of sophistication and sincere interest.

"Why do you plan to study medicine in England rather than here in America? I hear we've much the better schools."

"In the first place," Tim answered, "I am European. I'm not looking for the best schools, but for a way of life that satisfies me. I chose Great Britain as middle ground, neither American nor Continental, a place to study until the universities of Prague, Vienna, and Paris have something to offer again."

In the dim light Tim saw Fanchon nod thoughtfully. She said, "I'd like to see Phillip go to Europe—under the proper influences, of course."

Tim was silent, wondering what had prompted this observation. "Then why doesn't he?" he asked at last.

"After tonight's display, that should be apparent."

"Who is Phillip's master?"

"The family. Mother, Father, myself."

"His Uncle Felix?"

"Uncle Felix is a philosopher. Unfortunately he sees Phillip as an incarnation of Grandfather Dev."

"But Phillip is intelligent. He can break with this if he wants."

"No, he can't. He's too easily led, thanks to our riding him all his life," she replied reflectively. "He has little mental solidity

275

to back him up. This GCM proves that. He's deteriorating in a time when he should be building. He is a family tool. He has few friends because he has too much family. He hates Father . . . but you've seen that."

"I have."

"If Phillip were a lout, all this would be good enough for him. Father has kept him starved into submission, but one day he is going to find himself so restless he'll think he is going mad, or so bored he'll wish he were mad. The danger is that he may hate us all. Phillip's nature is to hate easily and to carry grudges to the bitter end. If we ever lose him, he'll never come back."

"Has he never loved?" Tim asked.

"Once. It turned out rottenly. Family again. . . . Care to hear about it?"

"Very much."

"He was fifteen. That winter he'd had influenza. Uncle Tony and Aunt Marie offered to take him with them to New Orleans for March and April to visit relatives. He met his cousin Anne, two years his senior. Actually their mothers were cousins, but Aunt Marie has always tried to keep the relation closer because of a fancied social prestige. Phillip fell in love with the girl, and as things always do with Phillip, it went all the way in a hurry. You know how serious he is. Judging from Phillip's subsequent behavior, I think Anne must have been remarkably wise; because he came home unbelievably older and quieter. There was a deadliness about everything he set out to do. He didn't utter ten words a day unless he was spoken to."

Fanchon paused and took a new cigarette from her bag. In the flare of his lighter, Tim saw that her face was strained.

"Someone found them in a situation that left no doubt in the minds of the families as to what had been going on. There was a scene with Anne's family doctor and the parish priest. It must have been pretty ghastly. Uncle Tony and Aunt Marie, may God damn their souls to eternal suffering for it, turned against Phillip. We'll never know what he went through down

276

there and alone. Yet he stuck it out and came home to face Mother and Father with his story. I've never loved anyone as I loved Phillip that morning in the library. He had the dignity and presence of mind of a man of fifty. Mother stood by him. I believe she saved his reason. Father, from the depths of his velvet-lined ignorance, would have crucified him. Phillip recovered from that episode very slowly. He needed friends then. He had only Uncle Felix, who did manage to hold him straight until he could think impersonally again. For years, I've thought that he might never love passionately again, that he would never be capable of it."

"And now?" Tim forced himself to ask.

"I think he is in love, though he is afraid to admit it." Tim was glad she could not see the deep color he felt in his face. Then, as if to relieve the personal sound of her words, she said, "Phillip has a startling capacity for enjoying himself. Paul and I took him East with us one autumn. I saw Phillip at the opera, the theater, in nightclubs. He was a different person entirely."

"What of the church?" Tim asked half-heartedly.

"There is little there for Phillip," Fan said with disgust. "He can live by an ideal if he must, but what Phillip worships, he must be able to touch."

Tim found definite challenge in her words. To his great horror, he knew he was not ready to answer it. "I—think we'd better go inside, Mrs. Cully."

She stood. "In a moment," she said tersely. "My brother's happiness means a great deal to me, Commander Danelaw."

"Would it help if I told you that his happiness is uppermost in my mind, too?" Tim asked simply.

"It is all I could ask of you."

Proudly she lifted her head and took his arm as they moved into the ballroom where the noise of the dancers was harsh against the smooth words Tim had just heard. Decidedly, Fanchon Cully was an unusually courageous woman.

They found Phillip and Paul and left the party that would

277

last until dawn. At the cars they said good night, and Fanchon invited them to dinner on the night before they were to leave for Seattle.

As she drove away, Phillip turned to say, "Do you mind driving home, Tim? I'm tired."

Tim took the wheel and headed out of town into the country where the wind was cold and a full moon rode the cloudless sky. Phillip sighed as the countryside flashed by them. Neither spoke until they had parked the car and entered the great, dark house by a back door.

"Let's look in the library. Mother may be up."

She was, dressed in an old flannel dressing gown, sitting by the fire with a closed book in her lap.

"Hi, *chérie*," Phillip said softly. He went to sit on the arm of her chair and to kiss her lips and ear. "I thought you'd be up."

"I wanted to apologize for spoiling your party tonight, dear."

"You didn't, darling. He did."

"I wanted the wine to be your grandfather's gift to you."

"I know. But where did it come from? I thought Father sold the cellar."

"Not the choice stock which was hidden. That's yours now."

From the depths of the chair in which she was sitting she lifted something gently and gave it to Phillip—a peculiar-shaped bottle.

"Brandy," she smiled. "Terribly precious. You'll find glasses in your rooms." She stood up and kissed her son's forehead. "Good night, my dear. We were all very proud of you tonight." She left her son and stood before Tim, beckoning for him to bend his head. She kissed him on the cheek and smiled. "Good night, Timothy. We are so happy that Phillip has you for a friend. And the ring is very handsome. Already it seems a part of him."

They watched her go. At the door she turned and smiled again. "Don't forget the fire, dear." The door closed silently. For many moments they did not move, but continued to look

278

at the door. Tim could not have guessed Phillip's thoughts at this moment. It was sufficient that his own mind was clear. For the second time that evening he felt he had been given a standard of behavior by one who loved the boy. He knew that in his future relations with Phillip he could not ignore them. He knew also that in adhering to them, his task would be easier.

Minutes later Phillip put the ornate brass screen before the fire and they took the bottle upstairs. The label had rotted away and the cork was inclined to fall to dust, but eventually they removed it and the ancient liquor was run gently into the crystal goblets. For a moment Phillip stared at it, the color of impure amber, as if he were hypnotized.

"It's almost like having him back," Phillip murmured. He lifted a glass and sniffed at the indescribably provocative bouquet that released the fragrance of the sun, wind, and earth of another century, another age. "It even smells of him." He gave the goblet to Tim.

"What was he like?" Tim asked.

Phillip looked around the room restlessly, smiling faintly as his eyes fell on the familiar objects. "I'll tell you about him, though I don't know much. Perhaps I should recreate for you the scenes I knew him in."

He went to the radio-phonograph and took out a stack of records. But before he put them on, he lighted the fire laid on the hearth and turned out the lights. Tim moved nearer the welcome flames.

"The time," Phillip said, "is about fifteen or twenty years ago. This was Grandfather's bedroom then and I'm supposed to be in bed across the hall, but he has sneaked me out for a bit of clandestine dreaming. I'm in his lap where you're sitting. His cigar smoke and brandy are mingling on the table at his elbow. The Victrola is pulled up close so he can crank it up, change records and needles without getting up. Fan is sitting at his knee, her hair in long curls, her skirts short, staring at the fire—'dreaming about the men she'll love,' Grandfather Dev says.

279

For a while Grandfather will talk to us—Fan and me. He'll tell us stories designed to dissolve our very reason: the cave of the winds, of birds called rocs, valleys where the stones are diamonds, and gardens where the pear trees bear pearls. This is a land of mists and silence, so limpid, so heartbreakingly tender that the mere telling of a nightingale's hesitant song brings tears to the eyes.

"We'd float away for minutes on end. I'd be all wide eyes and mouth, clutching my grandfather's coat to make certain I didn't lose him. Then Fan would ask a question and he would bring us home ever so gently. Then we'd discuss Fan's school and her friends and her ambitions. Then we'd have some music and Fan would Charleston for us. She was the best dancer in town. And here's the music we'd hear."

As he put the disks on the machine, he called off the names: "*Tonight's My Night with Baby*, Al Jolson with Carl Fenton's orchestra; *Sing, You Sinners*, Belle Baker; Al Bernard's *Beale Street Blues*; *Wang Wang Blues* by Bennie Krueger's orchestra; *Way Down Yonder in New Orleans* by Paul Whiteman; *Moonbeams Kiss Her for Me* by Nick Lucas, the crooning troubadour; *Barcelona*, with vocal refrain by Carl Mathieu; *Lonely Little Melody*, from Ziegfeld's Follies of 1924; *After I Say I'm Sorry*, 'a fox trot, tenor with cornet and piano,' it says."

Phillip set the needle on the first disk, and Tim smiled broadly as he heard the bouncy rhythm and the half-forgotten voice clown through the lyrics of the song. While they listened, Phillip brought cigars and held a match for his guest. They smoked and listened and fondled their brandy. But at last the final record fell into place and played itself through. Phillip stopped the machine and turned to Tim.

"That was Grandfather Dev. He loved laughter and gaiety. Those records became a fetish for me after his unexpected death —along with a lot of other things. Later I used to think that when he died my life had ended, too—not ended, but fallen deep in an evil spell that could be broken only by his reappearance. I

280

got over my Sleeping Beauty dreams, but I never got over Grandfather Dev."

Phillip pulled a chair closer and sat down. Talking as he did, he seemed warmer, friendlier, closer to Tim than ever before.

"You ask me what he was like and all I can tell you is of his stories of Greek heroes, my riding lessons, and his delight in my budding sexuality. I accepted him as an equal because he treated me with understanding and patience such as I've never since known. He never scolded me; he reasoned with me. And I sensed that Father was jealous of us; so, very loyally, I hated Father long before I had any reason to. Those are my memories. They used to come to life a bit for me through Uncle Felix—before the war."

"How did he come to know Mr. Mehl?"

"They attended some inexpensive school for accountants and the like in Paris. Grandfather was sixteen and preparing himself to work for some importing family in New Orleans. Uncle Felix was going to be some minor figure in the German diplomatic corps. They lived in the same pension for two years and dreamed dreams together.

"Grandfather Dev returned to America and married my grandmother, who was alone in the world with little money and much town house. She was very romantic and gave Grandfather a free hand. He converted everything to cash, except certain pieces of furniture she couldn't part with, and brought her to Oklahoma where she later died of influenza. She loved him very much. He did not marry again.

"He became a rich man and returned to Europe many times. During and after the first war he had not heard from Uncle Felix, so he went to look for him. He found him in Berlin, penniless, his wife dead, and incurably ill, the doctors said. Aunt Minna was nursing him and trying to earn their bread. Grandfather took them both to the south of France for two years and Uncle Felix recovered his health. By that time Grandfather had pulled enough strings to get them into this country. They settled here, Uncle Felix inheriting one-third of the estate."

Phillip paused and his eyes became thoughtful. "I've always felt that Grandfather Dev led a dual life. In one role he was an American banker. In Europe he was someone else. I know the first role well enough. Everyone hereabouts does. He is referred to as one of the finest gentlemen in the world, staid but friendly, humorous but godly, generous but hard to beat in a bargain, and above all a model husband and father. Yet I feel that he was none of these, that he was merely overplaying a part at which he was secretly laughing behind his fist."

Phillip shifted in his chair restlessly. "The townspeople say all these fine things about him, but not one will mention the fact that he liked his shirt fronts and cuffs edged with a bit of pleated piping and that he always wore the merest hint of rouge on his cheeks."

Tim watched Phillip's palms creep up his face and crush against his temples as if they would destroy his brain. Tim understood that with these words he had burst the bubble that enclosed years of tortured doubt within his mind. He saw at last the black, fearsome channels within that mind, the scars of incredibly savage battles that had been waged there.

And at last the man felt strong enough to do some battling on his own for the boy. His voice was casual. "Fifty years ago, when your grandfather was a young man, that was common enough among the men of Europe. Painting and personal adornment go in cycles, and always the male seems to be the gaudier when he sets his mind to it. Even now, just since the war, there has been a noticeable upswing in cosmetics, scents, and colored fabrics designed for men. I don't think it means anything, except that we are no longer predominantly pioneer in our culture."

"But I don't . . ." Phillip shook his head and stared into the fire.

"You can't inherit homosexuality, Phillip."

Phillip sat straight in his chair. He wanted to speak, yet his

282

mind was obviously in such turmoil that he could not bring himself to do so.

Tim rose and nonchalantly stretched his arms above his head. "I'm going to bed," he said. "If we start for the farm at six-thirty in the morning, I'm going to get some sleep. I've never seen a more comfortable-looking bed."

He unbuttoned his uniform and slipped it off. Phillip opened the windows and wandered out on the cold starlit balcony.

"Aren't you coming to bed?" Tim asked, picking up the pajamas that were laid out for him.

"Later, Tim." Phillip's voice sounded far away.

"Good night, then."

Tim stretched out between the luxury of cold satin sheets and blankets of cashmere wool that held the faint elusive odor of rosemary, lavender, wormwood, or chrysanthemum, as if they had been long stored against his arrival. He was very sleepy and his mind was at peace at last. His mouth throbbed from the bittersweet memory of brandy. . . .

Before he fell asleep, he was aware of Phillip fumbling through the papers on the bureau. When the door to the sitting room closed softly, Tim knew that the boy was examining the packet of letters his Uncle Felix had given him. Seconds later Tim was deep in dreamless sleep.

26

◇◇*◇*◇*◇*

*G*ood morning, farm families. Six o'clock and here's your radio reporter with the latest stock and grain quotations and the weather."

The radio was so low that for a moment Tim thought he was dreaming. He opened an eye and looked at the rumpled place beside him where Phillip had slept. Tim had not been aware of his coming to bed or rising. He had slept as if he had been drugged. The air was still, heavy, hypnotic, and the bedclothes were warm and smooth. He turned over on his side for another forty winks and saw Phillip in pajamas with a cigarette, listening intently to the radio. The sight made Tim want a cigarette— and want Phillip. He had his forty extra winks instead. When Phillip turned off the radio a few minutes later, Tim awoke again and watched Phillip walk through the doors into the spreading dawn outside.

Tim sat up, shook his head, and lighted a cigarette. He was certain that the boy heard the flick of the lighter, but he gave no

284

sign of it. Instead he breathed the cold air deep into him and lifted his arms over his head, rose on his toes, and arched his body like a bow toward the mountains already ablaze with the day's heat. Silently Tim slipped out of bed and went to him. The stones underfoot were cold and damp, but he barely noticed. He was aware only of the lithe trembling arc before him. Tossing his cigarette away, he took the boy in his arms and bent his head to the startled face. The action was so unexpected, yet so natural, that for a second the man felt the tautness in his arms bend against his body and he tasted the sun-warm ripeness of the boy, mingled with the chill brackishness of smoke.

Phillip's first response was complete, but quickly remembering his surroundings he released himself gently. "We must not. It's hardly an orthodox way to begin a day."

"I wish all of them began half so pleasantly," Tim smiled.

"I was wondering how I would awaken you."

They stood apart and Phillip showed no indication of embarrassment. He was learning to choose his weapons wisely, Tim thought with pride, remembering how he would have reacted to the same situation a fortnight ago.

"Aren't you up early?" Tim asked.

"No. We're the late risers. We'd better hurry if we want to catch Father at breakfast. You'll have time for a shower, though. Come along."

As Tim stepped from the bath, Phillip, already dressed and brushing his hair, indicated a stack of clothes on the chair nearby. "You'd better wear those today, Tim, or you'll ruin your uniform. They belong to Paul, but I think you'll be able to get into them. Fan brought them out for you last night."

Tim put on the brown corduroy shirt, a little tight through the shoulders but not uncomfortable. There was some difficulty with the denim jeans, but he got them buttoned at last.

Phillip, critically eyeing the bulge at the crotch, said, "Well, they say it pays to advertise."

285

Tim grinned and sat down to pick up one of the soft leather boots. "Why the fancy footgear?" he asked.

"Snakes," Phillip said briefly. "Three dangerous ones in the area."

They were the first down to breakfast, to Phillip's surprise. At Phillip's ring, Goldie appeared and the parade of food began. Coffee *au lait*, thick slices of ham surrounded by eggs, hot biscuits dripping butter and honey, and great ripe strawberries in yellow cream.

"Will this hold you until lunch?" Phillip asked.

"I thought it was to last all day," Tim said.

"We're having roast goose *à l'allemande*, apple dumplings, and all the trimmings out at the farm, prepared by Aunt Minna herself. I told you we were gluttons. Remember?"

"I can't say it has hurt you."

"Wait until you see Father this morning," Phillip prophesied.

When Julius appeared, looking sleepy and ill-tempered, Tim understood what he meant. Phillip got the morning papers from the sideboard.

"Good morning, sir. How did you sleep last night?"

"Stomach again," the man said petulantly. His skin had a gray pallor over its usual pinkness. He accepted the papers and after a comment on the weather to Tim, turned disgusted eyes upon the bowl of oatmeal and prunes that Goldie set before him.

"Sleep well, Mist' Froelich?" Goldie asked in her unctuous drawl.

"Stomach," Julius repeated wearily, unfolding his napkin. With effort Goldie looked unhappy for a few seconds before she left the room.

"Cream, sir?"

Julius accepted it. "Where is my dry toast?"

"I'll get it," Phillip said, rising. "Goldie must be making it."

"Ring for her!" his father commanded. When she appeared, he asked acidly, "Would it be asking too much to bring my toast *with* my cereal?"

286

"Yes, sir." Goldie looked unhappy with no effort this time. Phillip looked at Tim and lifted a shoulder almost imperceptibly.

Victoria appeared, fresh and smiling in a crisp linen dress and a pink sweater. Phillip rose to accept her kiss, and as she passed Tim, who was standing, too, she gave him her hand. Phillip seated her as she looked anxiously at her husband, asking, "Stomach better, Julius?"

"No."

"I'll have Goldie bring you some lemon juice."

Victoria turned to Tim, noticing his clothes. "Timothy, you look like one of the farm lads this morning." She cocked her head to the side and asked, "How much difference is there in your age and Phillip's?"

"Ten years, I think," Tim replied.

"The secret of his dignity is his uniform," Phillip laughed.

"And yours, too, young man, so don't be gay about it."

"A boy's best friend," Phillip said, making a face at her and picking up his suede jacket. "We're off. Anything we should do?"

"I don't think so, dear, unless your father has something."

"Be careful of those tires. And if you need gas, this is Texaco week."

"Yes, sir," Phillip said patiently but respectfully.

"Oh, yes," Victoria said. "Before I forget it, I can get your new saddle. I had a letter from that place in Virginia the other day."

"Fine. Do they still list those French officers' saddles?"

"I believe so. Shall I order you one?"

"What kind is that?" Julius interrupted suspiciously.

"It's like an English saddle only easier on the mount."

"Get him a Western saddle," Julius addressed his wife, ignoring his son, "like everyone else uses. We won't be different."

The silence, Tim knew, was storm calm. To his parents' evident surprise, Phillip said flatly, "Why?"

The silence became electric. Father and son faced each other

287

belligerently. Julius was trying to stare Phillip down, but the boy would not be routed easily.

"Because I said so," Julius said evenly.

"Without intending disrespect, sir, there must be a sensible reason." Phillip's tone implied that he was being reasonable. He stood erect and hurried on, "A saddle such as I want is easier on the mount. It weighs seventeen pounds to a Western saddle's seventy. It looks better in the show ring, and for jumpers it is imperative."

Phillip's argument would have made sense to a moron, Tim thought, but he knew that this was not the issue. Phillip was crossing his father for the first time as a man, and Julius' face proclaimed that he knew it.

He turned to his paper. "We won't be different," he said calmly. The interview was closed. Phillip might have won his argument, but he had lost unless he wanted to follow his quarry into the lair. He was not so foolhardy, but he did take one parting shot.

To his mother, he said with authority, "In that case, don't order anything. I'll wait until I can use my money." He tossed his coat over his shoulder and joined Tim at the door. "We'll be back about six. Goodbye."

His mother nodded, but Julius studied his paper, which was trembling slightly. Tim followed Phillip down the hall and out to the garage.

"You've just witnessed my bid for power," Phillip said. "I don't think I'd have tried it but for you."

"Then I'm sorry I am such a bad influence."

"Maybe you aren't."

"Suppose you had provoked a real break?"

"Simple. I'd have backed down and attacked at a more favorable time."

They got into the red pick-up and drove away from the house. Tim was amazed at the subtle change that was coming over the boy. He had a casual confidence that belied the seriousness of

288

the course he had chosen to follow. Through town, Phillip drove slowly, nodding, speaking to as many people as possible, much as his mother and sister had done the previous morning. On the other side of town they picked up speed again. At the top of a long hill, Phillip kicked in the clutch and let the truck coast.

"Saves gas," he grinned at Tim. "Father taught me that." And copying his father's pompous tones, he said, "Waste not, want not." Tim could not help laughing.

They drove in silence awhile until they approached a cemetery near the road. Two grave diggers were visible from the waist up.

"They're interring the Peters boy this afternoon. My age." Phillip shivered slightly. "Isn't it incongruous, the living doing service for the dead? There's such a distance between."

"You're afraid of death?" Tim asked with surprise.

"Afraid of dying before I've lived my share of life."

"That bothered me, too, once," Tim said.

"Not any more?" Phillip asked with interest.

"No. I've discovered several things I'm willing to die for."

Phillip turned this over in his mind. Suddenly he said, "I've nothing I'm willing to die for—except Fan, or Uncle Felix."

"I know," Tim answered. "But you will have. Then life takes on real complications."

Phillip nodded thoughtfully. He turned off the concrete slab on a dirt road, badly washed with gullies and holes. It was the worst road Tim had seen in America, he decided. The truck growled along in low for several miles, slipping dangerously close to ditches deep enough to bury it. But Phillip's hands were expert.

"As yet Devereaux farms can't boast passable roads. Our own fault. Inadequate tax system, crooked politicians, stupid voters. Take our ostrich attitude toward liquor. We're dry because of a lot of old women like Father who preach their Baptist morality and wouldn't know decency if they ever saw it. We're called the heart of the Bible Belt, you know. We quote the Golden Rule, but we say it in our sleep. Our missionary societies send representatives to Honduras instead of turning their funds to reclaiming the dust bowl. They keep the state from deriving any tax benefits from the huge amount of liquor that is bootlegged in by Eastern syndicates." Suddenly Phillip grinned. "I'm rabid on the subject. If I could, I'd change it if I had to resort to fireside chats."

The road had narrowed to a series of stone outcroppings and at last lost itself in a swollen stream about fifty yards across. Over part of it there was a bridge bed of logs lashed together and anchored to trees on either side. As the truck eased into the shallow water, Tim said, "I hope that thing holds us."

"It better. I helped build it."

They got through the stream, but as they started up the hill on the other side, the rear end of the truck swerved quickly and buried itself axle-deep in gummy mud. They were stuck. Phillip got out and took a shovel from the tool box. "Stay inside," he said as Tim got out. "I'll have us free in a jiffy when I get a couple of rocks from the hill."

"I'll get them," Tim offered.

"Better let me. City dwellers inevitably pick the ones that have blind, female rattlers under them." Phillip's eyes twinkled as he started up the hill with long, sure-footed strides. Tim picked up the shovel and started moving mud from around the rear wheels. By the time the boy had returned, he was sweating freely.

"If we ever duel," Phillip said, "remind me to choose shovels."

"What's wrong with my technique?" Tim demanded.

"Nothing, except it shouts you've never had the implement in your hands. Here, let me show you."

Tim watched him work, bending his legs instead of his back, keeping his arms close to his sides.

"I told you that you were playing my field now," the boy grinned, placing the flat stones next to the wheels. They got into the car and after two easy attempts, Phillip gunned the vehicle out and up the hill. At the top Phillip pointed to a herd of

290

grazing cattle. Their coats were so black they flashed a gun-metal-blue in the sun.

"That's one of our prize herds. Black Angus. Grandfather introduced them into this section. They're fine, but I'm a Hereford man."

"Oh, bv all means," Tim said with mock seriousness.

Phillip chuckled. "You know, Tim, I'm beginning to understand how I must have appeared to Pat's crowd in Seattle. You're the same way out here. You're amusing but not comical. I was wrong about several things."

"Then, I take it, it's time to talk."

"Yes. But wait until we get to my hill. We'll talk there."

They drove on until they reached the low stone farmhouse with its whitewashed fences and outbuildings.

"We won't stop by the house," Phillip said, getting out. "Uncle Felix isn't up yet." He waved to a farm hand driving a tractor which pulled a wagon piled high with loose hay. "Let's catch that and we won't have to walk," Phillip said, and they ran toward the tractor which slowed until they were atop the load.

"Taking this to the north barn, Jeams?" Phillip called, and the old man waved his hand. Phillip flopped on his back in the fragrant stuff and looked up at the sky. "It's like riding one of those clouds," he said.

They rode for a quarter of an hour, when the tractor stopped suddenly. The old man called, "Hey, Phillip, bet I jest seen sompin' you'd like."

Under his breath, Phillip said, "Oh, oh," and gave Tim a wink. "What kind is it, Jeams?" he called.

"Moccasin, I think," the old man replied.

"Have you anything to get him with?"

"Short-handled shovel or a rake."

"I'll take the shovel." Phillip climbed down and Tim followed, half-suspecting what was going on.

The driver, a white-whiskered old cuss with a battered hat and faded denim overalls, handed Phillip the shovel and pointed with a thick middle finger. " 'Tween thet rock and fence post. Beauty, ain't he?"

"Wonder what he's doing away up here?" Phillip said, approaching cautiously.

Tim had difficulty seeing anything until Phillip, with shovel poised, stood over a scattering of stone. Then, like a black flash of lightning, he saw the snake trying to move away through the weeds. But the shovel descended with the crunching power of a guillotine and with a quick motion descended again.

"Get him, Phillip?" the old man called delightedly.

"Right behind the ears," Phillip grinned. The old man cackled. Phillip lifted the headless writhing thing on his shovel and tossed it evenly over the fence where it tried in vain to crawl free. "About four feet, Jeams?"

"Aw, hell, son, thet's a five-footer easy." And turning to Tim, he said with admiring eyes, "Never seen sech a boy fer hatin' snakes. Me, I'm skeered of the varmits. Not Phillip. Kills ever' one he sees. I seen him fight a copperhead onct. Caught the devil with a tine of his pitchfork in the wheat field, right in the square of the back. Pinned him to the ground, then gets out his knife and goes atter him. Snake draws back in a S and strikes. Phillip takes a swipe with his knife. Sharp as a razor. Snake strikes again. Phillip swipes 'fore he can pull back. Takes thet snake's head off clean as a mole's ass. Thet Phillip's a gritty little bastard."

"Here's your shovel, Jeams. You can clean the blood off it."

"Aw, hell, Phillip, I'll leave it on and tell ever' one I done it."

"Okay, Jeams. We'll see you later."

The tractor moved on and Phillip turned to lead the way into the brush, saying, "Better stay behind, Tim. You'd step on a snake before you could see it."

"I don't need a second invitation after that encounter," Tim said. "I share Jeams' opinion: I'm skeered of the varmits."

"You'd learn to kill them if you had to."

292

"Why do you hate them so?" Tim asked.

"My fear is real enough. No phallic symbol, if that's what you're driving at. When I was eight years old I was running through the orchard and stepped on a moccasin. It coiled around my leg and bit me. I was literally paralyzed with fear. I couldn't move a muscle. I couldn't even scream. Fortunately, Oliver was just behind me. Despite that foolish grin he wears, he isn't an idiot. He got the snake loose and put on a tourniquet. Then he lanced the punctures and sucked them free before he carried me to the house. He saved my life. Now you understand part of my esteem for him. Back home, my leg swelled and I was pretty sick for a while. At the very word *snake*, I broke out in a cold sweat. I had nightmares all night, every night. I guess instinct told me I was in bad shape mentally. So I had a talk with Oliver.

"The first day I was on my feet again, he took me back to the farm and, armed with hoes, we went snake hunting. I was petrified all over, but Oliver kept talking to me and grinning his perpetual grin. We found our first one and Oliver held it with his hoe and talked me into killing it. It took me five minutes to strike that first blow. I wanted to run, to scream, do everything but stay."

Phillip had stopped to look at Tim as he told the story. His face worked with the emotions he was remembering. "That first blow did it. It released something in me. I killed the snake and with Oliver's knife I hacked it into pieces about an inch long. When it was all over, I was covered with blood and yelling like a savage. By the time we started home that night, I'd killed twenty-six reptiles and my fear was gone forever."

There was thick silence for a time as the two men looked at each other.

"That," Tim said, "is the most gruesome story of a child I have ever heard."

"Yes, isn't it," Phillip agreed coolly. "But it taught me a very valuable lesson. Nothing beats facing facts and fighting it out to the finish."

"Why do you tell me all this?" Tim asked suddenly.

"To give you an idea of what to expect if we ever come to grips."

27

When I dragged the sailor out of that naphtha fire my first day in Seattle," Phillip said, "I forced myself to think of this spot to fight off hysteria. Uncle Felix calls it my *prie-Dieu*."

They had reached a worn roll of shelfland high on the hillside, a place of few trees, a greenery choked spring, and a truly generous view of the misty valley not too far below them—a balcony of earth haunted by youthful dreams, Tim suspected.

"This is my grandfather's empire to me," Phillip continued. "Not the bank, nor the ranches or farms, cattle and oil, but this picture of the sweet land always waiting for me with the scents of cool pine and warm earth." Phillip shrugged his shoulders and turned his melancholy smile on his companion. "But I'm waxing poetic, Tim. You bring out the worst in me."

They sat on the acorn-spattered moss and leaned against the harsh trunk of an oak to relax after their climb.

"You know," Tim said, "if I had known all this about you, the episode in San Francisco wouldn't have happened."

"Why?"

"Your life is more complete than I had thought. I remember thinking the first time I saw you that you were curiously out of time and setting with the rest of the world. It must have been the GCM."

Phillip took out his pocket knife and started scraping the mud from his boots. For a moment he was silent before he said, "Don't flay yourself unnecessarily over Frisco. I didn't come to you in purity, you know. There was a similar experience years before, but of little consequence. That's what deluded me with you. I thought that you could offer me nothing, either. I was gambling. I lost." He paused again. "Of course, I'm sorry it happened, too, now. And yet, in some ways . . ."

"The ill wind, compensation, and so on?"

"I believe more of Emerson than that," Phillip said quickly.

"I know. 'Ne te quaesiveras extra.'"

Phillip studied his friend. "Every once in a while you give me the impression that my mind is looking into a mirror." He shook his head. "It isn't that I think that all experience is grist for the mill. I believe that there are many things I'll be better off never to know. Because of you, I've felt a great amount of stimulation, more than I can balance with understanding. That's dangerous because I am needlessly preoccupied with myself. Yet if I have been harmed, I think I'll survive it, if you leave me alone. You don't fit into my world, Tim. I've thought it over pretty carefully. There is an inclination toward homosexuality in me. You have revealed how strong it is. The longer I am near you, the greater it will become. So, I say again, there is no place in my world for you."

Tim traced the pattern of the moss beside him with a twig as he said, "Tell me about your world, Phillip. If I'm to be cut out of it so blithely, I think I've a right to know what I'm missing." Tim glanced up to see his own irony ignite in Phillip's eyes.

"I suppose I did sound melodramatic. But since you're asking for it, here goes." His gaze sought the horizon and grew reflec-

296

tive. "My father is a disciplinarian. He reared me as a stoic in some ways, and some might say it was a mistake. I don't believe it was. Many outstanding men have been reared by puritanical standards, and in my world I am expected to be outstanding. Ten million dollars and fifty thousand people demand tremendous consideration. I have fine examples and ideals to live up to. I believe in them because I have found nothing better to believe, and I am aware of the corrupt politics, ignorance, and indifference I must face. But I believe I am bigger and better than those evils. I'm the young zealot who wants to make the world better, mundane as that may be.

"My world is a reasonable one. My father, probably because he suspected my weaknesses, brought me up on hard work and sound business judgment. Mother and Fan taught me truth and humor. Uncle Felix and Aunt Minna shamed me into tolerance and mercy. All in all, they left the void for emotion for me to fill as I would, and there is the real test of my rearing—how I fill that void. It's up to me to set an example for the others who watch me constantly. Now that there has been a war and we face a period of moral giddiness, a greater burden is falling on fewer people to uphold those principles that make us a strong society. Our greatest weapon is our conduct, our personal lives. The social libertines will observe us and gradually return to stricter moral standards. Does that sound like bad theology?"

"No, you are making fairly good sense."

"You're very kind," Phillip said. He went on, "My first problem is to get the bank tucked firmly under me. This involves two fights. The first is going on now between my family and Francis'. I think I mentioned once how the bank was divided into thirds. In my generation it will boil down to Fan and myself against Francis. Uncle Felix' third goes to Aunt Minna who will leave it in four parts to Fan, Francis, the Catholic Church, and me. Francis, being Catholic, will control two-fourths, giving him as much power as Fan and I together. A deadlock. Then Francis sells his fifty per cent and hightails it for the choice social whirls in the South or East, leaving me to get along with some high-handed gang of thieves.

"In the past fifteen years we have grown rich enough to buy the Barrimans out, but they won't sell to us. So I marry Sybel Jo— and I'm sure I can do it despite Madame, because she knows that I'm the best prospect the girl will ever have. Joe Voth, Father, and I will get along. Already Joe and Father have made joint investments, mostly in oil leases and lakefront property up at Grand River Dam. Those deals were feelers and went through without a hitch. Father is satisfied that Joe Voth is our man. Joe can buy Tony Barriman out because they are close friends. I can buy out Joe at my convenience. That takes care of Battle Number One.

"When I face Father, I face the toughest battle. It won't take place for five or six years, but it will take place. Father refers to me as his retirement policy and it is a commendable idea. But when will he retire? My only chance at freedom is to be free of him. For five years I'll need him to teach me the intricacies of our particular bank. But once I know them, I want him *out*. No organization is big enough to hold us both. I've catered to him all these years and now he has to go. With luck I can get Mother to retire him. Otherwise something will have to be done. I've earned my heritage and I want it, free of him. Sometimes I think of Father and I ache with fury. Why did a man like Grandfather Dev have to die and leave me such a substitute?"

Completely fascinated, Tim watched Phillip's long fingers curl around the knife he was holding.

The low-pitched vibrating voice continued, "I remember the day Father decided I was going to give the valedictory address of my graduating class in high school. That was a fine ambition for him. He decided four years in advance, so as to give me ample time—ample torture. He called me into his study and outlined my next four years. And I, God damn me, didn't have the guts to protest.

298

"First he told me competition would be stiff, against students who were better endowed mentally than I, but that was to make no difference. No dates with girls the first three years, then night dates with Sybel Jo on Friday or Saturday. Be in by ten-thirty. No basketball or football. Instead, track, tennis, and golf. No concussions there. Debating and public speaking a must. No chemistry or trig, but bockkeeping, accounting, and modern farming methods. A lively interest in music—to keep me before the public who must see me grow up. Mother has a photograph of me on her dressing table now, in a drum major's uniform, complete with shako.

"I didn't question him. He could administer brutal whippings. I haven't forgotten one he gave me. After the first two or three, I learned to present him a placid exterior and do my thinking privately. About that time the whippings stopped. I never crossed him, but there were ways of suggesting the depth of my contempt to him. One day he is going to see it naked. I hope it kills him."

"Phillip! Ye gods, do you know what you're saying?"

"What?" Phillip turned a startled face to Tim, and seeing the disgust he had aroused, he shook his head dazedly. "I'm overwrought," he said slowly and closed the knife. "It's just that he seems so petty against Grandfather Dev and I can't forget the opportunities I might have had under his guidance."

"Then why don't you break with all this?"

"I've the talent. I haven't the guide. It's a little late to start thinking of being a concert pianist even if that's what I still wanted."

"And the diplomatic career?"

"Aim for an ambassadorship and wind up a dispatch carrier? No thanks. If I'm going to be buried, I prefer my grave to be here where I have a chance to dig myself free. When I told Father I wanted to enter diplomatic service, he looked as if I'd just told him I wanted to operate a string of whorehouses. But if I'd told Grandfather Dev, he'd have nodded and started watching me. A few years later he would have talked to me about it again and told me frankly what he thought of the idea. If he had approved, he would have started making plans: study, the selection of schools, the right people for friends. He would have moved quietly but certainly until he had the first foothold hacked out. Then the next and the next, all the while preparing me for the day when he would say: 'You are on your own. There is the road and here is a minute list of the pitfalls. Good luck, chéri.'"

"Rather pat, isn't it?"

"Damned pat. That's the way he did things. He'd have given me the essence of his facilities with the condition that I use it to project myself even further than he could have gone. Three generations of my grandfather and we might have produced . . ."

"That's all very fine," Tim said, "but how about the reverse of the medal? Suppose you faced the world without a cent, without the support of your family, with only your present knowledge and wits between you and the millions of others just like you?"

"I've thought of that, too," Phillip said with a sigh. "Before I made my decision I considered telling Father to take his retirement policy and jam it. I have a knowledge of banking, but I'd never work in a bank—unless I could marry the president's daughter."

"That's interesting. Why?"

"Working in a bank is dull, the pay is poor, advancement slow, risk of making mistakes or succumbing to temptation high, and I'm not proud enough to prefer a white collar. First, I'd decide what I wanted to do. Then I'd need a stake. I'd decide how many thousand dollars I needed and set out to earn it. I might start buying and selling cattle or go into oil speculation. If I needed several thousand dollars, I'd do manual labor to get it. It leaves the mind comparatively free. The body is healthy

300

and active. And I would be among the people who make the leaders. I'd be learning how to appeal to them."

"So you'd dig ditches?" Tim said with amusement.

"If the wages were high enough. But I think I'd go into the oil fields where a wise young man can make thirty to fifty dollars a day cleaning storage tanks or contracting roustabouts for earth work. The oil field has made as many millionaires as any other industry and I know the game fairly well."

"But suppose you were forced to go to a city where you know no one?"

"I'd try to get a job as a waiter with an eye to getting into the swankiest clip joint in town where the tips are high and the clients are fools."

"It wouldn't bother you to be a servant?" Tim challenged.

"Hell, no! This is the dawn of the workers' age, they say. Wages are at a peak. In five years, with a bit of personality and luck, I'd have my stake. In ten years we can expect another depression. Then the man with money buys at his own price. Land, cattle, and the beginnings of another empire. People hereabouts say that the oil boom made the Devereaux fortune. Perhaps it did, but it was the depression of '29 that secured it, the same depression that ruined a lot of new rich when oil went to ten cents a barrel under Hoover and the Republicans. This farm you're on right now is one continuous tract of two thousand acres. It wasn't continuous until after 1929."

"Your only thoughts are of money, then?" Tim smiled.

"I haven't heard of your giving away any of Danelaw Brewing."

"Nor will you. But have you no dreams that don't involve wealth?"

Phillip's face softened a little as he said simply, "Yes. I've a few, but they're farfetched without an income."

"Tell me about them," Tim urged.

"Well," Phillip began half-shyly, "I'd like to see God in everything the way Aunt Minna does. Please don't laugh. I really mean it, banal as it may sound to you."

"I wish I had the words to tell you how it does sound to me."

Their eyes met briefly. Phillip continued, "And I'd like to be free to travel over the world. I'd like to hear the wit of Paris first hand, and study the philosophy of the world's thinkers until I felt peace within myself, until I felt that I was self-contained. I'd like to have a wife like Fan that I could love and sons like little Paul-Phillip and friends like—well, like you without this other, of course. I'd like to sit on a beach somewhere for days and nights and see the light and tide come and go and yet always remain the same until my mind was so full of the pattern of things that I could face even death without a qualm. I'd like a house by the sea where there were breakers at the foot of a cliff below my windows every minute of the day, a gloomy sky nine days out of ten, and poetry and music and good conversation. But that's the minor theme of me. The major is here in this land where I can struggle with something that I'm forced to respect and yet is not too great for my talents."

Phillip took a cigarette and rolled it between his fingers. "So you see, Tim, beneath the shell, I'm just an ordinary guy with ordinary desires I don't expect to realize until I'm ancient and senile."

Tim smiled and lay on his back with his head on his palms. "How about going back to school to grow accustomed to our post-war world?"

"That's out. College was a let-down. Again I expected too much of it, I guess. That seems to be a consistent failing of mine. I thought of college as a state of preparation for living. I learned about one-eighth of what I should have learned. Everyone was in the same boat—too young, no sense of responsibility, twisted values, ivory towers, half-baked theories, and frustrated profs. All day I went through a lot of rah-rah and then crammed crap for mid-terms. At night I drank beer with frat brothers whose graves I wouldn't have pissed on, if I'd been perfectly

302

frank. We talked a lot and our conversations were as varied as fifty miles of telegraph poles. We were a bunch of bums destined to inherit the earth—we thought. That's not for me again. If I had a professional career ahead of me, I'd have to go back to school; but to get the equipment for living, I'm not going to college, not in the States anyway."

"Why does Europe attract you? You've admitted it several times."

"Because of Grandfather Dev, I suppose, and Uncle Felix. Once Uncle Felix said to me: 'Over there man lives in the shadow of disaster. He makes his days count, not financially but in another way, in the laughter of living. He knows about the sorrow that is great enough to make him laugh and the joy that is wonderful enough to make him weep.' " Phillip looked down at his companion. "Is that right, Tim?"

"I think it is."

"I'm not saying that Europe is better than my country," Phillip added defensively, "and I'm not one of those idiots who rants about culture, but if Europe can give me the necessary knowledge of life to live it to the fullest of my ability, I'd like to have it."

"Then why don't you go over for a few years?"

"I told you. I've made my choice. I've an inheritance to earn."

"Do you regret your choice?"

"That's the point of my argument, Tim. I don't. I want my hidebound unhappiness as it is. I want to work it out myself. This is what I am. This is my destiny. I believe in it. Yet you propose to destroy it for me. You would offer me a void, or at best a sham world. Up to this moment I will take responsibility for the mistake we have made. But from now on, your actions will be interference."

Tim knew that there was bluff, not heart, in his words.

28

$\mathcal{T}$he defense rests," Tim said, sitting up. " Now, I take it, is the time for me to justify my actions. Or am I condemned to silence?"

"Go ahead, Tim, I'm ready to listen." Phillip lay on his stomach and flicked his finger against a safari of ants.

"Do you mind looking me in the eye?" Tim smiled. "I've found you have a penchant for honesty only when you're cornered."

"Okay," Phillip grinned, rolling over on his back.

"My lap is free."

"Quoth the spider," Phillip laughed, moving nevertheless so he rested his head on Tim's leg. "Now. The only escape is to close my eyes."

For a few minutes Tim did not speak. He wanted to collect his thoughts; he wanted their playful banter to be forgotten before they talked again. He considered their ability to discuss their affairs with detachment a saving grace, their sense of humor a powerful incentive toward eventual freedom, but now he wanted sobriety.

"In the first place," he said, "you have based your observations on the supposition that the mind is free to act reasonably at any time."

"Isn't it?"

"I think it is rarely capable of functioning reasonably against emotion after a certain period has been reached. A period that is neither adolescent nor mature, but somewhere between. A period, in which it seems to me, you are now in the middle. Chronologically you've lived twenty-three years, but physically you're sixteen or eighteen. It isn't unusual these days. But sticking to the subject of the freedom of mind, do you think the average homosexual is such because he wants to be?"

"Why else?"

"For the same reason you didn't leave my hotel room in San Francisco an hour after you had entered it. You couldn't."

"But I did leave it the next morning. And for good."

"Shock. Bruner represented an avenging society to you. He aroused an emotion as great as the one you had just experienced. You experienced the first clash of emotions that the sexual pariah goes through far more often than we realize. Usually his mind is not as disciplined as yours. Desire wins. Does that sound logical?"

"I've never thought of anyone else in that connection, only myself."

"That's as it should be. You're no student of human problems yet."

"Until this year, sex has never been important to me," Phillip mused. "Now, suddenly, I find that everything hinges on it."

"Another indication of the swift, inevitable progress out of adolescence," Tim said. "But leaving that for the moment to approach another aspect of our situation: a while ago you used the term "interference," as if you were afraid of it. You could have used it as a scourge. On any number of occasions you could have cut me to pieces, yet in every instance I've seen you turn away from the opportunity. I have interfered in your life, Phillip, to what may be a criminal extent. But remember carefully and you'll find that always I have displayed respect and consideration for you. I have pointed a way and left the decisions to you. I always shall. You came to me because vaguely you realized there was something between us—admiration, infatuation, desire. Whatever it was, it was an exquisite torture such as you had never known. Is that right?"

"Yes."

"Here, then, are the reasons for my behavior. First, I love you. Writhe under the term as much as you must, but it is true for me. There was a point where I could have turned back easily. I may have to now, but it won't be easy. Second, I feel more than ever that we are alike. That is more important to me than it is to you at this time. Physically we seem counterparts, but basically there are elements you can't ignore. I've more to say about that later. Third, after Bruner blundered in, I did not feel that I could safely abandon you until I was certain that you could make a decision by which you could abide for the rest of your life. From the intensity of your shame, your decision to end everything between us was to be expected. If you could remain ashamed the rest of your life, you could keep your resolution.

"I'm giving you the other side of the question—an opportunity to see it that I didn't have. I've been over this ground before, and once I thought it was limbo, too. Now I know that it holds, not answers exactly, but milestones. . . . But I'd better begin at the beginning.

"Once I thought I had discovered my world, too. It was the world of art. I was seventeen, tired of school, tired of America. I longed for Europe. I wanted to study painting. I went to Italy. I was going to rank with Michelangelo, Titian, Rubens, the giants of painting. I was going to paint for the ages. I had some talent but I hadn't the rest of it. Art wasn't enough. I preferred

306

life. It took me two years to realize that. I knew I'd never be a great artist. I wouldn't be a mediocre one. I was disillusioned. For a while I played, but it didn't satisfy me. I sailed for Egypt. On the ship there was a French doctor going to the Orient to try out a cure for Asiatic cholera that he had been perfecting for ten years. For the first time in my life I felt a challenge in another personality. He agreed to let me come along—on my own since he was on a government commission—as a sort of assistant.

"Vincent Jardine was fifty years old, divorced, homosexual—though that did not come out for several months. First of all, he was an intellectual. He wasn't particularly unusual, but he and his work fascinated me. He aroused the most powerful emotions I had ever known. In comparison, nothing in my life had really touched me. And the more I was with him, the more I admired him. You'd have to have some of the experiences we had to appreciate them.

"First we went to Laos, but inevitably we went up into China and the war on our own. We were like birds hypnotized by a cobra. The war drew us to it—China and the Invader. The Orient is a great teacher, Phillip, but a monstrous one. She teaches all men the same lesson: passive acceptance of fate. Its effect on us was profound. Vince, the intellectual, showed the effect first. We witnessed the rape of Nanking. I tried to persuade him to come out, to go back to France. His cholera serum had failed. He had no reason to stay, I argued. But he was in too deep by then. It was a guilt complex. His morbidity was beginning to affect me. I knew that I had to make the break to save us both. I gave him an ultimatum and when he rejected it, I left him, stranded in the middle of hell, and went to India. He committed suicide.

"I began to realize what had happened to me in those years. Instead of facing facts, I ran—back to the States and a long period of drinking myself to death. I met Pat. We were married because I thought she was the answer. She wasn't. I haven't found the answer yet."

Tim paused and looked down at Phillip. The boy's expression was serious, attentive. Tim asked, "Are you beginning to see parallels?" Phillip nodded solemnly and Tim continued, "You tell me you have your world. You say your choice is made, that you are ready to make the best of it, to be happy in it. But are you? Can this world absorb all of your talents and satisfy all your needs? Are you advanced to the point where you can see it in perspective when it delivers a crippling blow, to laugh at it when it needs to be laughed at? What of Sybel Jo? Love and passion aren't satisfied by sex alone. And what of that which you are ready to ignore? When I go out of your life, what then? Can you encompass Devereaux with one problem still unsolved in your mind? Believe me, Phillip, if San Francisco had been anything but what it was, I would not pose these questions for you."

"And what is your solution?"

"I'm not sure. I think I've an answer, but I want more time. Whatever it is, it will be a few simple truths that we can rely on and apply to every situation."

"Tim—" Phillip's voice was cautious—"can you tell me about —Pat?"

"As much as you need to know, enough to convince you she cannot fit into your life, if you don't know it already." Phillip flushed guiltily and Tim said, "Yes, I know about the night of the Admiral's reception. She flaunted the fact before me. You need not be ashamed of it. Pat and I have lived apart for years. The break came when she refused to bear children—my sons. She hates you, Phillip, enough to destroy you if she can. You are her rival. I loved her until I knew her. Now I pity her because she can only torture herself to death. Yet she won't be happy doing that, since she can't torture me to death, too."

Phillip veiled his eyes and forced a thumbnail between his teeth. At length he burst out, "But I don't hate women. They

308

are an important part of my life. My mother, Fanchon, my cousin Anne—"

"Where is the woman you have loved better than yourself as yet?"

"There is none. Unless—"

Tim laughed. "I? Whatever we are to each other, it's hardly right to say that either of us is merely a substitute for femininity. The father-son relationship, perhaps, since we've both desired it so strongly, but not the other. Have you ever felt you were a substitute?"

"Hardly. It's something else, close, not marital but friendly, companionable, fraternal, comradely—all these things raised to the nth power. Has it a name?"

"It must have or we've lost touch with everything that is human."

"Tim, what does Proust mean by the German idea of homosexuality?"

"I'm not sure. Some dual standard of loyalty probably. I think I know where to get the answer in terms we can accept, despite its obvious delicate implications."

"Do you suppose it is the same as the Ancient Greek conception?"

"Possibly. You understand that well enough, don't you?"

"Yes. I can even sympathize with it. The Sacred Band of Thebes—one hundred young warriors, each fighting at the side of his best friend, the flower of an admirable society. It would be very easy to uphold honesty, courage, decency to the very last under those circumstances.

"And the Spartans who encouraged—even demanded—that each warrior adopt a young athlete for his own. Homosexuality was often the inevitable outgrowth but never the end in itself. The warriors went into battle in view of their young charges, the supposition being that they would fight the more fiercely. And the young favorites in the gymnasium, for their part, strove for perfection, supremacy; each reluctant to show pain or cow-ardice and thereby draw down disgrace upon his champion."

Phillip laced his fingers together on his chest as he talked. His eyes fondled the emerald against his dark hands.

"Their world needed such relationships. Its safety depended on the personal integrity of the individual. The fighting man was its most valuable asset. But our world. There is no place for such things. Sexual aberration is social disaster. Be different and be damned was never truer than here and now. The average individual doesn't dare show tolerance."

"Then wouldn't you say there is something lacking in such an order?"

"It's the best we have," Phillip said. "We'll make the best of it."

"And what are the rewards of this demanding world of yours?"

"That which is best for the majority. Happiness, perhaps."

"Personal happiness?"

"Personal pride in having done one's best."

"Rather idealistic," Tim observed.

"Perhaps. But nothing is emptier than the pursuit of pleasure."

"You're right," Tim agreed.

"You see, Tim," Phillip said suddenly, "your argument isn't reasonable. Suppose I granted your first point, that homosexuality is justifiable in certain instances and under certain controls. Then here is the catch: where does justification end and degeneracy begin? Society must condemn to protect. Permit even the intellectual homosexual a place of respect and the first bar is down. Then comes the next and the next until the sadist, the flagellist, the criminally insane demand their places, and society ceases to exist. So I ask again: where is the line drawn? Where does degeneracy begin if not at the beginning of individual freedom in such matters?"

"Perhaps it begins where the desire of the individual begins to actually destroy his fellow men."

310

"And would I not be destroying if I permitted myself to do as my emotions might prompt me? Would I not be destroying integrity?"

"Or more important, would you not be destroying yourself as you are at this moment?"

"Why do you constantly bring that up?"

"To make you think. Are you happy doing what you think is right?"

"Yes!"

"Your answer is too prompt. You impress me as a man who has embraced a religion fanatically—not because he believes in God but because he's afraid of going to Hell. Would you call melancholia a type of happiness? Tell me frankly, Phillip, how many times in the past ten years have you been happy?"

"I—I can't say accurately. Three, maybe four. A few days with Anne."

"But society says Anne is taboo for you."

"The birth of Fan's boys."

"Vicarious fatherhood for you."

"Really, Tim!"

"And the third time, Phillip, the third time you were happy, when was that? A night in San Francisco, perhaps?"

Phillip dropped his eyes. "I'm afraid so."

"Which leaves us with a problem in words: social versus personal inclination. You must decide."

"But, Tim, you haven't answered my first question: what is justifiable? What is degenerate?"

Tim looked at him closely. "That, Phillip, you must answer for yourself. That, if you are wise, will be your secret always; and, incidentally, your key to personal happiness, for that is the dividing line of your dual life." Tim took a deep breath. "And now, Phillip, one more point if you don't mind my going deep into the quick of your pride."

"So long as your motive is reasonable."

"It is. A moment ago you said that it would be easy to face

311

death under certain conditions. Suddenly I remembered seeing a small bottle of white tablets on your bureau in Seattle. I saw them again here in your rooms." Tim saw the muscles in Phillip's cheek tighten. "Are your ideals so weak that they require such 'or else' insurance?"

Silently Phillip took a cigarette and let Tim light it for him.

"I suppose I have to face that eventually," he said, flicking away his ashes, not meeting Tim's persistent eyes.

"It won't hurt you to do so now," he said.

"Very well. All my life I've known what I wanted. I won't accept substitutes."

"Ah."

"What do you mean by that?" Phillip asked suspiciously.

"A dangerous chink in your armor. Anyone can live an exemplary life if he always gets what he wants. But the wise man can accept all manner of substitutes and make the best of them. I know that you can do so, too. It's just that you don't want to. Have you another reason for the little bottle? One that I can believe?"

"I have one, though I'd hoped I wouldn't have to put it into words. For the past year I've suffered from melancholia. Because of it I've felt several times that I was near taking my life. I first noticed it just after the incident with my captain, or it might have been nearer the incident with Stuff Manus. We were at Majuro, on our way to Pearl. Majuro is a typical island in the tropics—heat, palms, a garrison of half-naked soldiers. We'd gone ashore for a beer party and a swim. But there'd been an accident on the beach. A swimmer had been lost. Two swimmers in diving goggles and with thin gray lines about their waists were searching the surf for the body. Just before we went back to the ship they found what the fish had left. He had been a big man.

"On board, we had mail from home. I should have been happy. But I kept seeing that mutilation on the beach. That night we had a movie on board. Betty Grable in flaming techni-

312

color. While the others watched it, I undressed on deck and slipped down the ladder into the calm water. A jellyfish touched my shoulder as I shoved off. It felt like a flabby, cold condom. I started swimming, admiring the slow fans of phosphorescence from each stroke of my hands. I swam straight out to sea, thinking how long it would take me to tire. I knew what I wanted. My only fear was that a shark or barracuda might deprive me of what I wanted to do. I wanted the act to be mine, deliberate, calm.

"I suppose it was the fear of fish that made me turn back. As I climbed up the ladder, I realized what I had done. I wasn't horrified. I was just sorry I was back.

"With the end of the GCM, I felt it disappear. But it isn't gone. I can't explain why I know, but it's there, waiting for me to need it. And still it isn't frightening. It's—comforting, a little world of its own when mine gets too complicated."

"Do you realize what you're admitting?" Tim asked.

"I do. I am mentally ill. Homosexuality and melancholia, a dangerous but usual combination. That's why I feared psychoanalysis. I was afraid of the truth, not because my commission as an officer depended upon it. Soon now I will be free of the Navy. Then I must decide what to do about it."

"Do you feel you need the help of a psychiatrist?"

"Not at all. I think I can weather my storms if I have a chance. The best psychiatry is that which we work out ourselves. And I'm no dolt. Innately, I think I'm as intelligent as the average doctor. And I've an advantage over anyone attacking my problem. I'm on the inside. Do you agree?" They smiled at each other.

"I agree," Tim said.

Phillip sat up, his gaze searching the valley and the horizon for a while. "This must be my life, Tim. It would help if you'd let me have it without—conflict."

"The decisions are up to you, Phillip."

"But I don't want to make them. I want you to say I am

313

right, that you can offer me nothing in comparison to all this." He indicated the valley with a nod.

"But perhaps I can. And if I think so, I shall tell you."

"And I shall listen. I respect you too much to do otherwise. That is why my decision will be so painful."

"Respect can't cause pain, Phillip."

"You want me to say 'love.' How can I when I've never known it?"

Tim did not contradict the boy. He stood up and offered his hand to rise. Phillip accepted it, saying, "Yes, it is time to go. We've had our talk but nothing is settled. Our progress has been in circles."

They turned and started down the hill, Phillip leading the way once more until they reached the floor of the valley. To Tim, this was symbolic. Phillip had to lead the way in the face of his own native dangers. But once he struck the level fields of cultivation, Tim could take his place beside him.

For his part, Tim was pleased with their talk. Unlike Phillip, he felt that several issues had been settled. Both had said what they wanted to say. And, above all, they had discussed their thoughts without emotion. This had pleased them both. It proved to them that indestructible as their feeling for each other was, it could be tempered. To Tim it had more significance. It indicated a safe foundation on which to build, not the sands of degeneracy.

And Tim felt that he understood Phillip completely. Already he knew what their future must be. He could have told Phillip about it, but that would have been an error. One didn't convince Phillip if one wanted him to stay convinced. Rather, one gave him the task and tools and let him do the work. Tim guessed that it would take him about a week. By then, they would be out of Phillip's territory. In the meanwhile, one more safeguard had to be made. As they reached the road, Tim made the first move in that direction.

"What do we do this afternoon?" he asked.

314

"Talk to Uncle Felix, I suppose," Phillip said with little enthusiasm. "Father sent me out to inventory my stock. Uncle Felix told me privately last night that he'd already done it but to come out anyway for a visit."

"Did you have something else in mind?"

"I'm afraid I did," Phillip admitted. "I was going to put new shoes on Pelops, my stallion, and sort of renew old acquaintances. You'll see him before we go back to town."

"Would you like me to take over your Uncle Felix all afternoon?"

"Would I?" Phillip's delight showed in his face. "Uncle Felix would like that. He'd never miss me. And we'll have a chance to talk at the bank tomorrow."

"Then it's settled," Tim smiled. "I'll exercise my German and you run along and play with your stallion."

"Yes, Father," Phillip said with mock docility, hardly able to choke back his laughter. But seeing the strange expression that shadowed Tim's eyes for only a second, his laughter vanished.

29

❖◦❖◦❖◦❖◦❖◦❖

*T*he day passed. After a memorable dinner of roast goose and thick bock in the stone-paved kitchen, ending with the long porcelain pipes from Munich, Phillip had escaped to the barn where he found My Little Pelops awaiting him. Their reunion had been a quietly glorious affair, each nuzzling the other for hours. After dark Tim and Phillip had returned home, tired with accomplishment and feeling very close. They had lingered over dinner and then gone up to bed and sleep.

Their last day, the friends were separated, Tim spending the day with Fanchon and her family, while Phillip spent eleven weary hours in the back rooms of the bank trying to devote his mind to the facts that were being poured over him by his father and Uncle Felix. His success was disgusting. Instead of studying "Time and Demand Deposits of Individuals, Partnerships, and Corporations," or "Reserve for Contingencies," he saw Timothy Danelaw's face, heard his words caught in the low, sibilant voice that could caress or demand with equal ease. And it was plain that Uncle Felix wanted to talk with him, but his father hounded the pair constantly. Not that Phillip really cared, because his mind was too full to do justice to his godfather's affectionate camaraderie. When he returned in two more months, they would talk then—acres of talk.

Phillip drove his father home, but before dressing to go to Fan's for dinner, he found his mother knitting at an afghan near the library windows. He dropped into a nearby chair for a few minutes' chat. His father left them to take his pre-dinner prescriptions. As Phillip had suspected it would, the conversation opened on Tim.

"What has he done to Fan?" Phillip asked. "She's crazy about him."

"I hadn't noticed anything unusual," his mother replied.

"We had ten-o'clock coffee at the hotel. Fan dropped in with him. She'd been shopping and he was carrying a bag with celery sticking out the top and leading Paul-Phillip, who calls him Uncle Tim already. Fan welcomes people, but always with plenty of reservations."

"Maybe she likes Timothy. Are you jealous?"

"Of Fan?" Phillip laughed easily. "Nothing can come between us."

"Oh," his mother answered somewhat dryly. Phillip realized that she hadn't been thinking of his sister. "Don't you like Timothy?"

"First rate."

"He's different from everyone else you've entertained. He seems so mature, yet so fresh. I like him." His mother laid aside the bright coverlet and smiled at him. She handed him a small notebook of clippings. "For your condolence calls. Take it to your room when you go."

Phillip opened the book idly and read a few obituaries from the local paper. But he closed it when it began to arouse morbid thoughts.

317

"Chérie," he said thoughtfully, "how much of all this mother sentiment is real?"

"What do you mean?"

"This: 'My Fine Sturdy Son Is Overseas—He May Not Come Back—God Bless America—et al attitude?"

"I don't like your cynicism, Phillip, but your question is interesting. I've thought of it often, having seen so much of it around town during the war." She paused as if arranging her thoughts for presentation. "Like a great number of things, I think the emotional root is sincere. But people love attention, so the flowering is sometimes gaudy. Hysterical churchwomen every Sunday, women who insist on embarrassing everyone for the thrill of sympathy. I think I'd say that most of the afflicted like a good show as much as anything. Of course, there are those whose grief is genuinely touching."

"And you?"

His mother glanced up at him. "I'd mourn you, Phillip. If you were gone I'd miss you deeply. But I've still your father and Fanchon. The best mothers are the sternest ones."

"Grandfather abhorred sentiment, didn't he?" Phillip had not been offended by his mother's attitude. He admired her for it.

"Secretly he did, though he was considered a model of correct behavior."

"Father doesn't believe in presenting two faces to the world."

"What do you mean?"

"He isn't a happy man."

"Do you mean you have to be two-faced to be happy?" Victoria smiled.

"No. I just mean Father isn't happy."

"He thinks he is and that's as important. I don't think it wise of you to compare your father and grandfather. That's why you have so little in common with your father now. It isn't good."

"Sorry. But is it necessary to lead two lives to be happy?"

"If you were told to put values on your demands of your world," his mother asked, "which one would you put first?"

318

"Privacy," Phillip said promptly.

"Exactly. Those who live before the public are entitled to their private lives. You should have discovered that by now."

"Then," Phillip mused, his mind rambling, "there is the vast responsibility of selecting what one wants to live for."

"Are you asking for advice, Phillip?" Victoria asked him bluntly.

"You wouldn't mind giving me some then?"

"If you are genuinely puzzled and think I can help," his mother said quietly. She added, "But you know it is my policy, if not your father's, to leave you to your own devices as far as possible. You are twenty-three. We've given you the best rearing we could. If you can't take care of yourself, there's been a drastic mistake made somewhere." She closed her lips firmly as Phillip plowed on.

"It's about Europe," he frowned. "If I'm ever to go anywhere and get ready for the grind of living, it will have to be when I'm discharged."

"You mean with Sybel Jo?" his mother asked a bit maliciously.

"I mean by myself. Europe or New York or Timbuktu—anywhere that I can get my bearings before I jump into the middle of Devereaux."

"That's up to you. You've enough money to go away awhile. If you need some time away from Devereaux, you'd better take it. A few months now might mean years later on."

"But suppose it's years instead of months?"

"Then it's years."

"And Francis sells the bank down the river?"

"That's a part of the price. Do you think you'd lose your opportunity entirely?"

"No. But it would set me back years in getting what I want."

"There's an old adage, Phillip, about eating cake."

Phillip's speculative mood continued all evening at Paul and Fan's table, where the wine was chilled and plentiful. Quiet and

319

keenly attentive to the others, he noticed that an unusual mood of comfort and understanding hovered over them. It was as if he, not Tim, were the stranger. This annoyed him.

After dinner, while Paul and Tim took the son and heir up to his nurse, Fan drew her brother's arm about her waist and suggested they go outside for a chat. His arm fit beautifully, Phillip thought; so he agreed. They strolled out to look up at the moonlit sky. From an open window on the floor above they heard childish laughter and Tim's distinctive voice.

"You should have heard Tim explaining honor to Paul-Phillip this morning," Fan whispered.

"I'd love to have heard that," Phillip said with a sarcasm Fan ignored.

"After a tedious explanation in a one-syllable vocabulary, Paul-Phillip asked: 'Uncle Tim, will I ever be old enough to get along without honor?' Tim gave me a helpless glance and answered: 'I certainly hope so.' It was delightful."

The lawn was wet with dew and they sat on a glider near the windows. They pitched their voices low so that when the men returned downstairs they would not be overheard. They sat very close, Phillip's arm still about his sister. She rested against his chest. Fan had always been extremely affectionate to him since the disastrous affair with Anne. It was as if she defied his desire to eliminate all manifestations of love from his behavior. Always she petted him lavishly, as if to prove that he need not be ashamed of showing his love. And this gesture of hers had benefitted him immensely. Never allowing their love to pick up any trace of passion, Fan had led him gently back to feminine society, laid the groundwork for his romantic inclinations toward girls of his own age, and founded his ability to come to her for confession any time he desired. Their "petting parties," as Paul referred to them, were one of Phillip's joys. Now he put his arms closer about her and settled her warmly for their chat.

"What's Tim's wife like?" Fan asked softly, hearing her guest and her husband enter the room behind them.

320

"Pat? After the divorce it will be easier to say. Tim purchased her like everything else he has wanted, and I suspect he trimmed off any edges that might have annoyed him."

"You could love her?"

"I might have once. Not now."

"I can't reconcile the two sides of Tim, the one I see and the one at which you've hinted several times," Fan said, wriggling closer to him. "He could be cruel—he could have a genuine talent for it—but not unless he were provoked."

"You like him, don't you?"

"Very much. I respect him, too. You should have seen him at the club this afternoon. We were on the terrace and Ellamae Grissom had her Tulsa crowd out to the pool. You know Ellamae—too, too sophisticated. Naturally they came on the run to see who Paul and I had the minute we set our clubs down. Well, Tim had them jumping through hoops in ten minutes, and loving it. And yet I had the distinct impression he was bored bloody well stiff all the time. Paul did, too."

"You've guessed who he is then?"

"Mother gave me the clues."

"Does she know, too?" Phillip asked uneasily.

"I don't think she wants to know. It's your life. Father, of course, suspects nothing."

"Poor Father."

"Yes, poor Father. Whatever his sins are, you're his punishment, Phillip. It wasn't kind about the saddle yesterday morning. Tim told me. He didn't like it either. He asked me if I couldn't do something about it. I told him that but for the war you and Father would have cracked up long ago. And," Fan said decisively, "don't be annoyed at Tim's frankness, or at mine. I gave him permission to be personal."

"What else did Tim say?" Phillip asked tightly.

"He said you were one of the most interesting young men he'd ever met, that it was possible for you to have an extremely brilliant life, and that, very selfishly, he wanted to feel he had

321

a part in it. In other words, he paid Paul and me the supreme compliment. He told us the truth." Phillip let this pass without comment. Fan went on, "He beats every other friend you've had all to the devil."

"I like my friends well enough."

"Everyone likes your friends. Why shouldn't they? Two and two make four. That's comforting, but not much to whet your mind against. Your friends are gaited, but no one will ever ride Tim. I think you're afraid of him, afraid of what he can do to that precious mind of yours."

Suddenly Phillip perceived that it was because of Tim that his sister had brought him out to talk. Characteristically Phillip changed the subject. "Do you really mind my marrying Sybel Jo? In Seattle?"

"Mind?" Fan said testily. "Would I mind inviting a cannibal to dinner tomorrow night?"

"You've never sounded off before."

"That's a Navy expression, isn't it?" she said momentarily sidetracked. "No. I've never sounded off because I didn't think you'd do it."

"I wish there was a way out. She and Madame are so god-damed silly out there." Fan laughed without humor and Phillip sighed lightly. "Why didn't you marry for money, Fan? You had the chance."

"Meaning?"

"Young Sauvage from New Orleans."

"I didn't realize you knew about him."

"You didn't expect me to ask questions at the age of eight, did you? He seemed eligible enough."

"I had reasons for refusing," Fan shrugged. "He was Catholic and we've been over that often enough. I didn't like New Orleans well enough to live there. I didn't love him. And, last of all—" her tone grew careful—"emotionally he didn't quite jell."

"Strange?"

"Not exactly. Later, perhaps, but it was something I sensed

322

about him—early development, a gaudy flowering, a short life. I'd have been running him in a year and his family would have interfered."

"And you don't run Paul, I suppose?"

"I do. But Paul and I want the same things. I only help him. . . ."

"I hope Paul-Phillip is like you," Phillip said with sudden tenderness.

"He will be, if it's possible." She covered his fingers with hers.

"Out of both our offspring, there ought to be one to carry on."

"More than one, with any luck at all," Fan assured him.

"Grandfather came close to losing out, didn't he?"

"Not so close. He had Mother, and toward the last he had started to believe in you."

"Why was he such a sphinx, Fan?"

"Something in his mind. He loved secrets."

"Did you know any of them?"

"No. No one did. And for the one thing you want to know, you'd do well to turn your energies on Uncle Felix, though I doubt that he would talk unless your life depended on it."

"It may, one day," Phillip murmured.

Fanchon pushed herself back so that she could look at him. Her face was a chiaroscuro of ghostly gray and heavy shadow in the moonlight.

"Phillip, everyone in the family, particularly Father, has pondered your questions. Was Grandfather Dev homosexual? Have you inherited the taint? That's one reason for your strange education, your hard work, your isolation, your enforced belief in principles you subconsciously hate. That's why Father hated his father-in-law and distrusted Uncle Felix, though God knows there is little to worry about on the last score. Uncle Felix is as straight as they come. But remember this, my dear, no matter what our grandparent seemed to be, there is no proof to damn him. *His public life was above reproach.* Just see that yours is, too, and you've fulfilled your first duty to society." .

They were silent for a while, searching deep into each other's eyes.

At last Phillip said, "I love you, Fan. Without you, I—"

She moved to him impulsively and kissed him on the lips. "I know, darling. Don't say it." They were silent again, each busy with thought.

"I've thought of psychiatry," Phillip said, "but I don't have the faith in it that I have in myself."

"You're right, too. You're like a man who thinks he needs a major operation when all he needs is the proper tonic. Psychiatry is for the herd, those who can't or won't think for themselves. It can only strip you to your essentials and prescribe common sense." She added with a smile, "And anyone who can teach himself Greek and analytic geometry as a pastime ought to be intelligent enough to do that. But the element you can rely on is this: you were reared as an individual by individuals who faced their problems and worked them out alone. We conquer, Phillip, or we go under knowing that we've done the best we could. If we are powerful, it's because we stand on our own two feet; and we know that if our money and position disappeared tomorrow, we'd still go on and make an excellent showing with our lives. But then you know that. What you don't know is this: Paul and I will take over the bank if you want to count yourself out of this conquering hero role that Father has reared you with. We'll stay on and fight Francis and we'll win. Nothing will ever be said against you by Paul or me. Only come to us when you feel that you possess yourself and want to take over the bank."

"Does Father know you're making this offer?"

"Heaven forbid! Even Mother might not understand."

"I'll stay, Fan. You go on East as you planned."

Suddenly they heard the telephone inside and Paul say, "Long distance for you, Tim." And then it was that Phillip understood all too clearly why his sister had offered to free him for an indefinite period. He felt his body stiffen with humiliation. He

324

felt Fanchon tense swiftly as she realized what he was thinking.

Her voice was unnaturally rapid as she said, "He's been using long distance all day—New York, Philadelphia, Washington. Something must be wrong."

"Not necessarily. He uses the phone as we use stamps."

"He's very rich, isn't he?"

"So I've heard." For a moment they listened to the hushed sounds of the well-bred neighborhood about them. Phillip said, "Fan . . ."

"Yes?"

"What has Tim to do with your offer to take over the bank?"

"Nothing."

Phillip knew she was lying to him and it infuriated him. He blamed Tim for it.

"Then what did you think I'd be doing away from Devereaux?"

"Studying, traveling. I know how you've always wanted to. You can afford a bit of an odyssey."

Phillip ignored her small talk completely and asked brutally, "Fan, how would you like to have a brother that minced around with a limp wrist and gushed over things real men don't even recognize?"

And her answer came like an unexpected blow in the stomach. "I wouldn't be the first woman to have such a brother!" she said.

Slowly he withdrew his arms from her. It was as if some lovely object in his life had been smashed before his eyes and now he could never look forward to the delight of beholding it again.

But Fan did not repent. Her nostrils flared whitely as her voice continued, "Do you actually think you could be a fairy? Do you think your background would let you mince anywhere? Do you think Tim Danelaw would glance at you if you betrayed the first hint of effeminacy?"

"And what's the difference between acting like one and thinking like one?"

"Keep your voice down, you little fool."

"Don't call me a fool, you she-pimp!"

"Phillip!"

His face burned with shame and his voice quivered as he said, "Please forget that, Fan. It's just that you gouged too deep." He covered his eyes with his hand suddenly.

Fan waited like an outraged judge for him to continue his explanation. His accusation had not offended her; rather, it had snapped her into an attitude of cautious respect.

At last Phillip said, "Even suggesting you'd countenance such a thing disgusts me."

"Why?" Fan asked flatly. "Am I such a prig I can't discuss such things?"

"Fan, you just told me that I had to keep my life above reproach—"

"Wait! I said your public life. Your private life is an affair with your conscience. I've suggested nothing to you, but evidently something of such a dubious nature has been in your mind for some time."

"Yes, it has. Any step in that direction takes me too far from what I want. I can't gain; I can only destroy. And suppose I couldn't return from it. Who knows where the heart is after such lotus dwelling?"

"That answer makes sense," Fan said. "Are you afraid?"

"Yes and no. I feel that my emotions are incidental. They can't rule me for long. Ruling myself is a point of honor. Stop it, and I stop."

"I see." She nodded and ran her thumb lightly across her strong oval fingernails as if testing a razor. "You're in worse than I thought, Phillip. Forgive my nastiness, but it was the only way of tricking you into a complete confession. Are you certain of what Danelaw wants?"

"I think so. Yes."

"And how do you feel about it?"

Suddenly Tim's words of the previous day leaped into his

326

mind and he uttered them: "Personal versus social inclination."

"And morally?"

"I don't give a damn!" Phillip said, his eyes unwavering. If his sister was capable of trickery, she was capable of knowing the truth. He hoped it gagged her.

It didn't. She asked quite frankly, "Then where is the crusade? As I see it, there might be certain advantages. If you love him and you don't love Sybel Jo—"

"I said nothing of love," Phillip snorted.

She shrugged. "Perhaps he is interested in you for reasons other than a sexual alliance."

"What do you mean?"

"He has no friends, no family. He is being divorced. He knows that we would accept him as something more than a guest."

Phillip shook his head. "No dice. What are you trying to say, Fan?"

"Control of the bank, the thing you say you want. Don't be furious," she added nastily, "I didn't want it to occur to you while you were alone. Some outsider will have to buy Francis. He could arrange that. He could even invest or lend you money, perhaps at a good rate of interest."

"Fan," Phillip said slowly, "I thought I was beyond redemption. Hell! I've got two great big white wings!"

To his surprise, she laughed lightly and for an instant it was as if no difference had sprung up between them. "I suppose I deserved that," she said, leaning back against the cushions. "Have you a cigarette?" He gave her one and held her light. "Are you too angry to see what has happened, Phillip?"

"I'm afraid I am. Please enlighten me." It was his turn to sneer.

"Another wall built around your boyhood just fell. From now on I'll be a human being to you, not a goddess. There won't be so much sweetness and light between us."

"There's a good deal less than there was ten minutes ago."

Fan laughed again, but she did not look at him. "I might

327

have done what I did more gently if I had had days instead of minutes, but you're leaving early tomorrow and what I've to say to you is better said now. You're caught in one of those futile situations in which life abounds, and unless I miss my guess you're going to make a decision you'll regret all your life. So here I go, giving you my support.

"You've been an idealist all your life. You rant about honesty, but you don't want it from those you love. That is because you're on the side, watching the game. You'll change when you get in it."

Against his will, Phillip felt himself relax. Even now Fan could still twist him about her finger. And suddenly he didn't care. Despite everything, he loved her. When her hand sought his, he held it gladly.

"Just now I shocked you," Fan continued, "but I had to do it. All your life, Mother, Father, and I have been in league to shape you to our ends. And frankly, I'm scared, scared that one day you'll see what we have done to you and throw us all overboard. My life would be dull without you, my dear. When I'm a very old lady, I shall value your esteem, and I'll want you near me often. Because then, Phillip, the mistakes you make now won't count, but your love will mean much.

"Just now when I suggested that you take Tim's offer for what it was worth, you told me the one thing I needed to know. In refusing, you told me how much you thought of him. You could marry a woman for her money and let her bear your children, but you couldn't sell a friend like Tim. Can't you see what that means, Phillip?"

"I—I'd never thought of it in that way."

"There are many things you haven't thought of, but you would, under Tim's tutelage. Believe me, I wish it hadn't been this for you. But now that it is, think it over carefully before you marry that girl, or turn Tim away. You like him and he likes you. I can imagine how you got off on the wrong foot with him. It doesn't matter. He wants your friendship, and for it

328

he'll pay you in virtues you can use all your life. He knows that buying a thing isn't possessing it. His wife has taught him that. So whatever you offer him, be sure it is genuine."

Phillip's mind raced back to that night in Frisco, and from myriads of words he remembered: ". . . only when you feel what I feel. It is no escape, no last resort. It may be madness but it is a lucid kind. . . ." Phillip was glad the darkness concealed his face.

Fan continued, "You are worried about the bank. You think you want it because it will make you like Grandfather Dev. How do you know you want to be like him? You know nothing of him. Personally, if the bank were lost, I wouldn't care. I don't think you need it. The leveling process has begun in earnest. There has been a war—a change of pace and tune. You will seek your youth in the present, not the past. Paul and I believe a diplomatic career for you would do the world and yourself far more good than the preservation of Devereaux. But Tim Danelaw can show you that, if you will listen to him. I can't believe that he will bring you to harm, whatever happens."

"But, Fan," Phillip interrupted her smooth voice, "I can't go to Anne or any other woman and say: 'Here, I've had my fashionable little affair. Now I'm ready to take you to wife.' What would you have done if Paul had said that?"

"If Anne can't accept you with all your propensities, you don't want her. That's why I invited her up in the fall, hoping to let you learn if she's the right one instead of Sybel Jo. And as to what I would have done if Paul had approached me with such a statement, I don't think he would have. I wooed Paul, you know. But if he had had such a past, here is what I'd have done. I'd have weighed my love for him against everything else. If it had been the greater, I'd have said: 'Very well, but that is past. Now you love me and from now on it is my job to see that you go on loving me.'" She flipped her cigarette away and turned to face him. "I challenge you to find a sounder marriage than mine. And I am bragging. It is sound because, as a good carpenter knows he has built a good house, I know my marriage. As the years pass, I change for Paul. There are no rules in the game—only a goal: his happiness, and mine."

"But the standards of decency never change," Phillip said tritely.

"Oh, Phillip, the good Reverend Plum would kiss you for that. You know very well that standards of decency and everything else shift whenever people progress. What I'm saying is this: your personal satisfaction is more important to me than the opportunity of pointing to your shining example above mankind and saying: 'That's my brother.' I won't sacrifice you. Father would. Mother might. I won't. Each of us has his own sphere. I have my family, Mother has Father, Father has his wealth and position. You can never be more than a satellite in any sphere except the one you create for yourself. So if Tim is a part of your future, you won't find Paul and me against you. Nor Mother and Father, so long as you present to them, and the world, the face they want to see."

Silence moved into the void where her words had been. But those words were already deep in his heart. And from there came his answer.

"I love you, Fan. I respect you."

They kissed.

"We'd better go in," she whispered. "And just pretend you had a dream out here. Later you'll accept of it what you want."

Tim was in the room alone, writing on the telephone pad. Paul was in the kitchen for ice. As Tim saw them, he straightened with a piece of paper in his hand and came toward them smiling. Suddenly Phillip felt shy in his presence. He shook the feeling off with difficulty and smiled, too.

"I've some news that may interest you," Tim said to them.

"Oh?" Fanchon asked. "And what may that be?"

"Joe Voth is broke."

Phillip saw his sister's eyes widen with surprise.

"What do you mean?" Phillip asked quietly.

330

"Just what I said. His first wife's money is nil. I'm surprised that this shrewd family of bankers let that one slip by."

"That's a very serious charge," Fan said severely.

"I know. That's why I'm giving you this number in Philadelphia. You can check for yourself." He handed the paper to Fanchon.

"But how did you know?" she asked rather sharply.

"Maybe I was looking for unpleasantness," Tim admitted. "Phillip mentioned certain investments. Felix Mehl said that Voth had sold those same investments. I thought that was strange. I also wondered why Sybel Jo wanted to get married. She didn't impress me as the sort of girl who would foul up as Phillip suspected. I had a friend of mine in New York do some checking. He found a long series of sales evidently brought on by Madame's extravagances and Joe Voth's financial schemes. His handling of his bank lately may not bear close scrutiny. You can see the rest. Sybel Jo's marriage would have cemented financial safety with connubial bliss." And Tim added calmly as if no bomb had been exploded, "Here is a check for my telephone bill, Fanchon. I just got the figure from the operator."

Fan took the check and tore it across twice. "Believe me, Tim, we owe you for a great deal more than a telephone bill."

Phillip felt that he should say something, too. He realized that Tim's action had saved him from another of his father's blundering mistakes. And he also realized that this put him farther in debt—so far, perhaps, that even reason could not get him out. But Tim had turned away to talk with Fan. Phillip continued to stare at a vase on a nearby table until its colors blurred.

30

$\diamond\!\!\!\bullet\!\!\!\diamond\!\!\!\bullet\!\!\!\diamond\!\!\!\bullet\!\!\!\diamond\!\!\!\bullet\!\!\!\diamond$

$\mathcal{T}$im and Pat were driving Phillip back to the base. It was not particularly late, only just past ten o'clock, but Phillip felt exhausted and strained. He had been back in Seattle three days. Much had happened, but nothing to give him the peace of mind he desired so deeply.

On the day he had arrived in Seattle from Oklahoma he had called on Madame at the hotel to break his marriage contract with her step-daughter. She had received him alone. Coolly she had asked him about his trip to New York. Evidently she knew nothing of his Oklahoma visit yet. Playing his hand straight, as if he did not know Madame's motives for trying to effect the marriage, he decided to make the most of what knowledge she had of his homosexuality. With superb genuineness, he looked uncomfortable, turned his cap in his hands feebly, stuttered a bit and said, "Mrs. Voth—" he declined to use her title, admitting its ridiculousness now that he no longer felt allied to her—"I cannot marry Sybel Jo. I think it would be a grave mistake. I imagine you know why."

He saw the controlled smile possess the woman's strong face. "So Bruner was right," she said softly.

"What do you mean?" Phillip asked quickly, raising his eyes to her.

"Rather an expensive price for a court martial," she said.

Phillip let his eyes waver. "Please," he said, "I'm trying to be fair to your daughter. My motives and actions are my own affair. And remember that gossip can be slander without proof."

Madame's smile grew bolder as she thought of the dirty work to be done in their home town. Phillip wanted to smile at the thought of the boomerang she would unwittingly release. She went to the desk near the windows and took something from the drawer. "Here," she said, putting her hand on the table near his. "Your gifts."

As she moved her hand, Phillip saw his engagement ring and the other baubles he had given Sybel Jo—the pearl pendant, the barrette, a cigarette case of gold filigree. Because they represented a good deal of money, he slipped them into his coat pocket with no qualm of emotion. Their presence in the desk indicated that Madame had expected his action and had evidently drawn up plans of her own. Later he had learned what they were when he heard that Sybel Jo and Francis had married two days after he had seen Madame. Tim, bringing him the news at the office, had said, "Francis thinks he's pulling quite a coup. Aren't you going to warn him?"

"I?" Phillip had replied with some surprise. "The family would never forgive me if I prevented him from crippling himself permanently now." And at the shadow that crossed Tim's face, Phillip had added quickly, "He loves her. Perhaps they will be happy. I hope so."

But that had been the most trivial of Phillip's problems. The loss of Sybel Jo was a great relief. It was promptly cast off and soon to be forgotten. The issue of greatest importance was Tim.

333

Once, before the night at Fanchon's, all of the boy's questions had begun with "How?" Now they all began with "When?" For his course was clear. Tim had effectively removed all barriers from Phillip's progress toward him, and there was no doubt about the final decision. When could he bring himself to make it? Constructed as he was, Phillip's mental processes were cautiously slow. Tim had impregnated his mind the morning on the hill. Fan and his mother had pointed ways of escape. Persistent thought was doing the rest. The time was here. A gesture or a word would plunge him into a world that was utterly foreign to him, but also so appealing to a part of him that at times he seemed to suffocate from its very absence. He felt like some amphibious creature that can live so long on land and then must return to water or die.

On the plane back from Oklahoma, Tim had set up the attitude which they had displayed to each other. They were friendly but impersonal. By not a glance did either of them reveal what was really in his mind. They worked together and with others in the offices of the flag. They tried never to be alone with each other, but on a plane no man could see, they were always alone together. They met Bruner and puzzled him greatly by their natural indifference to each other. Without knowing it, they almost cleared themselves of suspicion in the man's mind. They moved in the Navy crowd and in Pat's crowd, displaying the right degree of mutual consideration people expected of co-workers. It was their first stage of deceit. Beneath it all, as turbulent waters flow beneath ice, were the thoughts of the two men. Tim waited for the sign. Phillip watched the hours move by, knowing that soon he would close a door on everything in which he had once believed—and perhaps never return. He was alternately the victim of joy and despair, emotions he held severely in check. But always he waited.

And during this period he had one friend, Mike Mallory. Without having been told a word of what had happened, he seemed to know everything; and without saying a word, he

334

became Phillip's confidant. They never spoke of the matter, but Phillip knew Mike's sentiments, and he was glad for this silent approval.

The ferry docked at Amphib Island and the powerful car eased up the creaking ramp under Tim's hands. Soon Phillip would be alone again. The thought cheered him, for Pat was babbling about a bridge tournament, being exceedingly clever and tedious at once. After the solidity he had found in Oklahoma, Phillip found Pat's society hollow as a drum. He marveled that she had ever been able to excite feelings of inferiority in him.

At the officer of the day's shack, the car stopped, I.D. cards were produced, and they were logged in. As the young officer wrote their names, he said, "Froelich? Just a moment. There's a memo for you." He went inside the office and returned with a clip board from which he read: "Long distance call from Oklahoma. You're to call Operator Six. It's a death message."

Phillip's first reaction was panic, but he seized it and held it so firmly that the muscles at the base of his skull ached.

"Where can he take it?" Tim asked the O.O.D.

"Probably at one of the BOQ's at this hour, sir. The telephone office is closed and our phone has to be kept free."

Tim slid the car forward and drove quickly through the silent base to Phillip's quarters. No one spoke and Phillip was grateful. The word *death* burned angrily into his brain.

As the car came to a halt, he sprang out and ran to the entrance. Tim opened his door to follow, saying to Pat, "Take the car home. I'll get a taxi."

"I'm coming in, too," was her unexpected reply.

"Into bachelors' quarters?" Tim smiled. "I'm afraid not, Pat."

"Then I'll wait," she said firmly.

"No. You'll go home now." His tone did not change.

She grasped her evening bag with both hands and said with

335

desperate loathing, "Your interest in him is getting to be a bit sickening!"

Tim's body seemed to relax as he studied her sneering face. "As sickening as the cortege of men you've been sleeping with to arouse my jealousy?" he asked pleasantly. "What is it you want to say?"

"If you go in there now, you needn't come home. I won't be there!"

"I wouldn't think of inconveniencing you," Tim answered politely. "I'll pack in the morning and move to my club before you're up. You can reach me through my lawyer as you arranged previously. Remember?"

"You wanted this break," she choked accusingly.

"And now you've given it to me," he said. "Pity the clever girl who marries for money and then falls in love with her own husband." He got out of the car. "Good night."

As he took the first step away, she shouted, "Tim!"

He paused. "I don't think you'll want me to quiet you here," he said.

As he entered the building, he heard the gears grind into place and the car roar off. He dismissed the incident promptly and turned his attention to Phillip standing before the pay phone halfway down the dim corridor. Tim heard him murmur incredulously, "Uncle Felix? Instantly. Six o'clock." There was a broken sound that might have been a word or a sob as the boy let the receiver slide slowly from his ear and turned away.

Tim took the instrument and said, "Hello. This is Commander Danelaw."

Victoria Froelich's voice said, "Timothy. Thank God, you're there with him. He will need you now. Uncle Felix passed away this afternoon in a heart attack. We've been expecting it for months, but Phillip only guessed his real condition."

"I know," Tim said. He then extended his sympathy and promised to keep an eye on Phillip in the next days.

"If you can persuade him not to come home for the funeral,

336

we will appreciate it," Victoria said. "I don't believe it will be wise to draw this tragedy out for any of us. Services are in the morning at nine for just the family."

"I understand. Would you like me to call Francis and the Voths?"

"Thank you, Timothy." There was a pause and Mrs. Froelich said, as if they were in the same room, "I must leave you now. I shan't worry about Phillip so long as you are with him, and God bless you both."

As he heard the connection being broken, he turned to follow Phillip into his room, the door of which stood ajar. He found him standing in the darkness staring out the windows at the tremulous lights reflected in the bay. Tim closed the door softly and turned on the desk lamp, shading it to give a minimum of light. Phillip stirred and turned to stare at him as if completely bewildered by what had happened. Tim realized that in all the boy's years, this was his first real encounter with death since he had lost his grandfather. From an abstract conception, cold reality had emerged again for him. It was fantastic that he had escaped this experience so long. For an instant Tim was afraid that the shock might be too much for him. Phillip's first words allayed that fear.

"This is the beginning of the end for Aunt Minna." Phillip looked around the room as if embarrassed by Tim's attention. "I'm not going to break, Tim," he said, pressing his hands to his eyes.

"Of course." Tim was silent before he asked, "Phillip, would you like to—" He had meant to say "to pray" but instead he said—"go to the chapel?"

"Later, while the service is being read." He seemed to take it for granted that he would not be going home. "I'm very tired now."

"Would you like to sleep?"

"Yes. Yes, I think I would."

337

As he undressed, Tim gave him one of the sleeping capsules and saw him into bed. The man sat beside him until his breathing indicated he was asleep. Then Tim stood and looked down at the boy who slept with his arms above his head. He studied the incomparably splendid features of the head, the crisp way the hair curled up from the pure forehead, the shallow shadowed temples, the lashes that lay like bits of down against the cheeks, the straight nose and the dilating nostrils over slightly parted lips. Aesthetically these features were satisfying to him. But more satisfying was the knowledge that he held the boy's mind in his own. He understood its content and process well. There was beauty there, too—a treasure of it in the struggle between conscience and desire, in the ache and consolation in store for him. Tim remembered finding a book of Phillip's in his rooms back in Oklahoma and from the underlined words he had guessed the solace and challenge Phillip had found in them:

". . . The hidden harvest of luxurious time,
Sin without shape, and pleasure without speech;
And where strange dreams in tumultuous sleep
Make the shut eyes of stricken spirits weep;
And with each face thou sawest the shadow on each,
Seeing as men sow, men reap. . . ."

At last Tim knew what Phillip meant in his life. The boy was his last contact with a concrete world. When Phillip passed on alone, Tim would take his vows to medicine and to the support of a humanity he understood too well. Had Phillip been of the other sex, his life would change little at this point. With its sanction, he would be tied to society a little more, but his vows would still be made. He was glad Phillip was what he was, for in loving him he withdrew farther from all men and saw them in greater perspective. Phillip was his last benevolent gesture, the crystallization of his nature. That he would do the boy good was no longer doubtful to him. Not that he did or did not want to help him, that was not the question. He could not help ad-

338

vancing his friend no matter what happened, just as he would do his bit to advance medical science in his future research.

In Tim's life he had sought the homage of man in art, the comradeship of man in marriage. Neither had materialized. Now he sought to explore himself and ignore his fellow man. And in this point he knew that at last he was right. He longed to embrace his future, but first he must set his protégé firmly on his feet. This could be done only in one way, a long carefully traveled way. He would not be impatient.

Tim glanced at his watch and shrugged his thoughts away. He had much to do while the boy slept. He must go to his office, clear his desk, and leave instructions. He must pack some bags and move to his club. He picked up his hat, turned out the light, and with a parting glance at the figure sleeping in the moonlight, he left the room.

At six o'clock he returned and sat on the edge of the bed. Phillip awoke at his touch, blinked a few times, smiled, and then, remembering the news of the night before, sobered at once.

"You'll find it easier to face now. Last night you were rocky." Phillip nodded.

"Did you want to go back for the funeral?"

"No. Uncle Felix isn't there. Mother and Fan and Aunt Minna have each other." He paused. "I'd better call Francis."

"I called him last night. And the Voths."

Phillip looked at him gratefully and said, "I'll send telegrams."

"I sent them last night. Aunt Minna, your mother, Fanchon." Phillip sat up.

"Do you want to work today?" Tim asked.

"I'll manage." He tried to smile but forfeited the attempt.

Tim spoke quietly. "I've arranged with the Admiral to take a few days off. I've also chartered the plane to Fleurs-du-Mal Cove. We can leave as soon as you come from the chapel— if you want to come."

339

Phillip met his eyes. There was no uncertainty in them, as Tim had expected. In their clear depths there was an understanding of all the offer implied.

"I won't look away this time, Tim. I want to come."

Tim stood. "It's almost time for the services to start back in Devereaux," he said.

Phillip arose, washed, and dressed. While he was at the chapel, Tim packed a bag for him. They would reach the cove before noon.

31

◆◇◆◇◆◇◆◇◆

*O*nce more they were dropped into a world of clear greens and pure blues, of water, earth, and air, a world whose serenity seemed more civilized than civilization itself. Once more the plane taxied out of the cove to take off and quickly shrink to a dot on the inverted bowl of sky. And again they carried their supplies up the steep curving path to the cabin above the bone-white rocks. But this time they were alone. Climbing the hill, Phillip and Tim felt the front they had presented to the world slowly dissolve, the days that had occurred between their night in San Francisco and this moment dwindle and at last disappear. They felt equal in this experience, equal and joined.

Inside the cabin they faced each other. For a moment their eyes usurped the duties of speech. Phillip felt his breath hang raggedly inside his chest and his heartbeats catch sharply in his throat's hollow. He was rapidly losing himself in that strange, now familiar morass of swiftly rising sensitivity.

341

"Wait!" he gasped. "Not that again. Please." His breathing was short and thick. "It must be tied to something—something tangible. No moment such as this has the right to drift unanchored in the mind. I know that now."

To his relief, Tim nodded and turned away to light the fire in the fireplace. As naturally as if they had been in a circle of friends in Seattle, he asked, "How about a swim?"

"Yes," Phillip agreed. "I'd like that."

Below, on the jetty, they stripped and dove into the icy cove, momentarily quenching the consuming force that had threatened Phillip. For an hour they swam between jetty and rocks, crawling out with the first pull of ebb, dripping and weak yet glowing with awakened energy. And as they started back up to the cabin, Phillip dropped a hand on Tim's shoulder, a token of the feeling between them. When he thought of the intimacy it suggested, he blushed but did not remove it. At the top they turned for a moment to gaze down at the flower-like rocks rising up from the dark mystery of the ocean's floor to spread their strange beauty for few men to see.

"When I die," Phillip murmured, "I think my soul will come here—if it is damned."

And as they turned to enter the cabin, Tim frowned.

At the hour of sunset they walked to the promontory on the extremity of the cliff and stood against a new wind from the strait, savoring its salt and resinous smells. Soon there would be fog from the sea; already the sun was but a pale gold disk. A gull, seeing the smoke from their chimney, had come to wheel untiringly from cabin to jetty, knowing that he would be fed. Phillip tossed a pebble at him and laughed at the sharp glance he was given. Tim sat down, his back against a boulder, and looked up at Phillip. The boy moved nearer and knelt between Tim's knees which were drawn up before him. He took Tim's hands and held them against his face.

342

"Yes, Tim," he said, "at last I can say it. Above all mankind and myself, I love you."

"Thank you, Phillip," Tim said, detecting a slight tremor in the flesh beneath his hands. "Do you feel the need of justification?"

"I am a coward," Phillip said serenely. "An explanation would help."

Tim drew him close. "First, any regrets?"

"Of course, but they don't count now."

"Even so, what are they?"

"The regrets of the Sodomites—of all who have sinned against their God."

"So you do believe?"

"I do."

"I'm glad," Tim said. "You aren't afraid?"

"No. Now I shall seek Him in my way, not by way of Father's fundamentalist theology."

"And do you feel that you have sinned against Him?"

"Not against Him. Perhaps against you or myself, but not Him. Once you said we were alike. Now I know you are right. It is this finding of myself with two personalities that is the crux of our attraction for one another. Once I thought of you as a tempter. Now I realize the terrific strain you have been under, too. And now that the pattern is set and neither of us is equal to the task of breaking it, I know that our guilt is to be shared and respected. Once I thought the pursuit of pleasure as opposed to happiness was sinful. I couldn't understand why any reasonable man would be guilty of such a thing. Now I know that homosexuality or anything else is justifiable when it frees the intellect which can go only so far and then finds itself stopped. Then the vice becomes a vehicle of release. The sin lies not in the vice, but in the individual's failure to encompass it and live with it."

"Then what of your future?" Tim asked.

"A void. As yet I can see nothing there."

"You've given everything up for us?"

"I didn't really want the bank," Phillip said quickly.

"But you have the bank," Tim said, struck by the boy's fierce loyalty.

Phillip turned his head to look at him questioningly. "Tim, I won't accept your help in getting the bank."

"I see I've misled you. This concerns your Uncle Felix."

"I felt rather that I had failed him somehow when I was home. He kept wanting to talk, but I put him off because I thought he wanted to talk about you. Now it is too late."

"Not too late," Tim reassured him gently. "You see, he talked with me. He knew the end was near. He hoped he would live until you returned in the fall so he could tell you that he was leaving his third of the bank to you."

For a moment the significance of these words did not touch Phillip's mind. Supersaturated with emotion as he was, Tim guessed that he believed this some trick of his fancy. "But Aunt Minna?" he said at last.

"You are to provide her a quarterly allowance. She knew that."

"Did Uncle Felix tell anyone else?"

"No, only me. He wanted you to be prepared for any repercussions when your grandfather's will is finally read."

"Grandfather's?" Phillip asked. "What has that to do with it?"

"Everything. It was never read upon his death. And that's the point that amazes me, and shows me the character of men such as your grandfather and godfather, the trust they inspired in everyone who knew them. When your grandfather died, the Barrimans were in Europe, weren't they?"

"That's right. I remember Mother talking about the fuss Aunt Marie made because the interment took place before they returned. Mother and Father went away for a while, too."

"That's right. When the lawyers asked permission to read the will, your mother told Uncle Felix to take care of everything. So the will was never read. Considering the rivalry between you and Francis, one would think that the will would have been pawed over a thousand times. Millions were at stake, yet not one person ever questioned your grandfather's intentions or your Uncle Felix' honesty. And those two trusted each other as they did themselves. Their friendship would be a lesson to all men. If the will had been read, your Uncle Felix' intentions would have been known and all your lives might have been different. Your grandfather's power was split equally between the two heirs. Felix Mehl was to be the mediator. He was left his third of the fortune with the hope—and I think these were your grandfather's exact words—that upon Felix Mehl's death, the deciding third would be inherited by the heir most worthy in his estimation to carry on the Devereaux enterprises. There was no stipulation, only a hope.

"Your Uncle Felix chose you when you were twelve. It was a secret, of course, since he had no desire to see you and Francis pitted against each other any more than you were. He watched you grow up as you would. This is the result. He knew everything about you. So, you see, Phillip, your future has altered very slightly. Your responsibility to society is greater than before. You've many decisions to make and contrary to what you think, your life is not your own. Right now, you must decide how this will affect us."

For a few minutes Phillip was silent. Then he said, "My one hope for peace of mind in this thing was that we would be utterly alone, that we would hurt as few as possible. But now—"

"Would you have preferred my telling you in Seattle?"

"It doesn't matter. These hours were bound to be. I wanted them."

"And now?"

"I can't make a decision, Tim, not now."

"Still, you must think about it. The time for decision will arrive sooner than you expect. This is June. By the last of August—"

"All I can think of is you," Phillip said. "That suddenly my

345

life apparently lacks nothing, that you and I stand alone, to-gether, complete—that the demands of people I loathe—yes, loathe—are poisoning us already."

"*Pauvre, petit matou,*" Tim smiled. "You still seek perfection in neat situations. Will you ever learn what it is?"

As they talked, darkness had risen above the mountains and even now rushed down at them. The rocks below had colored pink, then coral, then yellow, and now loomed a ghostly gray. The gull had gone to sleep on one foot down on the jetty. Silently they rose and went back to the cabin, each deep in thought.

After supper they sat on the gigantic white bearskin before the fire and smoked while still pursuing their thoughts. At last Phillip got to his feet and went to his suitcase.

"To bed already?" Tim asked drowsily, watching him across the room of undulating shadows.

"No. I've something to show you."

He came back from the suitcase with the packet of letters that his godfather had given him at his birthday dinner.

"Do you know what these are?" he asked.

Tim nodded. "Your grandfather's letters. Your Uncle Felix had some doubt about your having them until he guessed the tortures of mind you were experiencing."

"There aren't many. I had no difficulty with the French, but my German is mostly oral. Would you mind helping me?"

"Not at all."

Phillip spread the dozen odd sheets on the fur between them, arranging them chronologically. Tim selected the first and began translating slowly for the boy. Even in translation the beauty of selection and arrangement of words was apparent. The letter was dated on the eve of the man's marriage. The place was Louisiana. The dry, brittle paper bridged more than five decades for them.

When he finished reading it, Phillip said quietly, "For the

346

first time since he died, I feel that I know him. He was a wonderful man, though certainly far removed from my childhood conception."

Tim read the next letter and the next, admiring the good taste, the exquisite manner in which even the most delicate emotions had been couched by Phillip's ancestor. And Tim saw how the influence of such a man might well ride above all other stimuli in the mind of a sensitive child such as Phillip had been.

At the fourth letter he paused. "Shall I continue?" he asked.

"No." Phillip stared into the fire. "All my life I've wondered about this one thing and now I know. I'm not sure that I should."

"Does he seem closer to you?"

"No. Now I realize that he didn't love me first in all the world. I used to believe he did. Everything in his life arranged itself behind his feeling for Uncle Felix. And yet no one ever really knew the truth. How can that be, Tim?"

"It was easy enough. He understood the world about him and was indifferent to it almost to the point of contempt. What it demanded of him he gave, but he was wise enough to keep his personal life on another level. He was a strong-willed man. He made his own rules, but he recognized that his real safety lay in his supporting what is accepted as right by the average man. Deceit was the price and the problem of his life. He accepted it because he knew what was genuine. He was no exhibitionist. He didn't give a tuppence for the opinion of the public; it was too easily won. His real life was remote. There is little doubt that he had a happy life. Too many things indicate that it was happy. And he did much good. . . . If you remember your Freud at all, you'll remember that he says often enough that the aim of psychiatry is not to correct the individual's faults and make him as other men, but to persuade him to live in harmony with himself and his fellow men. Actually that amounts to a sort of justification rather than a correction. The point of view is accepted in Europe on a wider scale than it is in America.

M

Your grandfather realized this very old problem was his, and he worked it out to his and everyone's satisfaction. Very likely he faced your blind alley once, but before naming it as such, he examined it carefully and found a way out. He climbed on top of his world and led it wisely and well. Certainly he brought beauty, comfort, and happiness to thousands of people. He set an example for living, incorporating all the virtues of his stratum he could, and in his own way he was sincere. He also demanded his right to happiness as an individual. There is much to be said for him, and few men could compare their lives to his and then condemn him. Perhaps now you can begin to see why you have always drawn a line between him and your father. One man was sincerely insincere; the other, insincerely sincere. Both have lived good lives. Both have been happy. It is up to you to choose your ideal. Do you understand?"

"Perhaps," Phillip said, turning his head away. "I'm not particularly quick about things. I solve my problems by persistence. I can't decide now."

"To continue as we are will put you in deeper."

"But if I decided now, it would be to continue with you as long as I can."

"And if you choose me, you must be ready to follow me through to the end, if that be the rest of our lives. Only then can you feel safe from homosexuality. If you broke this in the middle, you *might* succeed. Or it might lie dormant in your mind for years and then recur with fury enough to destroy you."

"And what is to assure me that it won't recur even after we have seen it through?"

"Nothing. There is always that danger. As you grow older you will grow wiser—if your mind is purged of fear. And a man who has reached perfection in his love and let it die in its own way and time is not likely to seek substitutes or even repetitions. He is happy in his memories—as your grandfather was."

"And do you believe we can reach this perfection?"

"We have reached it, Phillip. My ideas will be new and

348

frightening for a while. But if you believe in this strange emotion that is between us—and remember that we struggle toward a goal, that we are an experiment in personality over conventionality—I think we may succeed where others fail. First, we admit facts. Second, we decide upon the goals, and then we work to fill in between these points. To start, we might settle on a goal: for you, a compatible working relation between the personal and social demands in your make-up, a clear conscience, and a mind that can serve you freely the rest of your life. A set of principles to live by, the ability to gain the most from each day you live."

"And for you?"

"Your love. And, if and when you leave my protection, the knowledge that I have given you more that is good than evil."

"Posed in such a way, the problem seems capable of being solved."

"It is. Broken into their simplicities, all quantities have their denominators. Human beings have a bad habit of constantly bending toward complexities. Therein is our danger. On the other hand don't understimate your problem. But to state the facts, we might say that there are few psychological rules that are not particular, that is, as opposed to general truths. This gives us permission to work out our own difficulties. Second, between us exists an emotion that is real, genuine, inescapable —an emotion that allows no happiness without fulfillment. From this point we can conclude that certain voids exist in our personalities. Third, we believe we are strong enough to work them out by ourselves. If you choose what I am now proposing, there are certain ideas you must keep in mind. This may not last, Phillip," he said reluctantly. "To be fair to yourself, you must regard everything between us as temporary."

"Temporary?" Phillip's eyes held uncertainty and some fear.

"Unfortunately all things are temporary, *mon cher*. Try to regard it as a prelude to something even better. Man was not created to love man. *Cela va sans dire*. Your grandfather loved

349

a man passionately in his youth, but eventually he found the desire to part from him, marry, father children, and live a worthy life among his neighbors. From that passion evolved a friendship that was truly astounding. Yet there is every reason to believe that his sexual relationship with Felix Mehl ceased when they parted in Paris the first time. Of course, both men had a brilliant understanding of emotion. They believed in fidelity to the ancient laws of nature, yet they were not aloof from real need. You might call their relationship a tangent road, to use a simile. A tangent that touched the circle of their lives for only a brief instant. So long as it was a part of their lives, they traveled it, but when it moved away, they did not follow. They remembered to fulfill their duties as individuals to society because they had been taught to do so and they wanted to do so, thereby fulfilling the demands of equally important parts of their own personalities."

Tim looked at the boy sitting straight before him. Realizing that it was not only unwise but actually cruel to carry this point any further at this time, Tim said quietly, "You are aware of the name you now carry, Phillip, and some of the incurring unpleasantness. You are homosexual." Tim paused, but Phillip's gaze remained clear and steady. "An important thing for you to remember is never to identify yourself with any group. One of your great temptations will be to find companions and solace. Believe me, there is no safety or solace to be found in these groups. You are searching within yourself for answers and that is where you will find them. You've had excellent training living with society but apart from it. That will help you now."

"But has the homosexual nothing—no rights, even to a place in our social order," Phillip demanded angrily.

"The homosexual has a right to a place in our social order. Ordinarily, however, he has not the perspective to define that place or the courage to take it. A few have done so successfully because temperamentally they are capable of adjusting themselves, but the average slides further toward degeneracy for a

350

variety of reasons. Society sees him for what he is and condemns him. Not understanding his condemnation, he persuades himself he does not care, fights back by flaunting his nature, and thus drops lower and lower on the human scale. That is what you must not do, Phillip. You have the advantage of wealth and social position. It is up to you to see that they remain advantages rather than vehicles toward depravity such as you can only guess exists."

"But suppose I don't. What if I fail and become like the rest?"

"In the event that this experiment fails and you find yourself moving toward limbo instead of your goal, place yourself in the hands of a psychiatrist immediately. You will have no use for pride, reason, or anything else then."

Phillip said thoughtfully, "Oscar Wilde said that the only way to conquer a temptation was to yield to it."

"It wasn't his idea originally," Tim pointed out. "And he said and wrote many things he quickly forgot because he only understood them and did not believe them. Your grandfather took the same idea, lived by it, and died a happy man because he tempered it with common sense. He would not have dared to preach an idea to others who might have used it badly. He knew that it struck at the very foundation of his religion, his society, and hence his life itself. In his slow, quiet way, he lived simply, thought constantly, weighed all things carefully, and acted cautiously." Tim paused and added, "Forgive me for repeating myself, but I must do my best to make you grasp what you are facing."

"I understand," Phillip said, hugging his knees close to him. His body was bent as if already he was burdened with the task before him. "And yet," he mused, "you've told me only the worst to expect. Are there good things?"

"Many. To name a few: the joys and challenges of a solitary nature, years of a new kind of freedom, traveling the world, moving among people like your grandfather, Fanchon, the Admiral, the career you desire, and the possibility of returning to

351

Devercaux more like your Grandfather Dev than you could ever have been on your own, with the ability to see his town as he saw it and shape it wisely as he did."

"Yet you ask no stipulation for yourself," Phillip said.

"I make many. I shall always expect truth, industry, decency as you know it, fair-mindedness, fidelity, respect of yourself, tolerance of your fellow man."

"But for yourself?"

"My life is already shaped. You can only add to it in the things I have enumerated. Your happiness is most important."

Once more Phillip felt himself before the vast plain of the man's selflessness. Tim's analysis was perfectly logical. Despite the newly acquired responsibility of his inheritance, Phillip knew that his future course was determined. He would cast his lot with Tim. His love prevented him from doing otherwise. Phillip knew that once more his grandfather was at his side. The boy was ready to take up living where he had left it many years ago. But now the progress would be swift under Tim's guidance. The essence of years must be lived in days and months.

Tim, looking into the fiery hearts of the logs, spoke thoughtfully, "The Admiral wants me to go to the Orient with him in September. We could go together as civilians but with all the privileges of officers. It would be an excellent opportunity for you to see some of the Orient and a military form of government in action. Both would do your future a great deal of good, and we could easily afford a year before we go to Europe."

"I'd like that," Phillip said.

"Then your decision is made?"

"It is."

Phillip expected some demonstration of happiness from his friend. None came. Tim continued to stare into the fire.

Slowly Phillip gathered the letters between them together and put them in a neat stack. Then, crawling to the fire, he laid the brittle sheets on a blazing log and turned away.

352

32

❖◆❖◆❖◆❖

hus began a period of Phillip's life that in the years to come he was never able to describe satisfactorily because he was never to be free of it. For the first time in his entire life he felt individually free, yet never before had he been so enslaved. Concretely he was dumbfounded at the ease with which he progressed mentally; abstractly he grew wise enough to see the hopelessness of all wisdom in the face of a situation such as his. Later, when he was to think of it, he was to murmur simply: "I was happy."

Both Tim and Phillip felt that they were products of no age, citizens of no world. The people who surrounded them were another problem to solve. They planned their lives accordingly. Though Phillip kept his room and his personal effects at the base, he lived in quarters that connected with Tim's suite at the club in town. This was not a part of their original schedule, for they had agreed at the cove to see each other as infrequently as possible until they were both out of uniform—a measure of safety from and respect for the organization which had brought

353

them together. But in the taxi that took them from the airport into Seattle, the depressing thought of being separated had grown unbearably persistent. So when the driver had asked their destination, Tim, glancing at Phillip, had sighed and given the address of his club. The miasma they had created at the cove had refused to leave them. So another room had been taken. Later, when anyone asked him, Phillip admitted that he kept a second room in town, but he did not say that he had not occupied his old quarters on the base once in the seven weeks that followed.

In the morning they went to the base together and separated at the gate, Phillip dropping by his room for a few minutes so as not to arrive at the office at the same time Tim did. This might have seemed a small thing to others in their position, but it was not to them. They guarded their happiness and their reputations relentlessly. Each of them was sensible enough to know that one hint of scandal could level the structure of their lives.

At the office, they worked apart. When they met, they were friendly, impersonal, businesslike. Always they lunched in the company of others. In the afternoon they did not see each other at all. Phillip went to Mike for his orders. Mike had assumed a unique role in their lives.

After work, Phillip went to his room on the base and there Tim picked him up. Often they drove out of town for dinner, Tim having bought another car. If they dined at their club, they always saw to it that they were not alone. This was not difficult since they were both popular members and at the bar there was always an assortment of companions. Out of town they sought out-of-the-way places and returned to them infrequently. In their rooms they never answered each other's telephone. This subterfuge they labeled privacy.

On their weekends they went to places where they knew no one to fly, ski, sail, or swim, but most of all to talk and be alone.

From Bruner they learned that the newlyweds were back in Seattle after three weeks in Hollywood and that Madame was

354

back in Oklahoma. From Fan they learned that the town was agog over Phillip's inheritance, Sybel Jo's marriage, and Joe Voth's financial status—which had very mysteriously come to light the day Madame had arrived in town. "Naturally," Fan wrote, "the average Devereaunian who can add has come up with a good solid four, and he is delighted." Phillip chuckled and handed the letter to Tim, for part of it was addressed to him. Fanchon had quietly accepted the fact that the inevitable had occurred between them and now tactfully ignored it except in such little ways as writing to them together, which gave her, she liked to believe, some sort of an advantage.

They had not seen Francis and Sybel Jo, nor had Phillip seen Pat. Pat, Tim said, had made no change in her plans. She was not going to Reno until August. But she had been down to Carmel and Taos, "trying her wings," Tim grinned wryly.

It seemed they never had enough time to talk. They discussed everything. For Phillip it was learning a new language, a marvelously expressive language. The subject that fascinated him most of all was human behavior. Tim made it seem logical as he sought the core of things and explained them in terms Phillip could appreciate. Freed at last of his father's ethics, Phillip felt himself relax in mind and body. He began to look situations over in a more natural way. He became less abrupt. He suddenly found that it was easy to laugh, to live, to love. They talked of Phillip's future, a subject that had always been of topmost importance to him, and the boy amazed them both by saying, "The devil take it for now. I've more important things to think about." Phillip's old term describing Tim's painting technique, "off-center balance," took on a deeper significance with new ideas and developments.

Tim had a mind of myriad facets. He could be profound and witty within seconds of each other, and it was Phillip's greatest delight when the man concluded some serious discourse with the right pinch of Attic salt. And Phillip came to recognize a

355

certain natural division within their relationship—the intellectual and the sexual. It was the beginning of his real freedom.

Sexually their situation might have become baffling. Tim saw to it that it was not. Seeking identification which was necessary for justification, Tim showed Phillip the groaning shelf of literature on the subject—examples brilliant and commonplace from all nations and all ages. Phillip learned how widely discussed the problem had been and still was to humanity, and he became familiar with the various schools of thought on it. He heard it discussed as a fashion, an abomination, a disease, a philosophy. And from it all, Phillip drew one conclusion: that the answer lay only in the mind of the individual. As Tim had explained, there were no rules. Phillip came to accept this fact as an advantage. In seeking the reasons for his behavior, he came upon various parallels, both logical and absurd.

On the far-fetched side of the scale, he was quite ashamed of one parallel that had early sprung into his mind. But once he had told it to Tim, who laughed about it and explained it away, Phillip promptly forgot it. The idea had something to do with his beloved palomino stallion, that expensive animal that looked like a haze of bright gold dust in the hot Oklahoma sun. When his Uncle Felix gave the animal to him, Phillip promptly fell in love with it to the point of worship. In pondering this feeling, Phillip came to the conclusion that he worshipped the animal because it was just what it was—the male of the species in opposition to the female.

"My Little Pelops," so named because of one light shoulder, was a symbol of masculinity, beautiful with strength, great with power, yet tender, fragile, easily wounded, quickly dissipated, soon gone, and consequently a creature of delicately set action and delightful idiosyncrasies. And Phillip's youthful mind had enlarged upon this conception. The stallion came to represent an ultimate in attained perfection. It was a bangle of civilization, actually useless in a practical sense but capable of giving pleasure to those sensitive enough to appreciate it.

356

Then at his first show, Phillip had seen its effect upon others. Its phallic attraction struck like a blow. Phillip was aware of it before he comprehended it. He had seen certain women watch them both in the ring and later in the stables where they came to get a better view, silent, meditative, their eyes running over the beautiful specimen, their subconscious thoughts a hundred light-years from reality. He had seen men glance at the stallion with quiet respect and, he fancied, fleeting envy.

At Uncle Felix's suggestion, Phillip had put him up for stud, his services commanding a fee of one hundred dollars, a sizable sum in the early thirties. Because he was doubly registered, he soon was earning far more than his keep. He had become an investment, bringing more responsibilities. Phillip had hired a trainer and had taken a short course in husbandry, at last assisting in and directing the rites of breeding, often catching the dripping semen, putting it into the specially warmed capsule, and plunging it the length of his arm into the mare. Even his stallion's intimacy the boy was able to share.

Upon learning of these rites, Phillip's father, outraged and disgusted that "my son could do such a thing," had forbidden the practice. But Uncle Felix, armed with stud receipts for the past months, had prevailed against Julius' delicate stomach. Julius Froelich's attitude had had one effect on the situation. Until that time, Phillip had looked upon his responsibility with serious practicality. After his father's outburst, he began to listen to the crude jests made by the mares' owners who watched the breeding events. In spite of Uncle Felix' efforts to combat it, these processes took on the compelling fascination of that which is forbidden and evil yet necessary and desirable. His father's action had solidified a half-formed trauma.

Now all this was somehow parallel to Phillip's thoughts of Tim. But because he could now talk with freedom, Phillip related all this to his friend, discussed it, and happily discarded it once it seemed straight in his mind. Tim even made some tri-

357

fling joke about it at which Phillip smiled briefly and then concerned himself with other things.

Tim dissolved such fantasies in him and smashed barriers that kept them apart. He could dominate the boy completely, shake his mind as teasingly as a dog worries a toy, or lead it far into the long, dim corridors of thought. By merely talking to him, Tim could confine the boy to pure reason, exercising his mind with the precision of pistons firing in an engine, or he could release him into a field of sensual abandon. From his past, the man had a store of tales to delight a sage or to madden a greedy personality such as Phillip's.

But he used the boy well, leading him constantly toward the intellectual rather than emotional realms. Tim labored to prove his theory that the sexual element between them was merely a springboard to Phillip's self-mastery and to the clarification of his thinking. At times, Phillip bore him out completely.

There were occasional clouds on their horizon. Because Tim sought to preserve Phillip's balance, he would never let him forget that what was happening to them would not last. Phillip carried the idea a step farther and began to look for the first ruptures in their relationship. This could be annoying at times. Then, too, the infrequent recurrence of Phillip's ruthless independence and self-reliance had a strange effect on Tim. Seeing the boy's swift progress from hidebound tradition into sound thought, seeing him lay the foundation of a future that would certainly separate them as lovers, aroused his jealousy. Being the author and director of this experiment, Tim was constantly on the alert for the unharmonious in his protégé, but to master that which was discordant in his own feelings for Phillip, proved to be a far more difficult problem than he had at first supposed.

But all in all, theirs was an idyl. No longer were there nights and days, mornings and afternoons, but only minutes, each possessing the variety and uniformity of a thread of pearls. . . .

The incident that menaced all they had fashioned came from

quite an unexpected source. Phillip was studying a report on his desk one afternoon late in August when the phone rang.

"Offices of The Flag," he said absently, "Froelich speaking."

"Sir," a half-familiar voice caught his attention, "this is Stuff. Stuff Manus."

"Stuff!" Phillip cried, dropping the papers. He was surprised at the evident joy in his voice. There was really no cause for it. "Where are you?"

"At Pier 91. We just put in from tne East Coast."

33

◆◇◆◇◆◇◆

*S*tuff Manus is in town," Phillip told Tim when they reached the club that evening. "I'm having dinner with him."

"Must you?"

"I'd like to," Phillip answered carefully. "Won't you join us?"

"No. I'll wait for you here. Where will you go?"

"I don't know. He probably hasn't been able to find a room. I'll have to get him one. We may dine at the hotel. I thought of bringing him to the bar downstairs for cocktails if you don't mind."

"Of course I don't mind," Tim said irritably.

"What is it, Tim?"

Tim smiled. "Forgive me. I'm being dull. I guess I haven't transcended you yet."

Phillip touched his hand affectionately. "Impatient?" he asked.

Tim did not reply.

360

Phillip dressed with care, laughing at himself for the excitement that was within him. It was to be his first evening away from Tim in weeks. He supposed the change appealed to him. He thought of the episode with Stuff aboard their landing ship. He remembered the screaming rush of wind, the pounding, heaving deck beneath their unsteady feet, the cold sting of salt water on his face, the taste of blood in his mouth. He remembered the fear. But these things were no longer important. Tim had destroyed his past and loaded his mind with another set of memories. The sailor could never be of importance to him again. Still, he looked forward to seeing him. Phillip remembered their friendship with kindliness.

He did not say goodbye to Tim. He realized that he should say something to him but he was at a loss as to what it would be. He decided that to ignore the situation would be the wisest action. So instead of talking with his friend during the few minutes before he left, he spent the time at the telephone securing a room for the sailor. He took a taxi to the restaurant where they were to dine.

Though he was early, Stuff Manus awaited him in the richly furnished lobby. As the sailor saw him, he rose and they came toward each other quickly. They said hello rather breathlessly and their hands met. Their eyes went over each other eagerly in their pleasure.

Suddenly Phillip was startled as he recognized the strength of the emotion they aroused in each other. He smiled uncomfortably and released his hand. Some of the sailor's joy disappeared from his face.

"You look fine, Stuff," Phillip said.

"So do you, sir."

Conversation halted. They looked away in embarrassment, each recalling the stormy night in the Tropics, each knowing that it had been a mistake to renew this friendship.

"A drink, Stuff?" Phillip asked at last.

"Fine," Stuff agreed awkwardly.

361

Phillip had never seen Stuff with a haircut or in anything but old dungarees worn almost white. He was pleasantly surprised to find him freshly barbered and manicured and immaculately turned out in a tailored serge uniform. For a moment Phillip felt as he had once with Tim Danelaw, shy and inexperienced. But the thought of Tim sobered him and his poise returned.

Like Tim and himself, they were antipodes, yet possessing in their difference a harmonic sympathy for each other. They were a handsome, if unorthodox, twosome, and Phillip was aware that their appearance was provoking comments at some of the tables nearby. This had never happened with Tim. The fault must lie in Stuff, his too obvious admiration, his great size in comparison to Phillip's lithe slenderness. The boy tried not to be ill at ease. Loyally he remembered the sailor's position during that trying period aboard the landing ship. Deliberately he set about destroying the stiffness between them. Martinis arrived. They lifted slender stems in their fingers.

"To you, Stuff," Phillip said, looking into the blue-gray eyes that could be so damnably expressive.

Stuff shook his head. "To us," he corrected.

Phillip did not voice his objections.

They dined leisurely on the elaborate food Phillip ordered, courses arriving within hours of each other as their conversation grew interesting and Phillip forgot to summon the waiter. They spoke of ships and seas and wars and lands. Once again Phillip marveled over the genuineness that had attracted him to Stuff months ago. Every phrase the man uttered strengthened his admiration for that earnest simplicity, that direct charm the man possessed. The episode that had loomed so threateningly before them earlier in the evening seemed to be forgotten until, in their talk of their former ship and crew, Stuff asked about his court martial.

Phillip dreaded answering the question. "I didn't have a court martial, Stuff," he said.

"This Commander Danelaw?" Stuff asked. Phillip nodded,

staring at his coffee cup and caressing its handle with a long finger. "Tell me one thing," Stuff said quietly. "Did you love him?"

Phillip's eyes filled with anger as he looked up at Stuff, but the expression on the face he saw, so eloquently sincere and miserable, killed the protest on his lips.

He said humbly, "I love him."

The sailor rose and waited for Phillip to rise. Silently they left the restaurant. It was past midnight.

On the street outside Phillip said, "It's late, Stuff. I'd better go. Will I see you again?"

"No. We're shoving off in the morning for the South Pacific."

For a moment Phillip floundered for something to say. At last he asked, "Have you a room?"

"No. But it isn't far back to the ship."

"But your last night ashore," Phillip protested. "I reserved you one this afternoon—that is, if you want it."

"All right," Stuff said. "How about coming up for a last drink?"

"It's rather late . . ."

Stuff grinned and spread out his hands for inspection. "See," he said, "no strings."

Phillip laughed. "All right, Stuff, one drink, no strings."

In the hotel room, Phillip tossed his hat on the bureau and crossed the room to the open window while they waited for their brandy to arrive. He looked out over the city sloping down to the bay. A gentle melancholy was slowly possessing him.

At last he said idly, "It's very beautiful tonight, isn't it?"

"Yes, very."

Behind him, Stuff switched off the lights and came to stand close by. Phillip, guessing the man's intentions, turned to move away and felt himself firmly pinned by Stuff's arms. Once more he felt the unbelievable strength of the man.

Knowing how useless his protests would be, Phillip looked up

363

into the glittering eyes and asked quietly, "What about the 'no strings,' Stuff?"

"Is that the way you want it then?" Stuff's voice was less controlled.

"I think we'd better keep it that way."

"Why?"

"There is Tim—Tim Danelaw."

"And if there wasn't?"

"I don't know."

Suddenly Phillip knew what he wanted. He knew that unless something happened at once, he would commit an act he would regret all his life, an act of infidelity to Tim. The sailor's breath was warm on his face.

To save himself, he said thickly, "But I don't love you, Stuff."

"How could you—a guy like me?" He touched Phillip's face. "But I'll take you any way I can get you."

Phillip saw himself slipping closer to disaster, but he was powerless to act. His mind could not function. He knew he was lost. Tim was not here. His whole life was a mistake. The past months with Tim had been an abomination before God and man.

Suddenly there was a knock at the door. Taking advantage of the interruption, he pushed himself free of the sailor and went to turn on the lights, stumbling a little. He opened the door, took the tray, and handed the waiter a bill. He set the tray down and picked up his hat.

In the doorway he turned to Stuff who stood at the window. "Goodbye, Stuff, and good luck."

The sailor did not speak. He looked at Phillip with uncomprehending eyes, but he did not protest. Without closing the door, Phillip turned and walked slowly down the corridor.

Outside he started walking aimlessly. Out of the turmoil of his life a fresh wound throbbed. He had failed Tim and himself. Incapable of self-control even after Tim had granted him so many concessions to justify his nature, he had failed in his first

364

crisis. Now, more than ever before, he was pariah—in his own eyes as well as the world's. For he knew that even if nothing had happened in the sailor's room, the inevitable would have taken place if he had stayed. More important, he had wanted to stay. He wanted to go back even now.

He walked for hours and near daybreak he took a taxi to his quarters on the base. He could not risk facing Tim now with this knowledge. He had to think it out first.

Near exhaustion, he pushed his door open to find himself facing Tim Danelaw's accusing eyes. Phillip passed his fingers over his forehead. He knew now that everything was lost.

"Hello, Tim."

"I suppose there is an explanation," Tim said brutally.

"I suppose," Phillip answered in a dull voice.

"I called the hotel," Tim continued. "The clerk said you'd gone up about midnight. He didn't see you come down."

"I used the arcade entrance when I left," Phillip explained wearily.

"And I suppose you came here instead of to the club so as not to disturb me."

"That's right."

"Phillip! Don't lie to me!"

Phillip looked up dully. He shrugged his shoulders. "Very well, Tim, I won't lie to you. I did stay with Stuff." He paused and his voice rose as he continued, "I liked it. I liked it fine. There was something earthy about him that pleased me. I'd stay with him again if he weren't shipping out in a few hours. If I can find my pleasure so easily, I'm lucky!"

He swayed unsteadily as the silence rose up around him. He watched Tim come close and pause. He saw the blinding flash of fire as the blow struck him across the eyes.

34

$\mathcal{F}$or three days Phillip moved as a robot. He stayed in his room on the base every possible hour. And strangely enough it was Mike Mallory who came to his aid. It was Mike who heard the story of what Phillip had done. And it was Mike who succeeded in snapping him back to a semblance of reason.

"Where is your pride now, Phillip?" he said. "Where is that excellent training you've boasted of all your life? What are you going to do now?"

"Do?" Phillip asked stupidly. And he began to realize that it was only a part of him that was dead, a part that the world did not know existed. For a week or two more he had to keep up appearances. Then—then he would be free of the Navy and he would decide what to do.

He turned himself to his duties. He avoided Tim as carefully as he was being avoided. An immense lethargy had settled over him, the result of pain. It even seemed to be an effort to breathe.

366

Late Friday afternoon, just before the offices of the flag closed for the weekend, a yeoman brought Phillip an order to report to Commander Danelaw. The request set him on the keen edge of alarm, but he mustered the courage to knock and enter Tim's office. He found him standing over his desk with his hat on, hurriedly putting papers into a brief case.

"Get your hat and meet me in the car," he ordered curtly.

Phillip obeyed.

They did not speak until they were off the base and down the ramp of the Ferry Building. Then, racing through the outskirts of town, Tim said without emotion, "I'll give this to you fast and straight. You've got to get out of here in a hurry. In the first place, Pat is back and she's panting for blood—our blood. Quite naturally she went to Bruner, who has ample cause to hate us both. I don't know what they have fixed up yet, but I received a tip a few minutes ago that you are to be picked up for questioning by the authorities. That can mean several things. Most likely it is ammunition for Pat's divorce proceedings. We would both pay well to keep our names out of print. But she may want something more than money. Bruner's desires are obvious. But before I face them I want you out of the way. I want you to go up to Canada and stay there until I can get you free of the Navy and this part of the world. I'll speed up your discharge a few days. If everything goes well, you can return Monday. By Monday night you'll be a civilian. Will you agree to that?"

"Yes."

"Good. I'll drive you to the airport. You'll have to buy what you need. You don't dare go back to the base now. Have you any money?"

"About thirty dollars."

"Here. Here is about two hundred."

"Thanks. I'll return it."

Phillip spent the weekend in Vancouver—two long days of thought. Experience that had been piling up for him he now

367

sorted and sadly stored away in his mind. Late Sunday afternoon Mike Mallory appeared at the hotel to say that Tim had sent him up to drive Phillip back to Seattle.

In the car, Mike asked, "Have you decided what you're going to do?"

With no hesitation, Phillip answered, "I'm going back to Tim, on my knees if necessary, and ask for a chance to explain, a chance to live again."

"So the ivory tower falls at last?" Mike mused.

Phillip nodded. "If only it isn't too late."

Mike looked at Phillip and smiled. "Already it is working."

"What?"

"Tim's influence. You've changed. God, but you've changed. What a priggish little beast you were the first time I saw you. I thought Tim was on the wrong track, that you were just a good-looking kid and that was all. You are becoming what Tim saw in you from the first. And don't worry about being too late. For Tim Danelaw, you'll never be too late."

The next morning Phillip went to Tim's office. Cool, impersonal, and refusing to read what Phillip knew was in his eyes, Tim gave him a list of appointments. He accompanied Phillip to the door and told him to return when he was discharged to make his farewells to the Admiral. There had been no leak of information concerning Tim's skirmish with Bruner and Pat.

Phillip left the office and started the last lap of his naval career: the dentist's office, the doctor, X-ray rooms, Housing Office, BOQ clerk, the Captain of the Yard, Disbursing and Pay Accounts, Records Office with I.D. cards, dog tags, and fitness reports. He did not stop for lunch, but hurried through the red tape that Tim had cut for him. Two hours past noon Phillip was once more a civilian, free at last of four chaotic years. He went to see the Admiral, exchanged addresses (so they could send and receive Christmas cards, Phillip thought ironically), and shook hands for the last time.

In the corridor Phillip saw Tim. He held out his hand, but Phillip said, "Can't we go into your office?"

With a puzzled glance, Tim led the way. Phillip faced him clear-eyed, head high. "First, what of Bruner and Pat?"

Tim smiled. "An open and shut case of mutual blackmail in both instances. Bruner was the easiest. Do you remember the receipt of sales for movie equipment that you found your first day on the staff here and asked me about?"

"Yes. We decided it was sold without proper authority."

"That's right. The Lieutenant Van Meeter was Bruner. I checked in Portland. With that information in my possession, he changed his tune. He called his investigation of you off."

"Do you mean Bruner will go scot-free?"

"Oh, no. My silence means nothing. His case is in the hands of the provost marshal now. He is to be tried on three counts when they have all the information they want about him. It seems the worst one involves a carload of sugar turned over to black marketeers. There is another officer in on that with him. He also tried his hand at the knock-down racket on governmental appraised war surplus goods. He has been fairly clever, always standing behind another officer, and that's why he hasn't been arrested yet. The authorities want as much on him as possible. He'll get at least twenty years."

"Was Pat behind the investigation of me as you suspected?"

"She was another of Bruner's cat's-paws, I'm afraid. The important thing is that they are both quiet and likely to remain that way for a while. And now you are out of the Navy. You are safe."

There was a pause and the two friends looked at each other.

"And what of us, Tim?" Phillip asked tensely.

"Mike told me about the other night. Do you know why you lied to me?"

"Yes. I—"

"You need not explain. I understand. How do you feel now?"

369

"You are the only important part of my life, Tim. I can live without you . . . but I don't want to."

Tim's face relaxed and his old expression returned. He came to Phillip and put his hands on the boy's arms. "Then everything is as it should be. When I get back we will—"

"You're going away?" Phillip asked with disappointment.

"Only for tonight. San Francisco again for the Admiral. Tomorrow night we'll be together again."

They said goodbye, and at the door Phillip turned to speak to him in low, swift French before they parted.

In reply, Tim repeated the words that meant so much to them.

35

He was sleeping at the club. It was almost morning. A jangling bell aroused him. He picked up the telephone, but the bell jangled again. Sleepily Phillip stood up and pulled on his robe before he opened the door. Mike Mallory stood before him, strangely uneasy. Phillip stood aside for him to enter, knowing that something was wrong. Mike fingered a newspaper in his hands.

"Have you been asleep all night, Phillip?"

"Yes. Why?"

"Phillip, I've bad news. Very bad. Can you take it?"

"I can," Phillip said calmly, though he was icy all over.

"Tim—Tim's plane crashed in the mountains last night. He is dead, Phillip."

Phillip stared at his visitor stupidly for many minutes and at last looked away. He could not speak. Mike, unnerved by his immobility, began talking rapidly, incoherently.

"He was happy, Phillip. He told me he was. He told me every-

371

thing before he left. He said, 'Everything is all right at last, Mike. Phillip understands.' And I asked him what he was going to do and he said, 'I'm going to take him away for a while and we're going to live the best of our lives together.' He was happy, Phillip. You made him happy."

Seeing that his words were not penetrating Phillip's mind, Mike asked timidly, "Would you like to be alone, Phillip?" And taking the silence as an affirmative answer, he went out, leaving the newspaper behind.

Alone, Phillip turned to look at the closed door. His eyes found the big headlines, three black words: ADMIRAL'S PLANE DOWN. He shook his head, but he knew they were true. Timothy Danelaw was dead.

He had gambled with life for happiness, and miraculously enough he had won. But as he had put out his hand to receive his reward, it had vanished. Life and the game, both were a dream.

When everything is gone, there is no point in going on, dragging from this substitute to that, all the while falling lower and lower in the inevitable decline of hope and joy. Phillip thought of the sleeping tablets and knew they were not the answer. His last moments would not be passive ones. There was the other way. He thought of Fleurs-du-Mal Cove and the silent, relentless pull of ebb tide. He thought of the bone-white rocks rising from the black ocean floor. He went to the phone and dialed long distance.

Phillip stood on the jetty for the last time and removed his clothes. The day was cloudy, the wind chill. He looked at the restless gray water of the cove. Soon he would be lost in that great entirety. He dropped his last garment with the others and lifted his hands before him to dive.

The glitter of green caused him to hesitate. The training of two decades asked him what he would do with the emerald, that costly, beautiful toy. . . . The emerald . . . Tim. . . . Inside

372

the gold there were a few letters, enough to remind him of the words Tim had uttered on a night many weeks ago, words that held the meaning and essence of their love, words that were destined to be the last Phillip ever heard from his friend's lips:

And now, my life is a part of yours, and your life is a part of mine. Never again shall we stand entirely alone.

Slowly Phillip let his arms come to rest at his sides. Though he might be capable of destroying himself, he knew that he could never destroy that part of him which was Tim. Once more, even in death, Tim had intervened on his behalf. Now Phillip knew that he was strong enough to face the ordeal of living. In descending to the level of self-destruction, he had conquered it. He had found the one thing that was more powerful than death —love. Death was not strong enough to claim him without conquest. . . .

Phillip put his clothes on again and slowly climbed the hill.

EPILOGUE

When Sasha Alyson asked me for a new epilogue to this book, I recalled the advice of one who knew the story behind *Quatrefoil*. "Tell people as little of the facts as possible, even if they think the story is yours. You've written a classic love story for homosexuals; let the readers have their own illusions."

Now, after more than forty years in print, perhaps it is time to reveal some facts. So I wrote Mr. Alyson, "Q is not my story as many have believed. The model for Phillip was the most beautiful young man I ever saw, and I watched bitterly as his father destroyed him after World War II. He came home to marry and became a hopeless drunk, and almost certainly a suicide. Q is the life he might have had if he'd only had the courage to cut loose from his roots and survive."

Phillip and I were fraternity brothers at our university before the war. We were both quietly, very discreetly, homosexual but with one great difference. When dear Oscar's Love That Dare Not Speak Its Name smiled on Phillip, it turned him to stone. I, on the other hand, went prancing out to meet it. Somewhere between those two positions lay a blended story that would one day be called *Quatrefoil*.

In the atmosphere of the fraternity, Phillip and I quickly discovered our common ground. Inevitably we wound up stretched out nose to navel on the leather seat of my convertible one night. Phillip proved to be a tiny tiger until he climaxed. Then he was a scared little kid again, huddling in his corner, trying to get his clothes back on.

"It's okay," I tried to joke, "they say we're supposed to outgrow it any day now."

Instead of laughing with me, he said, "If our folks knew what we'd just done, they'd put us in prison, wouldn't they?" I laughed out loud at his absurdity. "Mine would," he insisted stubbornly. "Father would just love to get something like this on me!"

And there lay the key to his future, but I wasn't wise enough to see it yet. Phillip's father, a vicious bullying martinet, would die howling-crazy one day. But not before first driving his wife to suicide, with Phillip to follow her a few years later. Phillip could have saved himself by simply walking away, but he was too weak.

Only a few months after the attack on Pearl Harbor, I was in the Navy on my way to Guadalcanal. Phillip also entered the Navy at the end of that year. The first time we met during the war was by accident at the Submarine Officers Club in Pearl. He introduced me to the infamous French 75, a refreshing little libation of cognac and fine champagne over shaved ice, guaranteed to rot your socks off. When I ordered my second, he was finishing his third.

Phillip had blossomed in uniform. Even though it was obvious to anyone that he was a drunk, he was a charming one and everyone adored him. His beauty was startling. And the more he drank, the more delightful he became. Everyone, but everyone, loved Phillip. The thought crossed my mind — how would he keep it going back in Oklahoma, where that crazy father of his told him, and everyone else, when to breathe?

Phillip was never bold or aggressive in the least way. His passive role, almost the shy young maiden, was far more appealing. Certainly his partnerships were more romantic, but his disappointments were heartbreaking. The partners he always chose had to abandon him, or be sucked down with him.

Although I met the physical model of Tim Danelaw only once, and liked him, I knew his type very well. The Navy was peppered with them, from good financially solid families. They were often brilliantly educated, frequently married, and usually completely bewildered at having found strong tendencies of homosexuality in their personalities. Most came to accept this situation, some to glory in the brief opportunities. I encountered dozens of these men, many of their faces still vivid in my mind today.

After the war I got out of the Navy and enrolled in the School of Letters to become a writer. When I saw Phillip again, he had also returned to get his bachelor's, but I couldn't believe the change in him. The last time I'd seen him he'd glittered like a Christmas tree; now he looked as if he'd been stored in an attic for a couple of years. He was a sad, gray little fellow, who never smiled. Where the Navy had loaded me for bear, it had disarmed and defused Phillip. I honestly didn't know what I could do to help him. He started hanging around my off-campus apartment a lot, talking about moving in with me. He cut classes almost every day, because he was too hung over to get out of bed.

One day when I told him I wanted to write a gay novel with his story for the plot, he lifted a shoulder with indifference. After I outlined the plot I had in mind, he thought a while and then said, "If you do use me, I have just one request. Make me happy again. That's all. Just make me happy one more time ... please?" And to my horror, he started to cry, gut-wrenching sobs that shook him all over. I went to him, to put my arms around him, to comfort him, but he pushed me away as if he didn't want to be touched ever again, saying, "It's all over for me. Nothing's left." He started to drink from the bottle he'd brought with him, which rather repelled me. Gents just didn't drink from bottles in brown paper bags, by my code of rules in those days.

Another long drink and he looked at me dull-eyed. "Just make me happy ... one more time..." And he lay back on my bed and passed out. When I got back from classes late that day, he was gone, but not before being sick on the counterpane. I cried when I cleaned it up for I knew Phillip's life was over. When the six-weeks grades came out, Phillip's father came and took him home.

The next semester Phillip's brother enrolled at the university. He was only a year younger than Phillip. The two men looked somewhat alike, but were certainly not cut from the same piece of cloth. Reuben was his father's child, bold, aggressive, and probably ruthless. One evening he came to see me and have one of my famous martinis.

"Phillip asked me to come by and tell you he was being married next month, a small ceremony for just the family. He's working full-time at the bank now. He also said to wish you good luck with your writing. He made a point of that."

"How is he?" I'd never felt so helpless in my life.

"Doped up," Reuben said flatly. "Old Dr. Berger gives him pills in the morning to wake him up and pills to make him sleep in the evening. He looks and acts like a zombie. He eats almost nothing, gets no booze at all, and is watched, by some roughneck that works for Father, like a dog's dinner. Father screams at him all day long at the bank. Some of the best accounts are transferring to the other bank in town it's so embarrassing."

"Sweet Mother of Jesus in Heaven," I murmured.

"It can't last much longer. Phillip will starve to death if the pills don't kill him first. Just a matter of time." An ugly look came over his face. "When I take over, it'll be another story, believe me!"

"You!"

"Who else? Phillip will be dead this time next year and Father is so obviously insane, Judge Hearn has already started sounding people out about having him committed."

"Then why don't you do it now and save Phillip if you can?"

"Phillip doesn't want to be saved, and Father will have to make some overt move that will justify putting him away. Sympathy is beginning to build for Phillip, but I'm afraid it's too late."

I saw the announcement of Phillip's marriage in the society section of Sunday's paper, and on Monday's front page was the story of Phillip's death. His car had collided with a freight train going at high speed. Apparently the railroad right-of-way looked like a slaughterhouse. It occurred only a few miles from the family home.

I didn't learn until later that Phillip, getting hold of some booze at the reception, had found a car with keys in its ignition. The goon hired to watch him not in sight, Phillip had taken off as fast as he could. He died on his wedding day. Everything weighed objectively, it seemed appropriate.

The boatswain's mate, who would become Stuff Manus, used to have a tattoo of a dagger piercing a skull on his arm, above the motto "Death before Dishonor." I wondered if Phillip had thought of that tattoo and laughed gaily as he always did, while his car rushed toward that train. Death before dishonor, indeed!

I left the university by the end of that week for New York City. Though the semester was only half finished, the whole atmosphere sickened me. I was tired of pretty little boys with their pretty little toys in their velvet-lined worlds. I wanted to get down among the men who lived and fought with the ugliness of life that had killed Phillip.

And I had a novel to finish; a promise to keep. "Make me happy again ... just one more time ... please?"

I have tried, you poor, sad, doomed, gorgeous little sod! I did the very best I could for you. Now will you stop bothering me? Please? ... please?

THE AUTHOR

James Fugaté, using the pseudonym James Barr, wrote *Quatre-foil* in 1950. In the next five years he produced at least two other works of fiction with a gay theme: *Derricks,* a collection of short stories; and *Game of Fools,* a playscript. In 1965 Barr wrote a brief introduction to a paperback edition of *Quatrefoil,* then lost touch with the early homosexual rights movement. Alyson Publications was unable to locate him when we first reprinted *Quatrefoil* in 1982, but nine years later he came forward, and wrote the epilogue that appears, for the first time, in this new edition.

On the back jacket of *Game of Fools,* published in 1954, Barr is said to have earned his living as an oilfield roustabout. At that time, speaking of the potential for an organized homosexual movement, he said, "The time is not yet ripe. The homosexual minority is too amorphous to have need of a spokesman. At present the group must find and identify itself. Only time or a vicious persecution can hurry the process. But what an organization it could be if ever its individuals mastered their terror, sloth and inclination to pettiness! Can you imagine a group headed by such men as Michelangelo, Da Vinci, Proust, Gide, Tschaikovsky, Socrates, Wilde, Housman, Alexander, Caesar?" And he added, "The idea isn't as ludicrous as many people imagine."